MIRRORED

Also by
ALEX FLINN

BEASTLY
A KISS IN TIME
CLOAKED
BEWITCHING
TOWERING
BREATHING UNDERWATER
DIVA
FADE TO BLACK
NOTHING TO LOSE
BREAKING POINT

MIRRORED

ALEX FLINN

HARPER TEEN
An Imprint of HarperCollinsPublishers

HarperTeen is an imprint of HarperCollins Publishers.

Mirrored
Copyright © 2015 by Alexandra Flinn
www.epicreads.com

Library of Congress Cataloging-in-Publication Data
Flinn, Alex.
    Mirrored / Alex Flinn. — First edition.
        pages   cm
    Summary: A modern, multigenerational tale of Kendra, the witch
from "Snow White," who trains Violet, an ugly, lonely, and heartbroken
girl in the 1980s who transforms herself into "the fairest one of all" but
still cannot win Greg's heart, and Celine, Greg's daughter with Violet's
high school rival, Jennifer.
    ISBN 978-0-06-213451-6 (hardcover)
    [1. Beauty, Personal—Fiction.   2. Witches—Fiction.   3. Popularity—
Fiction.   4. Schools—Fiction.]   I. Title.
PZ7.F6395Mir   2015   2014041196
[Fic]—dc23   CIP
                                                                   AC

15 16 17 18 19   PC/RRDH   10 9 8 7 6 5 4 3 2 1
❖
First Edition

In memory of George Nicholson, who taught me so much

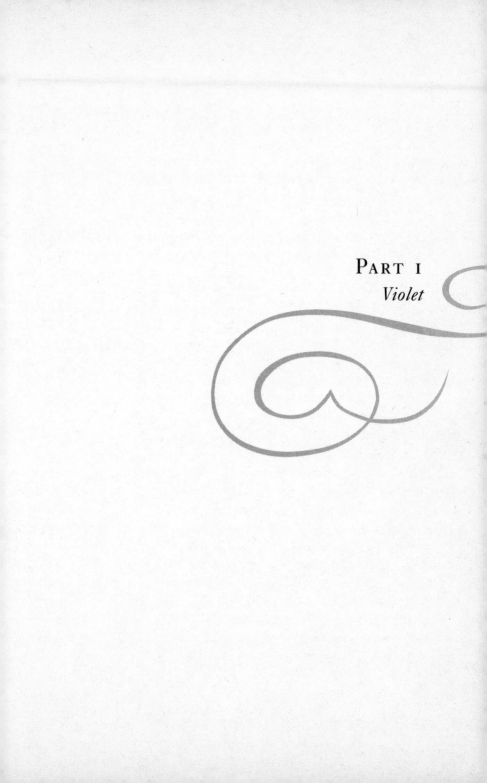

PART I
Violet

1

1982

I was a strange child. Strange looking, for certain, with buckteeth, red hair (and matching invisible eyelashes), a hooked nose, and barely the hint of a chin. My classmates at Coral Ridge Elementary teased me about these defects as if it was their God-given right. Maybe it was. After all, if I wanted to fit in, wouldn't I just act more normal?

But even if I could change my hair, my nose, my chin, I couldn't perform plastic surgery on my soul. Some secret part of me remained stubbornly different—brought egg salad when everyone else knew it was gross or used vocabulary words like *whimsical*, words no one else understood.

And shortly after my tenth birthday, I learned I was different in another way.

A special way.

That day, a rare, cold January day in Miami, I was walking alone on the playground. I had a jump rope. But when I'd asked the two girls who sat behind me, Jennifer Sadler and Gennifer Garcia, if they wanted to jump with me, they'd turned to each other with perplexed looks.

"Jump rope?" Jennifer's blond ponytail swung from side to side as she shook her head. "Who jumps rope anymore?"

"We do in PE." It was the only sport at which I excelled.

Jennifer rolled her enormous blue eyes. "Yeah, for a grade."

"We could do something else then," I said. "Kickball?" The Jennifers were part of a kickball game that included most of our class. I was never invited.

"Sorry, I think the teams are set." Gennifer Garcia wrinkled her perfect nose.

As I trudged away, trailing my red-and-white-striped rope, I heard Jennifer say loudly, "You are too nice to that girl. It just makes her think she can talk to us."

Gennifer laughed, then said softer, but still loud enough for me to hear clearly, "You can't just tell people they're freaks."

"Why not? It would help her to know."

Did being beautiful make you cruel? Were they really being cruel if I was so defective? And, if I were suddenly pretty, would I be mean too? Not that that would ever happen.

So I sat alone, shivering on a swing, looking at the toes of my navy Keds against the lighter blue clouds, when I spied a cluster of kids gathered around something. Ordinarily, I avoided unsupervised groups of my peers, but this particular group included, at its outskirts, one Gregory Columbo, a sensitive boy with coal-black hair and the warmest brown eyes I'd ever seen. Though he wasn't exactly nice to me, he wasn't mean. He was quiet, more the type to read a book than to play baseball. Now, he wiped at his eyes with his gray sweatshirt sleeve. And something else made me gravitate toward the group, something I didn't quite understand.

I jumped off the swing and went before I could chicken out.

"What's everyone looking at?" I wanted to ask Greg why he was crying, but probably, he was pretending not to.

Greg turned away, touching the side of his face with his fingers.

"Greg?"

"Leave us alone, ugly." Jennifer smirked. "It's just a stupid, dead crow."

Greg turned and I caught sight of his face. His cheeks and eyes were mottled red, like blotchy, red glasses, and I had a distant memory of him and a woman—his mother—standing outside his house, filling a blue bird feeder. Greg's mother had died the year before.

The crowd was dispersing except for two boys, Nick and Nathan, who stood over the bird, poking it with a stick. I hated them. Hated. I could see the crow now, shiny and black as Greg's hair against the dappled greenish-brown grass, one black bead of an eye staring at me. I stooped beside it.

"Eww!" Gennifer said. "Are you going to touch it?"

I glanced back to see if Greg was still there. Nick hovered over me with his stick. I fixed him with a stare.

"Don't touch that. It's disrespectful of the dead." I remembered my mother saying something like that. Nick laughed and began to respond, but I said, "Go away." I heard violence in my voice.

He backed away. "It's dumb anyway." Nathan and the Jennifers followed him off.

I reached down and touched the bird. It was not cold, not yet at least. But it lay as still as the airless day. Its licorice-black wings caught the light, reflecting green and purple. I felt the ground move with the thumping of my enemies' retreating sneakers. I shivered, then slid my hand underneath the bird. It felt like leaves. I turned my back to Greg. Then, I placed my other hand over it and picked it up. It was larger than both my hands, but it weighed less than air. I remembered someone, Greg maybe, saying in class that birds' bones were hollow so they could fly.

Without knowing why, really, I raised the bird to my face, opened my hands, and blew.

The bird blinked.

No, it hadn't. It was dead.

I stroked its smooth feathers. Behind me, Greg stood silent, but I could hear his breath. I found a tiny wound under the bird's wing. When I touched it with my finger, it seemed to disappear.

The bird blinked again. This time, I was certain it had.

"Are you okay, then?" I barely whispered.

It cocked its head toward me. Behind me, I heard a gasp. Greg. I did not, could not look at him. I whispered, "Are you ready to go now?"

Again, the bird closed then opened its black bead eye, and in my head, I thought I heard it say, "Do you want me to?"

"Whatever you like. Your family is probably worried, though."

"It was a boy," the bird said, "the one with the stick. He threw a rock. It hurt. It *killed me.*"

"It didn't kill you. You're alive."

The bird twitched its head. "It killed me. I was dead."

I couldn't understand this. "Hmm, maybe you should get away from him."

"I guess so!" said the bird. "Can you help?"

"How?" I drew in a deep, shaky breath.

"Just . . . raise me up."

I nodded, then stood, still holding the crow in both hands. I lifted it high above my head.

It rose, shifting first to one clawed foot, then the other. It spread its black wings toward the graying sky. They gleamed purple and green in the strained sunlight. It fluttered, then lifted into the air. I watched it until it was merely a small, black speck against the clouds. I turned toward school.

"Hey," a voice said behind me. "That bird was dead."

Greg. I looked up to where the bird had been. "No, it wasn't. It flew away."

"But it was *dead*."

"No." It seemed, now, very important for me to impress this upon him. After all, I could barely believe what I'd done myself. It couldn't have happened, but it had. "No. It was only scared. Nick hit it with a stick. It's okay now."

Greg glanced at the ground. I did too and saw an irregular puddle of blood, mixing with the dusty dirt. "Okay," he said finally.

"We're going to get in trouble," I said.

"I'll tell Ms. Gayton what happened, that you helped the bird." His eyes were just nice looking, the way his eyebrows came down in the center, all concerned.

I shook my head. "She won't believe you."

"She will. Teachers like me. They feel sorry for me because of—"

"Your mom." I was thinking they liked him because he was so cute, those big eyes.

He nodded. "I can get away with anything."

"They hate me." It was true. Even though I aced every test, teachers had no smiles for me. They liked the prettier girls, the ones who didn't care about learning but only copied one another's homework.

"I'll tell her you were helping me then," he said.

I thought about it. "Okay."

We began to walk. As we did, my hand brushed Greg's. I wanted to grab it, but I didn't.

He said, "That was pretty cool."

"I didn't do anything."

"You did."

"No." I said it too loudly, too emphatically, then regretted it. I sounded like I was lying. "I'm sorry, but the bird was probably just shaken up or something. I mean, it flew away like nothing."

I remembered the wound under its wing, the wound that had closed. *How* had it?

Greg shrugged. "Okay." He started up the stairs to the school building, taking them two at a time, keeping ahead of me. He thought I was weird, though I'd tried so hard to prevent it, though I wanted him to like me so much. I'd have done anything to make him like me. Anything.

I didn't speed my step. What would be the point? As I trudged along, I felt something, like a pair of eyes, peering at me through the trees. I looked back and saw a shadowy figure dressed in green like the leaves. Or maybe it was the leaves. I shivered, remembering what my mother had said about perverts who lurked on playgrounds, waiting for children alone.

"Hello?" I said.

No answer except a riffle of wind across the grass and my own footsteps.

I stopped, glanced back. No one there. A caw, maybe the same crow, echoed from the treetops. I felt each individual hair on my arms stand on end. My feet planted on the ground.

Finally, I ran after Greg to the school building.

Nothing unusual happened for a year or so. Maybe I made nothing happen. But then, one day something did. Something that changed everything.

2

From that day on, Greg and I became friends. Sort of. We didn't really talk much at school, but if a teacher assigned a group project, we chose each other as partners. We'd work at my house or usually Greg's, making brochures to entice people to move to the Colony of Delaware, or a travel poster for Mars. I loved going to Greg's house. His father was always building something like a flower box or a huge tree house, and he let Greg and me help. Once, when we were in seventh grade, it was a birdhouse.

"Violet loves birds," Greg told his dad.

"Do you?" His father's eyes were brown like Greg's, and he was tall, but not skinny. He had a belly, which seemed very dad-like. "So you're a bird expert?"

"Not an expert. But they're pretty."

"Right, she's not an expert," Greg said, laughing. "The first time I spoke to Vi, she was holding a crow in the palm of her hand. Since then, I've seen them follow her."

I stared at him, startled. I didn't know he'd noticed, but it was true. Birds seemed to gravitate toward me, animals too; even wild ones like possums and raccoons didn't scatter as they did when others approached. I kept that quiet, though. It didn't exactly make me seem normal.

"I think they even talk to her sometimes." Greg smiled. He had a dimple, just one, on the left side of his mouth.

"Right, Greg. Sure."

Greg's dad laughed along. "Well, if you could talk to the Carolina wrens, maybe ask them what's the proper opening size for their birdhouse. Or you could just look it up."

"Is that really important? My mom just bought the birdhouse she thought was pretty."

"Do you see many birds in it?" Mr. Columbo asked.

"No," I admitted. "Never."

"If you look it up for me, I'll build a birdhouse they'll use—and I'll make another one for your house."

"I think I'd rather come over and look at yours." I wanted to be with Greg, always. The Columbos felt more like a real family than mine, even though it was just two of them. At home, it was just me and my mother, who spent more time on her nails than talking to me.

Still, Greg and I went to the school library during lunch the next day. We looked up the information in a book, finding that the Carolina wren needed a hole between one and a quarter and one and a half inches. Mr. Columbo let me drill the hole myself and even, against my protests, made a second one for me. "You can still come over, Violet." His eyes crinkled around the edges. "You're welcome any time."

10

After that, Greg invited me over without needing a magazine project as an excuse. We walked home together, at least as far as his house, every afternoon and checked out the birdhouse. One day, we saw a small brown bird moving in. "Wow," I said, "your dad's going to be so excited." There had been birds in my own birdhouse since the first day, but I didn't tell Greg that.

Greg grabbed my hand and squeezed it. His own hand was cool, dry, and I felt a jolt of electricity run up my arm. "We've never had a bird in our birdhouse before, no matter what he said. They came because of you."

"Right." I could barely speak from concentrating on the moment, the dizzying tingle of his hand in mine.

"You should stay, at least until Dad gets home."

I nodded and walked into the house. I thought I could hear one of the birds say *Thank you*, but when I looked over at Greg, he hadn't heard anything. We spent the whole afternoon sitting side by side at the window, watching the wren build her nest, until Mr. Columbo called us in for dinner. Greg smelled of pencil shavings and Irish Spring soap, and even though he let go of my hand, I could still feel it against mine, far, far into the night.

After that, I went to Greg's house every day after school. We watched the wrens to see if there were eggs or babies, but we also sat on the sofa, eating brownies we made from a mix and watching *Family Ties* and *The Cosby Show*, shows about big, happy families like ours weren't. People at school called us geeks in love, and while I pretended to cringe, I secretly enjoyed that people thought it possible. Greg wasn't my boyfriend—not yet—but I wanted him to be.

But the summer before eighth grade, Greg went to sleepaway camp for two whole months. "It's like this really outdoorsy camp my dad went to when he was my age," he told me. "I hate it. I think it's supposed to make me a man."

"Sounds fun." I rolled my eyes, thinking he was perfect as he was. In fact, I was hoping he'd invite me to the Halloween dance at school in the fall. Halloween was my favorite holiday because it let me be someone else, someone better. Or maybe someone worse. I was hoping maybe, costumed as a witch or vampire, I would have the courage to lean in, to will him to kiss me. But that was a long time away. "Can I write you?"

"Sure. That'd be cool." He smiled his cute, one-dimpled smile. "I know my dad won't write that much, not like a mom would."

"I'll write."

Once he left, the long, lonely summer stretched ahead of me, and I wanted to write every day. I didn't, though. Some dim part of me knew that would look crazy, like I had no life, which I didn't. I actually did things like an Everglades bird tour, just so I'd have something to write about. I worked on the letters every day but sent them once a week. Greg wrote back twice, then stopped. I told myself it was because he was busy, then because camp was almost over. I'd see him soon. But when he got back, he was always busy. In rushed phone calls, he said he had family in town one day, shopping for school another. So I didn't see him until the first day of eighth grade.

I searched for Greg in the crowds outside. Usually, he wasn't hard to spot. He was tall and stayed on the outskirts. But I didn't see him.

Then, I did. He wasn't on the outskirts, but in the middle of the crowd.

Greg had always been tall, but now he was taller. Not skinny anymore, though. Suddenly his shoulders were broader, his face more manly. He was standing with some people, people like Nick and Nathan, Jennifer and Gennifer, people who'd always picked on me and ignored him. Popular people. Greg was laughing, his black hair shining in the sun like a crow's wings, his smile like the sun itself. I made myself walk past him, and even though he seemed to look right at me, he said nothing.

All week, I tried to catch Greg's eye, to find a way to talk to him, and all week, nothing. It wasn't like he was being actively mean. It was worse. It was like I was a stranger. He was just this boy, this suddenly popular, handsome boy at my school, and I was nobody he knew. It was like we'd never done all the things we'd done together, like he'd never been my friend, like I was some stupid girl with a crush on a stranger.

Thursday, I finally got up the courage to call him.

His father answered. "Violet! Long time, no see. We have a new woodpecker."

"Oh, that's great!" I smiled on purpose, hoping he could hear it in my voice. Maybe it would all be okay. "Is Greg there?"

But, when Greg got on the phone, I knew it wouldn't be okay. He sounded different, awkward, like someone wearing too-tight shoes but trying not to show it. "So, um, what do you want, Violet?"

Suddenly I didn't know. I didn't know what I wanted. I wanted everything to be the same as it had been the year before. Or not the same. Better. There had been the promise of something more, and now, it was gone, and I wanted to change that. I wanted to change . . . time.

"Are you going to . . . ?" *To what? Invite me over? Say hello in class? Do anything? Be normal?* "I haven't talked to you since you got back."

A pause. In the living room, my mom was flipping through television channels. I heard the *Family Ties* theme start. *I bet we've been together for a million years; And I bet we'll be together for a million more.*

Mom changed the channel, and *Entertainment Tonight* came on instead.

"Yeah, about that," Greg said. "The thing is, my friends don't like you."

"Your friends? What friends?"

"Jennifer Sadler and them. They say . . . you're bossy and mean to them."

I sucked my breath in. Unreal. Popular people always had some reason why you deserved for them to be mean to you. "And you believe that? That I could boss Jennifer around, that I bully *her*? All you have to do is look at the two of us to know . . ."

I stopped. That was the problem. He had looked at us.

"I don't know what to believe. I just want to have friends. I don't want to be alone."

"You had a friend. You weren't alone."

"You know what I mean. I've always had a thing for Jennifer."

I didn't know that. Why was he doing this to me? Why did Jennifer even want to be friends with Greg? But I knew. Because he was beautiful. And beautiful guys were catnip for Jennifer. A beautiful guy like Greg didn't belong with an ugly like me. The second she showed interest in him, he knew. I felt so stupid for thinking anyone would ever really like me, especially someone as great as Greg.

"I'm tired of people thinking I'm weird," he said.

"I thought you were weird, in a good way. I liked you the way you were."

"I don't want that anymore."

I stood, clutching the phone. I didn't want to put it back in its cradle. The click it would make would change everything. I felt like, if I just held on, I could hold on to my life. But Greg said he had to do homework. I hung up before he could hear me crying.

The next day, in civics class, Mrs. Davis assigned a group project, an ad for a mock presidential candidate. I tried to make eye contact with Greg, my usual partner, but he turned toward Jennifer Sadler.

"Does anyone not have a group?" Mrs. Davis asked.

I raised my hand, barely flipping up the fingertips, glancing around to see if anyone else raised theirs. No one. So humiliating.

Mrs. Davis asked if anyone only had two in their group.

"Yeah, us." Nick gestured to himself and Nathan.

"Okay, you can join them," Mrs. Davis told me.

"Great," Nathan muttered when I started over to them—as if I was going to be the liability in their group when everyone knew I was the smartest person in class and they were just about the dumbest.

"I can just do the whole thing," I said. "It's easier."

"Will you say we helped?" Nathan asked.

I looked over at Greg, who sat deep in conversation with StupidGennifer and StupiderJennifer.

"Depends. Will you refrain from being complete jerks for the duration of this project?"

Blank stares. I tried to figure out which word they hadn't understood.

I revised. "Will you be nice?" All single syllables.

They both nodded.

"Fine then."

I glanced at Greg, but he wasn't looking. Beside him, Jennifer mouthed, *Ugly.*

I realized what I had known, probably all along, what ugly girls since the beginning of time had been trying to deny: Beauty was all that mattered. I might tell myself that if people *really* knew me, they'd look past my weak chin and non-eyelashes, would see into my soul and like me despite it all. But, watching Greg giggle with Jennifer and Gennifer, I knew that was not the case. Greg Columbo had looked into my soul—but he still couldn't see past my nose. And, if he couldn't, for sure no one else could. I was disgusted at myself for liking him.

But I still did.

For the next week, Nick, Nathan, and I worked on our project. Or rather, I worked on our project while Nick and Nathan read comic books under their desks.

Tuesday, I asked my mother to take me to the drugstore for supplies. "I need a poster board, Sharpies, stencils, and one of those scissors with the cool-looking edge."

"Isn't this a group project? Can't someone else buy this stuff?" She squinted at herself in the mirror, looking for age spots. It would be hard to pull her away.

"They're sort of worthless. You know how it is."

"Where's Greg been lately? He was always a nice kid."

"He changed over the summer. Can we go to Eckerd's now? You can look at makeup while I find this stuff."

"Like I'd buy makeup from the drugstore." Still, she started toward her purse, since it must have been obvious I wouldn't change my mind. "Changed how?"

"What?" This was more interest than she usually took in my life.

"How did Greg change?"

"Oh, I don't know. Got too handsome to hang with me." I faked a laugh.

My mother, of course, was beautiful. Not beautiful the way every kid thinks her mother is beautiful, but actually beautiful. I'd barely known my father. He died when I was little, leaving Mom with enough money that she never had to work, never had to remarry "another old, rich guy," as she said. Mom had no photos of him she'd admit to, but he must've been really ugly because, for sure, I didn't get my looks from her side. She was tall, with the build of a dancer, blond hair the color of starlight, and eyes the exact shade of the Mediterranean Sea in photos of Greece. Her brows arched high, making her appear wide-eyed and innocent. Her lips were dark and pouty, the type I imagined boys wanted to kiss. No wonder she didn't know about some people having to do all the work on projects. I bet guys were falling all over themselves trying to do her homework

16

for her when she was in school.

Another mom would have said something about looks not being important or that I'd get pretty one day when I was older. That she said neither proved that she didn't believe those things. Instead, she said, "Oh, I guess that happens. Come on. Let's go."

As we started toward the door, I looked back into her mirror. She spent so much time in front of it, I half expected it to talk to her.

On Friday, I brought in my/our project. It was perfect, better than a professional graphic designer would have done. I set it up in the front of the room, noting the peeling tape on Greg's group's poster, the shaky handwriting on another. Mine—I mean, ours—was the best in the class. I took my seat, imagining that even my rivals were stunned by its beauty.

A lot of teachers, when we did group projects, handed out an evaluation form so students could grade themselves and their peers. The idea, I guess, was that if one person did all the work, he could rat out his partners. Like that would ever happen.

I sometimes gave bad grades, though. I had nothing to lose socially since everyone already hated me. Now, I picked up the worksheet and contemplated it. The first part was easy: evaluating myself. I'd been a joy to work with, of course. Cooperativeness: A; completed assignments: A; creativity: A.

I moved to the second section, where I was supposed to grade my partners. Of course, they deserved an F in every category. They'd done nothing. No, they'd done something. They'd left me alone. About that, they'd been completely cooperative.

I penciled in their names and wrote, *Cooperativeness: A.*

I'd promised, after all. I didn't like to lie, but they'd met every deadline because I hadn't given them any. And, as far as creativity went, I guessed they'd creatively managed to avoid work. I penciled in As for that too.

When Mrs. Davis collected the papers, I handed in mine with a clear conscience. Group projects were stupid. Teachers said they were supposed to teach us how it worked in the real world. I already knew. The real world sucked.

I saw Nick and Nathan hand in their papers, sort of smiling at each other. Of course, they were thrilled to have gotten away with doing nothing and still getting multiple As.

Walking home that day, I saw Greg walking with Jennifer. I'd seen him walk with her before, but I'd told myself it was for the project. Now, the project was over, and he was still with her. Were they going to his house to look at the wrens?

I couldn't breathe.

3

Monday, Mrs. Davis handed out grades for the projects.

Of course, we'd gotten As for neatness, artistry, and accuracy. But when I got to the peer-graded portion, I saw that Nick and Nathan had each given me Fs for the three categories of cooperativeness, completed assignments, and creativity. At the bottom of the page, Mrs. Davis had written: *Overall project grade: C.*

I felt my heart actually hammering against my ribs. This was not possible. I'd done all the work, even lied to give them As. That's what they'd been snickering about in class.

I went up to Mrs. Davis's desk.

"Stay in your seat, Violet. We're supposed to be working on our chapter outlines."

"I did that last night. I have to talk to you about this." I thrust the grade report at her and pointed to the Fs with a shaking hand.

She didn't take it. "Well, if you don't do the work on a group project—"

"I did the work. I did all the work." My voice sounded shrill, even in a whisper, and I felt like my face might crack. Everyone was looking up from their papers.

Mrs. Davis glanced around. "Violet, there's really nothing—"

"They did nothing!" I burst out. "I did it all."

She sighed. "What grade did you give them?"

"I gave them As," I admitted, "but that was because . . ." I took a breath.

"Because what?"

I looked at Mrs. Davis. She was almost six feet, big and broad-shouldered, with curly red hair. I bet she'd been picked on in school.

"Because I promised them I would if they left me alone."

"Left you alone?"

"I hate group projects," I whispered, knowing every eye was on me. "People are mean to me because of . . . my looks. Nick and Nathan didn't want me in their group. They bullied me into doing everything." I knew if I said I was bullied (which was true), she'd take it seriously. The school worried about bullying. Or, rather, they worried about fights. Never mind if people slowly died inside, year after year.

"They said I had to do the whole thing," I continued. "If you look at the handwriting, you can see it's all mine. And the project. I brought it in and set it up."

She took the paper from my hand. "Okay, I'll look into it. Sit down now."

A minute later, I saw Mrs. Davis looking at the project. Then she called Nick and Nathan up. After class, she called me back to her desk.

"I changed your grade and theirs. When I confronted the young men with the evidence that yours was the only handwriting on the poster—not to mention that they'd fooled around during all the class time in which you worked on it—they admitted that you had done all the work."

"Wow, thanks." I was sort of amazed she couldn't have figured that out without my telling her. "So what happened to Nathan and Nick?"

"I'm sorry." She looked down. "I'm not allowed to discuss another student's discipline with you."

Which was how I knew they'd really gotten reamed.

Sure enough, when I got to language arts class, I heard one of the Jennifers saying she'd seen Nick and Nathan going into I.S.S. I smiled.

That afternoon, I was walking home, smiling at the knowledge that my grades were again perfect. I walked alone, trying not to notice Greg taking off in the opposite direction with Jennifer, probably heading to her house. It was near Halloween, and the air had gone from summer-hot to chilly. A gust of wind swept up the empty street, and I shivered.

Then, suddenly, I heard footsteps behind me.

At first, they were distant. I resisted looking back, though I wanted to see if it was maybe Greg. It wasn't Greg. It wouldn't matter if it was Greg. There was no Greg for me.

The pounding steps got closer. And harder. I could tell now there were two pairs of feet. Boys' feet. Another gust practically knocked me over, sending leaves and dirt into my face. Usually, no one else walked this way, toward the outskirts of town. I sped up. As soon as I passed Salem Court, I knew they'd part from me. They had to be going there. I matched my step to the rhythm of theirs. Yet they grew closer. My backpack was heavy, digging into my shoulders, slowing me down, and my sneakers cut into my heels.

I, then they, passed Salem Court. They didn't turn. They were following me. That was the only explanation. No one was outside, no one to help me. There was one house, dark and lonely, with peeling, once-white paint. They said an old lady lived there, an old lady or a witch, but I'd never seen her. No kids, though.

Someone yelled, "Hey, ugly!"

I turned to see who had shouted. Nick and Nathan. They broke out laughing. "Look at that!" Nathan yelled. "She answers to ugly."

They were following me. And they were angry. I broke into a run. My sneakers were like blades, slicing into my heels, but I ran. I ran!

And, behind me, I heard them running too. Something hit the side of my head, hard. A rock. It stung, and I dropped my backpack to run faster, dropped it even though I knew they'd take it, knew they'd steal my books and scatter my papers to the wind. I ran as fast as I could.

Another rock hit me. "Stone the ugly witch!" And they were on me, pushing me to the pitted pavement, slamming my head to the hard ground. Their fists rained on me, on my face, into my stomach. I couldn't breathe. I couldn't fight them. The world should have gone black, almost did go black with the blows to my face, but instead, I stared upward at the blue sky. A bird, a black crow or maybe a grackle, sat on one bare tree branch. *Help me*, I thought.

Strangely, I remembered that day in grade school, the day I'd first spoken to Greg. *Help me.* Then, I was floating, no longer inside my body, but above it. I was the bird, perched high in the tree branches, waiting. I opened my beak and gave a mighty caw, spreading my wings and showing my black feathers to the sun. With my beaded eyes, I looked down at the girl, the ugly girl on the pavement, being beaten by two big boys. She looked tiny, shriveled. I cried out again.

Suddenly I wasn't alone anymore. And the sky was no longer blue. It was black with the wings of dozens, no hundreds of birds, blackbirds, grackles, crows, ravens, even larger birds, birds I'd never seen before, lunging and diving below, pecking at my attackers, at their faces, their eyes, not stopping even as the boys ceased beating me and began to beat at the birds. Their beaks pecked the boys' hands, their arms, drawing blood, and I watched from my tree branch, spreading my wings in joy.

Finally, the boys stumbled up and ran, the birds pursuing them down the street. Only one remained, a single crow, glossy wings reflecting the light in purple and green.

I watched from above. *I* was a bird. Then, I was a girl again, a small girl. In my body, on the ground. I gathered myself up. I felt no pain. I stood and walked over to get my forgotten backpack. The crow stood, unmoving, as if it had something to say to me in some secret crow language. Still, I walked around it, gingerly, carefully. I picked up my backpack. The street was again deserted. Nick and Nathan were truly gone. I wondered if I looked like I'd been beaten. I ran my fingers through my hair. Even though I was ugly, I hated to be messy. Why make it worse than I already was? My mother had taught me better. Finishing that, I trudged toward home.

"Hello?" A voice came out of nowhere.

4

I started. It was a woman, standing as if she'd always been there. Yet, I hadn't seen her before. The streets had been quiet, empty.

"Hello?" she repeated. "Are you all right? Did they hurt you?"

So she had seen? But how? There had been no one there. No one! The boys would never have thrown rocks at me with witnesses. They were dumb but smarter than that. Bullies always knew how to hide it.

Finally, I spoke. "I'm . . . I'm fine."

"I see that." She stepped closer. I noticed the crow was gone. It had been exactly where the woman now stood. "You don't have a scratch on you. How is that . . . Violet?"

A chill wind rippled through the trees. "How did you know my name?"

She shrugged. "Lucky guess, I suppose. Was I right?"

"You know you were."

She smiled. She had long, black hair and wore a dress of sheer, iridescent material, first black, then purple, now green, flowing around her. Her hair caught the strained sun and seemed to do the same. I couldn't determine her age. She was beautiful. "You look like a Violet, I suppose."

"No, I don't." First off, no one was named Violet. If you wanted to guess the name of a girl at my school, you might choose right with Jennifer, Kathy, Lisa, or Michelle. But I was the only Violet. "Violets are pretty, with their little faces turned to the sun, hopeful. I'm not pretty. I'm not hopeful either."

She walked closer. Her black hair blew around her face. "You could be anything you want to be."

I laughed. That sounded like something a mom would say. Anyone's mom but mine. "I can only be what I am."

"Sometimes, what you are is more than enough. How did you get those birds to come?"

"They just showed up."

"Pretty convenient, wouldn't you say? Ever hear of birds attacking anyone like that?"

"In a movie once."

"You won't hear about this time either. The boys will consider telling their parents, but, eventually, will decide it makes them sound guilty. Or crazy."

There were no cars anywhere. We were alone. Her eyes were a strange bright green, like a Sprite bottle.

"How about you?" she asked. "Have you had any other experiences with birds?"

"Who are you?"

"Oh, I'm sorry. I'm Kendra. I live here." She pointed at the house on the hill, the one I was sure was abandoned. "I'd ask you in, but, of course, your mother would disapprove of your coming inside a stranger's house."

Now her eyes seemed brown.

"Actually, I doubt she'd care." I knew the second I said it that it was the wrong thing to say. What if she was a kidnapper or something? But it just popped out. Besides, I'd never heard of a woman kidnapper.

"Ah, so she knows."

"Knows what?"

"That you can take care of yourself. And, of course, she's right. You can. Self-sufficiency is one of the few benefits of being lonely."

"How did you know . . . ?" I stopped. I was going to ask how she knew I was lonely, but of course, I knew: Anyone as ugly as I was would be lonely.

I started to walk away, then turned back.

"Once, I saved a bird."

I expected her to react with surprise or, at least, interest. Social interaction wasn't a huge thing with me, but I thought the normal thing to say was, "You did?" or "How did you save it?" Instead, she just nodded, as if unsurprised.

Maybe I should have walked away. Yet I always felt I owed people an explanation, so I told her the story. "I guess I didn't really save it," I concluded. "It just sort of felt like—"

"No, you did save it," she said.

"How do you know?"

"I was there. You were ten years old."

The hairs on my arms stood on end. How was that possible? I remembered the bird, the one I'd seen watching me. Then, the birds today, attacking Nathan and Nick. Were they related? Was it possible that the bird that day somehow remembered me, had told the other birds?

Crazy.

But the woman—Kendra—repeated, "I was there." Then she waved her hand in the air and disappeared. Where had she gone? A crow cawed from somewhere. I looked down. It was right where Kendra had been standing. Then, in a heartbeat, the crow was gone, and Kendra was back.

"How did you do that?" I felt breathless.

I knew the answer, though. Magic.

"There are people in this world who have powers, Violet." The sun was already beginning to set, streaking the sky behind her in strange shades of purple and orange. "I am one of those people. And so are you."

"That's crazy. If I have powers, why can't I . . . ?" I stopped, unsure, for once, how to express the thought: Why did everyone hate me, if I was so powerful?

"Think of what you know of witches. Does anything you have heard or read lead you to believe they are universally beloved?"

Witches. I turned the word over and over in my head, not understanding at first, as if it was a foreign language.

I thought about witches in books, the old woman in the gingerbread house, the green-faced crone in *Wizard of Oz.* But they were evil. The gingerbread witch had tried to bake Hansel and Gretel. The Witch of the West had captured Dorothy with an army of flying monkeys.

Kendra said, "I was ten when I first started noticing my own powers. But nothing big happened until I was thirteen. How old are you now, Violet?"

Thirteen. But I didn't, couldn't say it. I stepped back. If this woman was a witch, would she try to kidnap me? Bake me? Hold me hostage? I wanted to turn and flee. Yet my feet felt suctioned to the ground.

And I wanted to stay. I needed to hear what else she had to say.

Was she saying that she was a witch? Or that I was?

Kendra chuckled, not a high witch cackle, but a low sound from the bottom of her throat. "You think all witches are evil, yes?"

I didn't know what to say. If she was a witch, I didn't want to insult her—especially if she *was* evil. I noticed the street I'd just passed, Salem Court, named for a place where women were hanged as witches. In school, we'd learned they weren't really witches. Now, I wondered.

"I've only read about witches in books. Are they real?" I said to the woman who'd changed from a human to a bird. "Are they evil?"

"Witches are all different, just like everyone else. Some are nice, some not. What we all are, however, is lonely."

Lonely. The word washed over me like summer rain.

"But occasionally," Kendra continued, "I meet a kindred spirit, and when I do, I keep my eye on that person."

"Keep your eye on me? Have you been spying on me?"

I expected her to deny that, but instead, she nodded. "Since that day at the playground, I've watched you."

"As a bird?"

"Or with this." From the air, she produced a shining object, a mirror, surrounded by silver curlicues. She held it out. I cringed at my ugly face.

But she said, "This is a magical mirror. With it, you can see anything, anyone."

"How?" I reached for the mirror.

"Just ask."

"Ask." I had a hard enough time talking to people. What would I say to a mirror? They'd always been my enemies.

"Think of someone, anyone in the world you want to see, and the mirror will show you."

Without hesitating, I said, "Show me Greg."

My hideous face faded from view. The image changed to a room, a house I didn't know. Greg sat with Jennifer, books spread out before them, studying. Or, at least, Greg was trying to study. Jennifer was babbling on. I searched Greg's face for signs of annoyance. Greg took studying seriously, like I did. He'd once threatened not to study with me when all I'd done was ask if he wanted a glass of water!

But now, Greg smiled, then laughed—laughed!—at something Jennifer had said. He pointed at the math book just as Jennifer was trying to turn a page. Their hands touched. Greg turned away, blushing. He always blushed. I knew why he didn't mind Jennifer's chatter. Jennifer was beautiful, unlike me. Jennifer was everything I wasn't. The light gleamed off her blond, straight hair. I could feel my own frizz curling on my neck. Jennifer turned her fair, unblemished cheek toward Greg, and I could feel the hurt of the zits on my own cheek. Greg leaned toward her and then . . .

He kissed her! Greg actually kissed Jennifer!

The mirror fell from my hand and clattered to the ground. It shattered like ice against the black pavement. I jumped when a shard cut my ankle. "Oh!"

I knelt down in the splintered glass, not caring if the bits and pieces embedded themselves in my hands and knees. "I'm sorry. I'm so sorry. Oh, but I hate mirrors. I didn't do this on purpose, though." I picked up one of the larger fragments. It caught the waning sun, reflecting it into my eyes. I saw my own face in it, red, blotchy, a tear dripping from my too-light blue eyes.

And then, the fragment moved. I almost dropped it a second time, but I reached over with my other hand and caught it. The moving fragment sliced my palm. I wanted to cry out, but I didn't, couldn't speak, for at that moment, I saw what was happening.

The fragment, *all* the fragments, moved in the air like shimmering leaves, catching the light. As they fluttered together, my slice of glass slid from my hands. It joined the others, forming a silver oval. Then it flew into Kendra's hand.

I felt my mouth hanging open. I closed it. "How . . . ?" My finger had a heartbeat.

Kendra laid her hand upon mine. "Think about it. I'm sure you can work it out."

I flinched under her touch, but somehow, I couldn't remove my hand. When she finally pulled hers away, the cut had disappeared.

"What did you do?"

"Shh. People use too many words nowadays, always talking on the phone, in person. There is a place in the world, I believe, for thought."

I started to say something else, but I couldn't. It was almost as if someone was covering my mouth.

"Silent thought. One minute. Begin now."

I didn't want to think. I wanted to run. And yet, I couldn't because, more than that, I wanted to know. The mirror. The cut. The birds. Kendra was telling the truth about being a witch. And if she was telling the truth about herself, was it true about me too?

What did it mean?

I stared at Kendra. Her eyes looked green again. Finally, she said, "Are you willing to speak now?"

I tried to put it into words. "If I'm a witch, can I make things . . . ?" What was the word I wanted?

"Better? Maybe. Different? Yes."

"Happen. Can I make things happen?"

"Depends what you're asking for. World peace? End to hunger? Because, no, you can't do those things. No one has enough power for that."

Before I could stop myself, I blurted, "I want to be beautiful. Can that happen?"

It sounded so bare, out in the open like that, out in the empty street. Yet, it was the only thing I wanted, had ever wanted. Well, that and Greg. I knew beauty was nothing. But it was also everything.

"Yes, yes, I can do that. Or, rather, you can."

"How?"

She stared into the distance. The street was silent, no cars, no people, only that wind that picked up the dead leaves and whirled them around, finally sending them skittering away like so many winged insects.

Eventually, she said, "Not all at once. Changing things too quickly is how one gets discovered. But slow changes are fine. I've found that most people are stupid and unobservant."

"So how—?"

"Come here tomorrow." She pointed at the boarded-up house. Again, I remembered my mother—or probably someone else's mother—saying not to go with strangers. And yet I knew my mother wouldn't mind. If this woman could make me beautiful, she'd think it was a risk worth taking.

I said, "Can I see the mirror again?"

She drew it back out from the folds of her gown. Her eyes were brown now. "Don't break it."

"I won't."

I grasped it and brought it up to my face. I studied myself, crooked nose, freckles, frizzy hair, everything.

"Can I . . . can you change *one* thing now?"

She smiled. "Something small?"

"Something big. My nose. Can you make it smaller or, at least, not have a bump on it?"

She laughed. "Funny how society stereotypes witches as having long noses. In fact, it's the first thing most witches would change."

I noticed her nose. It was adorable, tiny, and turned up.

"Very well," she said. "Close your eyes. It will only be a moment."

I closed them. Around me, I heard the wind pick up, felt the dirt and rocks pelting my ankles. I wondered what she would do to my nose and, for the first time, I wondered what she *could* do. Make me even uglier? How could I trust someone I'd never seen before?

And yet, I knew I had nothing to lose. Still, I held my arms around myself, shivering in anticipation and maybe fear.

A moment later, she said, "Okay."

I opened my eyes. She was holding the mirror toward me. I stared at it.

It was my face, still my face, ugly, pale, blotchy, chinless. I still had no eyelashes and horrible hair. No one would notice the difference.

But there was a difference. The bump on my nose was gone.

"Oh." I turned sideways to admire it. "Oh, thank you. *Thank* you."

"Now do you trust me enough to come back tomorrow?"

I nodded. I still held the mirror in my hand, not wanting to stop looking at it. Finally, I handed it back to Kendra.

She smiled. "Power can be a wonderful thing, Violet, a wonderful, terrible thing."

I was still thinking about the mirror, about me, my face. I wanted to ask her how it could be terrible. But, when I looked up, she was gone.

I thought about power. A chill ripped through me.

5

When I found Mom, she was plucking her eyebrows. "Hello, Mommy."

She barely looked up. "Hello."

I just stood there. I wanted to see if she'd notice a difference. But she still didn't look. She plucked one hair, then searched for her next victim. Just when I thought she'd forgotten I was there, she said, "Violet?"

"Yes?"

She plucked another hair, still not looking up.

"You'd tell me if I had hairs on my chin, wouldn't you?"

I had to smile. My mother would never, in a million years, have a hair on her chin. A chin hair would be a flaw, and my mother was flawless. She didn't even have freckles. Not one.

I must have taken too long to answer because she said, "Oh, my GOD! I already have them, don't I? You've noticed, and you haven't told me. Violet, what is the point of even having a daughter if she doesn't tell you about your chin hairs?"

She abandoned her eyebrows and started searching her chin, positioning it in front of the mirror and rolling her eyes down to try and look. Well, that just summed up our relationship. I wanted to let her suffer, but I also wanted her to look at me, instead of her chin, so I said, "No, Mom, of course you don't have chin hairs . . . that I've noticed anyway."

I had to add that last.

"Are you sure? Can you look? Because I was talking to Marge Holcomb today, and since she's so tall, I was looking right at her chin, and you'll never guess what I saw there."

"A chin hair?"

"Haha. No. *Three* chin hairs. Three! That was all I could look at. I felt terrible for her." She laughed, the sound of a breaking mirror. "I would die if anyone looked at me and saw chin hairs." She laughed again.

"You're lucky you're not that tall."

"I am . . . not." Still, she searched her chin. "That's not the point, Violet. The point is, I shouldn't have any. Do you know how hard it is to see your chin? I hate getting old."

She still hadn't looked at my face. Unbelievable. "I don't think you have any. Want me to look?"

"Would you?" She broke into a smile, and like when I was a kid, it made me happy, so happy. My mother was smiling at me.

When I was little, I used to watch her get dressed to go on dates. She had the most beautiful clothes, nothing like other mothers. Silk blouses in jewel colors and strapless gowns like Vanna White on *Wheel of Fortune*. After she left, when the babysitter thought I was in bed, I'd sneak into my mother's closet and try everything on, clothes, shoes, jewelry, makeup, always arranging it back very carefully as if it were a booby trap she'd set to catch me in the crime of pretending to be her.

Sometimes, when she was home, I'd ask to try the things she used, the powders and creams that widened her eyes, blackened her lashes, and made her so pretty. I thought if I could look like her, she would love me, and maybe she would have—if I'd looked like her.

But I never did.

One thing she loved to do was watch pageants, Miss America, Miss USA, Miss Universe, Miss World. The girls in those pageants competed for scholarships, but their sparkly dresses and big hair probably cost more than they'd ever win. The contestants danced sexily onstage and then talked about ending world hunger. Some of the girls probably weren't even pretty before they applied all the hair spray, false eyelashes, and goo, and they did stupid talents like ventriloquism and hula dancing.

And yet, every time they crowned a new queen, the camera panned the audience, found their families. I knew those moms loved their daughters, loved them enough to take out a second mortgage to buy a case of hair spray. Which was more than my mother loved me.

So I was cherishing this mother-daughter moment even if it did involve hunting for chin hairs. "Move into the light where I can see you better. Maybe by the window."

Where you can see me.

"Oh, okay. Let me put on my contacts first. I always take them off when I pluck, to help me see close. But then I can't see anything. I can't even see your face."

"Sure." I handed her the case. I would have stuffed the lenses into her eyes myself had it meant it would happen faster. Could she tell?

Finally, they were in. She blinked at me. "Okay, then, where did you want me?"

In my corner. She still didn't seem to notice any difference. Was I so ugly that a little improvement didn't help? No, she probably hadn't adjusted to the contacts. "Come here."

The sun was close to setting, and the western-exposed window filled the room with strained light. I stood close. "Tilt your chin up." She'd be looking right at my nose in that position.

She obeyed. I held the tweezers, searching for hairs. None there. My perfect mother with a hair on her chinny-chin-chin? Impossible. But I pretended to search, waving the tweezers near her face, wondering if I should pretend to see something.

"Anything?" Her voice sounded breathless.

"I'm . . . not . . . sure." *Look at me.*

"Violet, you must be very certain. I have a date tomorrow, someone new, someone rich. I can't have . . . a hair."

No reaction to my new and improved nose. But, of course, she was too fixated on herself, her wonderful self, as she always was. Maybe if I found a hair, she'd look at me.

"Oh, here it is!" I inched the tweezers up to one downy, blond, regular peach-fuzz hair. I grabbed it. "Got it!"

A moan escaped her lips, and with that sound, I gave the skinny hair a mighty yank. My mother gasped.

"There!" I held the empty tweezers in triumph.

"You're sure that's all?" she asked.

"Positive." *Look at me. Look at me!*

But she turned away. I wanted to say something, anything else. Ask for help with my homework. Ask her to make me cookies? Hardly. Ask if she thought I was pretty. Ha. I knew the answer to that one without asking. I never would be.

Unless . . .

"Okay, Mommy, I have lots of homework."

I did have homework, but for once, I let it slide. I could do it at school. One B was hardly going to wreck my average.

Had I just thought that? I'd gone ballistic about the group project, about anything less than an A.

But the difference was, then, I'd thought it mattered. Now, I knew it didn't. Middle school grades didn't matter. Grades didn't matter. Or how smart you were. Or what college you got into. Nothing mattered if you didn't have the one thing that did: beauty. I was going to get it, and I wasn't going to wait.

I ran to my room and looked for a mirror. There was none over my vanity. I hadn't wanted one. Now, I did. I needed the truth of my ugliness, laid out before me, to see my work. I had no compacts, no powders or blushers, nothing with a mirror in it. Finally, I spotted the little jewelry box my grandfather had given me. It played music when opened, a plastic ballerina whirling round and round, the mirror behind her reflecting her every move. I broke the ballerina off and threw her aside, leaning on the spring that had connected her to the box. It kept spinning even after the dancer was removed. I tried to examine my face.

I couldn't see much in the tiny mirror, just my nose and my nonexistent lashes. How I hated my lashes! I tried to think back on the conversation with the witch, the conversation and what had happened before it. The boys. They'd attacked me, and suddenly, magical help had come. I remembered the other time the magic had come. The broken bird. What did those two experiences have in common? In both cases, I'd really wanted something to happen. Was that it? Was it enough? No. If merely wanting something to happen was enough, I'd be beautiful already.

And my mother would have a beard like Santa Claus!

No, it had to be more than wanting. There had to be some kick in the butt, something to jump-start the magic like cables on a car battery.

The anger. That would explain it. Maybe longing and need too. Ordinarily, I was what people in books called mild-mannered, accepting as an ugly girl needed to be. Pretty girls could have fits of pique, but girls who looked at me should be nice. Usually, I was.

But today, I hadn't been. How could I have? Nor that day with the bird. I loved birds, and I hated the kids who would harm one. Someone who hurt an innocent little bird would hurt me, or anyone. *Hate.*

I stared into the mirror as best I could, patted the spring that had now stopped wavering in the tiny gold frame. I hated my face, my eyelashes especially.

They weren't hard to hate, sparse and pathetic, almost invisible. I'd told myself that my ugliness made me stronger, a survivor. Now I knew I'd lied. Ugliness wasn't power. Beauty was. Those pageant girls knew it. So did the network execs who only hired beautiful airheads to do the news. They were making us stupid as a society. And Greg, my poor Greg, forgetting his best friends because of the beautiful, evil Jennifer. Beauty was power, and I hated it, hated Jennifer and Nick and Nathan, hated all of them, everyone. I wanted the power to hurt them.

I felt a strange tingling in my face. I expected to see that my eyelashes had grown instantaneously, but they hadn't. They were still short, still whitish. I squeezed my eyes shut against their hideousness, and I felt the room begin to whirl. The music box started playing *Swan Lake*, the story of a lovely swan. I remembered *The Ugly Duckling*. Me. I wanted to be the swan. The room spun around me, and when I opened my eyes, the colors kept swirling. I couldn't see my face. I felt like I couldn't breathe. I dropped the jewelry box. It clattered to the floor, still playing, spilling its contents. I felt myself falling too. Then, everything went black.

* * *

I woke, sprawled on the mint-green Berber carpet. I pushed myself up.

I started to stand when I noticed the music box lying open on its side, on the ground. It was just out of my reach, but I crawled toward it, expecting nothing when I looked in its mirror. Sitting up, I held the box close to my face, peered into the mirror.

The eyes that met mine were unrecognizable. Or rather, I did recognize them. They were my mother's eyes, deep blue, fringed with black. Whose eyes were these?

I struggled up. The clock said 7:30. Light streamed through the window. Time for school. I ran to the bathroom and peered into the sparkling, silver mirror above the sink.

It was still me. At least, most of it was me. Weak chin—check. Thin, fuzzy hair—still awful. But the eyelashes were the Maybelline-commercial lashes I'd wished for. The eyes themselves weren't really that different. The lashes just made them look that way. But, it occurred to me, I could change them too.

I could change them. I had the power to change anything.

Anything.

I could be the most beautiful woman in the world.

What I learned the next day in school was this: No one looked at me. Maybe they looked when I was younger, long enough to realize I was beneath their notice. But then, they stopped. So they didn't notice my eyelashes or even my nose.

Knowing this would've been a big time-saver, had I realized it earlier. I thought of all the hours I'd spent washing, brushing, and blow-drying my hair, covering zits in tinted Clearasil, or choosing outfits that wouldn't get made fun of. Had I known all along that I was invisible, I could have taken up a hobby. Or discovered a cure for cancer.

Even Greg didn't notice the change in me. In fact, he didn't look at me at all. Why did I care so much? Why did I still want him?

At least *I* was enthralled by my new look. I excused myself to look in the girls' room during each class, and I went in between too, seeing the same people, the druggies, cutters, and truants each time. The third time, I saw this girl, Molly, a brunette I'd known since kindergarten. She squinted at me through what I was pretty sure was a pot-induced haze and said, "Don't I know you?"

"Yeah, I'm Violet. We went to Coral Ridge together."

Her eyes flickered with recognition. "Ohhhh, I remember. You were the freaky chick who picked up the dead bird."

"It wasn't dead. People just thought—"

"Noooo, it was dead. You made it come back to life. Poof!" She made a sort of *abracadabra* gesture with her hands. "But when I told people that, they said I was on drugs."

"You probably were. How could I do that. I'd have to be—"

"A witch. I told them you were, but they didn't believe me. They said just because someone has a bad nose doesn't mean they're a witch."

Out of the mouths of potheads . . .

"Hmm, I see." I turned toward the mirror. Even though she was acting suspicious, I couldn't resist looking at myself.

"By the way," Molly said, "you look really good. The first time you came in, I almost didn't recognize you. You get a nose job or something?"

I nodded, watching myself in the mirror. I realized that, up until now, I'd wondered if the whole thing was my imagination. "Yeah. Yeah, I did. Thank you. Gotta get back to class."

It was real! It wasn't wishful thinking! It was real!

After school, I pushed through the crowds, past Nick and Nathan, who avoided me after yesterday. Once I was out of sight, I broke into a run. In minutes, I was walking up a driveway overgrown with roots and weeds breaking through the asphalt. The house's steps were covered in weeds too. Did Kendra really live here? I peered through the grimy window. Inside was dark, abandoned. Had it all been my imagination?

I remembered Molly's comments, the boys avoiding me. No. I hadn't imagined it.

I reached for the cobweb-crusted door, avoiding the dead leaves and insect skeletons. I knocked softly. The sound seemed to reverberate around the empty porch. No footsteps, so I was startled by the door opening.

The girl—because that's what she was—looked about my age with short hair that was actually purple. She wore a long, black gown that looked a hundred years old, and bizarre makeup with black sparkles highlighting dark eyes. She looked like a stunning vampire or something, a creature of the night. Was this even Kendra?

But she said, "Come in, Violet."

"Is it . . . Kendra?"

"Oh, I forgot." With a wave of her hand, she transformed into the older, dark-haired woman from yesterday, then back. "Everyone likes a change sometimes. Yesterday, I took a form that would make you comfortable, a middle-aged woman. But really, I can be anything I want."

I stepped inside. It was like the Palace of Versailles, marble floor and glowing chandeliers, all brand-new. She led me to a little sofa covered in tapestry fabric. How had she done it all? Witchcraft, of course. Could I do it too?

My heart whispered that I could.

"I see you've been experimenting." She focused on my eyes.

"What?" I tried to look confused. "No, I haven't."

She stared at me. "Of course not. I must be mistaken. Your eyes have always looked like the second coming of Elizabeth Taylor."

"Who's that?"

"Sorry, I date myself. She was an actress, lovely, violet-colored eyes, long, lustrous lashes. Some say she was the most beautiful woman on earth. Or the fairest one of all."

"The fairest . . . huh?"

"Sorry. It's something we used to say when I was a girl. No one says that anymore."

The fairest one of all. Man, would that be something. I'd have been happy just not being ugly, but the *fairest.*

"Okay," I admitted. "I guess I experimented with my lashes a little. I figured no one would notice, and no one did."

"No one?"

"This one druggie girl. But my own mother didn't."

Kendra nodded. "How did you do it?"

I shrugged. "Don't you know?" She'd probably been watching me in her mirror.

"I want you to tell me."

"Okay. I channeled my feelings, I guess."

"What do you mean?"

"Once, when I was in fourth grade, two boys got into a fight in PE. Instead of getting mad at them, the coach told them to channel that anger into the softball game we were playing. Choke up on the bat, and hit real hard. And it actually helped. At least, one of them got a home run on his next at bat."

"And this has what to do with you?"

"Just, that's what I did—channeled all the anger, the rage over the way people treat me, at girls like Jennifer and Gennifer, who wouldn't even let me play kickball with them in grade school, at Greg, for not noticing how awful they are, or not caring, anyway, for ditching me. I put all that in my head and concentrated on . . . my eyelashes."

She laughed.

"It seems trivial, I guess." I knew it wasn't.

"No, eyelashes are very important." She wasn't kidding.

"Is that how it always works? Does magic come from rage and hatred? It did with Nick and Nathan too."

But not with the bird. How had that happened?

"Maybe hatred and rage, maybe fear, maybe even love, though I've never tried that one myself. It comes from a strong emotion that overwhelms you like an ocean's waves. For me, it began with desperation. When I was your age, a terrible plague swept through my town. My father died, mother too. Then, one by one, each brother and sister was taken from me until, finally, I had only one left, my youngest brother, Charlie. And Charlie lay dying in his bed."

"That must have been terrible. No one could help?" I didn't have siblings, only my mother. But the thought of losing her was too terrible to bear.

Kendra had a faraway look in her eyes. "No, no one could help. I was thirteen and alone. Half the town lay sick and dying. The rest mourned as I did. Every day, Mr. Howe, the gravedigger, brought his wheelbarrow down our street, asking if we had any dead to bring out, and one by one, my family left me."

I shuddered. "What did you do?"

"I went to a woman, a healer in town. Her name was Lucinda, and she had been my friend, had told me that someday, I might be a healer like her. But she was gone too."

"Was she dead?"

Kendra shook her head. "She'd just disappeared. At that moment, I felt more emotion than ever before, emotions crowding inside me, crawling over one another, clamoring to get out like Pandora's box, anger, grief, desperation, loneliness, and they poured out of me and onto Charlie."

I remembered the night before, the room spinning, my vision going purple.

44

"So the emotions were what triggered your magic?"

"I didn't know at the time, but yes. When I woke the next day, Charlie was awake, alive. He was cured of his sickness as if nothing had been wrong. This had happened to no one else. Everyone who had sickened had died. There was only one reason this could have happened: me. I had cured him."

"Wow." It was incredible to think that such powers existed, that I could have them too. "Wait. When was this?"

Kendra hugged herself, her slim hands crushing down the black fabric of her dress. "The year the plague struck England. 1666."

"*Sixteen* sixty-six?" It was impossible. "So you're . . ."

"Immortal, yes. All witches are." With a wave of her hand, she transformed again, this time into a young girl from another era, blond braids streaming down her back. She wore a long, blue dress with full sleeves and a red apron. "It is a blessing, but a curse as well. One gets lonely. There are so few of us."

From another room, I heard a clock ticking. "So nothing can kill you . . . us?"

"Nothing but the flame. I have managed to avoid it these three-hundred-odd years, sometimes just barely." She waved her hand and was herself again, at least, the self I'd seen before. "Come now, let's work on making some magic."

I wanted to. I especially hoped to be able to work magic without passing out. Kendra made it look so easy.

"So, my friend, what should we try next? Something small."

"Does it have to be small? People at school wouldn't even notice if I showed up six inches taller. I'm invisible to them."

"You'd be surprised what people notice."

I thought of Molly from the bathroom. I nodded.

"And once people notice, they look for ways to use your magic against you. That's how people like my friend Lucinda disappear."

"But you said she was immortal, unless . . ." I shuddered, picturing someone being burned at the stake, the wood piled high around her, flames lapping at her feet. Would the fact that she couldn't die except by burning mean she couldn't asphyxiate, that her heart couldn't burst, but rather, she would have to be burned alive, watching the skin peel off as painful first- and second-degree burns gave way to the blessed relief of death?

"No," Kendra said, "she was not burned. She merely disappeared. Witches do. Now, let's find something suitably small. Your complexion, perhaps?"

I had a few blemishes, nothing terrible but, of course, I was self-conscious about them. I nodded.

"Hate drains the energy," she said, stroking my skin gently, like my mother never had. "It's not a safe emotion. That's why you passed out last night. Is there another strong emotion you can tap into?"

My first thought was love, my love for Greg. But that emotion was all tied up with other emotions, my hatred for Jennifer, my anger at Greg himself for ditching me when he suddenly became hot. I tried to think of happier memories, but they all failed me. I thought how I felt every day, how I felt alternately invisible, ignored, ridiculed. How I felt alone, even in my own house, with my own mother.

I remembered what Kendra had said about witches being lonely. "Would loneliness work?"

Kendra smiled, barely turning up her lips. "Yes, dear, I know it will. It is an emotion I use quite a bit myself." She reached toward me. Her hand was small and white, as if it had never seen sun. "Close your eyes."

She passed her fingers down my forehead and across my face. I closed my eyes gladly. The bright light against white walls was suddenly tiring.

"Now remember . . ." Her voice was soft, soothing. "Remember the loneliest you've ever felt."

So many memories to choose from. The time my school had Lunch with Your Child Day, and my mom was the only one who didn't come. She hadn't had time, she said, but she sure had time for dumb things like hair appointments. No, it was because I wasn't presentable, wasn't pretty. She was ashamed to be seen with me.

I'd thrown my sandwich in the garbage, feeling like the ugliest person in a world full of beauty.

But perhaps this memory edged too close to hate, to anger. I remembered other days, mundane things, walking home from school alone, remembered not having a partner on field trips and having to sit by someone else's mother who was chaperoning, party invitations handed out to everyone but me, no one talking to me except to ask me to please switch seats so their friend could sit there. I remembered . . .

"It worked." Kendra's voice interrupted my thoughts.

"What did?" I realized I was weeping, hot, salty tears seeping out from under my eyelids.

"Look."

I did, mopping at them as I looked. The mirror, Kendra's lovely mirror, was before me. I gazed into it. My skin was clear, unblemished, smooth, pink, like Mom's. And still, the tears kept coming, coming out of me.

Kendra's arms tightened around me. "There, my darling. Someday, you will be able to do this without crying."

"Will I?"

She stroked my back. "I promise."

"Can everyone do it then? I mean, does everyone have the power to channel their emotions?"

I hoped not.

"Oh, no. Not everyone. It is a rare thing indeed. No, my darling. You are special."

Special. No one had ever called me that before, not even teachers at school.

"Come, my darling. You have worked hard. Let me get you some gingerbread."

"Gingerbread?"

She shrugged. "I am sentimental. The witch who taught me, she made gingerbread."

I remembered the story of *Hansel and Gretel*, the children made into gingerbread. What if Kendra turned out to be like that witch, a cannibal bent on murder? Would I have the strength to run away from the one person who praised me and thought I was special? I stroked the smooth skin of my cheek, feeling Kendra's arm around me. I wasn't sure. I wanted Kendra to teach me. Desperately.

But the gingerbread she brought me wasn't shaped like children. In fact, it wasn't even a cookie, but a cake in a square pan. Kendra cut a still-steaming chunk for each of us and served it with glasses of cold milk. The hot gingerbread warmed my mouth and soon my tears were forgotten.

"What happened to the witch who taught you?" I asked.

Kendra brushed some crumbs that had fallen onto the lace table-cloth. They vaporized instantly. "Alas, she was burned." She looked down.

I waited for her to elaborate, to explain, but she didn't. There was only the sound of our forks on china. "I'm sorry," I said.

She shook her head and still didn't speak.

Finally, she said, "You should go home. Your mother will miss you."

I doubted that, but I said, "Can I come back tomorrow?"

"Best to wait a little. Thursday, perhaps, so as not to excite suspicion. I will see you then, my dear."

And suddenly, she wasn't there. The air felt chilly as, one by one, the objects in the room disappeared too, and I was all alone in the old, abandoned house.

I touched my cheek.

I wondered what else I could do.

7

I stepped outside. The door slammed shut. The sound echoed down the silent street. I trudged through the weedy yard. The sun had been shining when I'd entered Kendra's yard. Now the clouds blocked any sign of it.

Other than the brief, magical time when I'd had Greg, I had always been lonely. Yet the realization that Kendra was the only person *voluntarily* to speak to me in months chilled me. What was wrong with me? It couldn't just be that I was ugly. Yet it had to be. What else could it be? It had to. If it wasn't about my appearance, then changing it wouldn't change anything. And I wanted to change everything.

Everything.

Down the block, I saw a lone, white cat playing by the roadside. I remembered hearing that most white cats were blind. Or was it deaf? The cat was scrawny, maybe a stray, and, suddenly, I wanted to pick it up, take it home with me. I'd never asked for a pet. Could my mother really say no? I walked faster, suddenly wanting the cat, hoping it didn't have a collar.

Suddenly I heard a rumbling behind me. A car! I jumped, then ran under a tree, feeling the whoosh of air as the car sped by.

My heart was pounding. I screwed my eyes closed. Then, I heard a dull thud. My eyelids flew open. The cat! The cat, crushed under the wheels of some Mustang.

I waited for the car to stop, but it roared on as if the driver hadn't noticed. Or just didn't care.

Then, I was screaming, "Stop! No!" But the words were lost in the motor's roar, and the pounding of my footsteps on black pavement.

There was surprisingly little blood, only a bit coming from the kitty's mouth. Black tire marks marred its white coat. I held my hand to its chest, feeling for a heartbeat. There was one, but only faint. I knew it wouldn't last long.

I gathered the cat in my arms, hating the driver. How could people be so uncaring? He didn't even stop.

Something, a jagged, broken bone, penetrated the cat's coat. The loneliness and sadness rose up in my throat like bile, then came spilling out of my mouth in words like vomit, words I didn't understand. I just sat there in the road, rocking the cat back and forth, saying I didn't know what, and suddenly, the pointy bone retreated inside its body. The cat's heartbeat quickened, and then its whole being began to vibrate.

It was purring! Purring and rubbing up against me! I knew I had fixed it, my magic and I had. If my magic only did one worthwhile thing, saving the cat was enough. More than enough.

I picked up the cat and carried it home. To my mother's

questioning look, I said, "I found a cat. I'm going to keep it."

"Were you going to ask me?"

"No. I'll take care of it."

I stared at her, and maybe there was something in my eyes—or my new eyelashes—that made her say, "Okay. We'll have to get cat food tomorrow, but I have some old tuna tonight."

I fed the cat—whom I named Grimalkin after a witch's cat in a book—and took her to my room. She curled up on my bed and purred while I did my homework. She loved me already.

"The cat will have to stay outside while you're at school," my mother said the next morning. "We don't have any litter. It will pee all over the place."

"*She* will run away if I leave her outside." The cat had slept on my bed all night, between my legs, her purring lulling me to sleep. I'd awakened more rested than I'd ever been and had spent most of the morning admiring the cat's blue eyes and white whiskers. I had to keep her.

"If you feed it, it will stay."

"We don't have any cat food. Can't I just leave her in the bathroom?"

"Violet, do you know what cat pee smells like?"

I didn't answer, assuming the question was rhetorical. In fact, I did know, and I hoped my mother wouldn't notice the smell on a pair of jeans that had been crumpled on my desk chair. I'd stuck them into the washing machine and planned to wash them after school.

"The cat can come in once we get litter, but for now, it will have to stay outside."

I drew the cat into my arms. Most cats—I knew from painful experience—didn't like being picked up, but this one began to purr and rub her head against mine. "I can't just throw Grimalkin outside!"

"Uck, why give it such an ugly name? Call it something pretty like Tiffany or Courtney." My mother turned back toward her room. "It has to go out."

I went back to my own room. I considered skipping school, but there was a test in social studies, and I knew Mom would never write a note for me. Too much trouble. I shut the door, thinking perhaps I could hide Grimalkin inside. But she started to meow.

Finally, I waited until Mom was engaged in the delicate contour drawing that was her morning beauty ritual, then I took the cat outside.

"Stay there." I placed her on the step.

The cat looked at me as if she understood. She blinked once, then again in the morning sun.

"Stay there," I repeated.

She lay down on the step, curling herself into a ball.

"Perfect," I said, even though I knew the cat would probably be gone when I got home, and the loneliness was like a paper cut on my heart. Why couldn't Mom just get some litter? Be a human for once? But I knew she wouldn't, so I started toward school.

The cat stood and followed me.

"No," I said. "Stay."

But the cat kept following me, like Mary's lamb.

I remembered what I'd learned about channeling my emotions. The cat could not leave. She couldn't. It was completely unreasonable for me to get all involved with a cat, but I had. My loneliness made me unreasonable.

I picked the cat up and held her close, willing her to stay there, wanting her to. I was facing east, and the sun was already high and at the perfect angle to get in my eyes. I shut them, still feeling the warmth on my eyelids, on my cheeks, the purry warmness of the cat, who was not struggling in my arms. She nuzzled me, and I knew I couldn't go to school and leave her. I held the warm, fluffy, vibrating ball, rocking her like an infant. Behind my eyelids, I could see the sky changing colors, blue to red to purple and a burst of bright pink like fireworks. Stay. *Stay.*

Then, suddenly, I felt the cat's back feet digging into my stomach. She wanted to leave. You can't hold a cat who wants to go, and this cat did. I dropped her and opened my eyes.

The sun had gone behind a cloud, a cloud that hadn't been there before. I'd stood there longer than I'd realized.

I looked at the cat. She was chasing a squirrel. It went up a tree that overhung our neighbor's property. Grimalkin followed it. I knew she would be lost. The squirrel would go further and further, and she'd go with it.

"Stay," I said.

She did not, of course, look back at me. She followed the squirrel across the branch, toward the neighbor's yard.

But when the squirrel entered the neighbor's yard, Grimalkin didn't follow. Instead, she stopped, as if realizing she could go no further. She looked insulted, as cats do. Then she turned and ran down the tree trunk and stood at my feet. She began to lick her right front paw.

I glanced at my watch. Five minutes until school started. I had to leave, and I had to run. I gathered my books and lunch box, dropped in my trance. I patted Grimalkin's head, then started toward school.

When I looked back, the cat was still sitting under the tree, unmoving.

When I returned that afternoon, she was still there, waiting for me.

I visited Kendra after school the following day and the day after that and every day for the next two weeks. She taught me things, magic things. While she cautioned me not to alter my appearance too drastically, I did alter it some, straightening my teeth so much that my orthodontist declared, with a shocked expression, that I no longer needed braces. I also gave my hair a wavy, just-out-of-the-salon perfection. Finally, people noticed. At least, my mother complimented me on finally taking an interest in my appearance. Mom was great at making a compliment sound like an insult.

But Greg didn't notice.

Or, more likely, he didn't care.

Kendra taught me some party tricks, moving stuff with my mind like witches did on television shows like *Bewitched*. She didn't say anything about casting spells on other people, and I didn't ask. I knew she'd disapprove since she'd told me several times that my magic could backfire.

"Backfire how?" We were at her house, which was now decorated in some sort of British colonial, dark furniture and stuff with elephants on it.

Kendra adjusted her linen blouse. "Oh, sometimes the unexpected will happen, or you'll realize the magic you thought you wanted, you didn't want at all."

"All I want is to be pretty. And have friends."

"All?" Kendra asked.

Well, no. Not all. I wanted Greg to love me. And I wanted Jennifer to contract a bad case of leprosy, to help that along. But I didn't say that. Across the room, a brown spider crawled up a dining room table leg that looked like a lion's paw. I liked spiders. I never killed them. Unlike most people, I knew they weren't harmful, not usually. In fact, they killed mosquitoes and flies, bugs that spread disease.

The spider lifted first one leg, then another. Was it a brown recluse? Those could be harmful, resulting in skin death and terrible scarring. But even they didn't usually bite. People who got bitten by spiders brought it upon themselves. They weren't careful.

"Can you give me an example of backfiring?" I wondered if I could get the spider to come toward me. Kendra had taught me many tricks, but since the day of the cat, I hadn't used my magic on another living creature. I wanted to. It would be cool to be able to manipulate others, like maybe make Jennifer scratch herself like a gorilla. But, of course, I'd have to be able to do it so no one knew it was me.

"So hard to think of just one example," Kendra said. "I have been alive hundreds of years, and I seldom get the opportunity to tell my stories."

I laughed. That was obvious. For each bit of magic I learned, there was at least an hour of talk. But Kendra's stories were fascinating. She looked my age, so she was like a friend. Yet she'd lived hundreds of years. Someday, I'd be as experienced and smart as she was. "I'm sure it will be a great story."

Kendra leaned on an umbrella stand shaped like an elephant's foot and stared out the window into the waning light. "I once knew a tsar who had twelve beautiful daughters."

"A tsar? So you lived in Russia?"

"I've lived everywhere. But yes, this particular tsar was in Russia, and he had twelve daughters, each with so many suitors that the tsar could not decide—which was a high-class problem to have. He planned to have a month of balls and events and invited them all to a huge house party—or, rather, castle party. I was employed as a maid, so I knew of all the preparations."

"A maid? Why would someone with your powers want to be a maid?"

"A maid is an easy job for someone with my powers. A blink of my eye, I can clean the silver, fluff a hundred comforters, and try on all the jewels in the house. But a maid is where the action is. As a maid, I traveled on the finest ships, including the great *Titanic*, lived in palaces the world over. And people say things when the maid is in the room, secret things."

"So why aren't you a maid now?"

"Alas, there are few palaces and even fewer kings. The world has become more democratic, but also more boring. What happened in the tsar's palace could not happen today."

"What happened?" Across the room, the spider still crawled.

Kendra continued. "Many great preparations were made. Every stick of furniture was dusted to gleaming. Every sheet was washed in lavender to stimulate restful sleep. I was a lady's maid to Manya, one of the middle daughters. It was my job to make certain her clothes were in order and to do her hair. She had lovely titian hair."

"What is titian?"

"Oh, I am sorry. I forgot that people of your generation know so little. Titian is a dark red shade favored by an artist also named Titian who painted many red-haired women."

I nodded. Titian sounded so much prettier than my own carroty red hair. Perhaps I would change my hair to titian sometime.

"Anyway, Manya had red hair, so she liked dresses in blue and green with satin slippers to match. Since the party would last a month, I made certain she had thirty gowns (it would not do for a princess to repeat) and six pairs of dancing slippers, three each in green and blue. I took great pride in the hairstyles that I—or, rather, my magic—could accomplish. But one morning, the princess had a terrible illness."

"What was wrong with her?"

"I had no idea. It seemed like a sleeping sickness I'd seen on my travels, but there was no fever or cough. The princess simply couldn't stay awake. And worse, when I left her chamber to get help, I found that all her sisters were similarly stricken. They did not want to leave their beds, and when the governesses forced them to, they dragged around the floor as if half dead."

I wondered how all the princesses would have been so close in age. Were they sextuplets? Octuplets? But I figured Kendra wouldn't appreciate the interruption.

She continued. "We all ministered to the princesses, but none got any better. On the third day, though, I noticed a startling change. A pair of Manya's dancing slippers was missing."

"How strange." A missing pair of slippers wasn't my idea of high intrigue. My eyes wandered again to the spider. It had moved to the underside of the table and was starting to make a web. As Kendra talked on, I concentrated on the spider, the bit of thread emanating from its spinnerets. I wanted it to come over. Could I make it do so by just wanting it? To do magic without Kendra noticing was my goal.

"I looked everywhere for the lost shoes," Kendra said. "The princess had gone nowhere, so nothing should have moved. Finally, I asked one of the other ladies' maids if she had seen them. To my surprise, she reported that a pair of her princess's shoes was missing also!"

She paused when she said this, as if expecting some reaction. I had none, so I said, "Hmm." I was still staring at the spider, willing it to come toward me, concentrating all my love and hate, joy and longing into that one task.

"After polling the other maids," Kendra continued, "we found that, indeed, each young lady was missing shoes. A search ensued, and finally, we found a pile of slippers down the rubbish chute. Each pair had been danced into rags!"

I saw the spider's thread disengage itself from the table to which the spider had attached it. I tried to contain my excitement, to concentrate.

"It was so strange," Kendra said, "because Manya and all her sisters had done nothing but sleep. And, a few days later, another pair of shoes disappeared from each closet."

The spider raised a tentative leg and started the long journey down the table.

"The tsar was so concerned about his daughters' illness that he offered a reward: Any man who found the cause of his daughters' malaise could choose a princess to marry. Many young men came to take the test, but none could solve the mystery. Those who failed were brutally dispatched. Meanwhile, another twelve pairs of slippers were danced to rags."

The spider reached the ground and began to traverse the gleaming marble floor.

"One day," Kendra said, "I was out in the garden gathering flowers when a young man approached me. 'You are the maid to one of the princesses, I believe?' he said.

"I nodded, for I recognized him as a boy I saw sometimes in town, a boy who worked in the blacksmith's shop. He said, 'Then, perhaps, you can help me. It's about the princesses. The challenge the tsar has made. I want to try.'

"'You shouldn't,' I told him. 'It's a good way to lose your life.'

"But he told me he was very much in love with Princess Svetlana. He knew this could be his only chance to marry her. I asked him how he could be in love with her. He would barely have seen her. Svetlana was the oldest daughter and thought to be the most beautiful.

"But he told me I was wrong. Svetlana was an avid horsewoman. When her horse needed new shoes, she came with the groom. In fact, she came when any of her sisters' horses needed shoes also. 'She is so kind,' said the blacksmith's boy, 'so modest, not a haughty princess at all. She even has smiles for the lowly groom whom she accompanies. She treats him as well as a lord. Perhaps if I could win her, she could love a poor peasant too. This is my only chance.'"

The spider lifted first one leg, then the other, walking toward me, getting closer as Kendra continued with her story.

"I told him I didn't understand how he expected me to help. After all, if I knew what was making the princesses sick, I would already have solved the mystery. But he said, 'I think you have other skills that would help me.'

"I knew," Kendra said, "what skills he must mean, my witch skills. But how had he found out? I had done everything in my power to hide my abilities, for if I was discovered, I would be at best run out of town, at worst, tried as a witch. 'I do not know what you mean,' I said.

"But he told me his aunt was a witch. He knew how they

functioned. He had seen how things changed when I was about, the way the crows followed me and the horses reacted around me. And he said, 'I saw how Ivan Vangeloff's horse went lame when Ivan angered you.'

"There he had me. Ivan had been my beau, my ex-beau, a shop-keeper's son. When he had glimpsed pretty Katrina in the town square, he called upon me no more. I had seen his horse in the black-smith's shop, and, forgetting myself, I had bewitched it. Now I was paying the price. I would have to help the boy."

The spider came closer and closer. If I could perform spells upon animals unnoticed, I could probably do the same on people. A very interesting possibility. *Come to me*, I told the spider with my thoughts. *I have no wish to harm you. Not you.*

"So it was settled," Kendra said. "I would use my magic to give the blacksmith's boy—his name was Alexei—the power of invisibility."

I gasped. "You can do that?" It was all I could do to hold my gaze on the spider, for this seemed the most wonderful power of all. To go anywhere, spy on people, even.

"Of course," Kendra said. "It is just another way of changing shape. If one can shift one's own shape, it is nothing to change the shape of another, even to nothing."

"Wow." I sighed in amazement. The spider walked still closer, and I wondered if I could change its shape. If I made its legs longer, altered the color a bit, would it be a harmless daddy longlegs instead of a poisonous brown recluse? Could I transform its nature by shifting its appearance?

And, if so, could I change who I was, become an outgoing, happy girl, a winner instead of a loser? I'd have to ask Kendra sometime, maybe later, after I'd listened to her boring story about how having magic powers was somehow a *bad* thing.

"That night," she continued, "Alexei arrived, announcing that he would solve the mystery of what was happening to the princesses. The staff snickered, for the boy was small and pathetic. He was put up in a guest room, but as soon as the castle had gone to bed, I snuck him into Manya's room. Then, I made him invisible. The next morning, when the castle woke—except for the princesses—Alexei declared that he had the answer."

Kendra paused, and I knew I was supposed to say something.

"What did he tell you?" The spider was close enough now that I could make out details. Its legs were short and wide, bent like a crab's. I remembered a daddy longlegs I'd seen. Its legs were slender, arched like the supports on a bridge. I didn't know how to change one to the other, but I'd try.

"The blacksmith's boy said he had followed the princesses through a secret trapdoor hidden beneath one of their beds. He did not say how he'd been able to do so without being seen, and of course, no one knew.

"Under that door, he said, was a staircase, and down that staircase was a canal. The princesses, dressed in their best gowns and dancing slippers, traipsed down the staircase and entered the gondola. The gondolier took the princesses (and, unbeknownst to him, the blacksmith's boy too) down the canal to a secret dock, where they were met by twelve young commoners who escorted them to a secret ballroom where they danced the night away. At dawn, the princesses boarded the gondola again and went back to their rooms to spend the day in sleep.

"'Impossible,' said the tsar. 'Why would my daughters sneak out at night to dance with commoners?'

"But that night, we stayed up to watch the princesses. On my watch, one of the princesses got up, as if looking for something. But when she saw me watching, she fell back into fitful sleep."

Kendra's words got lost as I concentrated on the spider, then on the magic words I had learned and the ways I could use them. My vision blurred, but I struggled to remain focused. Just as I was about to give up, one of the spider's legs began to stretch, then another. The spider wobbled on its path, but finally, all eight legs matched. It skittered toward me, its body elongating as it went, the violin marking leaving its back. Success!

"The next morning," Kendra said, "we reported what we had seen. The tsar had the room checked and found the hidden door. The canal. 'It seems you are right, young man,' he said. The young man chose to marry the princess, Svetlana."

I tore my eyes away from the spider. "What's wrong with that? You said your magic backfired, but that's a happy story. A poor blacksmith's boy marrying a princess—it's like Cinderella."

"Ah, but Cinderella's prince wanted to marry her. That's why he searched the kingdom. Svetlana did not wish to marry the blacksmith's boy, and when she heard her father's declaration, she ran sobbing from the room. Indeed, all her sisters did. They wept all day, but, that night, the first of the royal guests were to arrive, and their father commanded the princesses to dry their eyes and come down to greet them. When I was fixing Manya's hair, I asked what was wrong."

"'Don't you see?' she asked. 'We don't want to marry the blacksmith's boy or anyone of Father's choosing. We do not wish to be auctioned like cattle. Svetlana was—is—in love with the groom. That is why she went with him to the blacksmith's shop. In fact, we all have secret loves, commoners we visit at night. But now that we are discovered, we will be married to princes. We shall go far away and never see our darlings again.' She sighed. 'If only I could dance with Viktor just one more time.' And, again, she began to weep."

The spider was within inches of me now. I reached out, and it crawled onto my hand. I stared at it, marveling at its coffee-bean-shaped body, its sunburst of legs. I had done that, changed one thing to another. I turned away so that Kendra would not see my smile.

"And so it came to pass," she said. "Svetlana married the blacksmith's boy, and each of her sisters also married a man she did not love. The end."

Mesmerized, I reached out to touch the spider.

"Ouch!" It bit me on the knuckle.

"What is it?" Kendra asked.

"This spider. It bit me." Already, I could feel the venom seeping into my system. "Help me, please."

Kendra looked at it. "Oh, don't be silly. It's a daddy longlegs. Humans aren't affected by their bites."

"But it's not a daddy longlegs. It's a brown recluse. I . . . changed it. Unless you're saying it's turned into a real daddy longlegs. Then it won't hurt me."

Kendra reached out toward the spider, and then, with a tiny tap, changed it back to its true shape. She placed it on the ground and shooed it away. Then she glanced at my hand.

A small, white blister began to form, but with the touch of her finger, that too was gone. "No. It is still a brown recluse. You can change a thing's appearance, but not its nature. Perhaps that, along with my story, is enough learning for today." She nodded at me. "Run along."

And I did what she said. What I had learned was valuable indeed: Any harm I did to myself, I could undo.

As I walked toward the door, I made certain to stomp upon the spider until it was just a brown blot on the floor.

9

That night, I decided Kendra was crazy. Oh, sure, she'd recognized what I was, taught me magic, and made me the powerful witch I was becoming. But that didn't mean she wasn't also crazy. Or senile. How could she say magic wasn't a positive thing? Even in the story she'd told, magic had ended the carnage.

Of course, Kendra was still my best, my only friend. I needed her. And I needed her to teach me too.

I thought about what I'd done with the spider. I'd been able to change its shape, if not its nature. I could do that to people. Changing their looks would be enough. That way, I could keep Gennifer and Jennifer the same shallow girls they were—trapped in fat, bacne-ridden bodies.

If you can't change their nature, something mean inside me whispered, *you can't make someone fall in love with you. Greg never will; you will find out the hard way.*

Stupid. I told myself I didn't need to change anything. Greg had loved me for myself all along, all the time we were friends. He just got sidetracked. He was shallow. Boys were. He wanted a prettier girlfriend. Since I was going to be the most beautiful girl in the world, he'd have to love me. I'd just have to get beautiful Jennifer out of the picture, to be sure.

I knew I'd have to change her appearance as I did my own, slowly, gradually, so it wouldn't be obvious, even to her.

As I drifted off to sleep, I made my plan. I would put it into action in language arts, the one class I had with Jennifer and not Greg.

The next morning, I stood by my locker, brushing my hair. I'd recently installed a stick-on mirror, so I could admire myself between classes. My classmates still didn't notice the difference in me, but I did. I straightened up. Greg was passing by, alone for once. I met his eyes with confidence, then looked away on my own terms.

Maybe that's what I needed, to be on my own terms. Probably Greg would eventually get tired of Jennifer on his own without any help from me. She was really stupid. It was silly of me to want to hurt her. After all, if Greg didn't like me for me, what good was he? Maybe I should—

"Hey, watch it, ugly!" Someone slammed into me.

"Sorry."

"Your face is sorry." It was Jennifer, Jennifer with brand-new highlighting and a face full of makeup. "You just exist to get in my way, don't you?" She shoved past me toward Greg, who'd stopped to wait for her.

Okay. Game on.

In class, we were reading *Animal Farm* aloud, painful because Mr. Cameron had students take turns reading and, apparently, some still couldn't. I read ahead, pages ahead, but then he'd stop to discuss it, and I wouldn't remember where we were. So, instead, I just zoned out as Colby Buckner read, "Man is the only real enemy we have. Remove Man from the scene, and the root cause of hunger and over-work is ab . . . ol . . . ished forever." I thought about pigs. The pigs in the story were supposed to be like the people in power. People were like pigs. If only the people who were like pigs could *look* like pigs.

I contemplated Jennifer, who sat two rows to the side of me. She wasn't even pretending to read. Her eyes fluttered closed, then open. Her forehead drooped forward. Her nose was adorable, slim, and turned up. What if it turned up a little bit more . . . ?

She saw me looking at her and mouthed, *Pig*.

I thought of everything Jennifer had ever done to me, the insults, taking Greg, the snickering, taking Greg. Then I thought of every-thing anyone had ever done to me. All my life, I'd been an outcast, a pariah, and why? Because I wasn't pretty enough? Because I was too smart to matter but not smart enough to play stupid? I closed my eyes, but I could see Jennifer's face, Jennifer's perfect, blue-eyed, laughing face, her enviable nose. Then, in my mind, it morphed into a pig nose. She squealed in horror, just like a pig, and held her lively, nail-polished fingers up to hide it. She squealed again, then started to cry. I smirked in satisfaction.

In the room, Colby was still reading. I put my head down, look-ing at Jennifer so she couldn't see me.

She was still whispering to Gennifer. Her nose was still perfect.

Why hadn't it worked? Guess I hadn't done it right. Maybe it was harder to work magic on others. But hadn't Kendra cured her brother the first time out? Hadn't I gotten the birds to fight off Nick and Nathan? I leaned my hand on my face and looked up.

Huh. My face felt different. My nose felt . . . piggy.

What? How could that be? I'd seen it so clearly in my mind,

Jennifer's face changing, not mine. Not mine!

Even as I held my hand up, I felt my nose hardening, my nostrils spreading even more. My head was heavy, and I remembered reading that a pig's snout weighed about a pound. I cradled my head in my hands like I had a headache, leaning to cover myself with my hair.

"Violet, will you read next?" Mr. Cameron asked.

I began to cough, still holding my hands over my face. I managed to gasp out, "Bathroom!" Around me, everyone was laughing. Without waiting for Mr. Cameron's response, I bolted to the girls' room, still coughing. I looked in the mirror and saw . . . my snout.

It was pinkish-white with black spots and stood at least three inches from my face!

What . . . the . . . ?

I ducked into a stall, shaking, and tried to bring up the magic. My thoughts were racing. How would I get out of here? What would Mr. Cameron say? Could I put my face back? I realized that, while anger had been an awesome motivator, fear was a terrible one.

Breathe. Breathe. Stop thinking about how you can't leave the building like this. Forget how you left your backpack in Cameron's class. Breathe.

Breathe!

I remembered the spider. How I'd changed its shape, slowly. If I could do that, I could do anything. Anything. Anything except give Jennifer a pig nose. I'd ask Kendra about that. Clearly, I still had a lot to learn about magic. Thank God for Kendra.

Finally, I felt my heart rate slow. And my breathing. It was hard to breathe through the snout. I sat on the toilet, breathing. Breathing. Breathing. Imagining my nose—not my nose, but Michelle Pfeiffer's nose, Diane Lane's nose, or model Brooke Shields's adorable, famous nose. Yes, that was it. Perfectly upturned with not too much nostril. I'd once read that it was nearly impossible to achieve this surgically. But magic surgery had to be better. The breathing, the heavy pig snout, the concentration made me feel weak, almost light-headed, and the metal stall walls began to blur around me. I held my hands up to my face and felt the snout shrink beneath them. Relief! I straightened my neck, held my head up, opened the door.

Even though I knew I was late, I couldn't resist a glance in the mirror.

It was perfect, almost too perfect. No, there was no such thing as too perfect. I would be perfect, all of me!

After school, I ran to Kendra's house.

"I tried to use magic, and it backfired on me."

"Backfired?" Kendra looked bemused—and maybe a little amused too, arranging herself on a red bench that looked like it belonged in the Museum of Modern Art. "How could it backfire?"

"Um, I don't know, turned my nose into a pig's snout. That's all."

Kendra chuckled. She was wearing a black lace ball gown that had barely made it through the door. "So you were trying to change your nose into this stunning creation—Diane Lane's nose, I believe—and it turned into a snout instead? Is that exactly what happened?"

"Not exactly."

"I didn't think so. Perhaps you were trying to give someone else a pig's snout?"

"How did you know?" Kendra seemed to know a lot of things—even knowing I'd copied Diane Lane's nose. Could she read my mind? Or was she spying on me with that mirror?

"It's about discretion." She pulled me by the arm to sit beside her.

"Discretion?"

"'Like a gold ring in a pig's snout, is a beautiful woman who lacks discretion.' That's from the Bible."

"You didn't strike me as the religious type," I said.

"I have nothing against religion. Since I'm never going to die, I don't have to worry about impressing God for the afterlife, but that doesn't mean I don't want to use my powers for good. Also, if you go around turning your enemies' noses into pigs' snouts, you'll get caught. That's why it's impossible to do."

"To do what?"

She waved her hand and produced two plates. "Gingerbread?"

"No, thank you. What's impossible?"

With another wave of her hand, the plates were gone. "Rules of magic. It is impossible to change someone without their knowing."

"You changed me the first day. You changed my nose." *Not as well as I changed it.*

"Ah, but you knew about it at the time. It was your choice. Once, I turned a proud, cruel boy into a beast, but he knew about it. To work magic on someone else, you must reveal yourself. It keeps others from being blamed. But had you changed your classmate's nose, she wouldn't have known how it happened. That's not allowed by the rules of witchcraft."

"So I can't even give her . . . zits? Diarrhea? A bad SAT score when she's a junior?"

Kendra shook her head. "Not without also giving those to yourself. It keeps you from abusing your power—and from making everyone suspect you. But you can do wonderful things for yourself, travel the world, give yourself incredible talents, never pay for cute new clothes." With a wave of her hand, she changed her dress to fuchsia. "You should hear me sing opera—I'm like a mermaid."

"All I want is for Greg to love me again. I don't care about that other stuff." I sort of wanted the gingerbread back. It was comfort food.

"Then you will have to win him back with your own looks and abilities—not by harming Jennifer. But it will be a difficult task."

"Why's that?"

"Because, my dear, he never really loved you in the first place. He was friends with you because he was lonely. With Jennifer, he has a whole circle of friends."

I remembered Greg and me, walking to his house after school, doing crazy science experiments like putting Mentos in Diet Coke so it would explode, checking our birdhouses daily. I'd had my first wren of the year last week, and I'd so wanted to tell Greg. But I knew he wouldn't care anymore. I guessed he'd never cared. I nodded, knowing Kendra was right.

"It's so unfair. Why do they hate me, Kendra? I always thought it was because I was ugly. But now, I'm not that ugly, and they still hate me. What's wrong with me?"

Kendra frowned. "I think you chose to like the wrong girl's boyfriend."

"But that's not fair. I saw him first."

"Since when are bullies fair?" Kendra asked. "Do you think they issue some sort of Bully Code of Conduct—only pick on people who deserve it?"

In truth, I guess I felt I had deserved it. Why would they pick on me if I didn't? I'd deserved it because I was an ugly freak. But now I knew they'd picked on me because they could, and maybe because I cared. Some part of me had once longed to be friends with Jennifer, to sit at her lunch table and go shopping at Dadeland after school. I couldn't explain *why* I wanted that. She was horrible. But part of me wanted to deserve them, the beautiful girls.

"I don't know why no one likes me. I thought it was my looks, but now, I don't know."

"I like you." Kendra put her arms around me. The dress was taffeta, a stiff fabric that felt like hundreds of Pringles chips when I hugged her. But I sunk into her embrace. She was the absolute coolest friend in the world.

"There, there," she said, "I love you. And, someday, others will too. You're going to be an incredible woman. You'll see."

"I don't want to be an incredible woman," I sobbed. I knew I was no better than anyone else. I'd only been happy to be smart because I was ugly. Really, I wanted to be beautiful and be loved. "I only want Greg!"

10

Over the next few years, I changed everything about myself. Everything I could, at least. My hair. The color of my eyes. My height. By seventeen, I was beautiful, tall with the body of a *Sports Illustrated* swimsuit model, strawberry blond hair that never got messy, and eyes the color of lavender dish soap—or, well, violets. I hadn't had a zit in four years, and even little details like the amount of space between my eye and my eyebrow (ideally the size of another eye) or my philtrum (the area between lips and nose—ideally about fifteen millimeters) didn't escape my notice. I was Pygmalion to my own Galatea, every part sculpted perfectly.

No one cared.

Or noticed.

I also developed talents, as Kendra had suggested. I could sing like Whitney Houston, dance like Paula Abdul. I used these abilities in school musicals and on the Cougarettes dance team. I was so talented they couldn't reject me even if they hated me.

Which they did.

It wasn't as overt now. I wasn't ridiculed, not usually. But even though strange men, and even women, approached me on the street to beg me to visit their modeling agency and new boys at school asked me on dates, I had no one to love me, no one I wanted. And, at the end of Cougarettes practice, when the popular girls got into their cars to go to the mall together, have dinner together, do homework together, I was the only one stuffing my pom-poms into my backpack alone. And watching Jennifer leave with Greg.

Yes, after all this time, they were still together. It was the one high school relationship that lasted longer than a rock star's marriage. They were voted Cutest Couple in middle school, and they'd be in this year's yearbook too. Greg was the star wide receiver, recruited by colleges. Jennifer was on dance team, at his side after every game. They belonged together.

And, of course, Jennifer got everyone else to hate me, just like she always had. Maybe now that I was beautiful, she saw me as a threat. Greg didn't care what a bitch she was. He didn't even know I was alive.

And yet, I still wanted to change Greg's mind, engineering ways to run into him without her. I tried different routes to my classes at school until I found ways to cross his path, just so I could say hello or look at him. I should have moved on, but moving on wasn't a thing with me.

Once, I passed him walking home from school. Greg had no car, but Jennifer had one, so she drove him most days, after her dance team practice and his football. But Wednesdays, she had Student Council (yes, I'd memorized their schedules), so Greg walked.

I had a car, a little blue Mazda Miata convertible I'd gotten for my sixteenth birthday. My mother was generous now that she was proud of me. Every Wednesday, I drove slowly from school, stalking Greg, fantasizing about offering him a ride. But, usually, someone else gave him one. After all, he was popular.

But that day, it happened.

As a bonus, it was raining, a sun shower that promised to get harder. Leaving the school parking lot, I saw Greg jogging toward home.

I pulled alongside him, onto the grass. "Want a ride?"

He wore black athletic shorts and a green tank top that showed every wet muscle. I longed to run my hands over him, to touch the hardness of his perfect body, the softness of that crow-black hair I'd loved since I was ten.

At first, he didn't seem to recognize me. He approached the car, squinting in the sparkly sun-rain. I smiled, showing my kissably puffed lips and that philtrum. I shook my hair a little. "Hey."

He backed away. "Oh . . . Violet. It's you. I probably shouldn't."

I feigned confusion. "Why not? It's awfully wet out."

"Yeah, I know." He was getting soaked.

"It's dry in here."

He was thinking about it. His hand approached the door handle. I wished I could control his mind.

"Why don't you sit in the car while you're working out the deep, philosophical problem of whether to accept a one-mile ride from an old friend."

He pulled his hand back a little. Way to go, Violet. But he looked at me, stared at me, actually, like he was seeing me for the first time. I parted my lips, knowing I finally had a tool, a tool more powerful than magic I could use on him. I stared back at him, lowering my eyelids. "We used to be such good friends, Greg." Showing my straight, white teeth. I was harmless. Beauty was always trustworthy. "Don't you remember?"

"Oh, yeah." A gush of air. He opened the door, letting the rain in, and himself. "I remember. You're right. It's stupid."

I tried not to grin. "You're getting the seat wet. Let me . . ."

I pulled a towel from my dance bag and began wiping at the seat, just the seat at first. "Let me get the other side too." I leaned across him, trying to touch him but make it look accidental. Like me, he'd become more beautiful each day. His arms were sculpted bronze ropes, and after I dried the visible expanse of seat, I began using the towel to stroke each muscle. "Sorry. My mom will kill me if anything happens to the leather."

"It's a great car." His voice sounded strained, as if he was struggling to keep it even. "You're really lucky."

"Yeah, my mom and I have been getting along better. Let me get behind you." I got real close to his ear.

"What?"

"Your back." I caressed it, moving him forward. "Let me dry it."

"Sorry." He obliged, and I dried behind him. We were close, closer than I'd been in so long. I felt a little breathless, but I tried not to let him know that my pulse was racing. I could have kissed him if I'd wanted. But I knew I shouldn't. Get him to trust me first. I dried the seat and his back, leaning close enough that my long hair brushed his chest as I did. I didn't dare touch his chest, his legs, on purpose. I wasn't that confident. But I dried his shoulders, his neck. He didn't try to take the towel from me. Was it because he trusted me or because, as I hoped, he didn't mind my touching him. My arm brushed his, and I felt his muscles stiffen.

"Guess that's good enough." I handed him the towel. "Let's go."

I pulled out. The car was tiny, and it had a manual transmission, which meant every time I used the stick, my hand was practically in

Greg's lap. His legs were long, so there was barely room to move.

"That was a great kickoff return touchdown you made the other day against Bradford," I said.

"Oh, you saw that?" But he looked pleased.

"Well, of course. I was there on the dance team. Remember?"

"Yeah. It doesn't always seem like those girls are watching the game."

He meant Jennifer. I grinned. "I watch you all the time, Greg. Of course I do. You're, like, the whole team." We approached a stop sign, and I downshifted, my hand brushing his leg as I did. "It's beautiful to watch you play, the way you got around those guys. It was . . . poetry."

"Wow. Thanks. That's really flattering."

"Doesn't Jennifer watch you?" Was I pushing my luck?

But he said, "Yeah. I mean, of course she does. She's my girlfriend. She just doesn't always seem to understand it. I guess football's complicated."

Which was why thousands of drunks could understand it. "Well, it's nice that she tries."

"Sure." He actually looked a little unsure.

What do you even like about her? But I didn't ask. "Well, I thought you were wonderful, a hero. And I heard there was a scout at the game."

He looked down, embarrassed. "Well, yeah, it's not really big colleges. Division Two."

"Are you kidding? Do you know how many guys would kill to be scouted by anyone? Your dad must be so proud." I patted his arm, loving the warmth of him under my hand.

He grinned. "Yeah. Yeah, he is."

We approached his house now. The ride was ending soon. I searched for something else to say. "How is your dad? Remember when I used to go to your house after school?"

"Yeah. We were just kids then."

"I know. But we had so much fun, didn't we? Like when we built the birdhouses?"

"Sure."

"And then, the wrens came."

He nodded. "I remember."

I wanted to ask him if he ever did anything like that with Jennifer, but I realized I might not want to know the answer.

He squirmed in his seat. "Look, Violet, I . . ."

"You once told me we couldn't be friends because I was too weird."

"I didn't say that."

"You did. I remember it like the answers to last week's vocabulary quiz. And, since then, I have worked really hard not to be weird, to be worthy of you. I mean, worthy of your friendship."

"Violet, I didn't ask you to do that."

"I know you didn't. I wanted to. I wanted to . . . be friends again. I missed you . . . that so much." We were dangerously close to his house. I was driving slowly. I couldn't drive any slower, but I couldn't let him out of the car without some kind of affirmation that we'd at least talk again.

"Friends?" He looked doubtful.

"Sure. Friends. Friends like we used to be." I wanted so much more, but there was time.

"I guess we can be friends," he said finally.

"That's so great!" I had to stop myself from doing a little seat dance. "So maybe I could drive you home every Wednesday."

He looked like he'd sat on a half-eaten Slurpee. He drew away.

"I don't think Jennifer would like that."

And, of course, you're not allowed to have independent thought. Does she really need to know?

"Well, then, maybe I could call you after school sometimes."

"I guess. Maybe. Well, maybe I should call you." We were right by his house, and he had his hand on the door handle like he might want to jump and run. "Look, I should go. Could you just—?"

"Sure." I pulled into his driveway, and he got out. I'd blown it.

"Thanks, Violet. We'll talk soon."

Then he got out and sprinted into the house.

I sat there a long time, staring at the closing door, then the seat which still, despite my towel drying, retained the damp imprint of his body. I curled over and lay against it until the seat got cold, and I couldn't feel him anymore.

I knew he'd never call me.

11

I got to see Jennifer three afternoons a week at Cougarettes practice. We wore cougar ears and drawn-on whiskers (okay, it may have
been slightly—just slightly—dumb). We danced at football games
and in competition. The juniors and seniors took turns choreo-
graphing, and this year was my first turn. I loved dance and didn't
just rely on magic for my talents. It wouldn't be as satisfying. I spent
hours working on my extensions and practicing jetés in the long
hallway between the bedroom and kitchen of our house, trying not
to kick my mother or the cat. I could leap higher than anyone. I'd
also spent a long time on the routine, forgoing homework to make
up the choreography. Kendra and I had gone to an Indian movie at
the local art cinema, and I loved the dance routines. I wanted to do
something like that. It would be different. Special! Like nothing

any dance team had ever done before!

Which would probably mean people would think it was weird.

Still, I had to try. If worrying about people thinking I was weird stopped me, I'd never leave the house. It wasn't like the girls in my grade were going to like anything I did. But there were eight new girls on the squad, three freshmen, five sophomores, none of whom knew I was weird. They weren't in any of my classes, so they didn't think I was a loser. I could impress them with my completely special routine.

That day, a Friday, I stepped in front of the group, trying to be proud, trying to at least *look* confident. I was, after all, six inches taller than I'd been in middle school with perfect 34 Cs and thighs like a Barbie doll's, that never squooshed together. Genetics didn't make bodies like mine, no matter what the magazines tried to tell us. But still, I stood before the group of fifteen girls in the otherwise empty gym, unsure how to start. I wondered if orchestra conductors felt like this, not completely confident that the violinists, oboists, or the guy playing the rainstick would obey his commands. Probably not. Probably everyone felt confident but me. Witchcraft didn't change the nature of a thing, so witchcraft couldn't make me confident.

But I tried to change my own nature. As I took my place before the group, I straightened my shoulders, shook my perfect ponytail, smiled, and tried to channel the other girls who'd stood in my spot before—the Nicoles and Julies and Merediths who'd stood confidently on the foul line with *Cougars* painted in green, and said:

"Okay, this is going to be awesome!" I clapped my hands, astounded by the awesomeness of it all. "I thought we'd do something different, a Bollywood-style routine!"

A few of the new girls nodded, like they knew what that meant, and one of them even said, "Like those Indian movies? That sounds so cool."

Encouraged, I went on. "So, for the first eight beats, this is what we'll do. Start with one arm out to the side, like this, in front of your chest." I demonstrated, picturing myself as the Indian actress in the movie I'd seen. "Then, shoulders up-down, up-down." Most of the girls copied me, but not all. I decided to keep going.

"Now, switch your arms the other way, and shoulders up-down, up-down."

Jennifer, who hadn't been following me, cleared her throat. Or, rather, she had a coughing fit, and most of the returning girls stopped dancing. They put their arms down.

"Come on, guys." I tried to act like everything was normal. "I don't want to go on until we have the first eight. Up-down, up-down, then switch."

I was screaming, but my voice got lost in the big gym.

Now, none of the returning girls were following me, but the new girls were, and the routine was pretty easy. So I decided to pretend nothing was wrong. "Freshmen, you're doing great! Show those seniors. Okay, one more time, then we'll move on. Up-down, up-down, then switch." Some of the new girls had dropped out too.

"Come on, guys!" My voice cracked a little. I looked at the fluorescent lights to keep from tearing up.

Suddenly Jennifer sat on the floor. Her cohorts, Gennifer and Meighan, followed. Then, the other junior girls, and the seniors.

Jennifer spoke. "What is this from, some kids' show? It's dumb even for you, Violet."

One of the new girls, the one who'd said it was fun, started to open her mouth. Then, she shut it.

"It's Bollywood-style, like movies from India. The Indian film industry—"

"Does anyone care about this?" Jennifer's hands were on her hips. "We're gonna look stupid. Why don't you think of something else, and we'll try next week."

I looked around. The adviser, Miss Levin, was supposed to be, um, advising, but she'd retreated into her office to call her boyfriend. And really, what was I going to do? Run to her and cry? Jennifer was the cocaptain. "Fine," I said.

"Great." Jennifer stood up. "I'm sure you'll be able to come up with something better if you . . . think about it more."

I stared at the light. I knew I couldn't come up with something better. What I'd done was perfect. Besides, even if I did, they'd hate it. I couldn't get a break with Jennifer. She had Greg, had everything I'd ever wanted. Why did she have to be such a bitch?

"Meighan, show us your routine," she said.

"Gladly." Meighan smiled and walked up front. For the next twenty minutes, she taught a routine based upon Madonna's "Papa Don't Preach," which was 1) borderline obscene; 2) copied from the music video; and 3) such an old song that all the teams had already done it. Everyone followed her like she was an innovator. Un. Freaking. Real.

I thought about how freeing it would be to throw caution to the winds and announce that I was, in fact, the Wicked Witch of the West and make all their heads explode. The news coverage: "High School Dance Team's Heads Explode." The T-shirts: "Guns don't kill people: Pissed-off witches kill people." There'd be protests by religious groups, complaining that taking prayer out of schools had caused my breakdown. It would be worth being ostracized, though. I was already ostracized. I didn't think they burned anyone at the stake anymore. And I'd be safe because I did it openly. That was the stupid rule, right?

But, of course, I was too nice. Scratch that—too much of a wimp—to do it.

When practice finally ended, I headed for the locker room, ahead of the others. It stunk of the sweat of thousands of freshmen. I got my gym bag, which I'd left on a bench. I wanted to change quick and get out.

Something was sticky.

Something was crawling on my clothes! Then, up my arms. Ants. Hundreds of ants.

From the doorway, Jennifer giggled. "Look!" She was pointing at me.

She'd covered my clothes in something. Syrup? No, honey. Jennifer had poured honey into my bag! On my clothes!

"Something wrong, Violet?" She came to where I was standing. A few other girls lagged behind her like the followers they were.

I stared down, remembering all those days in grade school when I'd eaten alone, all those times they'd made fun of me—*she'd* made fun of me. I felt the skin on my forehead tighten.

Don't stinking cry. Calm down. This was easy. It was a few ants. I could control higher orders of animal than ants.

I drew my clothes out of the bag. The honey, the ants, were all gone. I tried to keep my voice even. "Wrong? What could be wrong, Jennifer?"

She gasped, and her mouth quivered like Grimalkin's when she watched birds through the front window, knowing she could never get them, but longing. Sort of like I did with Greg.

I fixed her with a stare under the long lashes of my lovely violet eyes. "I know you would never do anything to my backpack, would you? You're so sweet and nice, and everyone loves you, and besides . . ." I fluffed my T-shirt in the air to show her how not covered in ants it was. "It's a bad idea to mess with me."

She laughed. "And why's that?"

I had a headache, and my eyes felt hot. Only crying would relieve it.

But I wouldn't cry. I'd rather have a headache forever. "It just is. You can figure it out."

I took off my leotard and stood there in bra and panties, not even trying to be modest, letting her and the others see every inch of my perfect body, more perfect than hers, more perfect than anything nature could make. My brain, I had no confidence in, but my body was excellent. I clenched my back teeth to keep from sobbing, but I smiled. "I know it would be too much to ask you to be . . . decent. So I'm just telling you to leave me alone."

She laughed. "Decent? Omigod, you are so crazy."

I pulled my T-shirt over my head, slowly, aware most of the girls were watching. I shrugged. "Who knows how crazy I am?"

I slid my perfect, tanned legs into my little white shorts, then slipped on my sandals, admiring the pedicure that never chipped. Jennifer had stopped laughing. Maybe she'd realized nothing was funny. Maybe she was scared.

They all remained silent as I left the room.

I stood outside, contemplating the blue and white afternoon. I lifted my head and squinted at the sun. A warm breeze set a nearby wind chime in motion. Across the street, a dog barked.

I allowed my face to break for a moment, feeling the hot tears running down my cheeks, the blessed relief of the dam breaking against the tension in my head.

I looked at the dog.

I had seen the dog before, a Doberman, wiry as a welterweight boxer and miserable about being fenced in. It saw me too and began to bark and fling itself against the chain-link fence. I felt its pain. I was fenced like that dog, fenced by people's expectations.

I lowered my eyes to meet the dog's. It was across the street, but it saw me. It calmed. It lowered its rump to the ground, sat, then curled into a ball. I held eye contact. *Good girl.*

So I couldn't do anything to Jennifer without bringing the same on myself. But could I have the dog do something to Jennifer?

I had nothing to lose by trying. Whatever I messed up, I could easily fix.

The dog was still staring at me. Its slender, black tail bounced up and down, as if it'd heard me.

"Good girl," I said aloud.

I examined the fence that contained it. Chain link already bowed down from previous escape attempts. It was almost low enough for it to scale in a single jump. Almost.

I visualized a weight, like an anvil in a cartoon, crushing down the fence. A wind whipped through the parking lot and across the street. The fence bowed. The dog sat, obedient, wagging its tail. This time, I pictured a steamroller, crushing it. The wind whistled through the trees. The fence bowed further, tapping the resting dog on the buttocks. It started, then woke.

"Stay," I whispered.

It stayed, but on the alert now, ready to spring.

The fence lay low on the ground, no protection at all.

Behind me, I heard laughter coming closer, then a voice from inside. ". . . so funny! Did you see her face when no one would do it?"

"Her routine wasn't that bad," another voice said.

"Oh, of course it was." I recognized Jennifer's high-pitched whine. "Anything she does is total poop."

"*She's* total poop," Meighan agreed.

"I can't believe she's even on the team," Jennifer said. "Where are the standards?"

The voices grew closer. I stared at the dog. *Good doggie. Stay one moment longer.*

"She's so ugly," Jennifer just kept going. "Disgusting, really." I heard the thunk-squeak of someone pushing the bar that opened the door. I moved to the side, out of the way, focusing on the dog, communicating. *Good doggie. Nice doggie. I'm your friend. And you're going to hurt the mean girl who hurts me—one bitch to another.*

Could I do this?

Suddenly my life started flashing before my eyes, but it was all Jennifer, like a collage of all the mean things she and her friends had done, said to me, the turned backs and mocking faces, Jennifer's voice in my ear, always, saying, "These seats are saved" or "Omigod, what happened to your hair? Did you brush it with a spaghetti server?" The pick-pick-picking on my skin, my hair, my nails, my body. "Are those new shoes, Violet? Where'd you get them—the orthopedic store? Can you believe what a suck-up she is, getting an A on the test when everyone else failed? Suck-up, asking questions in class. If I had that nose, I'd hide my face. If I had that hair . . . those eyelashes . . . that body . . . little bitch."

The dog was up on its haunches, backing up, then clambering, springing over the fence. The rage and hatred in its eyes matched my heart. The dog accelerated, dodging a passing car, intent on its target. Too late, Jennifer saw it charging toward her. "Oh, no!" she screamed. Her friends, true to form, ditched her, edging back into the building. Jennifer, poor, sweet Jennifer, was left all alone as the black beast's savage jaws came closer, closer.

And then, the dog was atop her, teeth ripping at her clothes, her arms. She was screaming, but her shrieks were drowned out by my own cries. "Bad dog! Bad dog! Not her arm!"

The dog sunk its teeth into Jennifer's cheek and pulled.

It was enough. The dog had done its damage. Jennifer's cries were still in my ears. I came from my hiding place. Jennifer's friends were in the door, cowering. It was just me, the dog, Jennifer, her face bloodied, with the teeth marks. I ran for the dog, breathless, as if I'd been running the whole time. I laid hands on the dog. "Stop!" I felt a jolt of electricity running from my body to the dog's. I pulled the dog off Jennifer. It stopped, motionless, as if Tased. I stroked the soft fur.

It was, after all, a good dog. It backed away, then trotted to its own yard. I went with it, as if I were taking it there, but partway back, I let it break away.

"Hide," I whispered.

I glanced at the fence. It sprung back into place.

I ran and knelt over Jennifer. Her face was bloody, flesh torn, and she was sobbing, holding her hand to her cheek. "Are you okay?" She whimpered in response. I pulled a damp towel from my dance bag and ripped it in half. I handed it to her. "Here. Apply pressure." I helped her do it. I was so nice.

Now that the danger was over, Jennifer's friends came back, all concerned, all, "Are you okay? What happened?" pushing me aside. Someone ran to dial 911.

Then, Greg was there. He must have been at practice. He knelt over Jennifer, beside me. "What happened?"

"It was a dog," I said, a little breathless just from being near him. "It came out of nowhere and attacked her. I pulled it off her."

"Where did it go?" Meighan said.

Jennifer was still screaming, sobbing, incoherent. But then, she formed words, painful words. "It was her." With her good hand, she pointed at me. "She did it."

"It was a dog," Gennifer said. "A pit bull."

"A white one!" said Meighan.

"It was her. It was her." Jennifer's voice rose to a violin's pitch. "She made it attack me."

Greg's eyes sought mine, and I made mine wide, confused. "Jennifer, the dog attacked you. I got it to stop. I helped you."

"Noooo! You didn't. You made it attack me. You made it because of what I did to your stuff." She was cringing in pain but still strong enough to accuse me.

"Poor Jennifer." I laid my hand on her arm. "You're in such

pain from that bad dog. But of course, I can't control the dog. And besides . . ." I moved my hand to her bloodied face. The wound was jagged, a lightning bolt from eye to mouth, streaks across her once-perfect nose. "Why would I want to hurt you? We're teammates, right? Friends." I stroked her hair until her eyes closed. "That's good. Probably better to sleep."

"You're a hero, Violet," someone said.

A siren sounded in the distance, distracting everyone. So I was probably the only one who heard Jennifer's voice, softer than the breeze in the grass, whispering, "You're a . . . witch."

I turned to Greg. "The paramedics are here. It sounds like she doesn't want me around, so I'll go."

"Thank you for helping her, Violet," he said.

I shrugged. "I was just so scared when it came after her. It was all, like, adrenaline when I pulled the dog off her. I mean, it could've attacked me. Maybe call me later and let me know how she's doing."

"Of course. You're a good friend."

I looked at Jennifer. My spell had her sacked out on the lawn, three Cougarettes over her. "Well, that's exactly what I want to be, a good friend." I smiled more at the sight of bleeding bitch Jennifer than at that thought. If I couldn't have Greg, I could at least have revenge.

But I meant to have Greg.

12

Greg called that night, and we talked about Jennifer. Jennifer. Jennifer—the pain she was in, the surgery she'd require, the way they didn't let him ride in the emergency vehicle and how mad that made him, the way they'd looked all over the neighborhood for the pit bull but no one had found it. Jennifer. Jennifer. Her name was like the bells, bells, bells in the Edgar Allan Poe poem, driving me mad.

"Did you see the dog?" Greg said, "the dog that attacked Jennifer? I thought it might have been that black Dobie across the street, but the fence was totally intact."

"No, it was definitely a pit bull," I said, not wanting to implicate the Doberman. "Big, white one. It ran away after I got it off Jennifer."

"You're really brave. Okay, I thought maybe Jen was confused about the breed. She's been kind of loopy from the drugs they gave her, confused in the head. She kept saying *you* attacked her."

I laughed. "I must have really sharp teeth."

"I know. I told her that was crazy, that you were always sweet and gentle. I still remember how you helped that bird when we were kids."

I smiled. "Of course I remember." I wondered what had happened to that sweet girl, the one who loved all living creatures. Kendra said you couldn't change the nature of a thing. The ability to strike out at my tormenters must always have been there. Now I was using it.

I didn't mind. I'd had enough.

"Thanks for keeping me posted. Will Jen be back at school soon?" I still didn't know how bad it was.

"Not for weeks. She has to have surgery for the scarring. The thing ripped off half her nose."

"Oh, that's terrible." It was. Plastic surgery might make her even prettier. I wanted Jennifer to know what it meant to be ugly. "Let me know if there's anything else I can do."

"I will. Everyone says you saved her life."

I winced. "Well, anything for a teammate."

"It's actually good to hear your voice, Violet."

"Is it? Then, maybe you'd want to—I don't know—meet at school to talk some more tomorrow."

"That would be great. I usually sit with Jennifer at lunch."

"I know." How I knew.

"We could sit together until she gets back."

"And talk about birds. Get your mind off things."

I hung up and went to bed happy, Grimalkin purring at my feet. Jennifer would be gone for weeks. Weeks! I had Greg all to myself. And now, I wasn't the frizzy-haired, hook-nosed loser I'd been. I was beautiful, talented, confident—at least on the outside. And, on the inside, I was the girl he'd liked all along, the smart girl. At least, smarter than Jennifer.

The next few weeks were the happiest of my life. Greg and I ate lunch together, studied together, I drove him to school. Even Jennifer's friends were nice to me. They'd seen me pull the dog off her. At first, Greg and I mostly talked about Jennifer, how amazing she was, but soon, we branched off into less-annoying topics, subjects like life, college (we both wanted to be environmental lawyers), current events, subjects an idiot like Jennifer couldn't possibly talk to him about.

We planned to see the movie *Dead Poets Society*, which was playing at the mall. "It wouldn't be a date," I told Greg. "We could just go as friends."

"I guess it's okay. Jennifer didn't want to go to that movie anyway. She said it looked stupid."

Jennifer's stupid. But I didn't say it. I didn't want Greg mad at me. I wished there was some magic I could work to make Greg see how awful Jennifer was, how we were meant to be together. I couldn't use magic to make bad things happen to people, at least not directly. But what about making someone fall in love with me?

I stopped by Kendra's house the day of our movie non-date. School was out now, and Greg was visiting Jennifer. I put the question to Kendra.

"Tell me again why I can't cast a spell to make Greg love me?"

Kendra winced. She hated the word *spell*. Said it smacked of mystical books and the silly TV series *Bewitched*, about a housewife who made magic by wiggling her nose. Magic, she said, came from deep within. It was a matter of harnessing it, rather than learning it.

"You can't make someone fall in love with you. Love comes from within too." She reached out her hand, an awkward gesture for her, and touched my shoulder. "Unfortunately, you had several opportunities to work your magic, so to speak, with Greg. It hasn't worked."

"It's so unfair." I bit my cuticle. "I have magic powers. I should be able to have anything I want. But this is the only thing I ever wanted."

"Is it really? The only thing?"

I thought about it, shredding my cuticle as I did. Of course it wasn't the *only* thing. But Greg was the main thing. Had I gotten him easily, maybe I'd be satisfied, but, as it was, I wanted more. I wanted to be beautiful, more beautiful than Jennifer, than everybody. I was. And powerful. I was that too. But that wasn't enough, or hadn't been. I was so sick of people making fun of me that now I wanted to be better than everyone, at everything. And obliterate my enemies. "Okay, maybe he's not *all* I want, but he's the main thing. That and world domination." I waited for Kendra to laugh, but she didn't. "But without Greg, I'll never be happy."

"Oh, dear." Kendra pressed her finger to her brow.

"What?"

"I'm just worried you'll never be happy."

I took another bite of my cuticle. This time, it bled, but I immediately stopped it.

Great. I could save money on Band-Aids. What an astounding ability I had.

Greg and I did go to the movie, though, which was about this boarding school teacher who encourages his repressed students to pursue their dreams, write poetry, seize the day. Then, one boy kills himself because he wants to be an actor, but his parents don't see it that way. Of course, the teacher gets fired.

"So that was a downer," I said to Greg as we walked through the mall afterward. "The message is that if you write poetry and think for yourself, you end up either dead or so beaten down you won't dare have an original thought again."

Greg laughed. "You're right. But most of us don't have parents as bad as that guy's."

"Speak for yourself," I muttered.

"I think the real theme was *carpe diem*," Greg said.

It was late, and the mall was nearly empty. I could hear, even feel our footsteps on the white marble floor. We were completely in step, just like when we were kids. I wanted to grab Greg's hand.

Carpe diem. Seize the day.

I didn't grab it. I was too scared he wouldn't take it. Still, our arms brushed as we walked.

"Do you believe that?" I asked. "Seize the day? Do what you want because each day might be your last."

"I do. Don't you?" He stopped walking to look at me. I could see us, reflected in the mall doors, him, tall and dark, me smaller, my hair flowing down my back. We belonged together.

I shook my head. "Guess I'm more cautious." Still I wondered how it would be to seize the day, do what I wanted. If I grabbed Greg now and kissed him, would he kiss me back? I looked up at him. His eyes met mine. It would be so easy to do that.

"You're so different than you used to be," he said. "It kind of shows how things can change. One day, you were this ugly duckling. Sorry. But look at you now—a swan."

"Thanks." He would kiss me back. He would.

"Or what happened to Jennifer."

"What do you mean?" I wanted to go back to talking about me, about how I was a swan.

"That dog could have killed her. And then, she'd have been gone, and she'd never have known how I felt about her. That accident inspired me. You saved her for me."

Saved her? For you? You've got to be kidding!

"Can I show you something? I've been carrying it around because I'm afraid I'll lose it."

And then before I could say no, no, I don't want to see anything that has to do with Jennifer, he pulled something from his pocket, a red velvet box, and held it near my face.

I backed away. "What is it?"

"It's a promise ring." He opened it. There was a silver ring with a heart and the tiniest diamond chip known to mankind in it.

"Promise? Promise what?" I felt like my legs might buckle under me, like I'd be on the floor.

"That we'll get married someday."

"Married? You and Jennifer?" I felt the bile coming up in my throat. I couldn't speak anymore.

Greg was nodding, grinning like an evil doll in a horror movie. "I'm giving it to her when she comes back to school. Unless you think I should seize the day and give it to her sooner."

"I . . . I . . ." I tried to speak but could only choke. I caught sight of myself again in the mall doors. I was so beautiful, so beautiful, so . . . so what? What good was it? It was everything I'd dreamed of, and it wasn't enough.

Suddenly the glass door shattered, blowing out like a bomb had hit it.

"Whoa!" Greg jumped back. "What happened? It didn't hit you, did it?"

But it wasn't like he threw his body over it to save me.

"N-no." I saw myself in another door. Then that shattered too. My magic was ungoverned, out of control, getting away from me, and I knew I had to stop before Greg realized it was me, then realized I'd hurt Jennifer. I veered toward the one open door, looking down, half closing my eyes so as not to see myself, and I ran. Beside me, Greg

95

was shouting, "Whoa! Whoa, watch out! What is that?" He put his arm around me, shielding me, and I wished I could pretend he was doing it out of love. But I knew much better. We ran through the parking lot. I dared look up, only to see myself in a car's windshield. It, too, shattered, but I hoped Greg didn't notice. I had to get out, get home, get away.

Finally, closing my eyes entirely, I got to my car. I told Greg I thought there was glass in my eye, so he drove us home, me seeing nothing. Thankfully, talk about flying glass at the mall drowned out any thought about talking about Jennifer. Jennifer. Jennifer. I excused my looking down by crying. From the shock of it, I told Greg. I didn't have to pretend. My tears were real.

I should have let her die. I had every chance, but I'd stopped it. Why? Why? What had Jennifer ever done but torment me? Why was I such an idiot?

I wouldn't make that mistake again.

I got home, finally, and groped my way to my bedroom, trying to avoid my mirrored closet door, the giant frame mirror over my dresser. I didn't wash my face or brush my teeth, fearing to enter the bathroom.

But when I stumbled to bed, something cold and hard touched my flesh.

A mirror. The mirror. Kendra's same mirror she had given me the first day. How was it here?

I stared into it. It didn't shatter. "Kendra?"

Thus summoned, Kendra appeared. She could see me too, for she stared at me. "My darling, what's wrong?"

"It's useless! He'll never love me! He *loves* Jennifer! He wants to marry her. Marry! They're seventeen! He's supposed to go to college and be a football star. And my magic is all out of whack. I broke stuff."

In the mirror, Kendra nodded, but her eyes narrowed. "Were you at Cutler Ridge Mall?"

"Yes. How did you know?"

"The news reported a bombing, broken glass everywhere. But they couldn't find the bomb."

"That was me." I was shaking, thinking about it. "I couldn't stop it. I don't know if I can stop it now. I'm afraid to look at anything."

"My darling." Kendra's face held all the sympathy I never got from anyone else. "When witches are unhappy, they generally make their displeasure known. It's unfortunate you were in such a public place, but you must calm yourself now."

"So what do I do?"

"Try to think about someone else. Try to be happy. Concentrate on other things. Your studies. You're such a smart, wonderful girl. Find someone else. Forget him. Let him go."

She was saying all the things my mother should have said, if she hadn't sucked. Yet it seemed like she was speaking a foreign language. "Forget Greg? I can't. I love him, only him."

"He doesn't love you. People get over failed romance all the time."

"No, never. Don't you understand? Everyone hates me. *Everyone.* They won't even do a dance routine if I choreograph it. They hate me, all of them. I even hate myself. I'm worthless. Worthless. Greg is the only one who ever cared for me, ever saw anything in me but ugliness."

"Shh." Kendra put a finger to her lips. "That's not true. I love you, Violet. You are my true daughter. And you'll find someone else, someone better. Someone who will love you."

I nodded, but I knew I wouldn't, couldn't. I would try to be happy, but the only way I could be was by getting Greg, by plotting Jennifer's utter destruction. I'd missed one opportunity. I wouldn't miss it again. Not just a dog bite, something worse.

I'd have Greg—someday—if it took everything I had.

"Kendra?" I asked. "Am I the fairest one of all?"

"Aw, honey, of course you are. Please get some sleep. It will be better. You'll meet someone else, someone who appreciates you as he never did."

I nodded. "Okay."

And then, she disappeared, and I was looking at my own face.

I was so beautiful.

PART 2
Celine
(The Present)

1

When I was eight, my Girl Scout troop went to a sleepover at the zoo. My mom, our leader, had agreed to do it even though animals terrified her—as long as the troop sold enough cookies to cover the cost. I think Mom thought it was a safe bet. We were rich, suburban kids who didn't have to work for much. But the thing is, everyone wants cookies. We figured if we each sold 150 boxes, we'd have enough for the sleepover *and* matching leopard-print bandannas. Then we nagged our moms to take us door to door or hold booths in front of Publix supermarket so we could make our goal.

Mom seemed way less excited than scout leaders are supposed to be when she announced we'd made it. I didn't blame her. She was really scared of animals, and with good reason. When she was in high school, she was attacked by a dog that had bitten her face and arms so badly she needed plastic surgery. After that, she freaked at every barking dog. More than one had come after her. So, of course, we'd had no pets. It wasn't just dogs that stalked her. A few times, birds had attacked her, and once, when we were bike riding, a squirrel jumped right into her basket, ran up her arm, and grabbed her face. She'd crashed, and I crashed into her. She shook for an hour. So my mother's fears weren't unreasonable. But I really wanted to do the sleepover, so she agreed. Besides, the zoo animals were in cages.

That night, we got to the zoo at six. After a dinner of hot dogs, Cool Ranch Doritos, and pink lemonade (I remember all the details because of what happened after), we went on a special after-hours tour. One of the docents, a strikingly beautiful woman with bright auburn hair, took us first to the reptile house. Mom clutched my hand as we watched the savannah monitor show its pointed teeth. We walked on. Quickly. Next were the wild animals who'd been brought in for the night. The lion roared. Beside me, I felt Mom stiffen. I hugged her in solidarity.

"It's okay, hon," said our tour guide, assuming I was the baby who was scared. "The cage is made of steel and has two separate doors. He's not getting out."

My mother laughed. "I know. I'm being silly."

"Not at all. Lions are powerful animals. Better to fear too much than too little."

"Thank you." Mom squinted at the woman. "You . . . you look so familiar. I wonder if we went to high school together." She touched the scar on her arm. "But no, you'd be too young. You can't be more than twenty-five."

The docent nodded. "I get that a lot. I seem to look like a lot of people."

We started to walk back to our sleeping quarters. The zoo at night was an eerie place, full of strange cries and creeping shadows.

Above us, the canopied trees seemed to move, even though there was no breeze. Then, I saw a shape.

"Look! A monkey!"

It wasn't in one of the trees contained in a cage. Instead, it was in a ficus tree growing near the path.

All the girls looked up, picking it out from the shadows. "Aww, how cute," my friend Laurel said.

"Is it supposed to be out here?" Mom said. "It's not in a cage. Did it get out?"

"Oh, Mom, it's just a little monkey." I heard her heavy breathing.

And just as I said, "little monkey," the creature let out a high-pitched shriek, swung down from the lower branch, then launched itself right at my mother. I stepped in front of it too late. It was on her.

From a distance, in the dark, it had seemed like a tiny monkey. Close up, it was way bigger, the size of a cocker spaniel, with long, powerful arms. My mother crumpled to the ground, and the monkey was grabbing her hair, pulling it over and over so her head was slamming, slamming, slamming on the pavement. The monkey sunk its teeth into her cheek, her chin. I screamed. I screamed and was kicking at it, over and over, get it off my mother, away from her! My mother must have screamed too, but all I could hear were my own shrieks, see the dark blur of my fellow troop members running for cover, the docent calling for help on her radio, my mother shielding her face, the monkey biting her arms, her legs. I fell backward from kicking, but the monkey was still on my mother, biting her.

Finally, someone came. They shot the monkey with a dart gun and pulled it off her. It was too late.

My mother was airlifted to the hospital, but the damage was too great. After a few days in ICU, they took her off life support.

My mother was dead.

"It was all my fault," I kept saying at her wake. Everyone was there, saying things I couldn't hear, didn't want to hear. My mother was dead. My mother was gone.

I couldn't even see her. It was a wake, not a viewing. The funeral home hadn't been able to fix her up enough to show. Despite her scars, my mother had been a beautiful woman. She'd taken great pride in her looks. She wouldn't have wanted anyone to see her looking less than her best.

"Of course it wasn't your fault," a woman's voice said above me.

I looked up to see an angel's face with bright blue, almost violet, eyes; fringed, long black lashes; all framed by wavy, auburn hair. I recognized her. The docent from the zoo.

"If anything," she said, "it's mine." She turned to my father. "I've been over and over it in my head, so many times, reliving it—how the monkey got out, how I should have seen it first, taken you girls to shelter. Warned her." As she spoke, a tear coursed down her face. She wiped it away, all the while staring at Dad.

"Do I know you?" he asked. "You look so familiar."

My mother had said the same thing.

"I volunteer at the zoo," the docent said. "I took the girls around . . . that night."

Dad shook his head. "It was the fault of the zoo management or whoever should have locked that beast in a cage. If volunteers were responsible for safety, that is a sad state of affairs. Poor Jennifer was terrified of animals, and now . . ."

"I am so sorry," said the docent.

Dad's eyes glistened. He looked at the woman again. "Really, though. You look so familiar."

The docent wiped another tear. "Don't you remember me, Greg? We went to school together. Violet Appel."

"Violet?" My father stepped closer, staring at her. "Violet, it's been so long."

I could barely keep my eyes off her myself. I hadn't seen her that well that night at the zoo.

My mother had been beautiful, and people said I was too. But this woman, Violet, was different. She was stunning. Like, I actually felt stunned to look at her, like electric shock.

My father took her hand and sobbed. "Violet!"

"There, there, it will be okay, Greg," she said.

They stood there a long time, Violet holding his hand, my father crying, until finally, she said, "I should let you greet the others."

Dad nodded. "I'm so glad to see you, Violet. Maybe we can talk later."

"Of course, Greg." Violet moved away. "I've missed you."

Dad said to me, "Violet was my best friend in elementary school. Such a nice girl. I haven't seen her in years."

At the time, I didn't think about it, but now I realize that Violet had told my mother she didn't know her. She'd obviously lied.

After the wake, she was back. She seemed to really want to talk to Dad. "After what happened, I quit volunteering at the zoo. I couldn't . . . I couldn't go back." She shuddered a little. "But I've loved animals since we made those birdhouses with your father." She touched Dad's hand.

Dad smiled. "I remember that. Dad was asking about you last time I saw him. He remembers all that old stuff."

"Grandpa made birdhouses?" Grandpa didn't remember my name, usually.

Violet knelt beside me. She smelled like roses. "Sweet child. Has your father never made a birdhouse with you?"

Dad said, "Jennifer was terrified of animals since the dog attack in high school—you remember. She avoided them, and yet, they couldn't seem to stay away from her. Cats peed on her shoes. A raccoon lived on her car for a month and wouldn't leave when shooed.

We had to sell the car. She had a job at an ad agency downtown, but she was forced to quit when pigeons ganged up on her on the street. Now this . . . " His face broke, and he began to sob. "I should have taken the troop myself! I should never have let her near the zoo."

Violet embraced him, rocking him back and forth while he sobbed in her arms. When I think about it now, it was weird, like he was a little kid. But at the time, it seemed so perfectly comforting that I hugged both of them. She said, "Don't blame yourself, Greg. There's no way you could have known."

We stood there, crying, the three of us, and somehow, Violet's presence made it better, made it almost right. It was like magic.

Two days after the funeral, Violet arrived with an animal carrier. From it, she drew a small ball of fur, orange and white. "Someone left her in my yard. My cat was my fondest friend when I was a lonely teenager, so I thought a kitten might help. A cat always helps."

I couldn't believe anyone as beautiful as her had ever been lonely.

She placed the kitten on the ground. I reached out, but she started to run away from me. Violet touched its back, and suddenly it switched direction and gamboled toward me.

"I asked your dad if you could have it," she said.

"Really?" The kitten pawed at my leg. I scooped it up, and it began to purr, like the small motorboats we used to rent on vacation at the lake.

"Really," my father said from behind me. "A child should have a pet."

That made me feel bad. The reason we hadn't had a pet was because of my mother, her fears. Now, I could have a cat. I'd rather have had my mother. But the kitten curled itself into a ball on my lap. It felt so warm.

"She likes you," Violet said, "but who wouldn't like a sweet, pretty girl like you?"

"Oh, I'm not pretty," I said, though I'd been hearing it all my life. In fact, I thought I was strange-looking, with jet-black hair and white skin like my father's, though I had my mother's blue eyes. I hated when people said I was beautiful because it was always something like what Violet had said, something that implied I should have no problems because of my looks.

Obviously, that wasn't true. If anything, my looks made people like me less. The first day of kindergarten, the kids had just stood around, staring at me. But then no one asked me over to their houses or to sit together at lunch. Mom had always said they were scared of me. That was why she'd volunteered to be the scout leader, so she could help me make friends. Once people got to know me, they forgot about my looks—sometimes.

But I wanted Violet to like me, so I didn't say any of this. The kitten nuzzled my face. Violet stood real close to Dad, smiling up at him.

"Your modesty makes you all the more beautiful," she said. "Maybe one day, you can come over and see my cat. I'll make you dinner too. I'm a good cook."

"Okay." I hugged the little cat.

"We'll make a date." Dad touched Violet's shoulder. "Thank you."

I named the kitten Sapphire for her blue eyes, and the next week, we had dinner at Violet's house. She made what she called "gourmet" mac and cheese, with some kind of weird smoked cheese in it and told stories about working as a lawyer for the US Attorney's office, putting criminals away in jail. I played with her cat, whose name was Grimalkin.

In the next few months, we spent more and more time with Violet until we were seeing her every day. I didn't mind. Violet had two passions, animals and her beauty routine, so some weekends, we went on nature walks, like in the Everglades, seeing alligators and birds and once, a panther. Other times, she did my hair so easily it seemed like magic, or we went for mani-pedis, stuff I'd done with Mom. Of course, Violet wasn't my mom, but having her around made it a little easier. And Dad was a lot less sad. I noticed the photos of my mother went from the living room to his bedroom. Then, one day, they disappeared. I found a big photo of the three of us in his closet. I took it out and put it under my bed, but I didn't let either Dad or Violet see it.

A year later, they got married. I wanted to be a flower girl in the wedding, but Dad said it wouldn't be formal, and it had to be small. "I'm a widower. It's only been a year since your mom died. We don't want a public wedding."

"Yes, no fancy dress for me, but I've got my man." Violet leaned over and kissed my father on the mouth. I looked down. They kissed a lot. "Besides, none of your dad's school friends liked me much."

"Why wouldn't they? Were they jealous because you were so beautiful?"

Violet looked at Dad and laughed. Then, she hugged me. "Oh, my sweet girl, you crack me up."

I didn't know what the joke was, but I laughed along anyway.

I wanted Violet to love me. She was the only mother I had, after all.

2

"Can you guys stop making out?" Violet was doing my hair for dance. At least, she was until my father came in. Then, she launched at him like a pumpkin in a catapult.

"We weren't making out. I'm just kissing my wife hello."

I rolled my eyes. They were always kissing, and since Violet had my hair in her hand, it was getting tugged. "I'm going to be late."

"Okay." Violet tore herself away from Dad and went back to brushing. "Your hair's so pretty. Black as a crow."

"A crow?" I wrinkled my nose. "Crows are ugly."

"Have you ever really looked at a crow, Celine?" Violet continued to brush my hair. I was eleven, old enough to do my own bun, but it was hard to tell Violet that. "I mean, up close? They aren't completely black. In the light, you can see purple and green. They almost shimmer. And each feather is lined up perfectly with every other one. So beautiful."

"Why do you love crows so much?"

"I love all birds. When I'm old, I mean to travel the world and see as many as I can. But crows and ravens will always be my favorite. It was because of a crow I met your father." She looked up at Dad. "Remember?"

"Of course. We rescued it on the playground. Some boys were throwing rocks at it, and Violet saved it."

"After that, we were always friends," Violet said.

I detected a false note in her words. She and my father hadn't "always" been friends. She'd just showed up after my mother died. But there was no point in saying that, particularly when she had my hair in her hands. Besides, I loved Violet, and I liked birds too. Sometimes, we went for walks and counted how many different kinds we saw. "Well, if you like crows, I'll like them too."

She hugged me for that, though her eyes were on Dad. Then, she put the last pins in and sprayed my bun. I always had the best hair in class.

But then, everything changed.

I was thirteen when I had my first period. I had it at school, of course, because that's just how things go with me. And, when I went down to the clinic to get a pad, one of my friend's moms was there. "Do you want me to call your dad?" she asked.

"What? No! He'll get all weird. Call Violet if you have to call anyone."

Laurel's mom got kind of an odd look on her face. "You and Violet actually get along, huh?"

"Yeah, she's nice. We're going bird-watching in Texas for spring break."

She nodded. "Okay. I wish your mom were here. This is a day

a mother and daughter should share. I can't believe it's been five years." She gazed at me. She and my mother had been best friends when they were kids. "You look so much like your mom."

"You think so?" I could barely remember her face. When I tried to picture her, I could only see the photo I still kept under my bed, her in the same pink dress, the same frozen smile. I couldn't remember the look and feel of her at all anymore. It was like the photograph had painted over my real memories of her. "I have black hair like my dad."

"Yeah, but those big blue eyes, they're Jennifer's eyes."

She looked about to cry, so I said, "It's all right." Because what else, really, was there to say? I just wanted out of there.

Finally, she called Violet and shared the news. "You can go back to class now," she said after.

I got out of there as fast as I could.

But half an hour later, Violet was there, carrying dark jeans and checking me out of school.

"You didn't have to," I said. "We're doing a lab in science. I sort of wanted to—"

"Science can wait. This is a special occasion for us girls."

I shrugged. It was sort of weird that she and Dad hadn't had other kids, but it was better for me. So I guessed if I had to act like her daughter, it was worth it.

She took me to Marble Slab Creamery. We both got chocolate with Oreos mixed in, and as we paid, the college boy at the register looked me up and down. I turned away, blushing like I always did when guys stared at me. Later, when Dad got home, Violet made my favorite dinner (still the mac and cheese) and filled him in. "Your little girl's becoming a woman."

I squirmed when she said that, squirmed more when he said, "A beautiful woman." With his hand, he turned my face toward him. "Like your mother."

"She doesn't look like her." Violet touched my dad's face. "She looks like you."

"More like Jenny," he said. "My lord, Vi, she's even as beautiful as you."

It was only for a second, so I thought I imagined it. But, in that instant, I saw Violet's eyes turn from lavender to black as a crow's. Then they went back to normal.

But that couldn't have happened. She wasn't a witch or anything.

"Do you think so, Greg?" Violet asked. "Yes, I suppose she is, just as beautiful."

She, too, gazed at me, and I saw hatred behind her smile. From that day on, she never looked at me the same way again.

And when we went to Texas over break, a red-footed booby swooped down and attacked my face.

3

Sophomore Year

When I get on the bus, wearing my usual hoodie, army boots, and jeans a size too large, Whitney Jacobs stage-whispers that I look like a bag lady, but Alex Abercrombie does a Parisian pass, brushing his hand against my ass to get by me. I ignore them both. *Eyes on the prize.* Laurel's holding a seat for me. She's near the back, where we live, waving and generally looking more excited than anyone has the right to look at six-forty in the morning.

I know why. And sure enough:

"Is your mom letting you go to the concert?" she asks the instant I sit.

The concert! I let down my guard and do a little seat dance to let her know I'm excited too, then say, "My wicked *step*mother, if that's who you mean, isn't in on the decision. But my dad says yes as long as your mom's going."

"Well, of course. What did he think, a couple of fifteen-year-olds are going to hitch to Orlando?"

"For Jonah Prince, I completely would."

"Can I get an 'amen'?"

And we squee in unison.

Whitney and her mean girlfriends look back at us and roll their eyes. I smile.

"Jelly?" Laurel says.

"Not of anyone who still says 'jelly.'" Whitney turns away.

"Is 'jelly' not a thing anymore?" Laurel whispers to me.

"Don't worry about it. She is such a hater." I pat Laurel's shoulder.

Jonah Prince, as everyone knows, is an incredibly gorgeous and gifted singer-songwriter. Previously the front man for the Boyz Band, he went out on his own when he noticed he was the only one with talent. And beautiful green eyes. And a hot British accent. I'm in love. Laurel and I host unofficial Jonah Prince pages on every social networking site I can think of, even Facebook, which only parents use.

Okay, so I have no life. I study, hang with Laurel, and listen to Jonah. But I know that, when we go to his concert in Orlando (where we'll get front row floor seats because we're in his fan club and plan to spend the entire night before tickets go on sale on the Ticketmaster site, entering CAPTCHA codes so we can get tickets the very first second the presale begins—and if that doesn't work, I'm spending a year's worth of babysitting money to buy them on StubHub), Jonah will pick me out from the crowd, his eyes attracted by the extraordinarily beautiful and artistic sign I'll make, and my total memorization of all his songs. He'll lead me onstage. I'll have the perfect outfit, of course, something that's actually figure flattering. Once there, he'll sing every song to only me, ignoring the boos of the other poor girls. I'll ask him to bring Laurel onstage to meet his drummer. After the concert, we'll talk for hours about the charity work he did in Haiti last year or the new songs he's composing. He'll ask me to come along on his tour, so I can get permanently away from my stepmother, who hates me.

Yeah, so it's a bit of a stretch. But it *has* to happen. There has to be something really good coming to me, to make up for Violet.

In some cultures, like the Greeks and Turkish, they believe in the Evil Eye. It's the idea that, if someone envies you, bad things will happen. Since that fateful day when my father said I was as beautiful as Violet, I've become more beautiful (don't hate me—I can't help it) and Violet's eyes have been seriously evil. Curling irons attack me, leaving scars. Tweezers rip out my eyelashes. Cleansers turn toxic and give me rashes. I avoid Violet—and beauty products—as much as possible. I wear no makeup, no hair spray. I don't get fake nails or even nice clothes. But people still stare at me. And Violet notices. And hates me for it.

"That's really trite," Laurel says, pointing to the chem notebook I'm studying for today's test. It has *J.P. 4-ever* written on it in pink highlighter.

"Nothing about Jonah Prince is trite."

"Do you even know what *trite* means?"

"Yes, I do." The bus hits a bump, and I steady my notebook, covering the writing with my palm. "But it probably makes us sound like nerds who use words like"—I lower my voice—"trite."

"Okay," she whispers, then giggles.

"Jonah is special. He writes his own songs and plays four instruments."

"Preaching to the choir. But my mom says he's just like Justin Bieber. Or someone named Bruce Springsteen, who was apparently famous when she was a teenager. Or the Beatles. Or Elvis. She says the names change, but the pathetic-ness of a teenage girl, scribbling initials of a guy she's never met, *will* never meet, is always the same."

"Laurel, I love your mom. She's the closest thing I have to a mom, and she lets me call her Gennifer. Plus, she's letting us use her credit card to buy tickets."

"And driving us to Orlando," Laurel reminds me.

"And driving us to Orlando," I agree. "Your mom is completely legit."

Laurel laughs because she knows that's something her mom would say, trying to be cool. Laurel and I have been best friends since we were born a month apart fifteen years ago, to moms who were best friends. I'm told that, usually, when people's mothers want them to be friends, they inevitably end up hating each other. Laurel and I are the exception. At this point, she's kind of the only person I hang with, but Dad says it's better to have one good friend than ten bad ones. Violet sort of rolls her eyes when he says that, but it's true. Also, it's Laurel's house I hide in almost every weekend. Laurel's mom knows how weird Violet is, so she lets me sleep over. Without Laurel, I'd spend my weekends watching my dad and Violet suck face.

Still, I say, "But your mom's old, Laurel. She doesn't remember what it's like to be our age. When Jonah sings 'Beautiful but Deadly,' it's like we've already met, like he's looking into my soul."

Laurel rolls her eyes. "Yeah, I know. Being the most beautiful girl on the planet is hard for you."

I look back at my chem notes. She knows I hate when people say I'm beautiful.

"Celine?" Laurel tries to look over my notebook. She's super-cute with wavy, dark hair. She thinks she's fat, but she's not. She's curvy.

"I'm sorry," I say. "I'm on a chemistry grind. I want to get an A so I can take AP chem next year. And this chapter is hard."

"All work and no play . . . ," she singsongs. "You know, you could go for a normal guy. Bryce Richardson is into you, and he sort of looks like Jonah."

"Bryce Richardson isn't into me." Bryce is the hottest guy in our class—and so knows it. I've seen him make fun of smaller guys, heavy girls, people with acne. I heard he wouldn't go out with one girl because her eyebrows were too close to her eyes. The guys with huge egos always like me. The right ones never do. I just want a smart, funny guy, but it's like guys my age are scared of me.

"I've seen Bryce looking at you," Laurel insists.

"I don't think so. You should go for him if you like him. I'm a little too sapiosexual for him."

"Sapiosexual? What's that? Sounds dirty."

"It means attracted to smart people. That kind of lets out Bryce Richardson."

She sighs. "I'm giving up now. Next order of business: *Oliver!* auditions are after school today."

I sigh and close the notebook. "Guess I'm done studying."

"You know you'll ace it."

I don't want to talk about this any more than I want to talk about why I don't like Bryce Richardson. But Laurel's totally obsessed with theater. "Why are we trying out for a musical again?"

"Because I need to pay my dues in the chorus—or, hopefully, a small but pivotal role—so I can get a lead next year."

"I'm sorry. I wasn't clear. Why am *I* trying out? I have stage fright. And no talent."

"Because you're my best friend. And because, if I'm in the play and going to rehearsals every day, you can't hang out at my house to avoid Lady Violet—unless you want my mom to teach you quilting. She'd completely love to do that."

Laurel knows how important Violet avoidance is to me. At least, she gave me the heads-up on the play. She made me watch the movie version a few weeks ago, and it was pretty good. I guess being in the chorus wouldn't be horrible, as long as I can be in back where no one sees me.

"Okay," I say, "so what do I have to do? Hopefully, not dance. Because I'm bad at that."

"Just a song. The drama teacher said 'Happy Birthday' was okay for chorus. They just want to see if you can sing on pitch."

"I think I remember all the words to 'Happy Birthday,'" I tell Laurel, "but we can go over them at lunch, just in case."

Laurel rolls her eyes.

When we get off the bus, Pierre Duval, a senior I don't know, is rolling by in his BMW convertible. "Nice jeans, Celine," he yells. "I'd love to get in them."

I move to the other side of Laurel and try to ignore him.

"I am not trying for the role of Oliver," the guy onstage tells the drama teacher, Mrs. Connors. "I may be little, but I'm not a kid. And I'm not cute."

I've noticed this guy before, even though he's a year ahead of me. He was in my bio class last year. His name is Goose Guzman. He has dark, wavy hair, olive skin, a wicked sense of humor . . . and he's maybe four and a half feet tall. Is it wrong to say I want to meet him *because* he's a little person? I figure he knows how it feels to be stared at for something beyond your control. Plus, he's funny—as he's demonstrating at the moment.

"You're definitely not cute, Goose," Mrs. Connors says.

"Thank you." He half smiles, lifting only one side of his mouth. "I'm also not a soprano." He makes his voice real deep when he says that.

"What part did you want to try for?" Connors asks.

Goose shrugs. "Bill Sikes. Maybe Fagin."

She sighs. "Bill Sikes is supposed to be a big, scary guy, Goose. I don't think—"

"Oh, I see how it is. You're being heightist." Goose stands up very straight. "Someday, when I'm the next Peter Dinklage or Warwick Davis, I'll tell people my high school drama teacher wouldn't cast me because I was too short."

I chuckle. The guy is awesome.

Connors rolls her eyes. "I'm not refusing to cast you, just refusing to cast you as Bill Sikes. I won't consider you for Widow Corney either, if that's okay. Maybe you can be—I mean try for—the Artful Dodger."

I remember from the movie that the Artful Dodger was a clever teenage pickpocket. Good call. Goose seems okay with that idea. At least, both sides of his mouth are now up. "Fine. Either that or Fagin."

Mrs. Connors shrugs. "Try for both. We'll see what happens. But who am I going to cast as Oliver? Most of the boys here are huge."

"Cast a girl," Goose says, "a little, cute girl. Cast her."

And he points right at me. I shrink down in my seat and try to think of some clever retort about how he doesn't seem to mind looks-based casting when he's not the one being stereotyped. But I realize it's probably not the same. Mrs. Connors looks at me and claps. "Splendid idea. Anyone under five foot three—except Goose—will read for Oliver." She walks over to me. "Can you sing 'Where Is Love?'"

I remember that song from the movie too. It perfectly described my life, a lonely child yearning for a lost mother.

But I don't want to be Oliver. I hate being the center of attention. This reminds me of second grade, when we did *Cinderella*, and I really wanted to be a mouse. I got Cinderella. Not only did I have to memorize a ton of lines, but all the mouse girls hated me. I glare at Laurel, who's five eight, then say to Mrs. Connors, "I only wanted chorus. I was going to sing 'Happy Birthday.'"

She sighs audibly. "Maybe just try?"

And, like the people pleaser I am, I say, "I guess if you have the sheet music."

Twenty minutes later, I'm standing onstage singing "Where Is Love?" Three other girls—girls who actually wanted to be Oliver—have already tried, and I could barely hear them. I could do that. No one's heard me sing before. I even avoid karaoke at birthday parties. I could waver off pitch on the high notes or sing so softly that no one could hear me. But when I get onstage, I start thinking about Mom, about how we used to bake cutout cookies at Christmas, and the Hannah Montana costume she made me for Halloween when I was five and thought Hannah Montana was cool. I remember all the crafts we did for Girl Scouts before that fateful day. And I start to sing about poor miserable Oliver, searching for his mother.

Halfway through, I see Mrs. Connors wipe away a tear.

When I finish the song, there's silence except a few sniffles. Sniffles!

Someone—Goose—starts to applaud and whistle. Thanks, dude. Then, everyone else applauds too.

I go back to my seat, sort of hoping no one else tries out. Maybe I want the part after all. I wonder if this is how Jonah feels onstage. That would be something else we could bond about.

No one else tries out. Mrs. Connors starts with the girls who want to play Nancy. Which is all of them, except me. So after Laurel and a few others go, I head for the ladies' room.

"She thinks she's all that," I hear one of the other girls whisper as I walk by.

So unfair! I want to round on her and ask what, exactly, I did to make her say that. Of course I don't.

When I come out, angrily, I pass Goose by the water fountain. "Hey," he says.

"Hey," I reply.

He doesn't quite reach my shoulder. He has these chocolate brown puppy-dog eyes. "You really moved me in there. My parents, they take in foster kids, and when you sang that song, it made me think of them, like, think of their *struggle*. Also, those are cool boots."

"Thanks. My mother died when I was little. The song reminded me of her." Why did I say that? I never talk about my mother. To anyone, let alone complete strangers. I hug my notebook to my chest. "Um, I'm Celine."

He nods. "I know. We had bio together last year. Goose."

"Oh, yeah. I didn't think you remembered me. I was just a freshman." He was always at the center of a group of theater kids, making people laugh, while I sat off by myself and acted studious because I didn't know anyone in the class. All my friends took Earth-Space, the normal ninth grade class, but I love science, so I was ahead.

"You were the one who stood up for the sub that day," he says.

"Oh." Ugh. I look down, embarrassed. But since he's shorter than I am, down is right at his face. "You remember that?"

"It was memorable." He waggles his eyebrows, smiling that half smile again.

Yeah. One day in class, we had a sub. A new one, probably fresh out of college, and he stuttered. Badly. Since the class didn't have assigned seating, he had to call roll. Which was painful. It took maybe ten minutes to call thirty names, but it seemed way longer because people were being so rude. He searched for C-C-Columbo and G-G-Guzman with everyone laughing at him. Well, almost everyone. I actually specifically noticed that Goose wasn't. But he wasn't telling his friends to shut up either.

When the sub reached the last name, Torres, his stutter made it come out Tit-tit-Torres, and everyone lost it, including the sub, who looked about to cry. It really bugs me when people make fun of someone who can't help it, and I didn't have any friends in that class anyway.

So I stood up. I had nothing to lose. I turned, faced the class, and just glared at everyone. And people actually stopped laughing, at least enough to hear me when I said, "What are you, four years old? I'm sure it's soooo funny."

Which is the bravest thing I've done since trying to kick the monkey off Mom.

And, for whatever reason, that shut everyone up. I knew people thought I was a bitch, but I sort of thought the same thing about them.

"It wasn't a big deal," I say. "I just wanted to get started with biology. I'm going to study nursing, so I need good grades in science."

Goose shakes his head like my dad does when he knows I'm lying. "Don't downplay how brave you were, standing up to a roomful of people. You weren't the only person who was annoyed, just the only one who said anything. I didn't. You were like a warrior."

I shrug and look away so he can't see my smile. Warrior. I like that.

"Serious badass. And you were brave just now, onstage."

Glad to change the subject, I say, "*That's* true. I was terrified. I'm probably the one person here who doesn't want a lead. Hopefully, I won't get it." Now that it's over, I'm backing off the fact that I really sort of want it.

"Oh, you'll get it." He points to my notebook. "So who's J.P.? Your boyfriend?"

He's looking at the writing on my notebook.

So. Embarrassing. I try to sneak my fingers on top of the writing.

"Um, actually, he's a singer. Jonah Prince." I realize this does not make me sound like a warrior-type. "It's dumb. My friend Laurel and I are getting tickets for his concert in Orlando this summer, so I was, you know, being a fangirl." I try not to look like someone who wrote three Tumblr posts about Jonah in the past week.

"Jonah Prince. That's the guy with the dance moves, right?" Goose executes a Jonah Prince–like spin. "I've got some moves of my own."

I stifle a giggle. He says, "It's okay to laugh. I wasn't being serious."

"I guess we should go back in," I say. "I think there's a dance audition." Which Laurel totally lied about.

"Wouldn't want to miss that. As you can tell, I'm a brilliant dancer."

That time, I do laugh. We head for the auditorium. Goose holds the door for me, then takes a seat with one of the better Nancy candidates. Another girl is onstage, singing "As Long as He Needs Me" off-key. I sit by Laurel.

The next day, when the cast list goes up, I'm Oliver. Goose Guzman is listed as the Artful Dodger, and he's hugging the girl he was sitting with, who got Nancy.

"I'm someone named Charlotte, and chorus," Laurel says. "We'll never rehearse together." But I can tell she's thrilled she got a speaking part.

"Congratulations. Yes, we will. Oliver's in almost every scene." *Le sigh.* "I'll be at your rehearsals and a bunch more. At least, it gets me away from Violet. And squee! Charlotte is a great part!"

"The beginning of a brilliant theater career," Laurel agrees. And we jump up and down.

4

That night, at dinner, I tell Dad and Violet about the play.

Despite a full-time lawyer job, Violet is an incredible cook. She scours food blogs and cookbooks and makes recipes that look like they should take hours, but still gets dinner on the table by seven. I think she stays up all night, chopping stuff. So, while normal kids are eating frozen breaded chicken breasts or even ramen, my family gets shrimp étouffée with grits or, tonight, beef Wellington.

God, how I wish we could eat frozen chicken breasts sometimes. I love frozen chicken breasts with barbecue sauce on them. It's such a mom thing to make.

I miss my mom.

But I eat everything in hopes that it will make Violet hate me less. It doesn't work.

"What's this in the middle?" I ask, picking at my steak, which has been rolled in a crust like a pie and has something gray that looks like pureed mouse in the center.

"It's really good." Dad smiles at Violet and rubs her back. "You're such a great cook. I don't know how you have time for this."

"We make time for those we love," she says.

And then, he kisses her. On the lips. With tongue. Long pause while I throw up in my mouth.

"But what is it?" I start to scrape it off, figuring they won't notice since they're so busy sucking face.

"Darling, don't do that. It's pâté, okay? It's delicious. It's . . ."

Liver! Do you know they force-feed the geese through a tube to make their livers more "buttery"? But I don't say it. I don't use any unnecessary words with Violet. I try to stuff the liver into my mouth to keep the words from coming out.

"Mmm. You're a great cook, Violet, um, Mom." In the beginning, she'd asked me to call her Mom, but it had seemed wrong. But, as years went by and everyone else had a mother, I changed my mind. It wasn't like Mom was going to know about it. And Violet was nice. Then.

Was nice.

She'd seemed happy about it. Dad said Violet had never had a good relationship with her own mother, a beautiful woman who'd joined us for Thanksgiving exactly once in the years Violet and Dad had been together, and who'd criticized the dry turkey (It was perfect, like everything Violet cooked) and left before dessert. I try to remember that when I get mad at Violet, but it's not easy.

"So I'm going to be in the school musical," I say, mostly to Dad. *"Oliver!"*

"Oh, that's wonderful," Violet says. "It's always so much fun to be in the chorus."

"Absolutely," Dad says. "Violet did musicals in high school, and she was on the dance team." He's so pleased we have something in common.

"That's so cool," I say. "I suck at dance. What were you in?"

Violet is actually momentarily happy, talking about herself. "Senior year, we did *My Fair Lady*. I played the lead, Eliza. And junior year, I was Irene Molloy in *Hello, Dolly!*"

"She was breathtaking," Dad says, and takes a big bite of his liver-y steak. "Just like this meal. I don't know how one woman can be so good at everything."

Almost like she's a witch.

"So breathtaking you never gave me a second look," Violet says. "You were busy looking elsewhere."

Dad looks down at his plate. "Mmm."

I know I have to tell them. "Actually, I'm not in the chorus. It's kind of a funny story. They were looking for a short girl to play Oliver."

"So you have the lead?" Dad says. "That's wonderful." Because he is just that clueless to how Violet will react.

She's already frowning. I say, "It's not really the lead. All the girls wanted Nancy."

"Don't be an idiot," Violet snaps. "The play's called *Oliver!* not *Nancy!*"

"But I'm playing a boy. I'll have to wear my hair in a cap and look ugly." She should love that.

"Maybe you should cut it off, immerse yourself in the role of a London street urchin. When I played Eliza, I talked in a British accent twenty-four seven."

So weird.

"I don't think that's necessary," Dad jokes. "Everyone can't be as dedicated as you, Violet."

I can tell he's trying to help me, but it's still annoying that he always takes her side. I chomp on my beef Wellington. "This is really incredible. You're a great cook, Violet." I chew real quick, like a rabbit, then take another bite. Dad and Violet are chewing too, which is better than tonguing each other.

"Anyway," I say when I've eaten enough to leave, "I'll probably have rehearsal most days. Laurel's mom can drive me when Laurel's rehearsing too, but otherwise, maybe you can pick me up on your way home?"

I'm looking at Dad, but Violet says, "Of course."

"Thanks." I take one last bite. "Mmm." Chewing.

"You must have a very beautiful voice," Violet says.

I can hear the jealousy tinging her own voice. But why would she be jealous? She's beautiful and talented herself. Why hate me so much?

Because she's a total wack job.

"I think it was more that no one wanted to be Oliver. They tried to talk this one short boy into it, but he refused. And the few girls who tried couldn't sing the notes right." I take another bite even though I don't want it, then stand.

"I'm sure you're being modest." Violet's stopped eating, watching me.

I sit back down, finish my bite, take another. When I've finished the whole gross, goose-torture experiment, I ask to be excused. "I have a lot of homework."

Later, when I go to wash my face, the soap feels hot on my cheek. I throw it aside and rinse off the water.

An ugly red welt spreads across my face. When I go to bed an hour later, it's even worse. I finally fall asleep with an ice pack pressed against my cheek. I put on Jonah's music to take my mind off it.

That night, I dream that Jonah and I are trapped in a burning building. He rescues me and takes me away, away from everything.

The next morning, my face is normal, like nothing happened. Before I catch the bus, I look for Violet. Dad's already left, and I want to remind her I'm sleeping over Laurel's. Violet's room is quiet. Maybe she left too.

The bedroom is carpeted, so my feet make no sound. A light shines from the bathroom. Violet's there. I can see her sitting at her vanity. In her hand, she holds a mirror, a big, round, silver one with a long handle. It's beautiful. There's a mirror over the sink, of course. Maybe she's trying to see the back of her hair. But no. As I stand there, staring, she speaks.

To the mirror.

"Mirror, mirror, in my hand, who is the fairest in the land?"

Who's the most batshit crazy?

I bolt from the room, but not before I think I hear the mirror say something back.

Now who's crazy?

5

We have a read-through after school that day. The second Laurel and I reach the auditorium, Goose runs to meet us.

"Please, suh, can I have some maw?" he says in a British accent.

I recognize Oliver's famous line and smile.

"Knew you'd be perfect for it," he says. "I practically discovered you."

"And how did you know that?" I try to give him some attitude— I'm a drama geek now.

"All right, you caught me. I threw you under the bus so I didn't have to play a little kid. I hate playing kids."

I nod. I get it. The same reason I hate playing princesses— typecasting.

"Anyway," he says, "enough chitchat. When Connors calls roll, say 'chop' instead of 'here,' okay? And pass it on."

"Why?" Laurel says.

"Everyone's going to do it."

"That sounds like those bad antidrug videos they make us watch in homeroom." Laurel puts on a stoner voice. "Hey, man, everyone's doing it."

"I'm sure this isn't going to end with one of us OD-ing on pot brownies." I look at Goose. "Right?"

"Right. So you're in?" When we nod, he runs off to tell other people.

When Mrs. Connors calls the first name, the guy playing Fagin answers, "Chop." Mrs. Connors looks a little uncomfortable but calls the next name, Willow something. The girl playing Nancy answers, "Chop." Then me, Bill Sikes, Mr. Bumble, all the way down to the chorus.

As the last name is called, all the older drama students yell, "Timber!" and pretend to fall on the floor like trees. They pull us uninitiated people down too. Mrs. Connors rolls her eyes and looks right at Goose. He grins at her, and she starts laughing too.

After the read-through (during which my Cockney accent is roundly ridiculed in case I was getting too full of myself), Goose comes up to me again. "How's J.P.?"

"Still unaware of my existence," I say. *And my identity as his future bride.*

"I heard one of his songs on the radio last night."

"Oh, really?" I hold my breath. Guys just looove to say that Jonah sings like a girl. Obviously, they're jealous, but it's still annoying.

But Goose says, "That song, 'Beautiful but Deadly,' it's pretty scathing social commentary about society's attitudes about appearance. I wasn't expecting that."

"Yes! Exactly! Most people don't get that. At least, most guys." Is he making fun of me?

"Guys like to hate on rock stars because they get all the girls. Me, I'm more confident in myself."

"I can see that." I smile. "You should go to his concert. Lots of girls to choose from."

"I'd probably get trampled by hundreds of screaming women. Not a bad way to go, though."

Laurel interrupts. "My mom's here. You ready?"

"Sure." To Goose, I say, "Concert tickets go on sale tomorrow. You'd probably be the only guy there. Big advantage."

"Good tip. By the way, if you need help with your accent—not that it's bad or anything—you could come over after school. My mom likes this British soap called *EastEnders*, and sometimes, we all speak in Cockney at dinner, just for fun."

"That *does* sound fun." A lot more fun than watching my parents make out. "I may take you up on that." Even though he obviously thinks my accent is bad.

"He's really nice," I tell Laurel as we leave.

"OMG," Laurel says. "You didn't actually buy that stuff he said about J.P. Guys do not listen to Jonah Prince. He's either making fun of you, or he's a total horndog and using Jonah to flirt. Like he'd be your type."

I guess she means because I'm pretty and he's short. Because, apparently, being beautiful automatically makes a person shallow. Like Violet.

"I don't know that I have a type." I don't like what Laurel is implying. Plus, it seems like she's judging Goose by his looks as much as people judge me by mine. I don't like to think that's true so I say, "Besides, I think he's dating Willow."

Goose has stopped to wait for her. I go back to him. "Say, Goose, what was your favorite part of the song you listened to?"

He thinks a second. "There were lots of parts I liked."

Laurel's nodding like, *sure.*

"Well, what was one part?" I ask, testing him, hoping Laurel's not right.

He thinks another second, then starts to sing:

If I could see you through your eyes;
And you could see me through mine;
The world would change for the better.
Only then could we feel love divine.

His voice is strong and mellow. He looks away as he sings, like he's suddenly shy about it. For a second, it's like Jonah's there, singing to me.

When he finishes, we just stand there, silent. Then he coughs. "I don't think I remember any more of the words—but I remember I liked it!"

I laughed. "It's okay. That's my favorite part too."

Willow/Nancy comes up to us. "I didn't know you were such a Jonah Prince fan."

"I'm full of surprises," Goose says. "You ready?"

"I am," she says. "My mom says it's fine if I come over on a school night, since I told her it was to watch *EastEnders* for the play."

"Great." He offers her his hand. "Your chariot awaits."

Willow leans in and kisses him. Then they walk off together. I give Laurel a look, like, *See?* because Goose and Willow are obviously a couple. She's also tall, at least six inches taller than I am, so they make an interesting one.

"See you guys Monday," I say.

"Have fun buying tickets," Goose says.

When I get to Laurel's mom's car, I text my dad to remind him I'm staying over. He doesn't reply. He doesn't care, of course, since it will give him more time to stay with his beloved, completely insane Violet.

6

Our fan club membership, plus incredible persistence on four different devices, gets us floor seats! After that, we get every calendar we can find (wall, cell phone, the agenda books they give us at school—the ones with inspirational quotes like, "If you reach for the moon, even if you miss, you'll land among the stars"—which isn't even accurate) and write countdowns on them. We start a series for Tumblr and Instagram too. One hundred thirteen days exactly. We plan to cross off each day together, to share the anticipation.

We sit at the kitchen table, and while Laurel's mom makes us eggs, plan the entire day out. "What should we wear?" I ask.

"We could get T-shirts."

"But then we'll look like everyone else."

"I know! I know!" Laurel starts jumping up and down in her

seat. She's so cute. "We could *make* T-shirts. That would really get his attention."

I try not to sigh. My fantasy of meeting my future husband does not involve looking like a screaming fangirl in a shirt that says *Waiting for My Handsome Prince* in glitter. I read once that Elvis Presley fell in love with his wife because she didn't think he was that big a deal. Her parents even threatened not to let her see him anymore when she broke curfew. Talk about hard to get. It's bad enough my only shot at meeting Jonah is at a concert. I have no idea how I'll get him to notice me, short of a miracle where his eyes meet mine across a crowded basketball arena, and he just *knows*. Still, I plan on leaving in his private limo. It's destiny. I believe in destiny, so why not?

"T-shirts are unflattering," I tell Laurel. "We should be different, rock some really fabulous outfits. We have months to plan and budget."

"Oh, okay." She looks sort of surprised. I don't usually show much interest in fashion. "So you're going to buy clothes that fit and stuff?"

"Yes. Okay. Hey, we could make signs. You're great at that artsy stuff." Signs are part of my master plan to get him to notice me. I had this idea about putting a line from the poem "The Love Song of J. Alfred Prufrock," which I read is Jonah's favorite poem. How cool is it that he has a favorite poem? I thought about putting "Dare to eat a peach," which is about taking chances. Or "Dare disturb the universe," which is about not being afraid to be controversial. No one else would know what it meant, just Jonah. He'd get that I'm more than a fangirl—I'm his soul mate. It would be like secret code. I decided not to tell Laurel that yet in case—you know—she thinks I'm crazy. Maybe I'm a little crazy, but you can't win if you don't try.

Over breakfast, while Mrs. Mendez reads the newspaper, we

discuss colors. "Jonah's favorite color is purple," Laurel says, "so we should use purple poster board."

"Won't everyone use purple because it's his favorite color?"

"Pink and purple?" Laurel amends.

I guess peach would be a bit much. I'm not even sure if they make peach poster board. Orange isn't the same. "Dare to eat a peach" is probably too weird anyway.

We decide to make two signs.

"What will yours say?" Laurel asks.

Suddenly embarrassed, I say, "I'm not sure yet. Maybe we shouldn't make it right away. It might get ruined."

Laurel nods. "The glitter will fall off."

"Last time I used glitter for a school project, Violet's lame-o cat, Grimalkin, rubbed against it, then licked herself. She yakked up glitter all over my bed, and all Violet cared about was whether the cat was okay."

"Grimalkin?" Laurel's mom looks up from the paper. "She still has that cat?"

"As long as I've known her, I guess."

"She used to talk about that cat in high school," Laurel's mom says. "I remember the weird name."

I forgot that Laurel's mom had known Violet in school. But that was a long time ago. I remember Dad had his twenty-year reunion a few years ago. So unless Violet got the cat on the last day of high school, it would be even older than that. "It must be a different cat. Cats don't live that long, do they?"

"Probably not. It was a white cat, I remember, solid white. She had a picture of it in her locker. We thought that was so . . ." Her voice trails off.

"You can say it. So weird." Violet's cat, Grimalkin, is white. It doesn't seem that old at all, though. "Maybe she just gives all her cats the same name, like Lisa on *The Simpsons*." Violet is exactly that weird.

"Let's make the posters here," Laurel suggests. "That way, Grimalkin Five won't eat the glitter."

I giggle. I know mine will be purple and gold, colors of royalty. But I'll wear peach to stand out from the throngs of girls wearing purple.

Sunday afternoon, Dad shows up at Laurel's house, unannounced. I gather my belongings . . . slowly, and come to the door when Mrs. Mendez calls my name for the third time.

"Hey," he says when I'm in the car. "We missed you."

"Really? I thought you and Violet liked having alone time. It gives you a chance to make out. Constantly." Since Violet stopped liking me, it seems like my dad and I never do anything together, so this was one of the few chances I had to talk to him alone.

"What's that supposed to mean?"

"It means no one's parents do that. It's super-weird and makes me uncomfortable."

"I don't think that's true." His arm sort of flexes, holding the wheel.

"Did you see how mad she was that I got the lead in the play? She practically burst into flames when I told her. She's never happy when anything good happens to me."

"Hey, wait, what's bringing this on?"

"She hates me. She's jealous. Or I remind her of Mom."

"That's crazy. You look much more like me."

His answer is so immediate that I know he thought about it before. I decide to ask him the question I've been wondering about.

"Why didn't you marry her in the first place? Why did you choose Mom?"

He brakes to avoid a squirrel that runs in front of our car. I pitch forward. Silence. Or as silent as it can get in our neighborhood with a lawn mower going, a small dog yapping its head off, all the tranquil joys of suburbia.

Finally, he says, "Believe me, that's a sore spot for Violet."

"I bet it is." It's like I thought. She hated my mother for taking Dad. And that's why she hates me.

"I'm afraid I wasn't very nice to her. We were friends, always together, and then, one day, I just . . . stopped. I knew Violet had a crush on me, but she was sort of homely and I just wanted Jennifer. There was never a time when I didn't like your mother. Jen was so pretty, so much more outgoing and confident than I could ever be. And, since she hated Violet's guts, I had to choose."

Wait. I want to rewind to the part where he said Violet was homely.

"You're saying you dumped Violet because she was ugly? Ugly?"

"Well, not dumped her. We weren't dating."

"But Violet was *ugly*?"

He shrugs. "I guess she was a late bloomer."

"So she had acne? Or was overweight?"

"No, not that. A bad nose and stuff. Not much of a chin. I don't know, she was homely. Everyone made fun of her. Stop asking me about it."

I feel a twinge of pity for poor Violet, ugly and with one friend, my dad. Then he ditched her for the pretty cheerleader. I push back the feeling that my mom was a mean girl. But I remember what Violet said about the cat being her best friend when she was a teen, what Laurel's mom said about her even having pictures of the cat in her locker, probably to get her through the day when everyone picked on her. It was sad.

But Violet isn't sad and pathetic anymore.

"No. What happened? Did she get plastic surgery?" I always knew Violet had work done.

Dad looks surprised. "No. I mean, I don't think so. She was just pretty in high school. It was sort of weird. Like one day I looked at her, and she wasn't ugly anymore. I don't know."

I shake my head. "You get that Violet is, like, the most beautiful woman I've ever seen?"

"I know. Some people are just late bloomers, I guess."

"You said that before."

We're in our driveway. Dad says, "Want to go out with us for pizza?"

I throw open the car door. "Not really. I ate at Laurel's. And I have homework." Both are lies. I start toward the house.

Dad follows me. "Hey, I think we should eat one meal together the whole weekend."

I keep walking. Violet intercepts him, kissing him. I start upstairs.

When I reach the steps, stupid Grimalkin throws herself at my legs, claws out, and rakes them down my calf.

"Ouch!" Reflexively, I kick at the cat to get her off me.

"Don't do that!" Violet shrieks. "She's old!"

"She attacked me out of the blue!" I scream back. Like when that monkey went after my mother.

The cat ran—ran like a kitten—toward Violet and rubbed against her legs.

After they leave for dinner, I go to Dad's closet, to a box where he keeps old yearbooks and stuff. I used to love looking at the photos of Mom and Dad, power couple. Mom was so beautiful in her dance team uniform and her homecoming dress. I never looked for pictures of Violet before.

First, I check the high school ones. Violet's there, tall and beautiful as expected, star of the school play in a big black-and-white picture, and on the dance team. The pictures could have been taken yesterday. Nothing has changed except her poufy 1980s hairstyle.

But when I look further back, to eighth grade, the name Violet Appel reveals an awkward, hunched girl with a crooked nose, an overbite, and no eyelashes. I only recognize her from the name.

In a group photo, with the middle school choir, she stands in front, one of the shortest.

In the high school dance team photos, tenth grade Violet is in the center of the back row, statuesque and beautiful.

Violet could have gotten a nose job.

She could have gotten a boob job, her eyelashes dyed, braces, makeup.

But you can't get surgery to grow six inches in two years, which is what she did.

The change is like magic.

7

I have *Oliver!* rehearsal every day after school. It's a great Violet-avoidance ploy, but also, I'm admitting to myself that I'm not completely miserable about being Oliver. In fact, I'm glad Laurel got me to try out. I've always thought I hated being the center of attention. Now I realize I hate being the center of attention *for my looks*. I'm sick of everyone fawning over my hair, my eyes, liking me because of how I look—or hating me for the same reason. But, as Oliver, with a cap covering my hair, I'm getting attention for my singing and acting. Not that I want to be an actress or anything, but it's fun for now.

Yesterday, we practiced a scene where Oliver's locked in the funeral parlor alone, overnight. At tryouts, people sniffled when I sang "Where Is Love?" Now they flat out bawled. It feels great that people care so much.

Today, we're practicing a scene Laurel's character is in. It takes place in the funeral home too. In it, a bully named Noah is picking on Oliver. He's a lot bigger, so Oliver just takes it. But then, Noah insults Oliver's mother, and Oliver goes nuts on him, pushing Noah into a coffin and kicking him. Charlotte, Noah's girlfriend, runs in screaming her head off. Laurel had to scream at the audition, and that's why she got the part. She's a great screamer. Once, she saw a marine toad eating dog food on her patio, and she screamed so loud the neighbors called 911.

I can so relate to Oliver getting mad at someone insulting his mother. Violet always makes little comments about mine when Dad isn't around to hear. Like last year, the lady next door commented that I was growing up pretty, just like my mom. Violet said yeah, Dad had been so taken with Mom's beauty (yes, she'd actually said, "taken with"—she talks like that) that he hadn't noticed how dumb she was. Mrs. Hernandez acted like maybe she'd heard Violet wrong. I felt like one of those cartoon characters, when they have smoke coming out of their ears. But, of course, blowing Violet up was out of the question.

Now, when Tedder Strasky, the guy who plays Noah, says to Oliver (me), "Your mother was a real bad 'un," I just picture Violet's face on Tedder's body, and I launch myself at him as hard as I can. I figure I can't really hurt him because Tedder's at least a foot taller than I am and outweighs me by a hundred pounds. But, to my surprise, he gives a yowl that doesn't sound like acting and falls on his butt, then slides to the edge of the stage. Goose and Willow are sitting in front, but they clear out real quick when Tedder goes barreling toward them. Tedder just sits there, winded, so I can't push him into the coffin.

When Mrs. Connors yells, "Cut!" Tedder turns to me.

"Man, you're strong, girl. I did not see that coming." He looks annoyed, even though he's trying to laugh.

"Oh, sorry." I look down. "Guess I really got into the part."

"No, it was good. It was kinda hot. I just wasn't prepared."

I ignore the "kinda hot," but say, "Thanks."

"Try not to maim the other actors, Celine," Mrs. Connors calls.

"Will do." I turn away, blushing, but not before I see Goose take his seat again and give me a thumbs-up. He mouths a word: *warrior.* Yeah, that's me. I roll my eyes.

We try it again, and now Tedder's ready for me. Connors says, "Remember what it was like when she took you by surprise. That was really good."

I'm hoping we're going to finish up with the funeral home scene so Laurel's mom can drive me home, and I don't have to bother Dad or, worse, Violet. But after I punch Tedder in the gut (gently) for the fourth time, Mrs. Connors says, "Good work. I think we can move on." She calls Goose onstage for the scene where Oliver and the Artful Dodger first meet.

"Thank God," Tedder says. "Do I get padding for the actual show?"

Everyone laughs, but I apologize again. Even though I think he's being a big baby at this point.

"Don't worry about it, little girl. I can handle you." I don't think he's totally kidding.

"You've got some real anger management problems, huh?" Goose says when he comes onstage.

Well, I do, but I say, "I feel really bad."

"Don't. Strasky's exactly like the character he plays. He was a huge bully in middle school. He actually did steal people's lunch money. It's not just a cliché. It would almost be worth playing Oliver to get a chance to beat him up."

"You could take him," I say. "He obviously has problems dealing with someone with a low center of gravity."

"I think he had trouble dealing with a girl—he couldn't just break your face. But I like that: low center of gravity. I'm not short. I just have a low center of gravity."

"Go out for wrestling," I suggest.

"Can't mess up my pretty face for showbiz." He poses like one of those guys in the Calvin Klein ads, except with a shirt.

Mrs. Connors calls for us to start. She blocks the scene up to the song and runs through it a few times. Then, she glances at her watch. "We'll start 'Consider Yourself' tomorrow."

I look at my watch too. Five-thirty. Too early for Dad to pick me up, perfect for Violet. I start down the steps.

"What?" Goose was walking toward Willow, who stayed to wait for him. But he stops and looks over his shoulder at me.

"Hmm?" I turn back.

"You sighed."

"Oh, nothing. It's just too early for my dad to pick me up, and Laurel just left. It's okay, I can walk."

"I was just about to offer you a ride." He looks at Willow. "You don't mind, do you?"

"No, no," Willow says in a fake Cockney accent. "We can give 'er a lift. You 'av to talk Cockney, though."

"What? Oh . . . um, I only live a wee bite awie from he-ah." It sounds more Irish than Cockney, but Willow nods. I remember what Violet said about speaking in a British accent during *My Fair Lady* rehearsals.

"We're gonna stop at Tawget first," Goose says. "Ye mind?"

"No, that's fine." I have to outline a chapter for chem, but I'd still rather get home closer to when Dad does.

"Why are we goin' to Tawget awl of a su'in?" Willow asks as we walk out.

"'Member wot I tole you?" Goose says.

Willow grins. "Oh, it's a prahnk."

"Not a prahnk," Goose says. "A sociological experiment."

"You 'av way too much time on your hands," Willow says.

I laugh. Goose does seem to have a day with a few more hours in it than everyone else's. In addition to the timber prank, the other day he got someone to hide a walkie-talkie in the dropped ceiling in the dressing room, then talked into the other one, yelling, "Let me out! Let me out!" Half the cast thought he was stuck up there.

"I'm still cracking up about the ceiling thing," I say.

"See there," he says to Willow. "And she is a h'independent observer."

Willow musses his hair. "I 'eard about this school where these kids released three pigs, labeled one, two, an' faw. The principal spent the 'ole day, looking fer number three. You should do that."

"As soon as I find someone to give me three pigs. Do you 'av any pigs, Celine?"

I shake my head.

"Maybe for the experiment, we shouldn't do the accents," Goose says. "It kind of makes us seem . . . weird."

"You think the accents make us seem weird?" Willow says. "Not, say, your personality?"

"I think that's a good idea," I agree, relieved.

We're in the school parking lot. Goose holds up his keys, and a blue Civic beeps. I'd assumed Willow would be driving, which was stupid. Still, I wonder how he reaches the pedals.

"Special pedals," he says, reading my mind.

"What?" I say.

"My car," he says. "I call her Nelly. She has extended pedals. People always wonder how I can reach. So I'm saving you the trouble of asking or rubbernecking from the backseat."

"That's cool," I say, embarrassed at being so obvious. And average.

We get in the car, a typically messy boy's car with crumpled assignments and McDonald's fry wrappers. "Sorry it's such a mess," Goose says. "I drive my brothers and sister around sometimes."

"Sure, and they're always leaving their chem homework." Willow uncrumples a paper she almost sat on. "You'd get better grades if you handed this stuff in sometimes. And fasten your seat belt."

"God, stop being such a harassenger," Goose whines, but he does the seat belt. "Mrs. McKinney said she'd take the homework late. She loves me. Everyone loves me."

"Don't know how you talked her into that," Willow says. "But remind me to staple it to your forehead tomorrow." She mimes stapling it.

"So what's the sociological experiment?" I ask.

"Yes," Willow says, "what is this grand idea that's keeping me from studying for my gov test tomorrow?"

"Selfies with strangers!" Goose says. He's turned toward me, backing up the car, so I guess he sees the blank look on my face as well as I see the grin on his. "You go to a public place, walk up to people, and take a selfie with them. Someone else films their reactions."

"And you don't get beat up?" This is so not something I can do.

"Not so far. I only did it once before. A few people got weirded out, but others thought it was funny."

"I'll get the person with a can of pepper spray." Still, I wish I were like him. I've spent my whole life hating when people looked at me. Goose seems to love being the center of attention. It must be cool to be so comfortable in his skin. "Can I be the one filming it?" I know I'm a geek, but I suspect Goose wants an audience more than anything else anyway.

"We take turns," Willow says. "It wouldn't be fair otherwise."

"Besides, you ladies are so hot, people'd probably rather have their picture taken with you than me."

Willow slaps Goose's shoulder. "Just for that, you're going first.

That way, if we get thrown out for harassing people, there won't be any photographic evidence of me being there." But she's laughing.

"Gladly," Goose says.

We're near Target now, and I feel a little nervous, but also, sort of anticipating. Goose pulls into the parking lot and parks near where an old lady is loading bags into her car. "How about her?" Willow asks him.

"The old lady?" Goose asks. "Easy."

Before I can even process what he's doing, Goose is out of the car and running up to the old lady. "Smile!" he yells.

"What?" the old lady says as he stands next to her. She's not much taller than he is, and at first she looks a little freaked out. "What are you doing?"

"Just a picture?" he asks. "Please? And I'll help you with your bags."

Finally, the old lady smiles, and Goose snaps the picture with his phone. Willow's filming the whole thing.

"Why do you want my picture?" the old lady says.

"No reason," Goose says. "You look beautiful. Can I help you with those?" He grabs one of her bags by the handles.

The old lady looks a little confused, but when Goose puts the groceries into her car, she smiles again. "Aren't you sweet?"

"Yes. Yes, I am. Can we all get a picture with you?"

She notices me and Willow, who is still filming. "Oh, aren't you pretty girls? Of course. You made my day."

We gather around. Goose takes a selfie of all of us, and we finish helping the lady with her bags. She tries to give Goose a dollar, but he says, "Free service."

"Well, bless you," she says.

We walk away, Willow saying, "It's easy if you're going to offer to load their bags."

"What can I tell you? I'm just a wonderful person," Goose says. "Now, I'm blessed too."

"I don't know," I say. "It could have gone another way, and she could have kicked him in the face when he touched her groceries."

"She did seem a little like a ninja," Willow says.

"I'm nonthreatening," Goose says. "We shouldn't approach anyone with kids, though. They'll think we're pervs."

"Good thought," I say.

Willow goes next, accosting a nerdy-looking guy our age in the entrance. He's happy when she runs up next to him to take a picture.

"He was looking at your boobs," Goose says when she comes back. "That's easy too."

"He was *not* looking at my boobs. Why can't you acknowledge my gifts?"

"I see your gifts. And so did he. Show me the picture then."

Willow gets out her phone and glances at it. "Okay, so he was looking at my boobs. At least I didn't have to do chores for him."

Next, we go to accessories and try on knitted hats and scarves. "Ooh, put on that red hat," Goose says. I put on a red hat and a striped scarf that looks like *Where's Waldo?* It's silly, but Goose takes my picture. "Model it, darling!"

Willow takes another photo with a different rando who also looks at her chest, but when Goose tries to take one with a girl our age, her boyfriend shows up and gets mad. We take more pictures of each other too, and a selfie of all three of us. Then, we head for the grocery section.

Goose says, "Your turn, Celine."

"Hey, I'm just along for the ride."

"No such thing as a free ride," Goose says. "You need to come out of your shell. You're in theatah now."

"You'd better do it," Willow says. "Otherwise, I'll never get home to study for my test." Willow looks around for a target. "How about her?"

She points to a woman. I can't tell how old she is, except she's older than us. She's in the frozen food section. She's wearing sort of a crazy outfit, a long, green, velvet skirt, black boots, and a black turtleneck. Her dark hair comes to her waist and has one purple streak. I'd actually love to get a picture of her to show Laurel. She'd like her style. And she looks nice.

"Okay," I tell Goose. "I'm going in."

I ready my phone, then run up to the woman, trying to be as confident as Goose and Willow. "Selfies with strangers! Smile!" And I snap her photo.

"Oh, look at you," she says. "So pretty. Is this some kind of school project?"

"Yes. Sort of."

"Okay. Well, glad I can help. What's your name?"

"Celine." I am sooo embarrassed. "Celine Columbo."

"Columbo." Her eyes narrow in recognition. "Any relation to Greg Columbo?"

"He's my father." Great. Now, she'll report back to Dad, and he'll think I'm on drugs. "How do you know him?" Hoping she'll say she hasn't seen him in years.

"Oh, I haven't seen him in years. I've known him since he was a boy, though."

Which is weird, because she doesn't look as old as Dad, nor does she have that Botoxed look of the fake-young. But then, I could say the same about Violet.

"Listen, we were just messing around," I say.

"I know. I'm Kendra, by the way." She backs up a few steps, staring at me, a weird expression on her face. "My, you are lovely, Celine. I'd heard you were, but I never imagined." She reaches up and touches my face, just staring at me. "So sweet and innocent."

Weird. I back away. "Listen, I have to go. You won't tell my dad you saw me, will you? I can delete the picture if you want. We were just kidding around."

Goose, who has been uncharacteristically silent during this encounter, comes up to me now. He says, "Hey, Celine, we should get going. Sorry, ma'am."

"Not a problem," Kendra says. "I won't say a thing to your dad. I doubt I'll see him anytime soon." She turns and goes back to choosing a bag of peas. We hightail it around the corner.

"Oh, God, kill me now," I say. "That was crazy embarrassing."

"What? I really liked hearing about how lovely you are," Goose says.

"Yeah, so sweet and innocent," Willow says. "So she's crazy? There's lots of crazy people. We've all done it, now let's get out of here."

She seems a little annoyed so I say, "Yeah, we should go."

We do, but Goose teases me the whole way home. I don't mind.

Goose drops Willow off first because she keeps griping about studying. My house isn't much farther. Now that we're done talking about the prank, I can't think of much to say. I always get this way, tongue-tied around new people. It actually takes longer than I thought because Goose makes a wrong turn. Fortunately, he talks for a while, about the play, about how they're having the cast party at his house, and it's going to be awesome. But then, there's silence. I say, "Thanks for driving me home. I hate having to ask my stepmother. And thanks for taking me with you. It was so much fun."

"Did you really think so?" He stops at a stop sign and looks at me. Sitting, we're almost the same height. It's mostly his legs that are short. "You seemed nervous."

"I was. I'm not good at talking to strangers. But I think it's important to face your fears." I think of my mom, how facing her fears had killed her. "I mean, sometimes, like being afraid of talking to people. Or stage fright."

"You're afraid of *me*?" He shakes his head. "No one's afraid of me."

I realize this sounds crazy. "Not afraid, exactly. But sometimes, with this group, I feel like I can't keep up. Everyone's so outgoing."

"So you're shy?" He nods like he's processing this new idea. "That's why you always sit with your friend and only talk to her?"

Do I do that? "I guess. Why? Did you think I was a snob?"

"Yeah, sort of. But maybe I just assumed that because you're so . . ." He stops.

"What?"

"Nothing."

"So what? What am I?" Though I know.

He shakes his head. "Nothing. I was going to say I'd see you in the hall at school, even before the play, walking by yourself, and I figured you were a snob because you're so beautiful. Okay? Usually, girls who are complete tens don't have a reason to be shy, so you assume they're snobby if they don't talk. But that was idiotic to think, so I wasn't going to say it."

Et tu, Goose? I wonder if other people think that, people who aren't as honest as he is.

I say, "When you pointed to me that day and said I should be Oliver, I could have killed you. I only tried out for the play at all because Laurel wanted me to. She's my best friend. I wanted to be in the chorus and dance in back, not be a star. I hate when people look at me. I hate when people think they know what I'm like."

"Like I just did. Got it."

"You're not the only one."

A car comes up behind us and honks. Goose starts driving again.

150

"Sorry," he says. "I shouldn't have judged you by your looks. You might not realize this, but people judge me by my looks all the time."

I smile. "No. It was a good thing. An opportunity. Once I got the part, I enjoyed it."

"You're awesome in the play. I tear up when you sing, 'Where Is Love?' It's . . . lovely . . . so sweet and innocent . . ." He laughs.

I laugh too, realizing the conversation had gotten too serious for him. I roll my eyes. "Anyway, I guess I have you to thank for me getting the part, since you didn't want to play it."

"Are you kidding? People would have come up to me, going, 'Please, suh, can I have some maw?' for the next year."

"And they won't do that to me?"

"It's cute when you're a girl, right?" He looks at my eye roll. "Guess not."

"I'm sorry you didn't get to be Bill Sikes like you wanted."

He laughs. "I didn't want to be Bill Sikes. I'm not stupid. I know I can't be Bill Sikes with a Nancy who could kick my ass. I wanted to be the Dodger. I figured by pretending I wanted to be Bill, I could guilt her into giving me Dodger, instead of making me be Oliver."

"Genius."

"That's me."

We're in my driveway now. I wish I could freeze time, freeze this afternoon and hang with him and Willow, instead of having to go home to Violet. Fun and laughter seem to follow Goose around, and I wish I could too. I like him, and suddenly it's really important that he like me. "So you don't think I'm a snob anymore, do you?"

"Nah, you went along with my stupidity, so you must be okay."

"I enjoyed it," I say. "Thanks."

"Any time you need a ride, let me know."

"Oh, you don't have—"

"Any time, Celine."

"Sure." I get out of the car and walk toward the house. Halfway there, I notice Violet gazing out the window at me. When she sees me seeing her, she closes the curtain.

I glance after Goose. He waited while I walked to the door, but now he's pulled to the bottom of our circular driveway. He looks back at me and grins. I wave.

I walk inside, yelling, "Hello!" Even though Violet was there two seconds ago, there's no answer. Sapphire is on the staircase. I bend to pet her. A claw flashes, and my arm is bleeding. I pull back. "Sapphire, you hurt me!"

As if realizing her mistake, she nuzzles my arm, then licks the spot she scratched.

"Oh, are you sorry? You should be. I don't know what got into you."

I remember Violet's face at the window, that odd, envious expression she's had on her face all the time lately. Could she have turned Sapphire against me?

Don't be crazy.

Almost as soon as I get to my room, Violet calls me for dinner. I think about saying I don't feel well to avoid it. But I'm actually hungry.

"Just a minute," I say.

I take out my phone and go through the pictures we took at Target; Goose, Willow, and me with the confused old lady. Then, all of us, trying on accessories. I'm looking for the one I took of the strange woman, Kendra her name was. I want to send it to Laurel. But weirdly, it's not there. I remember telling Kendra I could delete it, but I didn't think I had. Had someone else taken the picture, not me? No. It was *selfies* with strangers. I go through every picture on my camera roll, but it's like it was magically removed.

Finally, I go down to dinner.

Dad and Violet have already started. Violet stares me up and down, like she's trying to figure out who I am.

"Mmm, this looks good," I say, just to say something.

"What happened to your arm?" Dad asks.

"Sapphire scratched me. Can you believe it?"

"That's not like her," Dad says.

"I know," I say. "She doesn't even seem like she remembers she has claws."

"Sometimes, animals just turn on people," Violet says. "Like someone will have a pit bull for years, and then one day, it attacks someone. Or what happened to your mother."

Dad and I both stare at her. Outside, someone's mowing their lawn. Otherwise, it's silent.

I say, "I must have scared Sapphire. She acted sorry afterward. She licked my arm."

"Well, be careful," Dad says.

I glance at Violet. "I will."

Dad goes to the gym after dinner. Violet never goes. She's one of those lucky people who has a perfect body, seemingly without exercising. I go up to my room to do homework.

But later, when I go down to get a glass of water, I pass their room. Violet is sitting on the bed, staring into the mirror. It looks like she's talking to it again, a whole conversation.

What a weirdo.

I hear the words, *so beautiful.* But no, Violet's lips aren't moving.

Okay, so I'm crazy. But no crazier than Violet.

When Violet sees me, she turns the mirror facedown on the bed. I walk away.

So now, I stay away from cats, straight irons, beauty products, hair dryers, anything sharp, hot, caustic, or with the potential to become sharp, hot, or caustic.

And Violet. I stay away from her as much as possible. I go to Laurel's house most nights for dinner and all weekend, every weekend. Dad doesn't even seem to notice. When Laurel's mom picks us up for the fifth time in one week, she comments, "We're seeing a lot of you lately, Celine."

"I'm sorry. I sort of hate being home lately."

"You're always welcome, Celine. You do more chores than my own children." She glares at Laurel, who glares at me. It's true. I've been nauseatingly helpful at their house, doing all the dishes and volunteering for other chores so they won't get sick of seeing me so much.

"What's wrong at home?" Mrs. Mendez asks. "Does her name begin with a *V*?"

"Oh, it's not . . . Violet just doesn't like me that much. Guess I remind her of my mother."

"Yeah, they hated each other. Everyone else loved your mom, everyone but Violet."

"And now, she hates me. Only three more years until I leave for college."

"You can come over whenever you want, Celine. You can even just stay here if your dad says it's okay."

"Really?"

"Absolutely. I'd do anything for Jennifer Sadler's daughter."

"And my best friend," Laurel reminds her.

"Well, Jennifer was my best friend," Mrs. Mendez says. Then she stares out the window, like she's trying not to cry, or maybe like she's crying.

After a while I say, "So, what was Violet like when you were kids?"

Mrs. Mendez wrinkles her nose. "I hate to say it, but Violet was a total freak. We were a little mean to her, but honestly, it was hard to resist. Violet went out of her way to do weird stuff. Like, once, in fourth grade, she picked up a dead bird on the playground."

"A dead bird?"

"Well, it turned out not to be dead. But it looked dead, and it probably had some kind of bird disease. We were all grossed out, but Violet just walked over and picked it up with her bare hands. Like it was nothing. It was such a typical Violet thing to do."

"Violet loves birds," I say.

"Violet loved being a weirdo. For a while, we referred to anything incredibly weird as 'Violetish.' Oh, we were terrible. She was just . . . awkward. Poor thing." She sounds a little like the mean girls at school when they know they're being mean, but they just enjoy it.

"But you said the bird wasn't dead. Maybe she was trying to help it." I remember, now, Violet told me this story, a long time ago. She said they'd rescued the crow.

Mrs. Mendez shrugs. "I didn't see it, but Greg said it flew away."

"After she held it?"

"After she held it."

I think of something else. "My father said she was really ugly when she was a kid."

"Oh, yes, sooooo ugly. Poor thing. Crooked nose and no eyelashes. She looked like a parrot with no feathers." She smiles a little.

"And then, she got prettier?"

"It was like a miracle, really."

"And she didn't have surgery or anything?" I figured my dad, being a man, wouldn't be smart about stuff like that. A woman would know the truth. And maybe she was wearing five-inch heels in the dance photo.

"Not that anyone knew about. It wasn't like someone who got a nose job over summer vacation. I did that. With Violet, it just . . . happened. Everything in maybe a month or two. And she just kept getting more beautiful. More power to her, though. We were awfully mean to her."

I noticed she had gone from "a little mean" to "awfully mean."

"Including my mom?" I asked.

She stares out again before speaking, then says, "Not to speak ill of the dead, but especially your mom. She was brutal, even more so after she started dating Greg. Violet *always* liked him, and Jen couldn't resist rubbing it in her face. I think part of her attraction to Greg in the first place was that it made Violet so mad."

Which makes me feel a little sorry for Violet. I hate that my mom was so mean to her, and kind of my dad too. My parents were obviously like the Bryce Richardson and Whitney Jacobs of their class. I hate that.

At least, until I get home and the mockingbirds in our oak tree dive-bomb me.

And I see Violet watching me out the window, smiling.

And I remember that she's decided to be mean to me, to make up for it.

9

There's a song in *Oliver!* called "Who Will Buy?" In it, Oliver, who has survived the workhouse, being sold to a funeral home operator, and living in a den of pickpockets, has been taken in by the kindly Mr. Brownlow. He looks out the window at the beautiful morning—a beauty he knows can't last, not for him. He wishes someone would buy the wonderful morning and the feeling in his heart so he can remember it forever. He knows he can't.

It's my favorite song in the show, and it's how I feel about being in the play too. After that day with Goose and Willow, Goose gets everyone to include me when they do stuff after rehearsal or on weekends. I bring Laurel along, so suddenly, we're part of this cool, weird group of friends instead of sitting home every night with Violet and her disgruntled cat. Everyone's also raving about my voice. Mrs.

Connors says I should take drama and try for thespian conference next year. Laurel and I are both going to. This is the happiest I've been since I was a kid in Brownies, and my mom was alive.

And, like Oliver, I know the skies won't stay blue forever.

The play is this weekend. There are two more days before dress rehearsal, so we're staying late every night. I'm barely home, which is good because the cats are plotting to murder me. Grimalkin waited by my bed last night and attacked my leg when I walked to the bathroom. When I fell (hard!), Sapphire went for my face. It felt like an ambush. Appliances are still turning against me too. I've started taking baths because the shower never stays the temperature I choose. Dad says he'll call the plumber, but he keeps forgetting until he hears my screams.

But the show's songs are in my head all the time. Today, in the bathtub, I start singing, *Who will buy this wonderful feeling? I'm so high, I swear I could fly.*

When I walk downstairs to go to the bus, Dad and Violet are there, sharing coffee. Like, they're literally sharing it—she's sipping out of a cup that he's holding. *Kill me.* I brush past Dad to get to the refrigerator for my lunch.

"Hey, you sounded incredible up there," Dad says.

"What?" Violet stops drinking coffee. "Who sounded incredible?"

Dad brushes Violet's butt with his hand, a gesture that always makes me wince. He says, "I heard Celine practicing in the bathroom. She has a beautiful voice, just like her mother . . . oh, and you too, Violet. But, of course, she inherited it from Jennifer. I sure can't sing."

Violet looks like someone who found a pube in her ice cream. Then, she smiles. "How wonderful. The play must be soon."

"Yes, when is it?" Dad asks.

"Um, it's Friday and Saturday. But you don't both have to go if you don't want." I want Dad to go, not Violet.

"Of course we're going. What else would we do? Friday night? I'll put it on my calendar." Dad takes out his phone. "Is there preferred seating for parents of the star?"

"I'll check."

Violet's sitting there with a weird, strangled expression on her face. I know she'll ruin it somehow. "We're both looking forward to it," she says. But her eyes don't match her words.

When I wake Friday morning, I have no voice. None at all. I take a decongestant, but I don't have a cold, so it doesn't help.

No! I want to scream it, but nothing comes out, not even a shriveled whisper. I am literally speechless.

This is impossible. I've never lost my voice in my life. Now, on the first day of a play I have the lead in, it's gone.

I know Violet's behind it.

There have been so many clues, so many reasons for believing it's true, and only one reason for not believing it:

There's no such thing as witches.

But how can we know that's true, really true?

Throughout time, we've believed in magic, not cute, Disney magic that makes stuff fly around the room, but black magic, magic that caused plagues and brought down churches. That's why they burned witches at the stake. That was what they feared when they hanged women as witches in Salem. But the women in Salem weren't really witches. Not the women who died anyway. Real witches would have been better at avoiding detection. Real witches wouldn't have been captured. Real witches wouldn't have died. Real witches would have taken revenge on their enemies.

Like Violet had.

Violet was an ugly child. Dad says so. Mrs. Mendez too. The middle school yearbook confirms it. But now, Violet is beautiful without surgery or anything.

And my mother was Violet's enemy.

Twice, in Violet's presence, my mother was attacked by animals. The second time, an animal killed her.

Violet made them attack my mother. Violet killed her.

I am my mother's daughter.

So Violet hates me.

Now, objects and animals are attacking me.

Yet I know no one will believe me. I know my father won't. Why?

Because there's no such thing as witches.

I don't know what I can tell Mrs. Connors or all my friends in the cast. I'm letting them all down.

I knock on Dad's door. I want to go to a doctor.

"Come in."

When I walk in, he and Violet are still in bed, watching the morning news, wrapped up in each other as usual.

Nauseating.

Dad sees me. "Hey, it's your big day."

Violet smiles, happier than I've seen her in a long time. She waves but says nothing.

Dad says, "Would you believe it? Violet lost her voice. Can't say a word."

I point to my throat, gesture and nod, like, *Me too.*

The doctor can't do anything. He sees nothing wrong with me. "No cold. Throat isn't red. Nothing wrong with her tonsils," Dr. Alvarez tells Dad. "Seems like selective mutism."

I shake my head so hard my hair hurts my eyes, then I write a note. *I did not select to be this way.*

161

"I didn't mean you're faking. Perhaps a better term is hysterical mutism. Is anything upsetting you?"

Other than having no voice and a stepmother trying to kill me? No.

"She has a play tonight," Dad says, "a play she's been practicing for weeks. She has the lead."

"Maybe she's nervous," Dr. Alvarez says. "Are you nervous, Celine?"

I shake my head. On my pad, I write, *I want to be in this play.* My eyes are full of tears.

Dr. Alvarez nods.

"But the strange thing, Doctor," Dad says, "is my wife is having the same symptoms. They couldn't both be hysterically mute at the same time, could they? It would be an awfully big coincidence."

It would be except that Violet's faking. She cast some sort of spell on me, then pretended to lose her voice too so it would seem like an illness. That was obvious.

But I can't say it. I mean, aside from the obvious fact I can't speak, insulting Violet seems dangerous, considering she killed my mother. I'm just realizing that's what I'm saying about her. I believe that's true. I believe she murdered my mother so she could claim my father for her own.

And, if that's the case, I don't want to get her any angrier at me than she already is.

If she killed my mother, she could kill me next.

I get Dad to drop me off at school after the doctor. I have to tell Connors.

She sort of flips out when I do. It takes me a while to persuade her that I can't talk at all. She says maybe I'll be better for tomorrow's performance. I know I won't.

I attend both performances, in solidarity with the cast. I watch my understudy screw up my part. I cry softly in the audience because

162

softly is the only way I can cry. I tell Goose I can't go to the cast party. The cast party is for people who were in the cast. He begs me to come anyway, but I'd feel too awkward.

When I wake Sunday morning, my voice is back. Like I knew it would be.

So is Violet's. Like I knew it would be.

"It's like magic," she says.

Exactly.

10

I spend as little time at home as possible. I study with Laurel, stay at her house most nights, and only go home to refill on clothes or money or if I need something signed for school. My drama friends haven't ditched me (most pity me), so I hang with them too. When I do go home, I try to leave for the bus as early as possible.

Sunday night, two weeks after the play, Dad picks me up at Laurel's. I hear him in the kitchen, talking.

"So have you adopted my daughter?"

"She and Laurel love spending time together," Mrs. Mendez says. "It's so nice that they're friends. She said she asked you if she could stay over those days. Didn't she?"

"Yeah, she texts me at nine at night and tells, not asks."

"Is that true?" Mrs. Mendez notices I've entered the room.

"What's the big deal?" I ask Dad. "Violet doesn't want me around. I'm just granting her wish."

"That's not true," Dad says.

"It isn't? So if Violet had a choice between living with both of us or just you, she'd choose both?"

Mrs. Mendez takes the pot she's stirring off the stove, then starts for the door. I don't blame her. "I'll just let you two talk."

"We're leaving. Thanks for having her." Dad takes my overnight bag from me. "Violet loves you."

"Yeah, I can see the adoration in her eyes. She practically busted a gut from pride when I got the lead in the play. She wasn't crazy-jealous at all."

"We'll discuss this in the car." He opens the door and waits for me to go out.

In the car, he puts on his serious Dad voice and matching expression that he must copy from reruns of *Full House*. "Celine, Violet is a successful lawyer. An adult. Why would she be jealous of a teenage girl?"

"You'd have to ask her that. I just know she is."

"Violet tries. She just doesn't know about kids. That's why we didn't have any."

She has him so brainwashed. I wonder if *that's* witchcraft. "Give me a break. I'm not some baby crying. She was fine when I was a kid. It's now, now that I'm old enough to be a threat."

"Why would you be—?"

"Don't tell me you haven't seen the stuff that's happening."

He stares at the road, taking the Dad-eyes off me. "What stuff?"

Well, first off, my mother being killed by a freaking MONKEY.

"You ignore it," I say. "You ignore it all. You're so hot for her you don't see what she is."

"And what's that?"

"A witch."

Stunned silence. All I can hear is the car's air-conditioning, blowing too cold on my leg.

Then, Dad laughs. "Good one, Celine. I thought you were going to at least tell me she was a criminal, something that could be real."

"*This* is real. You know it. She reanimated a bird when you were kids. Then, she made that dog attack my mother in high school. Then, she made a monkey kill her. You were there when all those things happened. You saw it!"

"You're insane." My father is practically shaking. "You need help. I should—"

I stop talking. Violet would be completely happy to have him put me in some facility for troubled teens. I may be troubled, but I'm not crazy. I've just finally—finally—realized the truth.

But Dad's never going to see it. He'll never believe she's a witch even with all the evidence. No one would, I guess. But he's not even going to admit she hates me, that she hurts me on purpose.

The other, harder, truth is that my father loves Violet more than he loves me.

"Fine," I say, "maybe it's my imagination. But I'm not imagining that she doesn't like me. You know she doesn't want me around, even if you won't say it. So why can't I just stay at Laurel's?"

"You can go there after school sometimes, but you can't live there. You're my daughter."

We're pulling into our driveway now. I say, "Fine," knowing I'm going to do whatever I want. I jump from the car as soon as it stops moving.

"Violet has a good heart," he calls after me.

I don't answer. Anything I say would be worse than saying nothing.

I don't speak to Dad for the next few days. It's not obvious because I just go to school early and come home late. I sleep at home and avoid the cats like they're murderers—which they may be.

Friday, I'm standing, waiting for the bus with Laurel, when Goose comes running up to me. "There's been an accident! It's your dad."

"What? What kind of accident?" I flash back to the day with my mom, and it feels like a fist squeezing my heart. Would Violet hurt Dad?

"A woman came up to me and told me to get you. Your father's been in a car accident. He was airlifted to Jackson. That's all she said. I can take you there."

"Who? What woman? Did she have red hair?"

"No. She looked a little familiar, but I'm not sure from where. Come on."

I follow him and Willow in silence. What is this? Why would Violet hurt Dad? And who was the woman Goose talked to?

Please let Dad be okay.

We pull up in front of the emergency room. Now that we're here, it seems so much more real. Airlifted to Jackson. What if he's really hurt or . . . worse? "I don't know what to do," I tell Goose.

"I'll go in with you. Let me figure out where to park."

Then, I see Violet running toward me.

"That's my stepmother," I say to Goose. I start out of the car.

"I can still come with you. Just follow her, and I'll catch up."

I really want Goose to stay. Really. But I know he probably wants to leave. And I'm sure Willow does. It would be too weird to have them stay at the hospital.

"It's okay. Thank you. I'll go with Violet."

"All right. Let me know what's happening. Text me, day or night."

"Okay." I run after Violet.

Violet's hair is half up, half down. She's taken off her five-inch heels to go faster and holds her shoes in her hand. When I catch up to her, I can see that her face is tearstained. It's the one time I've seen her not perfect. She runs to the front desk. "I'm looking for my husband, Gregory Columbo. He was airlifted here. He was in a car accident." A huge sob rips from her throat.

"You're Mrs. Columbo?" a nurse asks.

"Yes." Violet's still sobbing. "Where is he? You have to take me to Greg!"

"Just wait a moment. I'll get the doctor."

"Please! You have to take me—" But the nurse walks away.

Violet follows her. "Maybe you shouldn't follow her in there," I say.

She looks at me like she's just realizing I'm there. "I have to. Time is ticking." I can hear her breath, shallow, like a panting dog's, and that's how I know she suspects what I do: He's dead. My father is dead. I go to put my arm around her, but she shoves me aside and runs after the disappearing nurse, through the emergency room doors. "Greg! I have to see him! Greg!"

She's intercepted by a female doctor in a white coat. "May I help you? You shouldn't be back here."

"It's my husband, Gregory Columbo. He was brought here. I need to see him."

"Yes, I was on my way out to you. I'm Dr. Martinez." The doctor is about Violet's age, short with blond hair in a messy bun. She looks like a mom, and her voice is soft. "I'm so sorry. We did everything we could, but he didn't make it."

"Noooooo!" It's a shriek. I feel tears spring to my eyes, and I wish Goose had stayed. I wish Goose had stayed. But Violet's reaction is much, much more. The sound is inhuman. "I have to see him! You have to take me to him!"

The doctor tries to get in front of Violet, who shoves against her.

"He was badly injured. It may be upsetting. In a little while, you can identify the remains." She places her hand on Violet's shoulder.

"No! Not a little while!" Violet's voice fills the room, and the doctor jolts back as if shocked. "You have to take me to him now! Right! Now!"

I hear glass shatter. The window on one of the doors has broken, but no one touched it.

"Very well. Just calm down," the doctor says. "You might want to have the girl stay here. She shouldn't see him like this."

"She can stay." Violet wipes the tears from her face, but they just keep coming. "I have to see Greg! Greg!" It comes out a wail.

"Follow me." I notice the doctor keeps her distance from Violet.

Violet follows, still breathing like a mastiff, practically running and almost overtaking the doctor. Despite the doctor's instructions, I follow, but when I get to the door she holds open, I stop.

My father—his body—lies motionless on a bed, a sheet covering most of him. Still, I can see that his head is bashed and bleeding. His face is almost unrecognizable. I stop. He isn't my father anymore. The doctor is right. I don't want to see him like that. But Violet elbows past me into the room.

"Greg!" She throws herself onto his body, embracing him, like she's trying to touch as much of him as possible, give her life to his, and she begins to make weird noises. It sounds like she's praying or speaking in tongues, but not exactly. Not exactly words, either. She isn't crying anymore, but her voice rises to a wail in the quiet room, and her whole body vibrates.

I remember what Laurel's mom said about the bird that was dead, then wasn't. Is Violet trying to bring my father back? Can she?

I would be willing to deal with everything about Violet if she could do that, anything to have him back, even for a minute, anything to make things right.

The doctor comes up behind me. "I'm so sorry. I shouldn't have let her . . . I'll get a nurse for your mother, with a sedative."

I nod, biting the back of my lips, then get out, "My stepmother. She adored him." I know it's true. If I ever doubted Violet's love, seeing her writhing, covered in my father's blood, changes that. Violet is insane with grief. I feel my own, like a weight on my chest. I have no one I can turn to. I have no one but Violet.

"I'm sorry for your loss," the doctor says.

Violet's on the floor now, still wailing. But now, I understand words. "Greg! Come back to me! I can't lose you so soon! I can't . . . I can't! I caaaaan't!"

I run to her, trying to avoid looking at Dad's body.

"Violet, let's get out of here. Looking at him can't help."

"He can't be gone!" she screams. "What good is it to be able to fix birds and cats when the only one I want is dead on a table?"

Birds and cats. But I lead her out into the hallway. I try to embrace her, but she falls to her knees. She throws her head back and shrieks so loudly that the floor seems to shake like the ground is opening. The doors rattle, and again, a glass window breaks. Then another. And another. How is this happening? Is her grief so huge that she could make this happen? Is there a tornado outside? Did Violet cause it? Is she really a witch?

I know the answer. If I didn't before, I know it now.

"Violet, stop!" I yell. "You can't do this. It won't—"

"Violet!" A woman is walking toward us. She's about Violet's age, with a beautiful face and dark hair streaming down her back. The woman from Target. Kendra.

Goose said the woman who spoke to him looked familiar. It was her.

She wears a black dress that looks like it's from another era. An orderly tries to stop her, but she stares at him, and he backs off. "Violet, I'm here."

"Kendra." Violet collapses in a ball onto the floor. "How did you know I was here?"

The woman, Kendra, kneels by her, embracing her. "I knew, my darling. I am always there for you, Violet. It's all right, my sweet."

"No!" she sobs. "No! He was my life! Now, he's gone. He's dead, and it's all for nothing. Nothing! It's all worthless. *I'm* worthless without Greg!"

The orderly who tried to stop Kendra is with Dad now, covering his body, covering his face so I don't have to see it again.

"This is a punishment!" Violet wails. "A punishment for what I've done, for what I am!"

"There, there, Violet." Kendra rocks her, like a mother with a small child. "There, there."

Between sobs, Violet says, "But Greg was the only one who ever loved me!"

"No, dear," Kendra says. "I love you. I love you, and I will be with you forever. Forever and ever and ever when everyone alive today is gone. I love you." She holds Violet for a long time, letting Violet's sobs shake them both.

Finally, she looks up at me. I know I'm staring, and I feel that my mouth is open. I shut it.

"You're Celine. We've met before," she says. When I nod, she adds, "Poor child, both parents gone. You and Violet are all each other has."

Horrible thought. My throat feels full at that thought, like I might never swallow again, like I might choke and die and be with my parents sooner, and be happy. But I nod. I breathe through my nose until I can speak. "But who are you?"

"I'm Kendra," she says. "I am Violet's sister."

11

Kendra, at least, turns out to be normal, though I'm still not sure about the sister thing. Wouldn't we have known if Violet had a sister? She talks to the hospital and police about my father's body. Together, she and I visit the funeral home and make the plans. Violet stays in bed the whole time.

"Celine?" Kendra taps my leg. I look up from my phone. I'd been thinking about sending a text to Dad. It seems like I should be able to. After all, it's only been a day. How can everything change in a day?

"I'm sorry, dear," Kendra's saying, "do you prefer dark wood like mahogany or cherry? Or we could get something light like poplar."

"What?" I put in Dad's name, text *I love you*.

"For the casket. I'm so sorry."

"They're all nice," I whisper. Now that I've sent the text, I can see the whole line of others, all from me, unanswered, saying I'm sleeping at Laurel's. I slip the phone back in my purse and jab my finger at a reddish-brown one. "That one."

Kendra nods. She plans everything and doesn't ask me anything else.

The day before the funeral, I go to school. It seems better than staying home with Violet, better than thinking about Dad being gone.

But as soon as I get off the bus, I realize it's a huge mistake. I stand there, not sure what to do, staring down at the sidewalk where the class of 2014 had painted lots of happy, green cougar paw prints, walking toward the school. All I can see are everyone's feet, yellow Converse, blue Converse, plaid Converse, flowered fake combat boots, white Vans, all walking with and against the paw prints, turning into an impressionistic painting as my eyes fill with tears.

"Hey, hey, why are you here? You shouldn't be here."

I'm still looking down, but I can see the top of Goose's head, one dark curl going into another. He looks at me, his eyes meeting mine.

"I just figured that out," I say, and then, I start to sob.

Goose begins to reach up to put his arm around me, then stops and tugs my hand instead. "Come on," he whispers.

"Come on where?"

"Shh. Quick. Get in my car. It's still early."

"What about you?"

"Shh. Be quiet. Have to be casual in case someone sees us. School doesn't start for twenty minutes." He tugs on my hand.

"Won't Willow wonder where you are?"

He looks away. "We broke up. I don't want to discuss it. Or anything. Be quiet."

He pulls me along, through the Converses, Vans, Keds, and I

follow. I don't want him to take me home.

"Don't worry. I won't take you home," Goose whispers, reading my thoughts. Then, real loud, so everyone around can hear, "We'll just go get that paper you forgot, then come back." He tugs my arm. He is brilliant at navigating through the legs of taller kids, and he just pulls me along.

I've stopped crying, at least. "Okay, let's hurry then."

Finally, we reach his car. The parking lot isn't crowded yet. The bus always gets there so early. I think I hold my breath the whole time we're buckling our seat belts and pulling out against traffic, but in a minute, we're free. Goose drives a block, then another, not looking at me. When we reach the park, he pulls into the parking lot.

"Are you okay?" he says.

When I collapse in tears against his shoulder, he says, "Okay, dumb question. Dumb question. Aw, Celine." He puts his arms around me. "I'm so sorry."

"I have nobody," I say. "There's nobody left."

"There's nothing I can say. I wish I could make it better, but . . . I'm going to shut up, like I never do." He holds me harder. His arms are surprisingly strong, and I sink against him and sob. My head, my neck, my jaw hurt. Everything aches with the emptiness that comes from wanting to talk to Dad and realizing I never will, never again. Goose just holds me.

Finally, when it's almost eight, I say, "I don't want to go home. I came to school because it feels so empty there."

"I understand. We can go to my house and watch TV or something. My mom's home. I mean, I'm not trying to lure you there for immoral purposes." He's trying to make me laugh.

"Your mom's home? Won't you get in trouble?"

"She works from home. She's an artist. And nah, she'll write me a note. She knows people need personal days sometimes. I needed a ton of them in seventh grade, when I took PE."

"That must've been tough."

"I'm not into sports . . . especially when people try to use me as the ball."

I finally laugh. "You're the best."

"I know. I'm awesome. We covered that. Come on. I hate missing Hoda and Kathie Lee. I hear they're doing makeovers."

I really don't want to go to school or anywhere else. "Okay. I love a good makeover."

"Girl, there is nothing to make over about you." He turns the key in the ignition.

"Yeah, just my life," I say. "I don't know what I'm going to do now."

We pull out of the parking lot, driving right past a police car. Goose nods at the guy. "Seriously, if you ever need a place to go, you can stay with us."

"Right."

"No, really. My mom is big on taking in strays. Stray dogs, feral cats, foster kids. She has a kind heart. She probably wouldn't even notice you're there."

"Great. I'm a stray."

"I didn't mean it that way. I meant you're a friend, and if you were in trouble, we'd help you."

"Okay."

He stops the car again. "Look at me."

Since there's not much choice, I do. The sun streams through the windows, and I blink at him.

He says, "I'd do anything for you."

I'm stunned for a second. It's a strange thing to say. Then, I recognize it. He's quoting the song "I'd Do Anything" from *Oliver!* I laugh. "Anything?" I parrot the song.

"Anything." He says it seriously, not a joke.

"Okay. Thanks. Can we go now, before we get picked up for truancy?"

He nods. "Anything." He starts the car again.

We pull up to a big yellow house with marigolds planted in the front flower boxes. "After you, milady," Goose says in a Cockney accent. A spotted cat jumps out of our way as we approach a black door that's a little wider than usual. "The woman who owned the house before us was in a wheelchair, so they had lower counters and stuff," Goose explains. "That's why the door's so wide, which we didn't need, but the other stuff was perfect for us."

I notice the cat doesn't try to murder me. I like that in a cat.

He walks in and calls, "Mom!"

The house smells of coffee, a homey smell. A blond woman, shorter than Goose and wearing light blue sweatpants, comes out of the kitchen. She's carrying an African American baby in one arm and a bottle in the other hand. "School's out a little early, isn't it?" She sees me. "Oh, I didn't know we had company."

"Celine, this is my mom, Stacey. Mom, this is Celine. She's having a rough day."

"Aren't we all?" She looks at Goose. "Don't you have a test in history today? You can't just blow off school for no reason." She has a southern accent. Over her head, I can see three kids, two boys and a girl, eating cereal at the island in their downsized kitchen. An orange cat is walking around. It rubs against my legs, but it doesn't try to attack me or anything.

"It's more than a normal bad day, Mom," Goose says. "Celine's father died Friday."

"Oh, my God." Stacey rearranges the baby in her arms so she can give him the bottle. "Oh, sweetie. I'm so sorry. You didn't want to stay home with your mother?"

176

My throat feels tight. "I don't have one of those either. She died when I was eight. I just have my stepmother now, and she's flipping out. I had to get out of there, but then, I couldn't handle school. Goose was really sweet and brought me here. I hope he's not in trouble because he was just being nice."

"Yes, my sweet boy. You poor thing." The baby turns away from her, but she coaxes him to take the bottle. He sucks for about a second, then starts fussing again. "I have to get them ready for school, but you stay. Of course, stay as long as you want." She adjusts the baby again.

"Thank you. Um, can I hold him for you?" I suddenly really want to be useful.

"You don't have to do that."

"I want to."

"Well, that would be nice, thank you. Do you want to sit on the sofa and hold him?"

I can tell she's worried I'll drop him, so I sit down on the squashy white sofa. She settles him into my lap. "His name is Jeron. After he drinks the bottle, you rub his back until he burps."

"Okay." The baby feels warm and a little sweaty, but when he is in my arms, he starts to suck on his bottle contentedly. "Good boy, Jeron."

"He likes you." Stacey disappears into the kitchen, where I hear her telling the kids to hurry. Goose sits next to me and starts flipping through the channels, which are mostly morning news shows and cartoons. He settles on *SpongeBob* for a minute, then changes his mind. Stacey walks through the room with the three kids behind her, wearing blue and white school uniforms. The two boys look about the same age, maybe eight, and they're dwarves or little people (I don't know which is the right term, and I'm afraid to ask). One has dark hair and looks a lot like Goose. The other has red hair and freckles.

The little blond girl is about five, an average-sized five-year-old.

"Are they all your brothers and sisters?" I ask.

"Yes," Goose says. "But if you mean did my parents have all of them, no. Tyler, the one with red hair, is adopted. His parents abandoned him. He's the same age as Tony, my other brother. Department of Children and Families contacted my mother because he was a person of short stature, and they thought she'd deal with him better than his parents had. She was fostering before that."

I file away *person of short stature* in my mental bank. I wonder if Tyler's parents ditched him because he was one. It seems impossible, but clearly, some parents suck.

"And Jeron is a foster kid, but we might get him too. We've had other babies that got sent back to their parents. My mom really likes babies. She had one that died, right after my sister, Isabella, was born. There's this genetic thing. So that was sort of the end with her, and she started fostering instead."

"So there are seven of you here?" I say. "Must get crazy in the morning."

He shrugs. "I'm usually out of here before they wake up." He flips through the channels some more and settles on a movie. "Oh, man, I love this movie. I love this! Have you ever seen it?"

"What is it?" Onscreen, a red-haired girl in crazy clothes and a hat is talking to a guy in even weirder clothes. All the extras look like corporate lawyers. Like, they're high school students who don't own jeans.

"*Pretty in Pink*. It's a John Hughes movie. He was, like, the god of teen flicks in the 1980s."

"Yeah, my dad made me watch *Breakfast Club* together last year. That was him, right? I loved it." My stomach drops at the realization that, now, I will never watch another movie with Dad. I feel my eyes starting to fill, but I inhale and try not to cry.

"*Breakfast Club*'s great too."

"Let's watch this," I say. "Did it just start?"

"Yeah, it's pretty close to the beginning. It's about this girl, Andie, from the wrong side of the tracks, and she likes this rich guy, Blane."

So I get totally engrossed in the story of red-haired, offbeat-dressing Andie and her best friend, Duckie, a short, weird guy who has a crush on her. People at school make fun of them because they're poor and also sort of weird. By the time Stacey comes back with the kids trailing behind her, Jeron is asleep in my arms.

"Oh, my gosh," Stacey whispers. "You got him to sleep? That kid never sleeps."

"I forgot to burp him," I whisper back.

Stacey says, "Hey, if he went to sleep, that's better. Do you want to try to put him in his crib?" She says it like she doesn't think it's a great idea.

"Nah, he might wake up. I can keep holding him if you want. I'm not going anywhere."

"We're watching *Pretty in Pink*, Mom." Goose has paused the TV.

"That's a great movie. Good music."

"If you like music from the eighties," Goose teases.

"Hey, *I'm* from the eighties," Stacey says.

The little girl is starting to sit down with us, but Stacey gestures to her to come on. "We'll be late, Isabella." To me, she says, "I'll take Jeron off your hands when I come back."

"It's no problem. It's sort of . . . life affirming." The same cat from before rubs against my legs again. I sort of jump. "Sorry, cats hate me."

"Oh, these cats are harmless." Stacey takes Isabella and Tyler by the hands and says, "Come on" to the other boy. He follows her out.

"She seems like a really great mom," I say. "You're lucky."

"Guess I am." Goose unpauses the movie. "This is my favorite part." Onscreen, Andie's friend Duckie is wearing a yellow jacket and doing a crazy dance to an old song, "Try a Little Tenderness," trying to impress her and obviously failing miserably. I giggle.

"That's love," Goose says, "when you're willing to make a total ass of yourself for a girl."

"Have you ever done that?"

"Not so far. Not on purpose anyway. But . . ."

"But what?"

"Nothing. I talk too much. Shh. Let's watch this."

I wonder what he means. Stacey doesn't come back for a while, and in the movie, Andie accepts a date with Blane, breaking Duckie's heart. Then, Blane breaks her heart by asking her to the prom, then canceling because his rich friends don't approve. My arm is starting to ache, and I ease Jeron onto the sofa, planting myself on the floor so I can keep him from sliding off.

"I don't see what Andie likes about Blane so much," I say to Goose. "He's got no spine. He doesn't want to admit to his friends that he likes her."

"I guess he's supposed to be hot," Goose says.

"He's not that hot. And hotness only goes so far." After seeing my dad spend seven years with beautiful but crazy, I know that for a fact. "After you've known someone a while, you stop looking, I think. Character is more important."

In the end, Andie wears a pink dress and goes to the prom by herself. But Blane apologizes, so she walks off into the bright prom lights with Blane.

And Duckie tells her it's fine!

Totally lame.

"That was a crazy-stupid ending," I say to Goose. "The girl had no pride."

"Right?" he agrees. "Did you know that in the original version of this movie, Andie wound up with Duckie, but test audiences didn't like it. So they went back and changed it. They re-filmed the whole ending to make it that bad."

"Really? Test audiences have no souls. She should totally have ended up with Duckie."

"Absolutely. You get it. I knew you'd get it."

"It was so stupid. He would never have said that." I imitate the actor who played Duckie. "'He's not like the others. Go to him.' It must have hurt the actor's soul to even have to say that."

Goose nods. "I agree." He switches the TV back to *SpongeBob*, which is still on. Or on again. Patrick is obsessing over getting nachos. "So you'd go with Duckie instead of hot Blane?"

"I told you, hotness only goes so far. My stepmother is obsessed with appearances, and it makes her crazy. Besides, I sort of think Duckie is cute. In his own way."

"Really? He didn't strike me as your type. You're still marrying Jonah Prince, right?"

I laugh. Does he think I'm silly for obsessing over a rock star? "Oh, absolutely." I turn over my hand so he can see the faded writing on my fingers, where I've written *J.P. 4-ever*. "We talked last night. He promised to take me to homecoming next year. On his private jet. And then we'll go to Paris and buy a horse—two horses, one for each of us."

"Get me a horse too."

"Oh, yeah," I agree. "He totally said three horses. Wanted to know what color you wanted. I said palomino."

"Good call."

We fall back into silence, watching *SpongeBob*.

"I'll miss school again tomorrow for the funeral," I say after a while.

"I was thinking about going to that too."

"Really?" I know Laurel's going, and her mom. But having more people as a buffer between me and Violet would be good. The thought of sitting there all alone with Violet is just freaky, almost as freaky as my father's body in a box in the ground.

"Would you want me to go?" Goose asks.

"Yes. Yes, I would so want you to go. But . . . you'd do that?"

"Like I said, I'd do anything."

"Okay," I say. "Can we just sit here and watch *SpongeBob* for the rest of the day?"

"Absolutely. Sometimes, watching *SpongeBob* is the best thing. *SpongeBob* never disappoints."

So we keep watching. My eyes feel about to close. In the background, I can hear Stacey talking to Jeron and making him another bottle, the next-door neighbor's lawnmower, and the squirrels outside, at war with the blue jays over a bird feeder. We watch maybe three more *SpongeBobs*, maybe more than that. I'm not sure because, at some point, I give in and I fall asleep.

12

After the funeral, Kendra moves in with us. She says it's to help Violet. I'm still not sure I believe she's Violet's sister, but it's good to have her there because Violet is definitely several pins short of a bowling alley. She doesn't go to work. She doesn't eat. She doesn't even cry.

Instead, she spends day and night sitting on her bed, staring into her hand mirror.

She doesn't talk to it anymore, just stares. I wonder if it still answers back.

A week after my father's death, I hear Kendra talking to her as I'm passing by on the way downstairs.

"Don't you think you should go to work?" she asks.

Violet draws a brush through her hair. She holds it up so the auburn strands catch the light. "I have no reason to go to work."

"Of course you have. Your job is important. You help people."

"I don't care about helping people. When have I ever?"

"As a girl you did."

"I'm not that girl anymore . . . thank God."

"I loved that girl," Kendra says.

Grimalkin brushes by me. She takes a swipe at me with one paw. I should go. I start toward the stairs again.

"Your beauty, then," Kendra says, and I stop again. "It used to be so important to you to be beautiful. Perhaps you could do some modeling, commercials."

I see a circle of light moving on the wall, as if someone was flipping a mirror over and over. The cat is stalking back toward me. I can't bring myself to kick her down the stairs, even though I hate her.

"I am beautiful, aren't I?" Violet's voice says.

"Of course you are, my darling," comes Kendra's reply. "But your hair is messy."

"Am I the most beautiful woman in the whole world?" Violet asks.

Kendra hesitates. "You are one of them."

"I mean, if I brushed my hair?" Violet asks.

Still, Kendra doesn't just say yes. *Just agree with her! Lie to her!* Besides, who is more beautiful?

"My dear, you are very beautiful. Any man would be happy to have a woman of your beauty."

"I don't want any man. I want Greg! I've only ever wanted Greg!"

From the bedroom, I hear glass break. I run downstairs before they can know I was eavesdropping.

That day, I forget my book for English class. I ask the teacher for a pass to go to my locker. When I get there, I find a mirror inside.

Violet's mirror.

Which is weird in and of itself because I didn't put it there and I didn't leave my locker open.

The hallway is silent. The white floors, unoccupied by hundreds of feet, gleam like ice. I don't want to touch the mirror. It might be poisoned or attack me. Violet's things tend to do that.

Yet, something compels me to reach for the handle. I turn it over.

Second weird thing: It's not broken, though I heard it shatter this morning.

I lift it and search for my face inside.

But my face isn't there.

Kendra's is.

"I need to speak with you," she says.

The mirror slips from my hand, shattering against the terrazzo. I look around to see if anyone has noticed, if anyone heard.

No one there. I debate running, leaving the splintered glass there, hoping someone will clean it up before fifth period. I have to. I grab *The Book Thief* from my locker and slam the door. It bounces open, so I hold it closed. I start to replace the lock. My hands are trembling.

As I do, before my eyes, the pieces of the mirror rise from the floor, hundreds of slices of silver, shining in the fluorescent light.

They dance before my eyes, then form into an oval mirror, neatly replacing themselves in the frame.

It flies up into my hand.

"Careful this time." Kendra's voice is a whisper. "I need to speak with you after school. Can you come to my house?"

"What? How? How are you doing this?"

"Isn't it obvious?" She smiles. "I'm a witch."

"There's no such thing as—"

"I know you believe in witches, Celine. You've been living with one for years."

Validation. Someone confirming all my crazy suspicions. I wish

I could tell Dad. Now, the victory seems hollow. A thousand times a day, I remember he's gone, and it's like he has died again.

I say, "You know . . . about Violet?"

"Of course. And I know you're not safe with her. But you have to get back to class. Come to my house after school. It's the big, gray one on the corner of Salem Court, the one that looks abandoned. Get your friend to drive you, the boy from Target."

"Goose."

"He'll drive you."

I know he would, if I asked. And I know the house. I didn't know anyone lived there. "How do I know I can trust you?"

"You don't. But you know you can't trust Violet. Also, if I wanted to kill you, you'd already be dead. I want to help you."

"Violet hasn't killed me . . . yet." My hand is shaking, rattling the mirror back and forth.

"Yet. Because of your father. Now, your father is gone."

"So you're saying . . . ?" She's saying Violet is going to kill me.

"My house. After school. With the boy."

Her face disappears from the mirror.

And then, the mirror disappears from my hand.

13

Two hours later, I'm in front of the abandoned house with Goose. I have no idea why, but Goose, at least, had been excited about it. "Really?" he said. "Someone lives in that house? She invited you? Cool. We always thought it was haunted. On Halloween, we dared people to touch it."

I nodded. "So did we. Laurel and I did it last year." I've explained as little about this as possible. It seems better to just let it unfold.

"So I get to go inside. Cool."

I laugh. "You said that."

But now that we're here, he seems less sure. The driveway is almost impassable, with weeds and branches scraping the sides of the car. At least two windows are broken, and the paint that used to be white is dirty gray, where there even is paint.

"You're sure someone's not playing a joke on you?" Goose says as he negotiates the driveway.

Considering she came to me inside a mirror, no.

"I don't think so." A flock of crows lands in the yard, settling on the bushes and in the trees. I wonder if they're friends of Violet's.

Goose puts the car in park. "You think those crows are going to shit on my car?" When I shrug, he says, "Maybe wait here while I look around, in case something's weird?"

"That's okay. I'm glad you're here, though." I open my door and step out. A branch scratches my arm. One crow caws. Then, they all begin to until the yard is filled with their cries.

Goose swears under his breath, but follows me to the doorstep. The house doesn't look any less abandoned up close. Leaf-covered cobwebs drape the door, as if it hasn't been opened in years. Grass and flotsam collect in the porch corners, and the doormat is almost entirely worn away. I knock. My hand chips away a layer of dust and dead bugs.

"Why?" Goose says.

"Why what?"

"Why are you glad I'm here? You won't let me be the big hero and go in ahead of you while you wait at a safe distance. What if someone comes after you with a knife?" He tries to stand in front of me.

"No one's going to come after me with a knife. And, if they did, I wouldn't sit in the car while you bleed to death on the steps anyway." It sounds funny, except when you think about it. "What I really need is someone to be here with me, experience it with me, so I'll know I'm not crazy."

At that, the door opens with a creak.

"Ah, I see you're both here," Kendra says.

She's holding the mirror.

Kendra steps aside so we can enter. My foot goes from dusty slate steps to . . .

. . . shiny black-and-white-checked marble floor.

The inside of Kendra's house is nothing like the outside. Everything inside is brand-new, and it's all black, white, or hot pink. It looks like a set for the musical *Hairspray* (which we're supposed to be doing at school next year), with pink walls, a pink jukebox, pink Lava Lamps, and a soda fountain with black tables and hot pink chairs. Kendra, wearing a fluffy, pink and black dress that could go to the prom, points to a spiral staircase that leads to a loft above the room.

"Follow me."

We do. The staircase is narrow, and, through the steps, I can see the room swimming pinkly below. I notice Goose is looking up at the ceiling.

"Are you okay?" I ask him.

"I have a thing about heights." He looks a little green, which clashes with the pink, and takes the last steps very deliberately. Soon, we're at the top in another black-and-white-tiled room with hot pink sofas. Kendra gestures that we should sit. I notice Goose takes the seat farthest from the stairs.

"Good to see you," Kendra says. "I wish it could be under better circumstances."

"You saw me this morning," I remind her. "At my house."

She nods. "Indeed, I did. But I will be seeing little of you from now on, I'm afraid."

"What? Are you going someplace?" Weird though she is, I sort of like having Kendra around, as a buffer between Violet and me. I can't imagine staying with Violet forever. Yet where else is there? Three of my grandparents are dead. My father's father lives in a nursing home. He probably doesn't even know Dad died.

"No. You are."

"What?" The pink fluorescent lights are disorienting. I look down, but the checkerboard floor seems to be moving. "What do you mean?"

"You're in danger. You're in danger, and you must leave that house."

Goose says, "What kind of danger?"

I look at my hand. It glows in the flashing pink jukebox lights. My head is light, spinning. I wonder if this is how it feels to be on drugs.

I say, "My stepmother is a witch."

Goose laughs, but an uncomfortable laugh. "Yeah, my mom can be a witch sometimes too."

"You are using the term *witch* in a derogatory way?" Kendra straightens her shoulders.

"Is there another way?" Goose looks confused.

"A literal way," Kendra says. "For someone who has magic powers and can use them for either good or evil."

"Oh. Right." He laughs again, unbelieving.

I'm saying nothing because my head is hot. I put my hand to my forehead.

"Besides, your mother isn't a witch in either sense. She has no powers, and she is a kind woman who takes in foster children."

"How did you know that?" Goose asks.

"I know everything."

"I guess Celine told you." He looks to me for confirmation.

Kendra shakes her head. "Celine told me nothing." She looks at me. "Are you all right?"

"I . . . the lights . . . all the pink. It's very pretty, but I think it's giving me a headache."

"I think life is giving you a headache. Understandable. How's this?"

She waves her hand, and in a second, the room changes to a French provincial décor, yellow flowered sofas and dark wood. Much calmer.

"Better. Thanks."

Huh. She just waved her hand and changed everything. This does not surprise me as much as it should.

Goose is looking at his hands like he expects them to melt. "Whoa. What the—"

"There are witches." I look around, trying to figure out a way of explaining what I don't completely understand myself. Even after the mirror, I can't quite believe this. "There are witches, and my stepmother is one of them. She used to be an ugly girl, and then, she made herself beautiful."

"She can do that?" Goose asks.

"Yes. And I'm afraid Violet is a bad witch." Kendra sighs. "She wasn't always so. When I met her, she was a little younger than you, a sweet girl, a victim. But, perhaps that's what made her what she is. She always wanted revenge on her enemies, and she got it."

Goose is up. He starts to pace, then sees the stairs and sits back down. I say, "Got it how?" Though I think I know.

"When she killed your mother."

Even though I thought I knew this, it still shocks me. Confirmation of my worst suspicions.

"You . . . you knew she did that? Why didn't you say anything?"

"Who would have believed me?" Kendra asks. "A woman is attacked by a monkey. Should I tell the police that Violet manipulated it? Do you think they'd believe someone can communicate with animals? Your father didn't, and he saw her do it twice."

The dog.

"And I couldn't risk being detected. Witches belong to no age, no time. I have no driver's license, no birth certificate but a family Bible dated 1652, no passport. Even my fingerprints have worn away. That happens in three hundred years."

"You've been alive three hundred years?" Goose says.

I say, "But you should have told before she hurt someone."

"That's what I'm doing. I'm telling *you* before she hurts *you*."

"Hurts me? You mean kills me?"

"Yes."

The air leaves the room. Silence. Goose has stopped, staring around the room like he can't believe it. Why would he? I barely believe it, and I've been living with a witch for years. I now realize there were so many signs I should have seen, little things like Violet's ability to whip up a recipe with dozens of ingredients in the half hour after she got home from work, like the fact that she still looked twenty-five years old, more than twenty years after she graduated high school. I was stupid. Dad was stupid. Still, I would love to go back to a time when I could not believe it.

And she wants me dead. Dead.

Goose looks at Kendra. "So you're saying her stepmother is an actual witch, she killed her mother, and now she's trying to kill Celine?"

"Yes," Kendra says. She says it like it's obvious.

"Did she kill Celine's father?"

"No. She loved my father." I look at Kendra. She nods that it's true.

"That she did. She loved him too much. It made her crazy. And now that he's gone, she has nothing and is even more insane. She's consumed by loneliness and her jealousy of you."

"Why is she so jealous of me? I know she is, but I've never understood it. I don't have anything she would want."

She wants me dead. I still can't believe it.

Goose laughs. "Even I know you're the most beautiful girl I've ever seen. Who wouldn't be jealous of that?"

I stare at him, stunned. He knows how much I hate to talk about my looks. At least, I thought he knew.

192

"I'm sorry, Celine, but it's the truth. You're beautiful, so beautiful it's almost unreal. And people hate you for it, even beautiful people. You can't ignore that anymore."

I wonder if he resents me. I hate this. My beauty has never done me a bit of good. It makes people hate me, makes idiots want to be my friend. I wish I could just be average. But I say, "Fine. But Violet is beautiful too. Obviously, she made herself as beautiful as she could with her magic."

"Yes," Kendra says. "As beautiful as she *could*. But there are limits to magic. Your innocence, your goodness, are part of what make you beautiful, a part Violet does not have. She lost it when she began to play with the darkness, and now there is nothing she can do to be as beautiful as you. As long as you live, she will always be second, just as she was second to your mother."

"Second? What about Keira Knightley? Amanda Seyfried? Tyra Banks?" I name the most beautiful women I can think of. "Should they be watching their backs too?"

Kendra grimaces. "Perhaps. But they don't live in her backyard, so perhaps she'll forget them. We'll keep her away from movie theaters, just in case," she joked.

"We'll have to keep her away from Celine, you mean," Goose says. He's standing again, and he comes to stand in front of me, all protective. "If Violet can't make herself more beautiful, why can't she just make Celine ugly, give her zits or something? Wouldn't that be enough for her? She doesn't have to kill her."

I mouth *Gee, thanks* at him.

Kendra says, "She could, but only if she reveals herself. She can change someone else's appearance only if they know about it. Otherwise, any spell she casts reverberates back to her."

I understand now. "Is that why she lost her voice when she made me lose mine?"

"Yes. But there are other ways she can hurt you, as she found a way to hurt your mother."

"You mean kill my mother."

"Yes." She sits closer to me. "You must go into hiding."

"Hiding? But how? I have school."

"School will wait. It has to." She places her hand on my shoulder. "Violet has confided her plan to murder you. I've offered to help."

"Help?" Goose says. "What kind of sick—?"

"I lied," Kendra says. "I told her she needs to withdraw you from school, say you're moving in with your aunt in another town. Then, I will take you away and murder you. I told her I'd help because she's been such a delight to me. And she was. She was like my own daughter." She looks down. "Where did I go wrong?"

"I'll tell you where," Goose says. "Where you didn't tell the world about her years ago, when you knew she had something to do with what happened to Celine's mother."

Suddenly Kendra is gone. The space where she was is just empty. Seconds later, she materializes downstairs.

"There's not a jail cell that can hold her," she says. She disappears again.

Then, she's back with us. "Besides, I didn't think it would get this bad. I loved Violet like my daughter. She was all I had. It's like how parents of killers always say they never suspected." She turns to me. "I will take you away, but to a safe location. Is there someplace you can go, to hide?"

I stare at Kendra. She looks different than the first day I saw her, younger. I have a feeling she can change everything about her looks, if she wants. She could kill me and disappear, and no one would know. I have to trust her because there is no point in not trusting her. It's like she said before: If she wanted to kill me, I'd already be dead.

"My friend Laurel. I always stay with them. Her mother was my mom's best friend. She hated Violet. If she thought I was in danger—"

"Ah, yes, but you do often stay there, which is precisely why it wouldn't work. Violet would immediately look there to see if you were hiding. No, it needs to be someone else, someone she doesn't know, a distant relative, perhaps. Or a friend."

She's looking at Goose, who has paced closer again. He picks up on the cue.

"She could stay with me, with my family." He holds out his hand. "I'd do anything for Celine."

"Yes," Kendra says. "I know."

And I know too.

Goose drives Kendra and me to his house. The whole time, my head is throbbing from the conversation with Kendra. Could it be true? Could Violet actually want to have me killed? But, of course. It makes perfect sense. Violet has never loved me, maybe not even back when she acted like she did. Did I think that, without Dad, the one thing that bound us together, she would suddenly want to be my mommy? Of course not. Her loathing for me would only increase. Without her darling Greg there, I was only a reminder of my mother, a girl she'd hated.

My stomach, my heart, my entire body feel empty: *There is no one now in the entire world who loves me.*

It's hard to remember a time when there was.

We're at a stoplight. Goose reaches over and touches my arm. "It'll be okay, Celine."

I shake my head. "How do you know that?"

"Because it has to be."

The light turns green, and we drive on.

It seems so drastic, to abandon school, abandon my whole life on the word of one woman, one witch. Yet what choice do I have? I've seen this all happen. I know it's real. Goose says he can talk his parents into letting me stay. He's so nice. Why is this guy I barely know so nice while the person who is supposed to care about me is so horrible?

Kendra insisted on coming along to explain it all to Stacey. "They need to know what they're getting into. It's not just letting a friend of yours stay a few days. It's not even the same as a foster child. They would be harboring a runaway. Your life is in danger. They'd need to keep you safe and tell no one."

Terrific. Why would they put themselves in that kind of danger for me?

"Would it ever end?" I ask Kendra.

"At some point," Kendra says, "Violet will have to move on. Witches always do. Then, you could start a normal life again, maybe go to college."

It doesn't seem like much of a plan, but there's nothing else to do. For some reason, I keep thinking about my AP exams. I won't even get to take them.

When we get to Goose's house, Stacey is browning meat on the stove. Jeron is hanging in a baby swing. The other three kids are spread out at the kitchen table, doing three different homework assignments.

"Oh, you brought company." Stacey wipes her hands on her apron. She gives Kendra's pink prom dress a quick up-and-down look. "My son always finds such pretty girls."

"Should I have worn something else?" Kendra whispers to me. "Is this too much? Should I change now?"

"No!" Goose and I both say, real quick.

"It's fine," Goose adds. "Mom, this is Kendra, and you remember Celine."

"Of course." Stacey moves the pan off the stove. "How have you been, dear?"

"Fine," I say automatically. "Well, except . . ."

"That's why we're here, Mrs. Guzman," Kendra says. "Celine has a big problem, and we're hoping you can help."

"I live to solve problems," Stacey says.

I look to see if she's joking, but the funny thing is, she doesn't seem to be. Her eyes are full of concern.

"Mom, what's an adjective?" Tyler asks.

"Stupid," Tony says. "*Stupid* is an adjective. Don't you ever do Mad Libs? It's a word that describes someone, like *fat* or *freckly*."

Stacey gives Tony a look. "Antonio, we don't call anyone stupid around here."

"I didn't call him stupid. I just said stupid is an adjective."

"Don't you need help sometimes?" Stacey demands.

"I need help *now*," Tony says, "with math."

"Oh, gosh." Stacey looks at Kendra and me. "Can you just wait one second?"

Quickly, she dumps the browned meat into a colander to drain, then she heads over to the two boys.

In the swing, Jeron laughs. Goose is so lucky to get to live with such a happy family.

Maybe I will be too.

"Can I help him with his math, maybe?" I ask.

"Oh, could you?" Stacey says. "But I thought you needed to talk to me."

"Goose can explain. I like math."

"Oh, good, because it's not my favorite." She walks back to

Goose and Kendra. "What can I do for you?"

I don't hear most of their explanation because I'm reading about the builder who needs 244 bricks to build a house and has to buy them in boxes of six. Isabella's crayons keep rolling off the table. I almost think she's doing it on purpose, to get my attention. Still, I keep retrieving them.

So the first thing I hear is Stacey saying, "I'm sorry, but you expect me to buy that?" She elbows Goose. "I'm sort of amazed you believe that."

"I know it sounds crazy." He looks up at Kendra. "Isn't there some way you can make my mother understand, like what you did at your house, with the decorations?"

Kendra lifts her hand to her chin. "Another parlor trick, so to speak? Oh, okay. But perhaps we should go into the actual parlor—meaning the living room—so as not to freak out the children."

"Good idea," Goose says. They walk around the corner.

Tony's doing better with his math, and I don't think I'm supposed to do it for him anyway. I sort of want to know what's going to happen. So I stand. I walk over to where the ground beef is draining and pour it back into the pan. I never get to cook at home, but Mrs. Mendez sometimes makes spaghetti with meat sauce, which I guess is what Stacey's making. There's a jar of sauce and a box of pasta on the counter. I don't know if Stacey wants to add anything else to the sauce, but I find a pot and put on some water to boil.

Suddenly, from the corner of my eye, I see a commotion in the living room. Lights are flashing purple and green, sparkling like falling fireworks. Small objects fly by. I run to see what's happening in time for everything to stop.

Kendra and Stacey are standing there with a very tall man. He's definitely at least six four, and he definitely wasn't there before.

"What the—?" the man says.

I do a double take, look at his face.

It's Goose, a foot taller than Kendra, where before, he'd been a foot shorter.

"You . . . did this?" Stacey is backing away, screaming, "Put him back!"

"How do I look?" Goose peers into the mirror on the wall, but since it's hung low, he has to bend down to see. "I can't tell because my face looks the same—all studly and hot. But look at you down there—so cute!"

"I liked you better before," I say. "Kendra, you have to put him back. What will people at school say?"

"They'll make me the star of their basketball team." Goose mimes a slam dunk.

"Put him back. Please," Stacey says.

"Fine." Kendra is pouting. "People say they want a demonstration. Then they get all mad when you demonstrate."

She looks up at Goose, then goes into a sort of trance. It all repeats, the room, the lights. At the end of it, Goose is back to normal. He stares up at me.

"You could make me an inch taller, couldn't you?" he says to Kendra. "Or maybe just give me better hair?"

She shakes her head. "That's how Violet got started. Little things."

"Celine, what's an adverb?" Tyler asks from the kitchen.

"A word that modifies a verb. Sort of like an adjective. They mostly have 'ly' on the end. Like, 'He grew shockingly.' *Shockingly* is an adverb."

"Thanks," Tyler calls.

"I put on some water to boil," I tell Stacey, who looks like she's about to fall over. "Do you need a glass of water?"

She nods, shakily, and I go to get it. She backs up to lean on the wall.

When I come back, she's saying to Kendra, "So you're saying that Celine's stepmother has . . . powers like that, and she's going to use them to hurt Celine?"

Kendra nods. "To kill Celine."

"Oh, sweetie." She takes the water from me. "I'll have to discuss it with my husband, of course."

"That's just a formality," Goose says. "He never says no to you."

"He's right," Stacey admits. "I still have to ask, though. But he'll be happy to let you stay. How could we say no?"

"Thank you. I'll help around the house. I'll tutor the kids. I'm really good at math. I'll—"

Stacey puts her arms around me. They only come up to about my waist, but the hug is warm and strong, like a mom's. I lean into her. She says, "It's okay. I know you will. You've been through so much. I want you to be safe. Every child deserves to be safe."

That may be the first time anyone has ever said anything like that to me.

When Mr. Guzman comes home he is *not* real happy about the idea. Kendra demonstrates her powers yet again (this time, by cleaning up the kitchen using only her mind—which I can tell Stacey appreciates). Then, they retreat to a bedroom to argue. Goose and I listen through the door.

"She's a minor," Goose's father says. "We could be accused of kidnapping."

"We're not kidnap—"

"Doesn't matter. You take someone else's kid, you're kidnapping. It's the law. We could try to get a legal guardianship."

"And then, everyone would know where she is," Stacey says. "This woman already killed her mother."

"And you believe that?" Mr. Guzman says.

"I do. And if you're wrong, and the girl dies, how will you feel?

You fight for people's rights for a living."

If the girl dies. Me. I'm the girl. My whole life depends on the outcome of this conversation. The outcome of this conversation and Kendra, which is a scary thought.

Next to me, Goose whispers, "He's a lawyer, unfortunately. My mom can talk him into anything, though."

Mr. Guzman says, "I know I do. I'm trying to protect my family here. You want to protect the whole world."

"Yes, I do!" Stacey yells. "It takes a village, Jorge."

"Why do we always have to be the elders of the village?"

"Someone has to be!"

"We don't even know this girl," he says.

"Maybe we should put the sauce on," Goose whispers. "I'm thinking we can probably still hear them from the kitchen."

"Good idea." I'm not sure I want to hear them.

"Your son knows her," Stacey says. "Are you saying you don't trust his judgment?"

"He's seventeen. He sees a pretty girl and—"

"Come on!" Goose takes my hand and hustles me to the kitchen before I can hear what he does when he sees a pretty girl. Kendra is sitting at the table helping with homework, her pink tulle skirt puffing out over the tabletop. The boys are finished with what they were doing and are on to a history assignment, which is the same for both of them. Kendra is holding crayons while Isabella colors.

"You're pretty smart," Goose says.

"I've done high school thirty-seven times," Kendra says. "I enroll whenever I get bored. If I went to your high school, I'd be the valedictorian without even using magic."

Goose laughs. "I may need some help with chemistry then."

"We can study together," I say before I remember that maybe I won't be studying, won't even be going to school.

"Your dress is so pretty." Isabella pets Kendra's poufy skirt.

"If you do a good job, I'll make one just like it for you," Kendra says.

"I think she usually adds an onion to the spaghetti sauce," Goose says.

I find an onion and a knife to start chopping it up. Tears fill my eyes, and I pretend it's the onion. I want to stay in this warm, safe house with Goose's warm, safe family. But I wish I didn't need to. I wish I could go back in time to when I was eight years old and everything didn't suck.

Kendra comes up behind me and whispers, "It's okay. If they say no, we'll think of something else. You're safe. I'll make sure of it."

But that's when Stacey comes into the kitchen and says, "You can stay with us."

"You talked Dad into it?" Goose asks.

"I didn't have to talk him into it," Stacey says. "He knew it was the right thing to do. Right, Jorge?"

He walks in behind her. "I can't ignore someone in trouble. Welcome to the family, Celine." He sticks out his hand. "Don't get us sent to jail."

I wipe the onion juice off on my jeans before offering my own hand. "I won't."

That night, Kendra invites me to visit her house after school tomorrow. She does it loudly, in front of Violet. "In fact," she says, "I can drive you to school in the morning too."

She tells me to pack any items I really want in my backpack. "Nothing Violet would notice missing. You're supposed to be dead. I might be able to bring you some other things later, but it's better to be safe. Violet is a powerful witch, so I'm not sure what I can slip past her. Take your favorite things."

It's amazing in a situation like that, how few things matter. I take photographs of my mom and dad, a bracelet my father bought me made of tiny golden seashells, some clothes, underwear, and toiletries. I take all my saved-up birthday money in case I need anything else, or for an emergency.

Last, I go to the computer and print photos off my phone: Laurel and me, wearing matching *I* ♥ *Jonah* T-shirts, me and Goose at Target. I put the latest Jonah Prince album on a disc. I delete the photos of Goose from the hard drive so Violet won't know about him.

I hand my phone to Kendra.

"I guess I can't use this anymore."

Kendra shakes her head. "Stacey knows you're coming tomorrow, late morning. She's ready for you."

I've already told Laurel I'm moving in with my aunt in Tennessee. I told her I'll be living in the mountains with little internet access. "I was thinking maybe you should make a sign that says, 'Dare to eat a peach,'" I told her.

"I'm not going," she said.

"You should. Take someone else. Just, you know, think of me when you're there."

She sighed. "This sucks."

I can't believe I'm not going to see Jonah.

Now I ask Kendra, "Can I write to Laurel ever?"

"Not for now," Kendra says. "It's too risky. What if her mother ran into Violet and said they'd heard from you?"

"That's unlikely. Her mother hates Violet."

"It's possible," Kendra says. "I'll help Laurel to . . . forget you."

"Just what I want, my best friend to forget me."

"I know, dear. I'm sorry." She's said it a hundred times. I know she blames herself. I can't say I don't blame her for parts of it. But she's the only person who can help me now. At least, I hope she can.

"How are you going to withdraw me from school? You're not a relative."

Kendra looks down a second like she's deep in thought. Her dark hair cascades over her eyes. When she looks back up again, the eyes that meet mine are Violet's. Her whole face is. And her hair transforms from brown to auburn. "They won't know that."

It's sort of terrifying. I want to go back to that time in my life when I knew nothing about magic, when I didn't suspect it existed.

I look around the room. This will be my last night going to sleep here. I've lived here my whole life. I lived here with my mother, back when I was happy. I wonder if I'll ever be happy again.

I guess it's up to me now. I have Goose's family to protect me. But I need to protect them too—from Violet.

15

The next morning, Kendra, disguised as Violet, takes me to school. I don't say good-bye to Violet, who is crying in her room. I amble down the stairs and to the front door, taking in each wall, each rug, each stick of furniture. I know I'll never be here again. When I get outside, I pause. The yellow birdhouse I built with Dad when I was ten hangs in our Hong Kong orchid tree, uninhabited. We had wrens last year, but now they're gone. I walk over to the tree. I glance up at Violet's window to make sure she isn't watching me. Nothing. I pull down the birdhouse from the tree.

"I'm ready," I say when I get in the car.

Kendra is wearing one of Violet's favorite work suits, black skirt with a bright purple jacket. She doesn't drive the car. It sort of drives itself. She doesn't even put her hands on the wheel.

I watch as the car stops for a school bus with no input from Kendra. "So Violet thinks you're just going to take me to your house after school to kill me?"

"Pretty much."

I feel a chill go up my arms. I remember Violet, when I was a kid, taking me to the park to feed the ibises, how I used to laugh as they pecked at the crumbs with their slender beaks, and Violet told me they were the first birds to come out after a hurricane. She didn't hate me then. How could she hate me so much now? What would be happening had Kendra not intervened? What if Violet finds out?

"Thank you," I say. "I know this is hard for you."

Kendra strokes my arm where the little hairs are standing on end. "I wish I had done more, sooner. I loved Violet so much I didn't see it, didn't see what she'd become. Love can blind us."

We're at school now. The car steers itself into the parking lot, and we get out.

"Act like you like me, so no one gets suspicious." Violet-Kendra takes my hand.

I pull away. "If we held hands, that would be suspicious. No girl my age would hold hands with her stepmother."

I walk ahead of her to the office.

When she finally gets someone to help her, she says, "I'm Violet Columbo. I'm withdrawing my daughter from school."

"Withdrawing from school? Why?" The woman's eyes immediately go to my waist. Oh, God, she thinks I'm pregnant.

"I mean she's transferring to another school. Here." Kendra reaches into her purse and pulls out Violet's driver's license along with a sheet of paper.

The lady looks at the paper. "Tennessee. Far away. We're sorry to see you go."

I look sad. It's not hard. I am sad. My whole life is over, school, taking drama next year, seeing my friends. It's almost like Violet *is* killing me, killing everything about me. I feel my face get hot around the eyes.

But, soon enough, it's over and I'm back in the car with a Kendra who looks like Kendra again. "What happens when my info goes to that other school?"

Kendra wrinkles her nose. "What other school?"

"The one in . . ." I realize what she means. "Oh, I see."

When we pull in to the Guzmans' driveway, Stacey has just pulled in too. She must be coming back from the kids' school. She's taking Jeron out of his car seat.

This situation is so . . . awkward. I don't know this woman, but I'm moving in with her.

But as soon as Stacey sees me, she turns around. "Welcome to our home."

"Oh, thank you." I want to hug her, but her hands are full, so full without me, fuller now. "You have no idea—"

"It's fine, sweetie. You're safe here. Come on inside."

I turn to say good-bye to Kendra, but she and the car are both gone. How does she do that? And will I ever even see her again?

I follow Stacey inside. I offer to take Jeron, but she says she's got him. She hands me her keys. "Lock the door behind us," she says.

I notice the door has three locks, the regular one and two dead bolts. She sees me looking at them. "I've fostered kids who were removed from their parents' custody. Drug dealers, really bad people. It seemed like a good idea to have some extra barriers."

I nod. I know that, if Violet finds me, no door will keep her away. And yet, here with Stacey, I do feel safe, safer than I've ever felt since I was little.

I lock all three locks. Each makes a satisfying clunk.

* * *

With Jeron on her hip, Stacey takes me on a tour of the house. "Your room's in the back, where it's quieter. You have to share with Izzie, I'm afraid."

"That's okay. She's sweet. I've always wanted a sister." The room has bunk beds. The bottom is made up with *Little Mermaid* sheets. The top is more sedate, but still pink, waiting for me. The walls are Pepto-Bismol pink with giant snails and starfish painted all over them. Stacey must have painted these, and I love it all.

"See if you think so in a week. We had to clean for a couple of hours to get it presentable for you. But Isabella helped. She's excited about having a big sister."

I smile, feeling good for the first time in a week. "I'll help her clean up. I'll help with all the housework."

Stacey doesn't protest or say I'm a guest. She just thanks me. I'm glad. I have no intention of sitting on my butt all day, sponging off them. It strikes me that I never saw Violet clean the house. She must have used magic. Still, I'm guessing I can figure it out.

Stacey shows me around the rest of the house. It's big and pretty and most of the walls are bright yellow, cheerful enough to maybe let me forget that, even though I'm with these great people, I'm a prisoner here. There's a piano in the living room, and I ask Stacey who plays.

"I used to, when I had more time. Now, the boys do."

"Goose plays the piano?"

She laughs. "Can't picture him sitting still that long, huh? I made him learn when he was younger. He complained so much, said the teacher was mean, but now, he plays great. I'll make him play for you."

I say, "I'm so grateful to you."

"Stop being grateful. This family, we help kids who need it. You need it. Besides, my spoiled son can talk me into anything."

"He's a talker." I grin.

"He wanted to stay home today." She steers into the kitchen and puts Jeron in his swing. She starts taking out stuff for a bottle.

"Can you show me how to make that? I want to help."

She hands me a canister of powdered formula and the bottle. She shows me how much water to add. "I only got him to go today by saying it might be suspicious if he missed too much. He's a little lazy."

"He gets good grades, though. I saw him at the honor roll assembly."

"Because I stand on his neck." She laughs. "Not literally. He doesn't like homework, though."

"I can help you with that too. I'm good at homework."

"Don't worry so much, Celine."

But I do. Still, I nod and offer to give Jeron a bottle.

After that, Stacey puts him down for his nap. "I have to get some work done now."

"What do you do?"

"I illustrate kids' books. I can show you my studio later. We built out the garage. But right now—"

"I know. You've got to work while you can."

"Make yourself at home. You must be exhausted from all the stress."

I don't think I am, but she probably needs to work, so I go to my—our—room and climb the ladder to the top bunk. I survey the room. The sea creatures watch me. I guess Stacey painted them. It's something my mom would have liked. When I was little, my room had a border of cows jumping over moons. I kept it long after I was too old, but eventually, Violet redecorated. From above, I can see that Isabella didn't do that thorough a job of cleaning. Clothes and papers are stuffed behind the dresser and desk. I'll offer to help her, or maybe just clean up myself.

But first, I want to shut my eyes.

I crawl under the crisp, pink sheets that smell of laundry detergent and bury my head in the pillows. I wish I could have brought my own pillow from home—I've had it for years, and it's smooshed just the right way—but it was too big. Also, my music, which was on the phone. I have the CD I made of Jonah, but no CD player. I'll have to ask Goose if he has one. Still, the bed is comfortable, and I close my eyes.

In the dream, I am little. Or, at least, everyone else is bigger. I'm someplace cooler than Florida, and it is fall, apple-picking time. I'm at an orchard with Dad. Then, I realize my mother is there too. She's so young and beautiful, her blond hair flying behind her. We are so happy, running, stumbling, falling through the piled red and gold leaves to trees heavy with fruit. Mom holds my hand as my father hoists me onto his shoulders. I reach for the sky, grasping a crimson apple instead. I start to bite into it.

It falls apart in my hand.

Something is crawling out of it. Insects. Maggots. And then, they are all over me, down my hand, up my arm, devouring me, my mother, my father.

"No!"

16

"Hey!"

Someone is shaking the bed, making the world vibrate.

I wake, staring at my hand. It is still there, still the same. Gradually, objects take focus behind it. I stare into the eyes of a blue stingray, then a red crab. Where am I?

I look down to where the shaking came from. Goose is there, by my bed.

"Are you okay? I wasn't going to come in, but you were . . . you seemed . . ."

"It was just a dream, just a nightmare." I smile. "I'm glad you're here."

He looks up. "Heights. My favorite."

"I'll come down." I gesture for him to move over, then throw my legs over the side of the bed and slide down.

"How was your first day?" he asks.

You mean, other than the fact that my parents are dead and I'm living with strangers because a crazy witch is stalking me?

"Great," I say.

"I doubt that."

"I miss my house, and my school, and everyone—and especially, my dad. But I'm glad you're here now. It's a lot less lonely." I reach for his hand. "You're so sweet."

He grins. "When my brothers and sister get home, you're going to wish for lonely."

"I doubt that. I've never had siblings. Laurel has a brother, though, and he messes with her, but they're always there for each other. I always sort of wanted a big brother."

He looks down. "I guess I can be your brother, then."

"I didn't know you played piano."

"One of the many things I'm awesome at. Want to hear me?"

I remember my promise to Stacey. "Don't you have homework?"

"What are you, in cahoots with my mother?"

"Maybe a little. Your mom is awesome."

"That's because you don't know her."

"I know she let me come live here. She's the best." I put my hand on his arm. "Come on. I can sit with you while you do it. I was taking chem this year too. I could do it with you. That way, when I retake it, I'll be all set."

I stop. Will I ever take chem again? Will I ever get to walk down the street again? Or will I be hiding forever? Goose is right. I barely know his family. I don't even know him that well. Did Kendra put some kind of spell on them to make them have me? Or did she just know they were the kind of people who would?

Goose says, "Okay, deal. But first, let's make smoothies. Our neighbor, Mrs. Ozanich, has a bunch of mango trees. She gives us tons of mangoes every year, and my mom freezes them. We still have frozen mangoes left from last year, and it's almost time for the new ones to ripen. So Mom says we have to make smoothies every day."

"I've never had a mango," I say.

"Wow, how can you live here and not have mangoes?"

We go to the kitchen and take out the frozen mangoes, yogurt, and juice for smoothies. We make enough for Goose's siblings too. "To keep them quiet," he says. Then, we start on chemistry. Mrs. McKinney is one of those teachers for whom copying from the book is a sort of religion. She's assigned them to copy fifty-plus definitions. I offer to read them aloud while Goose writes them.

"I'd rather do it the other way around, I read and you do the copying," he says, "but I guess they'd notice if I suddenly developed pretty, girly handwriting."

"How do you know my handwriting is girly?"

"Hmm, one, you're a girl, and two, I saw how you wrote 'C.C. loves J.P.,' which, three, is a girly thing to do."

"Oh, it is?" Of course I know it is.

"Yup. A guy wouldn't write that on a notebook even about his actual girlfriend."

"So guys don't express their emotions. Got it." I gesture for him to get out some paper.

"I didn't say that. Guys express their emotions by doing things."

"Like what?" I say,

"I don't know, taking care of a girl, fighting off bears, slaying dragons, repairing plumbing, going to work sixty hours a week to feed their families, like my dad does."

I think, again, of my dad, about how mean I was the last time we spoke. He thought Violet and I loved each other when he married her. I did love Violet then. How did it all go so horribly wrong?

Goose waves his hand in front of my eyes. "You there?"

I snap to. "Women do things for people they love too."

"Like what? Bake cookies?"

"I guess. Yeah, we make things nice, and cookies might be involved. What's wrong with cookies?" There was a sign up at Offerdahl's, the sandwich place near my house, that said, *Cookies Are Love*.

He laughs. "Nothing. I love cookies. What else?"

I make a mental note to make cookies for his family, maybe tomorrow. I'll ask Stacey if she has chocolate chips. Otherwise, there should at least be stuff for sugar cookies. "I don't know. I've never been in love—other than with rock stars who don't know I exist. Have you?"

He thinks about it a second before shaking his head. "No, not really." He gets paper from his backpack. "We should do this. I want to dazzle you with my musical ability before I get stuck helping my brothers with their homework. What's the first one?"

"Acid-base titration. That's t-i-t . . ."

"Ha! Made you spell a bad word."

"Idiot. R-a-t-i-o-n." I wait for him to finish writing. "It means a procedure that is used to determine the concentration of an acid or base."

"Got it."

The definitions take over an hour, and then he has pre-calc, which I can't help him with except by keeping his siblings away from him. Isabella has developed a little girl-crush on me, so I get her to help me clean up behind the dresser while Stacey helps the younger boys with homework. Then, Isabella and I set the table.

It's after dinner before we go to the piano, but Goose actually does dazzle me, playing the *Moonlight* Sonata from memory. Then, he takes out a book of vocal selections from *Oliver!* and makes me sing along.

"You're incredible," I say.

"I wouldn't say incredible. You mean because of my size?"

"No. I didn't say that. I would never—"

"No, you didn't. I'm sorry. People tend to underestimate me. When my mom first took me for lessons, the guy didn't want to teach me, said I wouldn't be able to play because my fingers would be too short or something. I believed him, but my mom found a different teacher, and she told me about this French dude, Michel Petrucciani. He had a genetic disease that not only made him small, but also made his arms ache when he played. He died young. But he became a really famous jazz pianist. They said he was a dwarf but played like a giant. So, after that, I knew anyone could play."

"I'd like to hear him sometime. But I just meant you play really well for anyone. I wish I'd learned. I was begging my parents for lessons when . . ."

I don't want to say it. It feels like I've been thinking about Mom a lot, like I'm always complaining.

"You didn't because your mom died?" he finishes.

"I love singing, though."

"I could teach you to play," he says. "You could practice during the day, as long as you don't wake Jeron. My mom will kill you if you wake Jeron."

"Really? You'd teach me?"

"Sure, why not? I think they sell beginner books for older students in the school bookstore. But we have my brother's books for now. It's a little babyish." He pulls one out from behind his book. There are cartoons of birds sitting on a musical staff. "Okay, it's a lot babyish, but it shows all the notes. You start with middle C." He gestures for me to sit down. I do, next to him, hip to hip. He picks up my hand and places it so the thumb is on a white key that's next to another white one. "Each finger has a number. The thumb is one, forefinger is two, and so on. That's how you know which finger to use, so you don't tie yourself in knots. CDEFG."

He guides my hand, playing each one. My blue nail polish is chipped. I'll have to ask Stacey for nail polish remover.

"What's that?" Goose points to a burn scar on my finger, the one from the curling iron.

"Oh, it's weird. It's a burn. Violet could make appliances . . . turn on me. I know it sounds crazy."

"Nah." He strokes it with his finger. "Poor little finger."

"It didn't hurt that much."

"Mom wants you to take out the garbage." Tony comes up behind us. "And I'm supposed to practice."

"You could go a week without practicing. You only want to practice now because I am."

Tony grins. "Recital's coming up."

I stand. "I'll help you with the garbage."

"No. You can't go outside," Goose says. "It's not safe."

"I just feel like I should help more. Your family is helping me so much—"

"You helped me do a ton of chem busywork. It would've taken twice as long without you. I hate that crap. I'll be back in a few minutes."

"You're not going to watch me play, are you?" Tony says.

"Only if you want me to," I tease.

"I don't."

So I go into the family room and watch a reality singing show with Stacey and Isabella. A few minutes later, Goose comes back in. He stands in the doorway, motioning for me to come over.

"Goose wants to talk to his girlfriend." Isabella giggles.

"Shh," Stacey says.

I head over to him. "What?"

He pulls me away. I can hear Tony practicing an unrecognizable song for the tenth time.

"There was someone out there, watching me," he whispers. "Don't go near the windows."

"Someone? Like who?" I'm whispering too, so Stacey won't hear. Or someone outside.

"I don't know. I heard rustling. I saw . . . a shape. Our neighbor, she's outside gardening a lot, but not at night."

He's worried. So am I. If Violet's watching Goose, she's as good as found me. How would she, so quickly?

"I'll check," Goose whispers. "I just want you to stay away from the windows, okay?"

The doorbell rings. We both jump.

"I'll get it!" Tony starts to get up.

"No! You keep practicing. You have a recital coming up—and it's not sounding real good at this point." Goose walks to the door. "And remember, no one's supposed to know about Celine being here."

"I know, I know," Tony says. "It's your dear little sister that's going to be the weak link there."

Goose waves him off. At the door, he says, "Who is it?"

"It's me," says Kendra's voice.

Goose starts to open the door.

"Wait. How do we know it's Kendra?" I ask.

"Only Kendra would know you know Kendra," she says from outside.

Good point. Still, Goose opens the door warily.

A woman who looks nothing like Kendra stands there, a blond housewife in yoga pants. She steps inside. "Close the door."

I do, and as I do, she melts into Kendra again, dark hair, purple-streaked, wearing a veiled black hat and high-heeled boots that make her look from the Victorian era.

"It's done." She looks at me. "You're dead."

I draw in a breath. "You mean—"

"I mean Violet believes you're dead. I brought her the proof she sought."

"What proof?"

She opens her hand. I step back. In her palm is an object, a finger. *My* ring finger, wearing a turquoise ring my dad brought back from a trip to Arizona. The blue nail polish is chipped, and on the knuckle is a burn scar. I look at the finger that is still on my hand. They're identical, other than the blood.

And suddenly, it all becomes real, too real. I feel a tightness in my throat. My vision looks black, gray, like someone is fiddling with the lights, and my head feels tight.

And then, I'm on the floor. Someone is pressing a wet rag to my forehead. Someone else is holding me.

"Celine?" It's Stacey who's cradling me in her lap. "Are you okay?"

"Yes, it was just . . ." I search for Kendra. Gradually, she comes into focus.

"I shouldn't have shown it to you. Sometimes, I don't think."

"Yeah," I say. *Yeah, seeing my severed finger was a little jarring.* "Will it work? Will she believe I'm dead because of that?" Stacey's stroking my hair like a mom.

Kendra says, "She knows I'm a witch, so she knows I can make things up. But she trusts me. If she stops trusting me, she'll get suspicious."

"So that means—"

"It means I have to pretend I adore her when she completely disgusts me. Ah, well, if anyone can do it, I can. I've had centuries of practice."

I take Kendra's hand—the one that isn't holding my finger—and squeeze it. I know I'm not the only one Violet has hurt.

17

That night, when I go to sleep, I dream of the orchard again. But this time, when I reach for the fruit, I fall from my father's shoulders to the ground, into a pile of apples, some ripe, some rotten. Down, down, I sink deep into them, and they multiply like cancer cells, massing around me, eating me alive. I look up, searching for my father's hand, but he is doing nothing to save me.

I wake, sweating, sobbing. I reach out, searching for the nightstand, the clock. There is only air. Gradually, I remember where I am. Goose's house. Safe. For now. Objects take shape in the darkness. The buzzing of a thousand bees becomes a ceiling fan. A monster in the corner becomes Isabella's giant stuffed bear, the kind people win at the fair. I try to sleep, but now, I am awake. I can't listen to music because I left my phone with Kendra. I don't want to disturb the family, especially Isabella, but the more I lie here, the more terrified

I become, thinking of Violet coming for me. Not only for me, but for Goose and his parents, his siblings, even little Jeron. I'm putting them all in danger. They are all at risk for me, and there's no end in sight. Kendra has no plan. Maybe I should run. Or just give myself up to Violet.

In the darkness, I climb down the ladder. My backpack is still there, packed. I take out jeans and a T-shirt, put them on. Isabella stirs in her sleep. I stand still until she settles back in. I pick up the backpack and my shoes.

In the family room, I sit on the sofa to put on my sneakers. I leave the lights off. I don't know where I'm going. I have my birthday money, over a hundred dollars. Maybe I could take a bus somewhere, somewhere far from Violet, then look for a shelter. I start to tie my shoelaces.

The lights go on, blinding me. I blink, then look toward the door. It's Mr. Guzman.

"Night owl, huh?" he says.

"I had a nightmare. Then, I couldn't sleep, and I feel . . ." I stop.

"What?"

"Nothing. Just insomnia." I know if I tell him I feel guilty about being here, he'll just try to reassure me, tell me how much they want me here. I am already taking enough from these kind people, who are risking so much for me. I don't need to burden them with my guilt too.

He says, "Are you okay? What was the dream about?"

I notice he's dressed for the office already, carrying a briefcase. I remember what Goose said about how hard he works.

"I don't want to make you late," I say.

"I'm not late, I'm early. I like to read the paper when it's quiet. You're . . ." He hesitates, looking me up and down. "You sleep with your jeans on?"

I nod.

"Shoes too?"

"I was just putting them on."

"I can see that. My question is why? I know you can't be thinking of taking a walk."

"I was thinking about leaving." It just pops out.

He doesn't reply, only nods. I add, "I guess I just . . . I feel bad, making you hide me."

He shakes his head. "You didn't make us do anything. We volunteered."

"I know, but—"

"But nothing. We're responsible for you. You think if you left, we'd just forget about you, like a cat that shows up on our doorstep for a while, then leaves?"

"I guess not." I really thought he didn't want me to stay. I know Goose and Stacey pressured him to keep me.

"My wife and son didn't talk me into anything," he says, reading my thoughts. "I'll admit I was . . . hesitant to take you in, but now that we committed, we're in this. If you left, we'd have to look for you. We couldn't just leave you out there on your own, in danger. The police would be involved. Do you want that?"

I shake my head.

"Me neither. So why don't you go back to bed for a while? It's not even six."

"Maybe I will." I stand and start to go.

When I reach the doorway, he says, "Celine?"

I turn back.

"I have a big trial today. I've been preparing for months, and my client stands to lose big if I do a bad job." He pauses, staring at my feet, still in sneakers. "I don't have to worry about whether you're going to run away, do I?"

"No, sir. You don't need to worry. Thank you."

222

I go back to bed until Isabella wakes me, wanting to know if I can braid her hair. Goose has already left for school.

I practice the piano all day, except when Jeron is asleep. That's when I make oatmeal cookies from the recipe on the box of oatmeal. I learn Tony's whole piano book. That day, after school, Goose brings me an *Adult All-in-One Piano Course* book and a book of Jonah Prince's greatest hits. "I stopped at the music store in Suniland. So you have something to write 'I heart Jonah' in," he says.

I'd wondered where he went. I flip through the pages. It has "Beautiful but Deadly," my favorite song, and all these pictures of Jonah.

"I heart your family," I say.

"You should've known we'd be awesome, having met me."

"I did. I just didn't know *how* awesome. You're so lucky."

"We don't want anything to happen to you," he adds.

I wonder if Goose's dad told him about my escape attempt. I hope not. I don't want him to know. And I don't want anything to happen to them either.

Later, in my room, I cut one of Jonah's pictures out very carefully, with scissors, and tape it up next to my bed. A souvenir of the life I used to have, when I cared about things like rock stars.

That night, I don't have any nightmares. Instead, I dream I'm with Jonah. It's the same kind of weird dream I used to have, where he rescues me. This time, I'm a princess, like Sleeping Beauty, comatose in my golden bed. Jonah comes through the window and kisses me. I wake and gaze into his eyes. A handsome prince! He rescues me, taking me into his strong arms. We're in love, will be in love forever.

Of course, I know it's not real. Still, I wonder if the dream means I'm safe.

18

When you're little, you think it would be cool not to have school, to just sit home and watch TV all day, every day. When my mom was alive, and sometimes even in the early Violet years, I used to love staying home, eating soup, and watching *Fairly OddParents*.

Let me tell you: It gets old real fast. There's a definite limit to how many game shows, courtroom dramas, and soap operas a person can watch—especially if that person isn't eighty years old. When you find yourself *really* rooting for the uniformed soldier to win the hot tub in the showcase, it is time to turn off the TV.

I do. I study for classes I'm not taking at school. I'm way ahead in Spanish. I research different ways to French braid Isabella's hair. I practice on her dolls. I bet she has the best hair at school. I listen to the Jonah Prince CD I made, and Goose loans me an old iPod he has. I make cookies almost every day, which makes me Tony and Tyler's favorite person. I also get good at the piano real fast. By the end of the first week, I can play Minuet in G by heart. But, when I tell Goose I want to learn *Für Elise*, he says I need to learn to play scales first.

"Okay, that should take a day," I say, feeling jazzed.

"You need to play them well," he says, "two octaves, twelve different scales, and that's just the major ones."

I roll my eyes. "Fine. Teach me."

"You're welcome." He sits beside me on the piano bench. He's wearing some cologne that smells citrusy. Then, he starts in on C, showing me how to sneak my thumb under the first two fingers to reach the F. His hands are small, but he makes up for it with speed and skill, then he tells me to try. I do.

"Arch your hand more." He reaches for it, lifting my palm.

"Next, you're going to hit my knuckles with a ruler." I stare at my fingers, remembering the one Kendra held in her hand.

"Only if you don't practice the right way. Again."

"Such a power trip," I say. "You've just been waiting for someone to boss around."

"Nah, I've had siblings for years."

I've noticed that, since I've been here, Goose comes right home after school. I know he didn't before. He hung out with friends, went to their houses, played pranks at Target. Even Stacey commented on how much he's around. Thank God for Goose. I'd explode from loneliness if he didn't spend the hours after school with me. I don't care if I have to help him with his homework. I'd *do* his homework for him if he wanted. He is my best, my only friend now.

Today, I ask what I've been wondering about for weeks. "So . . . why'd you and Willow break up?"

"The F major is a little different than the first few," he says. "You use the first four fingers, then roll the thumb onto the C."

"Goose?" I say.

"I'm ignoring you," he singsongs.

"Fine. Don't tell me."

"It was mutual," he says. "Now, you try."

I start the scale, but I don't remember where I'm supposed to use my pinky. So I stop.

"So, okay, mutual's good," I say.

"Yeah, we *mutually* decided that since she's a senior and I'm only a junior, and we're not in love or anything, she should date someone who'd look better in her prom pictures."

He plays the scale for me again, so I can see where my fingers go. "You actually don't use your pinky at all," he says.

"You're kidding," I say. "I mean about Willow, not the pinky. She said that to you?"

"Not in those words." He points to my fingers, and I try again. I get it sort of right.

"What words, then?" I cross my arms in front of my chest. I'm done playing until he talks.

"Well, for context, you have to know that when I took her to homecoming, her mom made me stand on a step stool for photos. And I was still a head shorter than her."

"That's because she's super-tall." When he gives me a look, I say, "Well, partly."

"Oh, completely. It was definitely her freakish *tallness* that was the issue." He stands up. Have I overstepped? But he says, "So then, when I asked her about prom, she said she thought maybe she should go with someone else. Not anyone in particular, just 'someone else,' like anyone but me. Then, she said—actual words here—she didn't want me to have to find a tux because she knew it was hard for me to rent in my size."

"Seriously?" I say. "Well, it's her loss."

He shrugs like he did before, but doesn't sit down. "I wasn't in love with her. She wasn't 'the one.' It just sucks to get dumped."

I nod. "She sucks. You'll meet someone better."

He sits back down. "I guess." He gestures at me to try again.

I do. This time, I get it perfect, but he yells at me to arch my hand. "You're hitting extra notes with your palm."

"Okay, okay." I start again, arching my hand sarcastically high. Goose seems to think it's perfect.

"Good. Again," he says. When I start to play, he says, "Sometimes, I get tired of always being the court jester."

I'm not sure I heard him right, over the music. I stop playing. "What?"

"Nothing."

"I think it was something." I cross my arms again.

He gestures for me to play again, but I don't, waiting for him to elaborate. He says, "People only like me because I'm funny."

"That's not true."

"It is true. Like, last year, in English class, we had to write a poem and read it aloud. I don't know if you know this about me, but I write poetry."

"How would I know that?" I start to play the scale again but also sneak glances at him out of the corner of my eye. He has strangely long eyelashes, and, in the lamplight, they make a shadow on his face like a moth flying.

"I guess you wouldn't," he says. "But I do. This should have been an easy assignment. But I knew that, if I read some teen angst poem, or even something about a tree, people would've busted a gut laughing. It would have challenged their image of me in a way they wouldn't want it challenged. So I wrote a limerick and got a C. But at least when they laughed, they weren't laughing at me."

"Are limericks that easy to write?" I finish the scale. "I thought they were hard."

"They're easy if you write about a girl from Nantucket," he says.

"I'm surprised you even got a C." I laugh, but then say, "Okay, so here's what I think about that. First off, you're too hard on yourself. People love you. You're super-popular. You could be class president if you wanted."

"Yeah, right. If they love me, they love me because I'm funny."

I shake my head and go on. "They like you because you're *fun*. You're the most fun person I know, which is different than just being funny. Secondly, you don't know if they'd have laughed because you didn't give them a chance. You were the one who didn't want to challenge their image of you. You chickened out."

"I know what would've happened."

"Maybe. Maybe not. But third, you're probably right. You probably do have to change who you are some to be popular. Everyone does. When I was in middle school, Whitney and the mean girls wanted me to be in their clan. But they only liked me because of my looks, and I didn't want to be a mean girl. So I decided just to stop trying, not have a group. That's why I'm not popular."

He thinks about it, then says, "Okay. But I wasn't *normal* not popular before I changed. You could be popular if you wanted. Your looks are enough. My looks are another story."

I nod, acknowledging that's probably true. I know what it's like to look different, but I can't pretend that being beautiful is the same—at least outside of Violet's house.

I say, "Tell me about it." Because I know he wants to, even if he won't admit it.

"I'd rather teach you the G major scale," he says.

"Let me guess. One sharp, so it goes like this." I play exactly the same fingering as C major, but starting on G with the F a half step higher.

"That was right," he says, looking sort of stunned.

"I'm gifted," I tease. Actually, the G major scale was in my piano book, right before Minuet in G, and I worked on it. "Now, tell me your sad, sad story, and I'll tell you mine. Bet I win."

He laughs. "Challenge accepted. Okay. So, when I was a kid, I had no friends. Zero. I was smaller than everyone, and no one wants to hang out with the weird-looking kid. Occasionally, people would be *nice* to me, like take obvious pains to include me, to show they weren't assholes. Or because their parents told them to. But I was never the kid who just got invited to hang out after school."

"That sucks," I say.

"It did. And there's more. Once, when I was nine, this kid, Coleman, invited me to his birthday party. I was excited because, usually, I didn't get asked. People would hand out invitations at school, and every boy would get one except me and this kid, Ricky, who picked his nose until it bled. But Coleman invited me. So I showed Stacey the invitation, and the next day, I told him I could go."

"Okay." I finger the G major scale again, to distract him from the fact that he's actually expressing an emotion for once, instead of being a total *guy* like he usually is. "So then what?"

"He said, 'Oh, I only invited you because my mom said I had to ask all the boys.' I felt like someone kicked me in the stomach."

"Ouch," I say, wanting to reach back through time and hold that little nine-year-old boy's hand. But I play the scale again. I hate Coleman. I don't even know him, but I hate him.

"Yeah. Anyway, I wasn't really invited, so I didn't want to go. Obviously."

"Obviously."

"But I'd already told my mom about it, and I didn't want to tell her why I'd been invited either. She was so happy. She bought this big gift, a Lego *Star Wars* starfighter set. So that Saturday, I faked a stomachache to get out of it. Stacey was so upset. She kept asking me if I felt better, telling me it was okay if I went late. She was worried I wouldn't get invited again if I blew it off. She was even a little mad at me. Finally, I told her the truth. Man, did that reek."

"What happened?" Though I can imagine.

"She cried. She flat out bawled. She kept saying how cruel kids were, threatening to call Coleman's mom and tell her. I begged her not to. It wouldn't make things better. Finally, I told her to please stop talking about it. So then, she gave me Coleman's gift. I spent that day making a starfighter with my mommy because I had no one else to make it with."

"Stacey's the best, though." His story is so sad I sort of want to cry myself, but I suppress it. "Do you want to show me A major?"

"Nah, that's enough new stuff for one day. Work on those. Try with both hands."

"Okay." I start playing C major, but softly.

"Anyway," he continues, "one day right after that, I told a joke in class, just by accident, said something funny. I don't even remember what. I'd been funny to my family all along, but never in school. I was too shy. But everyone laughed. Actual positive attention from my peers. I liked it. So, I decided I was going to be funny all the time. That weekend, I went to the library and got all these joke books and books of insults, and when I got to school, I started telling them. The first kid who insulted me, I said, 'You're so dumb, you're flunking recess.'"

I laugh. "That's funny."

He rolls his eyes. "Yeah. If you're nine, it's hilarious. Everyone laughed and started making fun of him, instead of me. So the next time someone insulted me, I said, 'Is that your nose, or did the *Millennium Falcon* park on your face?' I thought of that one myself. I was a huge *Star Wars* freak, and this guy had an enormous nose, so it was perfect. It was easy to come up with jokes when I did it ahead

230

of time, not on the spot. And people laughed at that too. The next week, someone invited me over to his house for real, not just to be nice. It was the same guy I'd told the nose joke about. Turned out he liked *Star Wars* too. And he respected me now."

"Or feared you," I say.

"Nah, we were friends. We still are. It was Tristan Hernandez."

I gape. That was the guy who played Bill Sikes. Tristan's huge (as is his nose), and they're best friends. "You're kidding."

"Nope. So ever since then, I've spent every spare moment thinking of funny things to say, coming up with pranks and stuff. It's hard work. But no one makes fun of me anymore. They want to be my friend. I'm cool. But they don't know the real me."

"Do I know the real you?" I hold my breath, awaiting his answer.

He shrugs. "This is him. You like him?"

"He's a good piano teacher," I say.

He smiles, showing a dimple on one cheek, but not the other. "Thanks."

Silence. I want to say something else, tell him he's *not* that ugly kid he obviously thinks he is, that he's funny and charming, but he's also handsome, especially when he smiles. Sure, the first thing I noticed about him was his size, but his beautiful, brown eyes were a close second. But that would be awkward, so instead, I just sit there with a dumb grin on my face, playing F major.

Then, we both speak at the same time.

"Is the real you *ever* funny?" I ask.

"It's not that I'm never funny," he says, then laughs when he realizes what I've said. "Of course I'm funny. I'm hysterical, obviously. Just not all the time. I have deep thoughts too."

"Got it. Deep thoughts. I'd hate to think it was all a lie. Can I read your poetry sometime?"

He looks away. "I shouldn't have told you about it."

"Why can't I?" I stop playing and make my lips an exaggerated pout.

"'Cause it's embarrassing. What if you hate it? What if you think it's stupid?"

"I wouldn't. I'm your friend."

"Right. Friends." He nudges me over and starts playing "Clair de Lune," a piece he says he plays to relax. He's still not making eye contact. The music is soft and gentle, moonlight over a river. "Okay, how about this? Someday, I might leave a poem lying somewhere, where you can find it. Just don't ever tell me you read it, okay?"

I roll my eyes. "Guys are such idiots. Don't want anyone to know they have souls."

"Soul? What's that? I sold mine to the devil in exchange for piano-playing ability." He keeps playing, showing off, not looking at me. Now, the music sounds like falling water. "Hey, this is huge for me. You're the only one I've ever said this to. You're the only one who knows the real me, the me that gets pissed off at the world sometimes, the me that thinks it's not fair."

"Life's not fair," I say. "I know a lot about getting pissed off at the world."

He nods. "I bet you do." He keeps playing, his arm brushing mine with each arpeggio, stronger, then softer, like a river, flowing toward the ocean, then crashing into rocks. For a minute, it's only the sound of the piano. The piano and our breathing.

Then, at the highest point, he says, "Okay, your turn. How old were you when your mom died?" and I wonder if he's timed his question, as I timed mine, so I'll think he's not listening, concentrating on playing.

"Eight," I answer. "So you were not getting invited to Coleman's party, and my mom was planning the Zoo Sleepover of Death. They said it was a freak accident—I mean, she got attacked by a freaking

monkey. One day, she was there. Then, she's gone, just like my dad."
I suck in a shaky breath, closing my eyes and letting the music flow
over me. It's so beautiful and a little sad. I still can't believe my dad
is gone forever. I barely had time to process it before I had to deal
with this, with Violet. "It feels like I'm sleeping over a friend's house,
and when I get home, he'll be there. I regret every time I stayed
at Laurel's and wasn't with him. Who knew it was my last chance?
Violet took it from me."

"You've been through a lot." Goose stops playing, giving me his
full attention now that it's not about him. The silence seems louder
where the music used to be.

I say, "When my mom died, people were really nice, at first.
They brought so much lasagna our freezer was full for months. They
offered to watch me after school. I had tons of invites. But then, it
sort of stopped. It was like everyone forgot us. They'd do things with
their families, and wouldn't ask us, even if they used to when my
mom was there. The only one who was still friends with me was
Laurel."

Laurel. I swallow hard. Yesterday, Goose left his laptop on the
kitchen table when he went to school, and I saw Instagram photos of
Laurel and this girl, Britney, wearing matching pink shirts that said
Waiting for My Handsome Prince. I bet they're going to the concert
together too. Britney's willing to wear the lame-looking T-shirts, and
she'll be sitting in my seat. *My* floor seat with *my* best friend seeing
my Jonah Prince. The concert's in two weeks.

Still, I say, "Laurel was my best friend, and her mom was my
mother's best friend since they were kids. One day, I was complaining about how no one ever wanted to hang with me anymore. She was
playing at our friend Cassie's house, but Cassie hadn't asked me." I
start playing C major again, just with my right hand.

I say, "Laurel, she got this sort of weird look on her face. She said

233

that Cassie had told her that her mom didn't want her to play with me anymore. Her mom said that when girls didn't have mothers, they went wild. She thought I'd be on drugs or something. I was eight, and her mom already had me pegged as a future crack addict. Laurel said she wasn't going to be friends with Cassie anymore either."

"So your mother was dead, and your friend ditched you too?" Goose said. "That's harsh."

"Friends, plural. All my friends ditched me. Maybe they weren't all as mean about it as Cassie, but they totally forgot about me. The only one who stayed with me was Laurel. I think maybe the others never really liked me in the first place. Their moms were friends with my mom. She was the leader of the Girl Scout troop. Once she was gone, they didn't care about me, and neither did their kids."

"How could they not like you?" he says. "You're so . . ." He stops.

"Beautiful?" I roll my eyes.

He shakes his head. "That wasn't what I was going to say. I was looking for the right word."

"What word is that?"

He thinks about it. "Fierce. That's a word. You're fierce. People think you're like this fragile flower because you're so little and pretty. But you're really strong. You've been through all this, and it hasn't broken you. And it hasn't made you less sweet."

Wow. That's maybe the greatest thing anyone's ever said to me.

I say, "I guess they don't see that about me. And I don't even know if it's true. I feel so alone. My parents . . . my dad. I have nobody. Nobody." My eyes fill up with tears. They just do that randomly now, but usually not in front of anyone. Just out of the blue, I'll be wallowing in self-pity. I hate it, but sometimes I can't help it, with all that's happened. The piano keys swim before me so I can't see which is which.

Goose sees. He puts his arms around me and pulls me toward

him. "You have me . . . us. I know it's not the same."

I sniffle, then sob. His hold on me tightens. His arms feel so warm, and he smells of lemony cologne.

"I'm an orphan," I say. "I wish I could just take care of myself."

"I'll take care of you. I'll get my parents to. They took in Tyler and Jeron. They can take you in too. It doesn't have to be temporary. You can stay here forever."

"That's crazy." But I remember what his dad said, about not treating me like a cat. Maybe it isn't crazy.

"It's not crazy," he says. "It's okay. You'll never have to go back to her or anywhere you don't want. We'll take care of you, Celine. I know it's not the same as having your parents, but I . . . we'll love you, my family. You'll never be alone."

"But . . ."

"Shh. Just stop . . . stop thinking I'm wrong, okay? I'm telling you the way it is. While I am around, you will never be alone. I know I'm not a big guy, but I'm big enough. We all are."

He takes me by the shoulders and backs off, making me look at him. His brown eyes hold conviction. He believes what he's saying. It's incredible. I've only known him a few months. Who knew there were people out there who were so kind? I'm not used to it.

"You're so . . . why are you so sweet to me?"

He laughs. "That's me, Mr. Sweet." He lifts a hair out of my eyes, wiping a tear. "You win."

I say, "Win what?"

"The pity prize. You said you were going to win, and you did."

"I don't want to win. I don't want pity."

"I know."

I bury my face in his shoulder and sob with abandon.

He holds me tight, and he lets me.

The days go by. Slowly. Stacey and Jorge attend spring concerts, and Isabella comes home with a dance recital costume that makes her look like a duckling. So cute! I help her sew the straps to be the right size. Tony's piano recital has happened. The school year is almost over. When Kendra had arranged for me to live with the Guzmans, we had agreed it would be temporary, a few months, a year at most. Then, she said, Violet would get past it, move on. Once I was off Violet's radar, Kendra would help me create a new identity, move me to a new town, get me a new family, sort of a Witness Protection Program with witchcraft.

The part I had pushed back in my mind, the part I'd avoided acknowledging, the part I'd definitely never told Goose's parents was this: Violet never "got over" anything. She hadn't gotten over her love for my father, whom she'd met at age ten. And she'd killed my mother years after she'd last seen her in high school. She'd stayed, like an alligator waiting, mouth open, for its unsuspecting prey, until my mother had felt safe. Only then did she strike.

Of course, she thinks I'm dead. Maybe that will help.

Still, it won't be as easy as Kendra thinks. I had secretly hoped to be able to go to the Jonah Prince concert with Laurel in June. But it's late May, and I haven't seen Kendra since the day I moved here. Will I never go to school again? Never have friends, other than Goose? Never have a boyfriend, marry, or have children, just stay here like one of those kidnapped girls who lives her whole life in someone's walls—albeit with really nice people? Would that be enough for me? And what about the Guzmans? Always sheltering me, swearing the kids to secrecy about me, that had to be hard on them.

One day, after practicing *Für Elise* for two hours, I retreat to my—our—bedroom to listen to my Jonah CD. Goose is doing math homework, so I don't want to disturb him. I bring the book Goose got me, to look at the pictures. I wish I could get a copy of *J-14* or *Tiger Beat* that would be sure to have pinups of Jonah. But it's not like I can ask someone to buy me something so silly—even with my own money. So all I have is the songbook. That, and my dreams.

At night, I listen to Jonah on my headphones, and I try to conjure up the dream I had about him again. I know it's just a fantasy, but my reality is so crazy-awful. But instead, I dream of apples, rotten, exploding apples. Lately, I've dreamed of being rescued, but the guy who saved me wasn't Jonah. At least, I don't think he was. I couldn't see his face. Still, I can feel my rescuer's arms around me, his lips on mine. I seek out his eyes and know that I am safe!

Only to be awakened by Isabella's snoring. They should take her to be allergy tested! Actually, something in the air is giving me allergies too. It hangs heavy, filling my lungs, making me feel like I'm half asleep all the time.

My fantasies are taking over my life, and I will go insane.

Could work. If I'm locked in a mental institution, Violet won't find me. I could make friends, insane friends. I can grow old and fat, pretending I'm in Jonah's arms.

Le sigh.

Today, I'm listening to "When I See Your Face" when Isabella comes in.

Isabella is the one person who keeps me firmly grounded in reality. It's pretty hard to live in a fantasy world when a five-year-old keeps begging you to play with My Little Ponies. Fortunately, I really *love* playing with My Little Ponies. Isabella insists on being Pinkie Pie, but she lets me be Rainbow Dash sometimes. I think it's important for her to learn to share. I gave Goose money to buy her Pinkie Pie's helicopter, from me, for her birthday.

"I like this song." She does a little dance around the room.

"Do kids your age like it?" I ask, hoping they don't. If kindergarteners like the same music you do, that's bad.

"I don't think they've heard it." She points to the songbook in my lap. "Who's that?"

"That's Jonah Prince, the guy who sings it." I turn over the book so she can see the color photo on the cover.

"You have his picture up by your bed too."

"How do you know that?" I ask, wondering if she had climbed up onto my bed. I knew she could. Last week, when she couldn't find her tap shoe, it had turned up under my pillow.

"I can see it." She points to the picture and, since I'm sitting on the floor, I can see it's clearly visible from her perspective. Which means Goose sees it too. At worst, he knows I ripped out a page of his gift. At best, he thinks I'm a lame fangirl who keeps a rock star's picture over her bed. Of course, he already knows I wrote Jonah's name on my notebook.

Okay, so I *am* a lame fangirl.

They said on *Entertainment Tonight* (which I watch because I am now the only teen on the planet not on social media) that Jonah's dating this Teenz Channel star, Allegra Kendall. They also say he drinks and parties a lot. Not exactly my type, but it's his music I love. Besides, I know I'm not really going to marry him. I just want to go to his concert like a normal girl, and maybe fall in love with a normal boy someday. I'm not actually insane . . . yet.

Now, Goose comes in, so he must finally be finished with his pre-calculus. "Yay, you're done!" I stand and try to block his view of the photo.

He looks at Isabella, who's still dancing. "Did you ask her about the mangoes?"

"What about the mangoes?" I love the smoothies we make, but I thought we were out of frozen mangoes.

"Good news—Mrs. Ozanich brought us new mangoes. They're ripe again. My mom wanted us to cut them up and peel them, to put in the freezer."

"Sounds like fun." If Goose said this, it would be sarcasm, but I actually like helping. Feels like earning my keep.

"Yeah, fun." Still, we head to the kitchen where the counter is stacked with a dozen mangoes, red, orange, and gold, and oozing sap. I think of my dreams, of the apples. Could these too all turn to muck and maggots? But I haven't had the dream in a few days. I feel safe. The mangoes are beautiful, the colors of sunshine.

I pick one up. There are two peelers, and I hand one to Isabella. "Do it over the sink," I tell her. Since the kitchen is fitted for smaller people, she can do this easily. It's harder for me. When I first moved here, I kept leaning on counters that weren't quite where I expected, but now I'm used to it. Still, I'll let Goose cut them up.

"*Ferris Bueller*'s on tonight," Goose says.

"What's a Ferris Bueller?" I ask.

"Celine, didn't you ever watch TV?"

"Maybe not as much as you did." Laurel and I watched a ton, but it was all stuff like *Bridezillas* and *Say Yes to the Dress*, stuff you wouldn't share with a guy friend.

"Cultural illiterate. Well, it's a John Hughes movie, the same guy who wrote *Pretty in Pink*. *Ferris Bueller's Day Off* is my favorite. You have to watch it."

"Okay." I try to slide the peeler under the mango skin. It's not as easy to peel as an apple, but at least it stays whole in my hand. Suddenly there's a knock on the window.

I look out. It's someone I don't recognize, an older woman, dressed up with a hat, like a Jehovah's Witness. But they usually come to the front door.

She mouths *Kendra* so I understand.

Goose sees too and starts toward the door. I glance at Isabella. Goose says, "Hey, isn't your dance show on, Isabella?"

"Mom says I have to do this, right?"

"Nah, we got it," he says. "Why don't you go watch?"

Isabella goes to the family room and, again, Goose starts for the door. But, then, Kendra is in the room.

"Oh!" She puts her hand down onto a pile of mango peels. "What a mess." In an instant, the mangoes are peeled and chopped, flying into the Ziploc bags we had for them, and the kitchen is cleaner than before.

"That's better." She turns to face us. "I have good news. I think Violet has decided to move on."

"Really?" That so does not sound like her.

Kendra nods. "She was talking about taking a job transfer to another office, another city. She says no one in this town has ever liked her, so she should go someplace new. I encouraged her. I told her she could travel, as I had. We could even travel together. She agreed that she could forget Greg better if she didn't live in his house. Wasn't that emotionally healthy of her?"

"Very." *It sounds fictional.* "Other than the fact that she only got there by thinking I was dead."

"We take what we can get," Kendra says. "She's applied for a job transfer. Once she leaves, I really think you can move on with your life."

"Move on?" Goose asks. "Like she can go back to school? And get a foster family?"

"Well, she has to move, of course. Violet thinks she's dead. She can't just show back up at school. Violet would still be her guardian. She'd find out. I'll take Celine someplace far away and exotic, like France or Italy, or maybe Ohio." She touches my cheek. "I've decided it would be safer if you live with me, like my daughter."

"Wow. France?" Goose says.

I look at Goose. I know he's thinking the same thing I am: We'll never see each another again. I'll miss him.

"It will probably be several weeks still," Kendra says. "Don't get too excited yet."

Goose looks down. "No, not too excited." He turns to Kendra. "Hey, you want a smoothie? We have all these mangoes."

She shakes her head. "Can't. Allergies. But thanks."

And, before I can say *Witches have allergies?* she's gone.

Goose looks up at me. "I guess you can go to summer school now, to catch up."

I nod and try to smile. "Yup. In France."

"Maybe you could talk her into Ohio. At least they speak English."

"It's still really far from Florida."

He turns away and starts feeding mangoes into the blender. "Yeah. Really far."

We make smoothies. They don't taste the same, though. Mangoes are usually sweet. These were so pretty, but they taste like turpentine. Then, we try to go into the family room like nothing is wrong. After all, nothing is. This is what I wanted, to be away from Violet forever, to be free. It's not like Stacey and Jorge were planning on keeping me forever. It's not like they need another kid to add to the five they already have. It's not like they'll miss me the same way I'll miss them. They have each other. It's not like—

"Sit by me!" Isabella shoves her mother over to make room.

Stacey and Isabella are watching a reality show. Jorge is on his laptop, and the boys have disappeared into their rooms. Since Isabella is taking ballet-tap, we've all gotten completely addicted to this show about dancers and their crazy stage moms. Now, one of the moms is threatening to quit because she doesn't like her daughter's costume.

"She quits every week," Stacey says.

Two grown women are screaming and stomping their feet. It's like a traffic accident. You can't stop watching. But I say, "This is so nice."

"What is?" Goose says. "*Dance Moms?*" The dance teacher is screaming at all of them.

"Just . . . this. Watching TV together. My family never did that. You're so lucky." Where will I be a year from now? With Kendra in Ohio? Or France? But I don't want to watch *Dance Moms* with Kendra. I want to stay here and help Isabella do her hair every morning, help Goose with chemistry, learn to play something a little harder on the piano.

Stacey laughs. "Well, you've come to the right place. That's all we do together around here, watch TV. Can't get anyone out for some exercise."

"You know, they've got power yoga on every day at six. I was thinking we could do it together." Maybe if I pretend I'm not leaving, I won't have to. Yeah, that'll work.

"That'd be cool," Stacey says. "Maybe DVR it for Jeron's naptime."

After *Dance Moms*, the rest of the family goes to bed. Goose says, "*Bueller* time."

"You should go to bed too, Goose," Stacey says. "Don't you have a test tomorrow in chem?"

"Day after tomorrow," he says.

"Still, you need to sleep. Your grades are important to you. You want to get into a good college."

"We'll just watch half," he says. "Please. Celine's alone here all day."

"Alone?" Stacey laughs.

"You know what I mean. I just want to spend some time with my friend."

Stacey frowns. "Okay. But just half the movie."

"Absolutely." Goose waits until she turns the corner into the hallway before he whispers, "Nah, we're watching the whole thing."

"She's right, you know. You shouldn't ruin your GPA. Junior year is the most important for college."

He rolls his eyes. "What you're not understanding is that I'm a genius. I get As without studying."

I remember what Willow said about him not handing stuff in. "Can you get them without sleep?"

"Sleep's for babies. Sit down, and stop acting like my mother." He sits and pats the seat beside him. "You're going to love this."

I do. It's a funny movie about this cool guy, Ferris, who skips school with his girlfriend and his very reluctant best friend, Cameron. They outsmart his parents and the principal and go to a fancy restaurant, a baseball game, and an art museum.

Goose says, "It's true what Ferris said in the movie. Life moves pretty fast. If you don't stop and look around once in a while, you could miss it."

I notice he's wearing that cologne again, the lemony one. Probably, whenever I smell lemons for the rest of my life, I'll think of him.

I want to stay with him.

I say, "That is true. I probably haven't looked around much lately. Maybe once I stop hiding out in your house I could do that. Except I'll miss you."

He looks sad, then suddenly smiles like he's trying hard to. "We should run away for the summer, go backpacking or something."

"My stepmother . . ."

"We'll go someplace she'd never look, like the Grand Canyon."

"I'd like that. It's supposed to be beautiful."

Goose glances at the TV. "Oh, wait—this is my favorite part. Ferris is in a parade."

And then, in a second, he jumps up onto the coffee table, imitating Ferris. "'And I'd like to dedicate it to a young man who doesn't think he's seen anything good today,'" he lip-synchs with Ferris. "Give me Izzy's hairbrush."

I give him a look like WTF, but hand him the hairbrush. So when Ferris starts singing "Danke Schoen," Goose does too. *Danke schoen, darling, danke schoen. Thank you for all the joy and pain.*

I can see the actor, Matthew Broderick, on the television, and Goose doing a perfect imitation of his every expression, every gesture.

"You've obviously seen this movie a lot," I say, laughing.

He ignores me, still singing, *"Danke schoen . . ."* and dancing. Then, he holds out his hand. I take it, and I dance with him. It's fun, and for a while, I forget that my life is a mess, that my family is gone, and I'm never going to go to school again. Goose is good at making me forget the bad stuff.

How will I live without him?

But that night, when I go to bed, I have another nightmare. Again, I'm picking apples with my parents. This time, when I pick the ripe, green apple, it turns black, then melts to molasses. The molasses spreads up my hand and turns my arm black. Then, my whole body. It consumes me until I am gone.

I wake, remembering something: Violet's maiden name. Appel.

Violet is the apples. They destroyed my family, and they will destroy me.

The dreams mean I will never be safe. She'll find me sooner or later.

Even though I can sleep all day, I never get enough rest because my dreams keep me up all night, worrying, not just worrying about Violet and Kendra but worrying about the Guzmans, what they're risking, keeping me. Despite Jorge's assurances that they want me, I can't help but think they'd be better off if I just disappeared.

Of course, if what Kendra says is true, I'll be disappearing soon anyway, and that worries me even more. Where will I go? Who will I live with? Will I ever have any friends? And what if Violet finds me anyway? I can put these questions out of my head in the day, but at night, they dance in my head like sugarplums on acid, keeping me awake for hours.

But, the night after *Ferris Bueller*, I decide to turn in early, to read until my eyes shut without my help. I know Goose has that chem test the next day, and I want him to study. But when I get to our room, Isabella is still coloring.

"You should put that away," I say. "Your mom's going to tell you to soon."

Isabella has been very cutely obedient. Doing everything I say. Goose says, jokingly, it's because she looks up to me. I think it's just because I'm new.

But, apparently, the novelty has worn off because she says, "I'll wait until Mommy tells me."

"And then, about ten minutes more, I bet. And then, she'll be mad and take away TV tomorrow. Don't you want to watch *Liv and Maddie* together? It's our favorite show. Come on, I'll help you clean up." I start gathering her crayons. It's a big box with a hundred twenty, and I know she likes when I put them in rainbow order, so I start with the reds. "You get the oranges."

She does. It takes forever because she's just a little kid and some crayons are in the middle between red and orange, like mango tango. Finally, she hands me the ten oranges, and I fit them next to the reds. "Now, start on yellows, and I'll do greens."

She picks up a lemon-yellow crayon and holds it aloft.

"Do you love my brother?" she asks.

The question startles me for a second, and the magic mint crayon slips from my fingers. Once I catch it, I consider her question. I know any answer I give will be trumpeted not only to her brothers but to the neighbors and everyone at her school. I also know that five-year-olds only define love one way: a boy and a girl K-I-S-S-I-N-G. Neither yes nor no will yield a good result.

I think of Goose at the piano, playing music like falling water.

Finally, I say, "Of course I love all your brothers. And your mommy and daddy and you too." I pick up the screamin' green.

"I meant my brother Goose. Are you his girlfriend?" she says.

"Silly!" I laugh. "We've never even been on a date. We're friends."

Blue violet, red violet, violet blue . . .

Isabella rolls her eyes. "I mean—"

"Izzy! Time for bed!" Stacey's voice mercifully interrupts us.

"In a minute!" Isabella says.

"Now. Brush your teeth. I think I saw something crawling around between them earlier. I'm checking your toothbrush."

Isabella thrusts the various yellows into my hand and walks out, huffing.

After she leaves, I quickly gather the blues and violets and purples, then the neutrals. I'm in bed with my eyes closed and the pillow over my face by the time she comes back, safe from questions I can't safely answer.

Fortunately, she doesn't revisit the subject the next day. I feign sleep in the morning until she's gone. In the afternoon, I'm listening to Jonah when she gets home. She shares my Jonah obsession to a major degree now.

"He's soooo cute!" she says.

I laugh. "You're, like, five years old."

"Six. You know I had my birthday last week."

"Okay, six. Sorry. You're not supposed to be obsessing over rock stars."

"Why not? You do." She turns away, singing "Yes, Baby, Yes," and shakes her hair to indicate she wants me to braid it again. I oblige. I saw a style with a braid across the forehead, and I've been wanting to try it. I get her hairbrush and start brushing out her golden waves.

"Well, I'm older than you," I say. "I've been obsessed with Jonah for, like, a year, and I'm getting less obsessed." It's true. Without

Laurel's influence, it's less fun. "Do you know I was supposed to go see him in concert?"

"You were? Like, see him in person? Wow."

"I know. My friend Laurel and I got tickets the first day they went on sale. We had floor seats right near the stage where he could see us if he looked down, and we were going to make posters so he'd notice us."

"What were the posters going to say?"

I can't tell her about *Dare to eat a peach*. Not only will she not get it, but it also sounds completely stupid when I say it out loud. So I say, "But now, Laurel's going with this other girl, Britney. It makes me so mad. I really wanted to go." I want to cry, not about Jonah. That was a complete fantasy. But about Laurel, being trapped inside, basically losing my life.

"That's what you're upset about? A stupid concert?"

It's Goose. He was late coming home from school today, and I've been waiting for him. I finally mastered *Für Elise*, and I've waited to play it for him, my only audience. Now, he's standing in the doorway, staring at me with something like disdain.

"Jonah Prince, really?" he says. "You're stuck here all the time. You've had to quit school. My parents are taking risks having you here. I never go anywhere anymore, just so I can entertain you, and you're upset because you can't go see Jonah Stinking Prince and his diaper pants?"

His words are like a bee sting, or a hundred. I turn on him.

"It's not the only thing I'm upset about, and you know it." Even more, I want to cry. Why is he being such a douche? Can't he see that Jonah is a *symbol* of all those other things? Like having to go to Ohio or *France* with Kendra. Like maybe never seeing him again? "You don't have to stay home for me. No one told you to. Go out with your other friends if they're so great."

He looks at me, sucking in a breath. "Maybe I will. And maybe if you'd stop playing his insipid music night and day, I could actually think straight and study."

The chorus of "Yes, Baby, Yes" is playing. Those are pretty much the only lyrics. It is insipid. Still, I say, "You said you liked it. Were you just playing me?"

"Yes. I mean, no." He rolls his eyes. "I was being nice."

"Yeah, well, maybe you should keep *trying* to be nice."

He stalks over and pulls the plug on the speaker. Isabella starts screaming that he's in her room. Finally, he leaves. I scramble up the ladder to my bed to cry, but not before I rip down the photo. I don't want to throw it out, though. It's from the book Goose got me. Even though Goose hates me, it has meaning. Instead, I hide it under my pillow. Isabella turns the sound back up as soon as Goose leaves, louder than before, so Jonah is screaming, "Yes, baby, yes!" but when I close my eyes, I can't picture Jonah's face, only Goose's face, disappointed and angry at me.

Stacey calls us for dinner, but I say I feel sick. I'm mostly embarrassed. When Isabella comes back to the room, I pretend I've gone to bed early, even though it's only seven and still light out. Eventually, she leaves.

A little later, there's a knock on the door. I ignore it, even when I hear Goose's voice, saying, "Celine? Come on, Celine. I didn't mean it. Come play the piano with me. Or just talk to me. Anything."

I bury my head deeper under the pillow, ignoring him, even though I know I'm being a brat.

"Celine?"

I don't answer, and finally, he goes away.

But I don't sleep. I can't. I stay awake, listening to the muffled noise of the television, the whirr of the blender making more smoothies, the boys fighting and flushing toilets. Goose knocks two more times, and I want to talk to him, but now, I've pretended so long that I can't. Of course he was totally right. It's dumb to fantasize about a rock star I'll never meet. I know that. Eventually, Isabella goes to bed and all the noise gives way to the wind chimes on the patio and the stop-start of the air conditioner. I'm lying there, wide-awake.

Hours later, I hear a knock on the window.

"Celine?" The voice seems to be coming from inside my head. Kendra.

I slide down to the floor and pad toward the window in my bare feet. When I get there, I have to look down. She is disguised as Stacey. But her voice is still Kendra's.

"Celine? May I come in?"

"Come in, then," I whisper. And immediately, she is there beside me.

"It's, like, midnight. What is it?"

She melts into her own face and grows about a foot. "I'm sorry, Celine. I think I was wrong last week. About Violet. She's not leaving."

What else is new?

"And I think she might be onto me. That's why she lied. She may know I helped you."

This is worse news. "So she knows I'm alive?"

"I'm not sure. But you should definitely lay low."

"How much lower can I lay? I'm in total hiding." I have another horrible thought. "Does she know I'm here? Are the Guzmans in danger?"

She shakes her head. "I don't think so."

"You don't *think so*?" I glance at Isabella, sweet Isabella asleep in her bed, her French braids still intact. "How about you *know* instead of thinking? I can't put them at risk."

"I'll find somewhere else for you to stay, another place, another town. Just don't talk to anyone right now. Don't even trust me if I come to your window."

I'm thinking maybe I shouldn't have trusted her in the first place, but I don't say it. She's trying to help. If it weren't for her, I wouldn't even know about Violet's intentions. I'd probably be dead. My head is awhirl with jumbled feelings, but mostly regret, regret that I have to leave here, leave the people I love, people who have protected me. Goose, whom I adore despite his recent meanness. Yet I don't see any other way.

"How will I hear from you?" I ask.

"Through the mirror, only the mirror," Kendra says.

And then, she's gone.

21

I stumble back to bed and find the mirror under my pillow, as I knew it would be. But now I can't sleep at all. I have to go away. I have to leave to protect the Guzmans. It's not fair to them. I should rest up, then sneak away in the morning. It's hours before I sleep again, and then, I am awakened too soon, by a hand in the darkness.

"Celine?"

Goose. He's climbed up the ladder even though he's afraid of heights. He nudges my shoulder. I smell that citrus cologne he's been wearing.

I have never been good at giving people the silent treatment. When Laurel and I would fight, we'd say we were never speaking again. That would last an hour. I can never handle someone I love being mad at me. One of the most heartbreaking things about my father's death is that I was so mean to him. I would have broken—if he hadn't died. I don't want to leave on bad terms with Goose. I may never see him again.

So I say, "What, Goose?" not even sounding mad.

"I'm so sorry. I . . . it wasn't you. I had a crap day. I got a D on a pre-calc quiz."

"A D?" He's good at math, usually. At least, he understands the chem math a lot better than I do. "Ask if you can do extra credit, maybe."

"Yeah, maybe. That's not the point. The point is, I was a douche, and I'm sorry. I'm upset that you're leaving, mainly." He doesn't know how soon I'm leaving, and I decide not to tell him. He'll just try to get me to stay.

"Okay," I say. "But listen. You can do stuff with your other friends, you know. Just leave me home playing ponies with Isabella. I like it, and I'm not going anywhere." A total lie.

He tries to brace himself on the rail of the bed. "I know. I want to hang with you. Can't you tell that I . . . ?" He stops, then drops down to the floor.

"Tell what?"

"Nothing. I don't remember what I was going to say. But we have fun together, don't we?"

"So much fun I ruined your grades?" I know the D is because he was hanging out with me too much.

"That's my fault, not yours," he says. "I know you're lonely, no matter what you say. I'm sorry you can't go to the concert. I know it was important to you."

"It's not that big a deal. I know the Jonah thing is stupid." He must think I'm such an idiot. "I was more upset about Laurel. Laurel's going with someone else. It feels like she forgot all about me."

"No, she misses you." He kicks the floor. "Shit. I forgot to tell you. I saw her the other day, and she said she misses you so much. She doesn't understand why she hasn't heard from you."

"Oh, wow." Now, I feel worse because she probably thinks I forgot all about her, and I can never tell her otherwise, tell her I miss her.

From below me, Isabella yells, "Would you guys be quiet! I'm trying to sleep. I'm going to tell Mom you were in my room."

"Okay, I'm sorry." Big talk from a kid whose hair I do three times a day. To Goose, I say, "I'll come down."

We go to the kitchen, and over Cheerios, Goose says, "Maybe they'll do one of those 3D concert movies next year, and I can take you to it."

I smile. "You're so sweet." Even though a 3D movie isn't the same as actually being in the room with Jonah. But I think of what Kendra said. By this time next year, I will be in some other place, far away from everyone I know.

Or I could be dead.

"Listen, you'll get out. You'll come back here, or I'll go to Ohio. Or even France. We'll do stuff together. You heard what Kendra said. Violet will move on. No one's that crazy."

You don't know Violet. "You're probably right." I don't want him to worry any more than he already has.

"Of course I am. What are you doing today?"

Leaving. Suddenly, I just know it. I have to leave, have to protect them from Violet. That's more important than anything else, even than seeing him again. "I don't know. I guess I'll practice the piano a lot. Your mom has a PTA meeting, and then, she's taking Jeron for a checkup, so I'll be all alone."

"I wish I could stay home with you, so you won't be lonely."

"I'm fine. Really. You should go suck up to your math teacher."

Forget me.

"I will."

I watch him trying to catch a stray Cheerio that's floating away like a little life ring. This is probably the last time I'll ever see him. I stare at him, memorizing his eyes, his dimple, everything about him. I don't want to go. Yet, what choice do I have? A lock of hair falls into his face, and I reach to move it. He looks up at me, raising an eyebrow.

"Violet always told me people treat you better if your hair is neat," I say. "Besides, it covers your beautiful eyes."

I remember what Dorothy said to the Scarecrow: *I think I'll miss you most of all.*

He smiles halfway. Our eyes meet, and for a second, we just stare at each other. He smiles big. "Yeah. My hair should be more of a priority, I guess. I should get going."

But he stands there, still staring. Suddenly, I want to tell him lots of things, that I don't really care about Jonah, for one. That no one in my entire life has ever been as nice as he is, for another. It's weird that you can just meet someone, and right away, they mean so much to you. But if I say that to Goose, he'll know something's up, that I'm running away, and I don't want him to know. I don't want him to stop me. I don't want to leave, but I have no choice.

I wish I could stay here. With him. Forever.

So I wait until he's picked up the cereal bowls and is on his way out before I say, "I really appreciate everything you and your family have done."

He shoulders his backpack. "Please stop thanking me. Anyone would do this, anyone decent."

"Guess I don't know many decent people."

"Why don't you get some more sleep?" he says. "I'll see you later."

It's just barely light out. I say, "Okay." I want to hug him, feel his arms around me one last time. But, instead, I wait until he closes the door, then go back to my room.

I watch him out the window, feeling like my bones may crumble, as he runs to his car in the morning rain. Then, I watch the car's taillights get smaller and smaller until they disappear entirely.

I lie in bed, tears running down both cheeks, my fist in my mouth so as not to wake Isabella with my sobs. I will never see him again.

And he is the only one who ever rescued me, truly rescued me when I really needed it.

I sleep, fitfully, dreaming of apples, exploding like the bomb at Hiroshima, taking me up in a mushroom cloud to the top of the world. The dreams make me sure that leaving is the only way. I'm not safe. Nothing will make me safe. At least, if I leave, I won't endanger others. I can't put the family I've come to love in danger.

When I wake, Isabella is gone, Stacey and Jeron and the boys too. I'm sorry I can't say good-bye to them, but I can't. I stuff my few possessions back into my backpack. I take the songbook Goose bought me, not as a souvenir of Jonah, but as a souvenir of Goose, of our time here.

I go to the bathroom to brush my teeth.

On the counter, I find a sheet of paper.

It's a poem, the poem Goose said he'd leave for me someday. I see the title, "Going to Target With Her." I smile and feel like I'm about to cry at the same time. It's about that day at Target, with Willow. I'm a little surprised that he would write a poem about Willow, or leave it for me, when he said he wasn't in love with her, when she dumped him. Then, I read it.

Going to Target With Her

Going to Target with her
Driving the ass-backward long way to Target to spend more time
with her

Rather than cramming for the test I need to ace
Time I couldn't have gotten otherwise
At Target with her
Trying on cheap, stupid, beautiful red and purple Target hats,
Trying to make her laugh and pose for pictures I take
Telling her we're there for a different reason
Lying that we're there for a different reason
When really, I just want to be with her
At Target with her
Hoping her tiny, white butterfly hand will brush against mine across
* the displays of socks and gloves,*
And she'll see me differently.
Differently than everybody else.
But she doesn't.
Taking pictures of her trying on stupid hats
Taking selfies, but really, training my phone on only her
At Target with her
Goofing around in frozen foods
At Target with her
Her and another girl, the girl I was supposed to be at Target with
The girl I used to think I maybe liked until the first day I met her, the
* first time I heard her voice, the first time I talked to her*
And I knew
That she was the arrow that hit the target that was my heart.

The paper smells like his cologne, just a little. Underneath the poem is a photo, a selfie Goose took that day. He'd taken it of all three of us, but in the photo, you can only see part of Willow's arm.

Training my phone on only her.

I stare at it a second, realizing that I, not Willow, am the "her" of the poem. The poem is about me, about that day at Target.

Driving the ass-backward long way. I remember how long it took to get there and, especially, back, how Goose made a wrong turn on the way from Willow's house to mine. Stupid. He asked me to go because he liked me.

Maybe loved me.

Loves me.

I remember what he said about showing me his poetry: "Okay, how about this? Someday, I might leave a poem lying somewhere, where you can find it. Just don't ever tell me you read it, okay?"

But how could he expect me to say nothing?

I sink to the floor, reading it over and over to see if I could be wrong, yet I know I'm not.

I wanted to leave today, right now, to protect him, his family, from Violet. I love them and need to protect them. This makes it worse. He endangered himself because of how he feels about me. Yet how can I leave without talking to Goose? If I leave, he'll think I ran away because of the poem. But that's not it at all. Not at all.

The doorbell rings. My pulse quickens. Is it him? I know he skips sometimes, or takes "personal days." But he wouldn't ring the doorbell, unless he forgot his key. I want to see him again, so much. Maybe he did forget his key. I'll check. I start for the door, then go into the bathroom to put the poem back where I found it, facedown on the pink tiled counter. Maybe he changed his mind about showing me. Maybe he came home because he wants to get it back. I sprint for the door.

But when I bend to look out the peephole, I see only an old woman holding a Publix grocery bag of mangoes, standing in the rain.

Kendra.

I have to get her to help me leave tonight, after I talk to Goose. I open the door.

She looks confused. "Who are you?"

Not Kendra.

Through the mirror, only the mirror. That's what Kendra said. But this isn't Kendra. She must be the neighbor, the nice lady with the mangoes. I make up a name. "I'm, um, Mary, the Guzmans' cousin. I'm staying with them awhile."

"Pretty girl." With her free hand, she reaches out to touch me. She is old, with wrinkles atop her wrinkles, white hair piled on her head. I back away. Stupid. She's just an old woman, a *nice* old woman. I step forward, letting her touch me. The rain is falling, but she doesn't seem to care.

"Thank you, ma'am. Stacey's not home."

"I came to bring her these." With great effort, she lifts the bag of mangoes. "Do you like mangoes?"

"I do." They smell overripe, rotten. "We've been making smoothies from them." I start to take the bag from her, but she pulls it away.

"Have one plain." She reaches into the bag and takes out one that is mostly scarlet, about the size of her clawed hand, perfectly firm with no brown spots. "Nothing like a mango, fresh from the tree, juicy . . . succulent."

"Thanks. I'll have it later."

"Oh. Okay, if you don't like them." But she keeps holding it out in her veiny, spotted-brown hand. "I always save the nicest ones for my neighbors, and this is the best one of all. Isn't it pretty?"

I nod. It is beautiful, so red it almost glows. The most beautiful mango I've ever seen.

The old woman is looking down. She drops the hand holding the mango, slowly. "It's just, they don't last very long."

It's so ruby red.

"I . . . okay. I'll try it." I hate to hurt her feelings. She seems like a nice old lady.

"Just one bite. You've never had one fresh picked, I'll bet. Why, when I was a little girl, we used to put a straw right into them and drink the nectar. You should try that."

"I don't think we have a straw, but another time." I reach for the mango. It is hot, probably from the sun, though it's morning, and the light isn't too bright yet. I examine its surface, looking for the perfect place to bite. It is smooth as porcelain, red and yellow as flame, no green, every part as perfect as the next. "Looks yummy."

"Try it then. It won't make you fat, if that's what you're worried about." She laughs.

Her lips are so wrinkled, and there are hairs sprouting atop them. Suddenly, I don't want to bite it, but what else can I do? Throw it back into an old woman's face? Just a small bite. I choose a red part and sink my teeth into the thick flesh. The bite mark shows a crescent of yellow, like the sun.

Only after I've bitten it does the old woman look up at me. I notice her eyes. They're not old at all, and they're familiar, so familiar.

It's the color. They're not blue.

They're violet.

The bite of mango catches in my throat. I choke as I fall to the ground.

I hear her laughter.

PART 3
Goose

1

I decided yesterday in chem that I was going to stop being in love with Celine.

Okay, that sounds a little arbitrary, but life is arbitrary. It was arbitrary life that put her in my path, that made her audition for that play, that let me fall in love with someone so completely unattainable.

And I need to butch up. My grades are sucking wind. I'm getting a C in pre-calc because I can't stay awake in class. Every day, I sleepwalk through school, just waiting for the time when I can go home, when I can see her, talk to her, stay up all night watching John Freaking Hughes movies with her, hoping our hands will meet across a bowl of cut-up mangoes or teaching her piano just so I can sit next to her on the bench.

And every night, I crawl into bed an hour before I have to be up for school, wondering why I haven't told her how I feel.

But really, I know.

I'm afraid. Who wouldn't be? What guy wouldn't be scared to declare his love to the most beautiful girl on the planet—a girl who could have anybody, even a rock star? Why would she want *me*?

But maybe she could. Maybe she appreciates my intelligence, my talent, my sense of humor, my low center of gravity. Maybe she's special enough to see who I really am.

So, yesterday, I made my plan. I would walk in there, find her, and say, "Celine, I love you." No. Too bold. Maybe I'd say, "Celine, I was thinking I'd like to make you dinner. No, not mac and cheese, but something special, a special dinner for the two of us, like spaghetti with crumbled-up hamburger in the sauce, like my mom makes. Okay, maybe my mom will just *make* it for us, but then, she'll leave us alone so we can have dinner together. Like a date? Yes, like a date. Actually, a date." I could say that, couldn't I?

Maybe.

Yes. Yes, I could ask her out. Or in. I've asked girls out before. That wasn't scary. And they've accepted. I didn't have to declare my love for her and ask her to marry me. In fact, that would be creepy since I'm only seventeen, and it's not 1940. I could just ask her on a date. What was there to lose? I was, after all, saving her life by hiding her from her wack job stepmother. That had to be a point in my favor, a way out of the friend zone and into the end zone. And, if I asked her out, and she laughed at me, I could just pretend I was kidding. I'm a super-big kidder.

I decided that's what I would do.

The experiment about acids and bases, the pre-calc class, and the reading of *The Kite Runner* all sort of ran together after that because I was contemplating the possibility, the impossibility that she might actually love me. It wasn't so crazy, was it? I was a great guy. And she had said herself that she thought that Andie should have ended up with Duckie. I was confident that I was at least as good-looking as Duckie.

I mean, if Duckie was four foot five inches tall.

But, except for that, I was actually better looking than Duckie. I didn't have that 1980s bouffant hairdo that you could tell had been weird even then because the cool guys in the movie didn't have it. And hadn't Celine herself said I had beautiful eyes? I do have beautiful eyes.

A year after *Pretty in Pink*, John Hughes did another movie, *Some Kind of Wonderful*, about a guy who falls in love with the popular girl, ignoring his tomboyish female friend, who adores him (and who was actually hotter than the popular girl, but I digress . . .). But in the end, he realizes it's the nerdy friend he wants. *Some Kind of Wonderful* ends the way *Pretty in Pink* should have, with the hero, Keith, running after Watts and giving her "a kiss that kills."

That's how I wanted my story to end too.

I was actually semi-confident, but when I went in to talk to her, she was babbling about how much she loved Jonah Prince, how she wanted to go to the concert so she could meet him. I pictured his eyes (under one of his stupid backward baseball caps), meeting hers across a crowded stadium, and I remembered one universal truth:

Girls like hot guys.

And a second truth:

I'm not one.

So I sort of freaked out on her, which was stupid because it wasn't her fault. But we made up this morning, and everything is fine. But then, I had to leave that stupid poem in the bathroom. I thought it would be easier than telling her how I felt, but now, I realize it's worse. Because, if she doesn't feel the same way, there's no way I can back out, no way I can laugh it off and say I didn't mean it. It's there, in black-and-white. I wrote a *poem*. About her. And if she thinks I'm a pathetic loser, I can never go back.

So the question is, what kind of drugs was I on when I thought leaving that poem was a good idea? Like, did Stacey spike my cereal milk with absinthe? What other explanation could there be?

So, even though I *need* to go to school to keep from actually failing math, I turn around and head back home. I consider calling my mom. I could ask her to find the poem, to rip it up before Celine sees it. But I don't want her to read it either, don't want her to know about it and think, *Isn't he cute.* So I wait at McDonald's until it's time for her to take my brothers and sister to school, and then, I head home. Hopefully, I can pick up the poem before Celine wakes up.

And then, I'll tell her in person or maybe just walk up to her and kiss her, which somehow works for guys on sitcoms.

Sure, maybe. Ten years from now.

But, when I get to the house, something is different. The front door is open. It's raining and the rain has come in. There are mangoes, red and gold, scattered down the steps.

Then, I see Celine.

She's spread out across the entranceway, her feet against one wall, her body slumped against the other, like she's just asleep. But no one sleeps getting rained on.

"Celine!" I run toward her through the driving Miami rain. "Celine!"

She doesn't move.

I grab her wrist and, at the same time, put my head against her chest, hearing her heartbeat, feeling her pulse. She isn't dead. She isn't dead!

Yet, she isn't moving.

"Celine!" I start to shake her hand, furiously. I get closer to her ear. "Celine, wake up! Wake up!"

She doesn't move. I have to call my mother, or maybe 911. I take out my phone. My hands are shaking as I dial it. I look around as it rings.

A shiny red-gold mango lies by Celine's bare feet. It has one crescent-shaped yellow bite missing, just one. How did it even get there? She must have opened the door to someone. Why did she open the door? She knew not to!

"You have to help me," I tell the 911 lady. "I think she's been poisoned!"

"Who's been poisoned?"

"My . . . friend. She was lying on the floor when I got home. Send someone quick." I can barely remember my own address. It's like everything that's happened before this moment has been a dream.

"Okay. Is she breathing?"

"Yes! Yes, but she's not conscious. She's lying on the floor. Send someone quick!"

"Someone is coming, sir. Did she hit her head?"

"I told you. I think she's been poisoned. Hurry!"

"What do you think she ingested?"

I look at the mango. It's crazy to say I think she had eaten a poisoned mango, but what else could it have been?

"This is going to sound crazy, but there's a mango here, and I think it might have been poisoned."

"A mango?" the lady says, like it's the most normal thing in the world. "Does she have allergies?"

I hadn't thought of that, but I say, "She eats them."

"Is it stuck in her throat? Did you attempt to remove the obstruction?"

"No. I mean, I don't know if there's an obstruction."

She tells me to sweep my finger through Celine's throat to see if there's something stuck in there. I slide Celine's head onto my lap, then ease my index finger between her lips and into her throat. *Shit, please don't die.* She gurgles a little, but there's nothing there. "Please hurry!"

"They're coming, sir. They're on their way. Don't hang up."

"No, there's nothing there. I'm sorry." I hold Celine tight.

"It's okay. They're coming. She's still breathing?"

"Yes. Yes."

She asks me some other stupid questions, who Celine is, who I am. Finally, I hear the siren in the driveway. I watch as they take over, then take her away.

2

Accidental overdose. That's what the paramedics and, later, the doctors at the hospital, think it was, and that's how they treat it. I know it was neither, but they won't listen to a kid. They do all the stuff I already did. They check her vital signs and hook her up to a bunch of tubes, then take her to the hospital. They pump her stomach, give her charcoal. The whole time, I feel like it's *me* they're hooking up to all these machines, me who can't speak or move, who's clinging to life. They ask me questions I can't answer. They want to know what I think she OD'd on. Nothing, I tell them. I tell them to test the mango. I brought it with me. They act like that's crazy.

They also want to know where her parents are. "She doesn't have any," I tell a nurse for the fourth time. He's a burly Cuban guy twice my size. They've wheeled Celine out, away from me, into some curtained-off area where I can't see her anymore. I wonder what they're doing to her. "Her parents are dead. She lived with her step-mother, but she was abusive. She took her out of school. If she came to my house, she was probably running away."

"Do you know where she lives?" the nurse asks.

"No, um . . . I was at her house once, but I don't really remember." Not that I drove by there twenty or a hundred times or anything. But I'm buying time. If Violet comes, maybe she'll finish her off. She could tell them to unhook her oxygen. Or unhook it herself. Or put something in Celine's tube. Or use magic to kill her and make it look like an accident. I'm hoping maybe if I say she was abusive, they won't let her in. And it's not a lie anyway.

The nurse turns over the clipboard he had all ready to write the information. "Okay, let me know if you remember. The police will probably want to talk to you too."

The police? Maybe they are taking this seriously. "Then I should probably wait until my parents get here."

My mom shows up soon after, then Dad. Dad says they can try to file papers to become Celine's guardians. He says I did good, even though I was skipping school and what's that about. He also says we probably have to tell them about Violet.

"But she'll kill her, Dad." I picture Celine, before they took her away, so white and still. "She already almost died."

"We won't let her," he promises.

I give them Violet's name and address. I actually don't know if they have a landline, or any phone number. Celine would know, but she's suspended in some still, white place with too-little air. "She's a really bad person, though. Celine was afraid of her."

That's completely true. I remember something Celine showed me once, that first day we played the piano.

"Violet burned her. Celine showed me the scar. It's on her ring finger."

And that's when Violet walks into the emergency room.

And starts crying.

And begs to see "my darling, darling Celine."

I try to follow her when they take her out, but the nurse stops me. "Family only," he says.

But Violet says, "It's all right. He saved her, didn't he? He was like a brother to her."

I stare at her. She knows why, and she stares back. As she does, her eyes turn from blue to brown, then back again.

Kendra.

Kendra with Violet's ID and insurance cards . . . and her face.

I breathe in, a shaky breath, and follow her into the curtained area where Celine lies. "We're going to admit her to the ICU," the nurse says. "We don't know what she ingested."

"Try everything," Violet/Kendra says. "It might be something you don't suspect. May I speak to a doctor?"

"Yes, ma'am. Just a moment." He excuses himself and is gone.

I stare at Celine. Her face is white as her pillowcase, and she doesn't look sick, only sleeping. She is so beautiful, her dark hair fanned out beneath her, a frame for her doll-like face. Celine hates being called beautiful. She says people judge her for it as much as they'd judge someone else for ugliness. But her beauty is so undeniably . . . there. Of course, it's the first thing you see. But, gradually, as I've gotten to know her better, I've forgotten it, forgotten how frightening that beauty is. She's become just Celine, a girl I know, the girl I love, Celine in motion, talking, singing, playing with my sister, lusting after Jonah Prince.

Now, a motionless shell, the outer beauty is all that's left. It crashes over me like a wave, taking me down into it. I'm choking, drowning.

Celine's beauty isn't what I love about her. It's what I hate about her because it's what makes her so unattainable. I love the girl inside, but I'll never have her.

Now, it's more than her beauty that makes her unattainable. What if she never wakes up?

When I first noticed her, it wasn't because of her looks. Well, not *just* because. It was because she was really brave, really fierce. She stood up to a roomful of sophomores who were picking on this stuttering substitute. She shamed us all, including me. I should have done what she did, but I didn't want to stand up to my friends. From that day on, I wanted to know Celine Columbo. It took a year, but when I finally did, she was everything I'd imagined. She was beautiful on the inside, like those ABC Family shows say you're supposed to be.

And now, she's dying. I reach out my finger and touch a little peach-colored freckle on her arm right above where the tube goes in.

"Ahem." Violet/Kendra interrupts my drooling reverie. I look up at her.

"Why is she like this? I thought Violet wanted to kill her. I mean, not that I want her dead, but this . . ." I jut my hand toward Celine.

I hate that Kendra looks like Violet.

"Violet did try to kill her. She didn't die because I used enchantments to protect her as best I could. But I couldn't defend her completely, and I can't wake her."

"What can?"

"Violet, of course, but that isn't going to happen."

No, it's not. "Anyone else?"

Violet/Kendra shakes her head. "I don't know. Usually, with spells, there are hoops to jump through. The feather of a golden bird, the scale of a dragon, but until someone tells you . . ."

"You don't know." I look back at Celine. Her chest rises and falls with her breathing. She's still breathing, but for how long? "Is there a time limit? How long will she stay like this?"

"Indefinitely, as long as she's nourished and hydrated. I assume they'll feed her intravenously."

"So someone could just tell them to disconnect it."

"Someone could."

We exchange a look. We both know who that someone is.

Earlier this week, I was playing the piano with Celine, sitting beside her on the bench, our hips touching, her hand so close to mine. Why didn't I take her hand? Why didn't I beg her to run away with me, someplace where no one would find us?

Because I'm just a kid. I can't do anything.

I have to do something.

"I have to talk to her," I say.

"Talk to . . . ?"

"Violet. The real Violet."

Violet/Kendra shakes her head. For a moment, I see a glimpse of her real self. "You're getting overconfident, talking to me disguised as Violet. The real Violet won't speak to you, much less do what you ask."

"Maybe she will."

"Maybe all the world's children will join hands and sing 'Kumbaya,' but it's unlikely," Kendra says. "I've been trying to talk to her for weeks. You see where that's gotten me. And she likes me."

"What do you think I should do then? Just leave Celine here to die? Or stay in a coma for the next fifty years?"

I look at Celine again. I remember that day she came over, right after her father died. She fell asleep almost in my arms. I'd watched her sleep for over an hour, and it gave me hope. She felt that comfortable around me. Maybe I'll never have what I want, but just knowing that Celine is alive on the planet makes the world better. At least my world.

Kendra's smile is sad. "No, I guess not. You love her very much, don't you?"

"Is it that obvious?"

"I saw it that first day at Target. That's how I knew you would help her."

"I'd do anything for her. I mean, I'd prefer not to die for her, but if that's the risk in talking to Violet, I'll take the risk."

"Don't take unnecessary risks, though," Kendra says. "Talk to her in a public place, her office building or the train station."

I hate the Metrorail station. It's an elevated train with views of the city, and I can't stand on the platform without holding on to a wall the whole time. Even then, it's terrifying. "Where does she work?"

"I'll show you. And take this with you."

From nowhere, she produces a silver mirror with a handle. It's about a foot long, and when she hands it to me, it weighs maybe ten pounds.

"What's this for?" I ask.

"If you look into it, you can see whoever you want. We can stay in touch that way."

"You don't have, I don't know, a phone?" I turn the crazy thing over. It looks like Marie Antoinette might have owned it, all curlicued and fancy. And I'm supposed to talk into it?

"Sorry. I can't make that kind of technology. Mirrors are easier. If you get in trouble, let me know. Otherwise, try not to let Violet see it."

"Why? What will happen if she does?"

"Bad things."

She doesn't elaborate any more than that. I probably don't want to know.

I take Celine's hand. It's tiny and white, with little pink nails like shells. And it's cold. I clutch at it, warming it up. Finally, the orderlies come to wheel her to the ICU.

"What's your plan?" Kendra says as she leaves.

I laugh. "I wish I had one."

But it's really not funny because my whole plan is just to talk to Violet. What else can I do?

And yeah, I'm terrified. But I'm more terrified of what will happen if I do nothing.

3

Violet's office building turns out to be a skyscraper with balconies, way worse than the train station. Until I change my mind and go to the train station. Then, that's worse. The escalator going up is three stories high with soaring views of the surrounding tall buildings. And by "soaring," I mean sickening. My stomach feels like I swallowed a wad of chewing gum. A quarter of the way up, I picture myself plummeting from the height, tumbling over and over to the ground, then farther, down to hell. Halfway up, I picture myself jumping. I close my eyes, remembering a news story I saw once about a guy who fell twenty-three stories through what was supposed to be a stable glass floor at a hotel.

About me and heights: I avoid them. Florida is a flat place, so it's not that hard, but there have been moments. My earliest memory of being afraid of heights was being about five years old and going to Tom Sawyer Island at Disney World. Tom Sawyer Island is one of the lamest attractions in the parks. Only little kids go on it. To reach the island, you have to cross this skinny, rickety bridge, supported by barrels floating in the water. I got halfway across, and I couldn't go on. I was sure I was going to die, and I stood in the middle of the swaying bridge, screaming like a girl, while the people bottle-necked behind me yelling in a very un-"Happiest Place on Earth" manner for me to get out of the way. Finally, my dad and a Disney employee dressed as Huck Finn picked me up and carried me off, to the cheers of the assembled guests.

This turned me off to theme parks. Obviously. I tell people it's because I'm not tall enough for the rides, but I actually can go on all the rides at Disney. You only have to be three foot eight to go on Space Mountain. I just don't want to. Other things I avoid include rock-climbing walls, rope courses, skyscrapers, hotels with high balconies, and—oh, yeah—the Metrorail.

"Are you okay?" Kendra has decided to accompany me, at least this far, probably in hopes of talking me out of it. Which she never will. I wanted her to stay with Celine. My mother is at the hospital, but Kendra would be better protection. We rehearsed things for me to say to Violet, but now, they're out of my head.

"You're turning green," she says.

"It's not easy being green," I try to joke. I feel the hospital cafeteria tacos in my throat.

"I didn't realize you were this big a chicken."

"I'm no chicken." But I still don't open my eyes, preferring to stare at the red and black shadows behind them. "I have a problem with heights, but I'm here. I'm in this. I'm brave. Brave—whoot! A chicken would say, 'Oh, well,' and go home."

"Yes, he would." Kendra touches my arm. "You're going to want to open your eyes now and step forward, brave boy. You're at the top. You've arrived."

I open them just as my left foot hits the metal at the top of the escalator. I made it. The first half of my journey seemed to take as long as a drive to Fort Lauderdale with my brothers fighting. The second, with the distraction of my annoyance with Kendra, took seconds. For an instant, the floor swims below me, and I stumble. But Kendra takes my arm and points to the turnstiles. "Wait for Violet inside. No scary heights, and she comes through here most days around 5:10. And be careful."

My watch says 5:07. We cut it close. When I turn to thank Kendra, she is gone. I hurry to buy a ticket. Then, I notice I have one in my hand. It wasn't there before. Thanks, Kendra.

Her "be careful" rings in my head.

I go inside, and wait where Kendra told me. I don't know what I'll say when Violet gets here, but I have to try.

If I feel like the climb was the scary part, that all changes when Violet shows up.

I've only seen the real Violet twice, once for a brief second as she rushed into the hospital, the other time at the funeral. Both times, she was frantic and messed up, miserable about her husband's accident. She still looked inhumanly beautiful.

Now, her beauty is something else.

Kendra spoke of Celine's beauty as being from within, a light of kindness and innocence. Celine and I joked about it, because, who talks like that. But it was true. Celine has the face of an Old Master's *Madonna*.

Violet is a comic book super-villainess. Catwoman? Harley Quinn? Elektra? No, she's Poison Ivy, Batman's nemesis, live and in person in the Metrorail station with long, bright auburn hair and a body you can't help noticing, hugged by a bright blue suit that shows off her curves—and her eyes.

Those eyes. They're blue, almost purple, and huge. And evil. I can see them even through the mobs of commuters. In high-heeled boots, she sticks out above the crowd and way over me. Every guy in the place pivots to stare at her, and more than a few women.

She is the most intimidating person I have ever beheld. I practically expect to see vines sprout from her hands. A girl in front of me smacks her boyfriend, who's staring.

And I have to confront her. Now. Preferably before she goes out to the scary trains.

I pursue her. "Violet!"

She looks around, hearing her name but, at first, not seeing me. I shove through all the legs. Some guy calls me an asshole. It's rude, but this is life-and-death. No time to apologize.

"Violet, wait!"

She turns and stares. She looks at me like I'm a mangy dog or a leper. Maybe I am.

"May I help you?"

"Violet." I'm panting. "I'm Goose, Goose Guzman. I'm—"

"I know who you are. You're my stepdaughter's little friend." She emphasizes *little*. Her eyes bore into me, and I see something like revulsion at my appearance. "You brought her home once, and to the hospital, when Greg . . . but Celine is gone now. She's living with her aunt in . . . Tennessee."

People are stopping to stare, and I realize we must look like characters in some fantasy movie. Their eyes give me courage. Violet can't do anything to me in front of all these witnesses.

Nothing except *not* help Celine.

"You know that's a lie," I say. "You didn't send her to Tennessee. You sent Kendra to kill her. But Kendra didn't. You know that too, because you saw Celine this morning."

Violet looks away. "I don't have to listen to your babbling, dwarf." She turns on her heel and walks toward the glass-brick escalator, the one that will carry her—and me—even higher to the train platform.

"Wait!" I run after her, trying to get in front of her, or grab her hand. But she eludes me, striding through the crowds so I have no choice but to pursue her up a second scary escalator. I want to take the elevator, but I can't risk losing her.

I'm shaking when my foot hits the bottom step. By the top, I can't breathe, much less speak. I stumble after her.

"Why?" I gasp out. Everyone's staring at me, but I don't care. I follow Violet. The train station is laid out with a platform in the middle, north and southbound tracks on either side. She stands on the southbound side, too near the edge, away from the crowds of people.

The train station overlooks the city. How great if it was underground, like the New York subway, where the only drop is onto the tracks themselves. Instead, I can see for miles and miles, practically to my house. I hang back, or try to, but Violet seems to realize my fear for she steps closer to the edge, her beauty silhouetted against the blue and silver skyline, teetering on four-inch heels. I could push her over. It wouldn't help Celine, though.

"Why do you hate her so much?" I'm shivering, though the day is hot and windless, a June day in Miami.

She smiles, then laughs. "Come closer, and I'll tell you." With her hand, she beckons me. Yep, she definitely knows I'm afraid.

I edge closer. When I'm near a high place, I always picture myself plunging, flying at first, then diving down, dropping like a . . . well, dropping like a guy falling off a train platform. Must concentrate. I look into Violet's eyes, but they're almost as scary as the height.

I will myself forward. When I'm five feet away, far enough that, if I fell, I wouldn't go over, I stop. I try again.

"Celine loved you," I say. "When she first met you, she did. She told me how wonderful you were. You got her a kitten. You did her hair, and then . . ."

"And then, she turned into her mother. I hated that bitch." Violet's voice is a knife in the noisy station. "She was cruel and heartless. She never loved Greg. She only took him because I wanted him. You can't imagine how she bullied me. And Celine is the same."

I hear the wind down the tracks. "I think I can imagine being bullied. But Celine isn't like that. She's not a bully. I've seen her stand up for people, not bully them."

"Please. She's exactly like her mother."

"I wouldn't be friends with her if she was like that."

Violet smiles and gets a little gleam in her eye. "Is that what you are, dwarf? Friends? Because that's not what I see."

"What do you see?" But I think I know. And I guess she's just going to keep calling me "dwarf" like she's some evil sorceress.

Which, I guess, she sort of is.

She throws back her head so her orange hair streams down her back. "I see a beautiful girl, using some loser who's in love with her. I see Jennifer all over again."

I shake my head. "She's not like that." But I wonder. Violet is half right. I am in love with Celine. Is she *all* right? Am I just deluding myself about Celine?

No. That's not true. Celine was nice before she knew me, definitely before she needed me. If anything, I was using her, pretending to be her friend in the hope of being something more.

"Believe what you want." Violet takes a step backward. "I've seen the look on your face when you're beside her on the piano bench, holding her hand, trying to edge closer. Or when you watch TV together at all hours of the night. It's the same look I used to have with Greg, sad, longing. Pathetic."

"How did you . . . ?" But I know. Magic. All those things

happened in the past few weeks, after Celine had moved out. Violet had watched us the whole time. She'd known Celine was alive, waited until she could harm her. I take a half step toward her, saying, "What did Celine do to you? What did she do that was so awful that you want her dead?"

Violet thinks for a moment. "She is a constant reminder that her father preferred someone else to me. Even when we were married, he never really loved me. He was enthralled, but his love was all for Jennifer."

"But her father's gone. Either way, he's gone. Couldn't you, in his memory, just be the bigger person? Just let his daughter live?" In the distance, I see the train coming. What if I fell onto the track, if I was swallowed up in it? I feel dizzy, like my head is an escaped balloon, floating in the fluorescent lights above me.

Violet chuckles. "You're really afraid, aren't you?" When I don't answer, she says, "With a blink of my eye, I could send you hurtling over that track, then crash! Down onto the sidewalk. They wouldn't even recognize you."

I feel her words as if she did it. But I say, "Why don't you?" Trying to keep my voice steady, though I hear it shaking.

Violet smiles. "I know that, whatever I can do, Celine can hurt you more, hurt you the way Greg hurt me. That's better, my little friend." The train is pulling into the station now, brakes squealing, covering the treacherous view. "My train is here. I have to go. I'll do you a favor, dwarf. I won't kill your darling."

I feel my knees start to give way, but I catch myself. "Really?" Sensing a trick.

"Really. But I won't revive her either. She will sleep forever. As long as you both shall live, you can fantasize that she might have loved you, if only Evil Violet hadn't taken her away. You can worship her shell of a body, wrap your little tiny arms around her, and dream

284

that she is yours instead of knowing the cruel reality, as I did with Greg."

Her eyes are mesmerizing, like Christmas lights.

"And what reality is that?" I barely whisper it.

"That someone beautiful like her could never love a little freak like you."

Her words snap me out of my trance. I stumble forward, wanting to hurt her. The train screeches to a stop, but I barely notice it, the people, the height. My heart is banging like crazy, and I advance toward her, remembering every kid who ever made fun of me in elementary school, every fear I had about Celine, every doubt I had about myself, sinking that anger into Violet.

"You know, Violet, I may be a freak, but I have a family that loves me, unlike you. I have tons of friends, unlike you." *I'm saying this to a witch?* But I don't care. I can't stop myself. The words just come out, like vomit all over the yellow, rubber barrier that separates the train from the station. "You're a beautiful woman, and it hasn't helped you. Your beauty is nothing, worthless."

I take a shaky breath. I look up at Violet, and she's smiling.

She laughs. "Anything else?"

"Yeah. You're evil, and you've paid the price. You have no one. Greg is gone, and everyone else hates you."

I look up to see if I've hurt her. I want to hurt her. But her face is immobile, unreal.

I add, "So, sometime, you may want to ask yourself which one of us is really the freak."

And, before she can change me into a toad, I turn and walk toward the elevator. When I look back at her, the train doors are just opening. Yet, she is gone.

I'm sweating when the elevator comes. I take it down, then sit in the train station for half an hour, trying not to hyperventilate, wanting my mother. Finally, I summon Kendra with the mirror. She walks with me back to the hospital.

"I'm sorry, but not surprised. If a good talking to was all it took, I would have done it. It is, alas, her nature to be cruel." She touches my shoulder. "I am sorry."

"I'll find another way."

Celine is still in the ICU, beautiful and dead-looking. I think of what Violet said about her being a shell. It's not true. I want to take her into my arms, give some of my own life to her. I could give her ten years, twenty, half the time I have left. I would if I could. Was Violet right? Would I rather Celine be like this forever than face her rejection?

No. I love Celine, and part of loving someone is wanting the best for them, even if the best for them isn't being with you. I'm not Violet. Even if Celine will only ever be my friend, I want her alive.

But how can I make that happen?

I gaze at Celine's pale white face, and I feel the weight of utter hopelessness upon me.

It's Sunday now. Celine is still in the ICU, stable, but no different. The doctor assured Violet/Kendra that Celine has a good chance for recovery. Of course, the doctor doesn't know about the magic.

Friday and Saturday, day and night, I sat in a hard, metal chair by Celine's bed, holding her limp hand, squeezing it, willing her to squeeze back. The nurses didn't even try to kick me out. Kendra said it was okay, and I guess they felt sorry for me. Maybe they realize I can barely move. I feel petrified, not like when people say they're petrified meaning scared, but actually petrified like wood, like parts of me have turned to stone, and if Celine doesn't come out of this, maybe I'll just turn to stone beside her. Of course, I can't help but think of what Violet said about worshiping Celine's shell of a body. How long can I go on, waiting for someone who may never awaken?

Forever.

Violet has been true to her word. She hasn't been here. Still, I won't leave Celine alone.

When I went home to get my clothes Friday afternoon, the poem I left for Celine was still on the bathroom counter, facedown, exactly where I'd left it. She never saw it. And that was when I realized, I wanted her to. Even if I was going to be totally crushed by her reaction. When you love someone, you have to tell her.

I lean close and whisper in her ear, "Please wake up."

But she doesn't. I squeeze her hand. I have my American history exam tomorrow, and I've been reading aloud to her from the book. In between World War One and World War Two, I tell her all the things we can do together if she wakes up. After Korea, I beg her to wake up. Vietnam, the Cold War, "I miss you so much." Now, I've studied all I can, so I just watch her.

Stacey's texted me about a dozen time, telling me I have to sleep at home tonight, long texts about how she understands I'm upset, but I have to finish out the year. Finally, I text back that I'll be home by nine.

It's a little before eight when Kendra shows up. She's disguised as Violet, and I shudder. As soon as she closes the curtain, she changes into herself, red hair melting to purple-streaked black, her clothing turning to a long, black dress.

She looks excited. "I've figured out what will help Celine."

"Really?" I clutch Celine's hand, hopeful.

Until the next words out of Kendra's mouth.

"Yes. A handsome prince! I remember once, there was a girl who slept for over a hundred years. It was a curse like this one, except a fairy placed it. The girl pricked her finger on a spindle and fell down as if dead. A century passed—they didn't even have feeding tubes then—and everyone forgot her until, one day, a prince came riding

288

by on his horse. He kissed the girl. She woke and they lived happily ever after."

I try to keep my voice even. "So what year was this?"

Kendra thinks about it. "The kiss happened in 1675, but the princess went to sleep a century before."

"And this was in Europe? England?" I feel suddenly tired, like I could just put my head down on Celine's bed and go to sleep.

"Or Germany, maybe. One of those countries."

"One of those countries with princes riding around on horses?"

"Yeah." She finally gets my meaning. "Oh."

"This is America, Kendra. No princes here."

"There could be. It probably doesn't have to be from a reigning family. One of the Romanovs was mayor of Palm Beach for a while— the great-grandson of the tsar of Russia."

Palm Beach is about two hours' drive from here. "Do you know him?" I ask.

"He died in 2004."

Not helpful. I shake my head. "Could there be another way?" But, even as I say it, I remember her saying the other princess slept for a hundred years. A hundred years before they found a way to wake her. Celine might live a hundred years in a state of suspended animation.

But I won't.

I take a long look at Celine, the shell of Celine. Is this all I'll have of her, ever? I want to shake her, slap her, do anything to wake her, but it won't work. No, that's not what I want. I want to take her in my arms and kiss her. But I'm no prince, just some poor slob who loves her. She's not mine to kiss.

Suddenly I have to go. I can't look at her anymore today.

"You'll stay?" I ask Kendra.

Kendra smiles sadly. "Don't worry. I won't leave her."

I turn toward the door.

"You know, Goose, the prince was also her true love."

I shrug. No help there.

When I get home, I can't sleep. Even though I've already spent the whole day studying, I lie in bed, reading the flash cards I made, because it gets my mind off Celine. After a while, I guess I drift off.

At three, I wake up. The lights are on. There are three-by-five cards all around me and only one thought in my head.

Jonah Prince.

5

"He is, technically, a prince," I tell Kendra. "And Celine's not-so-technically completely hot for him, so maybe he's her true love. There's no royalty in Florida, unless you count Disney World. I know it's a crazy idea. . . ."

"No," Kendra says. "It might work."

"Really?" I'm impressed with myself. We're in Celine's hospital room, where Kendra guards her motionless body. I try not to look at Celine. It makes me sad that she looks like a beautiful doll that should be displayed in a plastic bubble.

"Sure," Kendra says. "I've seen people get off on technicalities before. But how are you going to get Jonah Prince here? Isn't he, like, a rock star?"

"I figure that's where you come in. You could use your magic powers to just . . . zap him here so he can kiss her."

Kendra rubs her forehead, the way my mom does to smooth out wrinkles, except Kendra doesn't have any wrinkles. "I can't do that with people. Even if I could, I wouldn't."

"Why the hell not? What kind of lame powers do you have?"

Kendra huffs a bit at that. "What if Jonah Prince was onstage, or just sitting down for dinner with his family, and he suddenly disappeared. People would freak. It would be in all the papers . . . and everyone would know that witches are real."

"And that would be bad?"

Kendra nods. "You've heard of Salem, witch burnings in Europe?"

"That was a long time ago."

"Women are being burned as witches in New Guinea to this day. I can't take the chance. And it isn't the right way. He must come of his own free will."

"Wow." I reach over and run my hand across Celine's. It feels cold, but I warm it. "Okay, but you can still help me, right? If I get him to come?"

Kendra nods. "I can help you."

Under my hand, I can feel Celine's pulse. Touching her makes me feel better, knowing she's still alive, warm, real. I turn toward her. In the elevated bed, her face is close to mine, so close I could kiss her, close enough to hear her breathing.

Instead, I lean my head against her shoulder and close my eyes.

I remember something, the argument Celine and I had about Jonah. I raise my head.

"There's a concert coming up. He's going to be in Florida."

An hour later, between Kendra's mirror and my phone, I know everything I need to know about that concert. It's next Tuesday night in Orlando. I can't tell where he's staying, but Kendra promises to spy on him with her mirror and let me know as soon as he checks in.

Kendra is pacing back and forth in Celine's room. "Okay! So all you have to do is go to Orlando, locate Jonah Prince, and ask him to come back here and kiss Celine." She counts these things off on her fingers like they're done. "Easy-peasy!"

I can't believe she just said *easy-peasy*. I mean, aside from how annoying that phrase is, it won't be. "You get that he'll have tons of bodyguards, right? Big bodyguards, possibly with guns."

"I have confidence in your ability."

Glad one of us does.

"And you get that he's a serious asshole?" I say. My research about Jonah also revealed an uncomfortable number of accounts of him urinating in public, sideswiping bicyclists with his Maserati, spitting on people, wearing diaper pants to meet the president—the list of douchery goes on and on. What did Celine see in this guy? "He's not necessarily going to be helpful."

She shrugs. "If you don't want to do it, I'm sure I can keep Celine comfortable here."

"It's not that I don't want to." I look at Celine, noticing for the hundredth time the two little freckles on one side of her nose. I have always been a person who pushed myself, someone who tried to ignore limits and strived not to give in if someone said I couldn't do something, whether it was playing the piano or climbing the jungle gym or being the Artful Dodger. But this sounds . . . really hard. And if it does work, I'll lose her to Jonah.

And yet, if I don't do it, Celine could die. Who's to say Violet—the real Violet—won't sneak in and put some real-world poison in Celine's feeding tube. At best, she might live in a vegetative state. I have to try, at least.

"No," I say. "I will do anything for Celine. And that means overcoming any obstacle."

* * *

The main obstacle turns out to be my mommy.

"No. Are you crazy?" She's tenderizing meat with a mallet. With it in hand, she is four feet of scary. "Of course you can't do that." *Whap!* "You can't drive to Orlando on your own." *Whap!* "You can't sneak into a rock star's hotel room." *Whap!* "What if you were arrested?" *Whap! Whap! Whap!* "You'd never get into college." *Whap!* "You could get shot." *Whap!* "I won't let you put yourself at risk in that way. Let Kendra do it."

Funny how you never get over fearing the wrath of Mom.

I tell her, "Kendra needs to stay here with Celine. What if Violet comes back?"

Another series of *whaps!* I jump at each one. She keeps pounding as she says, "What if Violet does come back? What if she comes after you? Or our family? No!" *Whap! Whap! Whap!*

"But I love her!"

It's the first time I've said it to anyone. I've only just started admitting it to myself.

I feel naked.

At least Stacey stops pounding.

"I love her," I repeat.

Stacey sucks in a deep breath. "I know you do. We love her too. And we've done a lot for her. She's a sweet girl. But, don't you see? We have to think of you first." Stacey puts down the mallet and holds out her arms like she's about to hug me. But, when she walks toward me, I dodge her.

"If she dies, I will never forgive you."

I turn and leave. There is silence. Then, the pounding starts again, louder.

In the dwindling days of classes, I contact Jonah Prince's agent, publicist, producer, the Florida Citrus Bowl, where the concert is being held, and the local news, all with the same sad story. My friend is dying. Maybe a visit from Jonah Prince will help. No one bites. The guy's a total douche, and everyone who works for him knows it.

I give Stacey begging looks every time I pass her. When that doesn't work, I stop looking at her completely.

On Sunday morning, two days before the concert, I make the decision I always knew I'd make.

I'm going to Orlando with or without my parents' permission. Stacey hid my car keys. I hate her for that. Hate. But I will find another way.

I have never wanted anything the way I want this.

How can my parents not understand that it's like my heart is trapped inside her?

6

A few years ago, I heard about the show *Game of Thrones*, starring Peter Dinklage, a guy about my size (and my personal hero), as Tyrion Lannister, the sometimes heroic, sometimes not, son of a lord. I begged my mom to let me watch it. She protested that the show was TV-MA, with tons of nudity and violence in it. She suggested *Little People, Big World* as a substitute.

Because what any normal, red-blooded teenage guy really wants to see is a show about a bunch of little people, operating a wedding farm.

But I gave it a shot. Also, I read the book, *A Game of Thrones*, which is over eight hundred pages long. Then, I started on *A Clash of Kings*. And I begged my mom again. I pointed out that, if I wanted to see boobs, I could find them on my phone, just by Googling *boobs*. It wasn't about boobs.

It was *mostly* not about boobs.

That time, she let me. She'd watched the show herself by then, and she said okay—if I promised not to be influenced by the characters' drinking and whoring. I swore I wouldn't hire any prostitutes without asking her first.

Then, I marathon-watched the whole series in a single weekend.

Best. Show. Ever. For a lot of reasons. But, especially because of Dinklage. That's not just my opinion. If you look at any poll about people's favorite characters, Tyrion is the hands-down winner, besting even the hot blond dragon chick who gets naked a lot (okay, I like her too). Whether that's because people love to champion the underdog or because of the character's quick wit, I don't know.

But I sort of lied to Stacey. Tyrion's character had a huge influence on me. Here was a guy who looked like me (only old), using military tactics, wearing armor, and marching into battle with an ax. A hero . . . even if he usually got injured. And the legions of *GoT* fans found that believable. It made me see that a hero had nothing to do with size, made me want to be a hero too, realize I could be.

But how many battles do you get to fight in the twenty-first century? How many fair maidens are there to rescue from the cruel king?

Celine is my true love, even if I'll never be hers.

It's time to be a hero. And a hero must have a quest.

I have one.

And I'm starting on the freaking Metrorail.

The train to Orlando leaves at 8:10 a.m. I've never taken a real train, the kind that goes to other cities, instead of the lame commuter trains. The pictures on the Amtrak website make their trains look like the ones that go to Hogwarts.

And the best thing is, they stay firmly on the ground.

The worst thing? I have to take the Metrorail to get to the Amtrak train.

Have I mentioned I hate the Metrorail?

Oh, and lying to my parents. That's another bad thing. But I'm so pissed at them, so pissed that they won't let me go, that I don't care that much.

When I was a kid, I was a really bad liar. My mom said she trusted me completely because I was so bad at covering my tracks. Like once, when I was eleven, I took the leftover Fourth of July fireworks from the garage (in November). I was going to set them off with my friends, but I left such a trail of matchbooks and wrappers that I got caught red-handed before the first crackle. Dad said he was concerned that I lacked the logic skills to be a more proficient liar (yeah, he talks like that; he's a lawyer). Since then, I've improved a little, but I still don't lie much. It sounds nerdy to say, but I'm close to my parents, or I was. When I lie, it weighs on me. Besides, everything always comes out.

This definitely will. Sneaking out and training it to Orlando to stalk a rock star—hard to hide. It might even make the paper, and not in that good way parents like, like when you earn your Eagle Scout or sing at a charity concert or have perfect attendance for thirteen straight years. No, this would be more like the stories you see on the "Florida Man" Twitter feed, the guy who collects all the stupidest, craziest things done by folks in the Sunshine State: There was "Florida Man tries to remove face tattoos with welding grinder," and "Florida Man caught with sushi sampler stuffed down pants," not to mention the classic, "High school graduation canceled after Florida Man etches massive penis on football field." I can be, "Florida Man arrested in former boy band star's dressing room." The humiliation. It has never been my ambition to be a Florida Man.

But it's worth it if I can save Celine.

That's what I try to remember when I go to my dad—to *lie* to my dad—before he leaves for work.

"Hey, can you drive me to the train station? I want to go to Jackson to see Celine."

He looks at his watch. "It's awfully early."

It is. It's 6:30. Dad usually leaves at 6:45. I'm counting on that to be able to make the 8:10 train.

I say, "I got up early so I could get a ride. So I don't have to bother Mom since she took away my car keys." I swallow. Angrily.

He shifts from foot to foot. "You have to understand—"

"I will *never* understand. Never." He frowns, but doesn't say anything. I add, "Look, all I want is a ride to the train. It's on your way. But if you can't help me with this one little thing, I guess I'll figure out the bus."

I can't. I would never make it on time if I took the bus. But I try to sound casual anyway.

He shakes his head. "It's okay. I can take you. Be ready in ten minutes."

I don't take much with me. I don't want to arouse suspicion. With any luck, I'll be talking to Jonah before people notice I'm gone.

I put Kendra's mirror, a book, and my sweatshirt in my backpack from school, enough to look normal, not enough to look like I'm running away. I take all the money I saved from my jobs tutoring kids on their monologues for drama auditions, close to five hundred dollars. I cashed out my bank account.

I turn off my phone and leave it on my desk. If anyone tries to use it to find me, they'll get nowhere.

I wish I didn't have to lie. But nothing else worked.

At 6:42, I'm in the car with Dad.

"How's she doing?" He's trying to make conversation.

"No difference."

"She could still recover," he says.

I know he doesn't believe it. Still, I say, "I know."

We drive in silence. The streets are pretty empty without people going to school. Even the joggers and dog walkers slept late. It's cloudy, and I hope I can get to Amtrak before it starts to pour.

We reach the Metrorail's "kiss-and-ride" lot. There's a huge escalator leading up, just like at the downtown station I went to with Kendra. Dad eyes it dubiously. "You're going up that? I remember Tom Sawyer Island."

Yeah, thanks for reminding me. But I say, "I love her. If the only way I can see her is this train, I'll do it. I don't give in to fear like some people."

He starts to say something, then stops. I hope he's not going to offer to drive me to Jackson, but he just gives me sort of a pitying look and rubs his forehead with two fingers. "Let me know if you need a ride home."

"Thanks." I get out of the car.

I'd asked Kendra if she could transport me magically to Orlando, but again, she'd been unhelpful. "The only thing I could do is turn you into a crow to fly there."

I declined, but now, as I head upstairs once again, I wonder if it would have been easier. A bird is in control of itself, its wings, its destiny. As it is, I'm at the mercy of stairs and tracks I didn't build, putting myself at risk.

But, as I told my father, I can't give in to those fears.

So, as the escalator bears me up, instead of closing my eyes, I concentrate on the sky.

"Where's your mom?" the lady at the Amtrak ticket counter asks me.

"My dad dropped me off. I'm seventeen."

It's one of those high counters I can barely see over. The woman stares down at me. "I can't sell you a ticket without your parents."

"Actually, you can. I . . . I mean, my parents and I looked this all up on your website. Minors who are sixteen or seventeen can travel without restriction." I look at my watch. Seven forty-five. The train leaves soon. "I'm seventeen. Look, here's my driver's license. I'm visiting my grandma in Orlando. If I don't get off that train, she'll worry about me."

I've experienced this before, the disconnect between my size and my age. Adults don't like to sell tickets to an R-rated movie to someone who's as tall as their eleven-year-old. I don't mind getting in places cheap, but they'll be handing me kids' menus when I'm fifty. Maybe I'll grow a mustache.

"I'll have to get my supervisor."

"No. You don't." I'm trying hard not to lose it because yelling will make me seem younger. I tap my driver's license on the counter, which is above my head. "What you need to do is look at my license and check my age. Then, sell me a ticket so I can go see my grandma. Please."

She doesn't answer.

I say, "Please. She's an old lady, and she misses me. The train leaves in twenty minutes, and the next one isn't until twelve."

Finally, the woman relents and takes the license from me. She compares my face to the photo, checks the birth date, counts on her fingers. "Oh, you are seventeen. I'm sorry. You look much younger."

"What can I say? I have a great moisturizer."

"I could use some of that."

Huh. She doesn't get that I'm kidding. How cute. Just print the ticket.

"Okay, will that be one way or round trip?"

"One way." Part of me says I should buy round trip to avoid this problem when I come back, but I'm really hoping to come back in Jonah's private jet. Why be pessimistic? "I may stay the whole summer."

I get to my seat right before the door closes. There's a bunch of Boy Scouts in the same car, probably going to Disney. They're running around like someone gave them too much sugar. In fact, someone did give them too much sugar. There's a box of donuts open on one seat and a mom is offering around another. Wish I could take one. I forgot breakfast.

"Would you like a donut?"

"Uh . . ." I look around, realizing the Boy Scouts are all wearing matching navy blue T-shirts and matching baseball caps. I'm wearing a navy blue polo. I could make this work.

"Yes, please." I take a jelly, not looking up. I know from my siblings that little kids hate jelly. It would've been left anyway.

"Aren't you polite!" The lady musses my hair.

As soon as she walks away, I scarf down the donut and head for the bathroom. I take out Kendra's mirror. "Show me Kendra."

She appears. I can tell she's at the hospital. "How's Celine?"

"The same."

I want to ask to see her, but first I say, "Any updates on where Jonah's staying?"

"He's still on the plane. You could keep an eye on him in the mirror too."

"I will. Can I see Celine first?"

"It won't make you happy." But Kendra turns the mirror away anyway. She's wrong. Just seeing Celine's peaceful face, knowing I'm helping her, at least trying to, helps. Maybe it won't work. In that case, I'll have plenty of time to be miserable. But, for now, I'm hopeful.

"Thanks," I tell Kendra.

Before I leave the bathroom, I ask the mirror, "Show me Jonah Prince."

It does, as if it's a television. Dude's in an airplane seat, first class. No—a private jet. He takes his gum out of his mouth and sticks it underneath the shiny walnut trim on the wall beside him. Gross. Even though he can't hear me, I say, "Please, guy, please be everything she thinks you are, everything she wants you to be. It's crazy, but you're her only hope."

I take my seat, which is next to one of the moms from the scout troop.

"I think you have the wrong seat," she says. "Where's your mom?"

I look up at her. "Back in Miami."

"Oh." She starts a bit. "Sorry. I thought you were from my troop. I had an empty seat next to me." There's an edge to her voice.

"I bought my ticket at the last minute. I'll be quiet, though, at least quieter than this group."

"You'd kind of have to be." She eyes a group of boys who are playing soccer with a squashed Bavarian cream donut.

"Where are you headed?"

"Happiest place on earth. I need a drink."

It's eight-thirty in the morning.

"Kidding." She must see my rising eyebrows.

I can tell she wasn't. "Sure. Where are you staying? I mean . . ." I realize this sounds stalkerish. "Are you camping? Because you'd really need a drink then."

"No, thank God. We're staying at the All-Star."

The All-Stars are the cheaper Disney hotels, which are still pretty expensive, but nowhere Jonah would stay.

I nod. "So you have a bus picking you up?" I'm forming a plan in my head.

"I certainly hope so." The donut sails past us at eye level. "Guess I should do something about that, huh?"

My mom wouldn't put up with that crap for one second, but I say, "They'll get tired soon."

"They never get tired."

Finally, one of the other moms takes the boys to the lounge car. The mom by me follows her, probably to get that drink. I take out the mirror and set it up between me and the window.

"Show me Jonah Prince."

They're off the airplane now. Jonah's surrounded by people, bodyguards, an older, balding guy I think is his agent, and a girl I recognize from TV, Allegra Kendall. She used to be on this show Isabella likes, *What a Girl Needs*, and she looks, basically, like every other teen star, the Demi Lovato model, with long, dark, wavy hair, brown eyes, and a ton of lipstick. She teeters on high-heeled boots and waves at a group of people inside the terminal as they walk across the tarmac.

"Can you be a little polite?" she says to Jonah. "Like, look up at them."

"I'm dead tired," he says.

"It's that pill you took on the plane. Live in the now, Jonah. They're your fans." She says it through her teeth, still smiling and waving.

"I have a concert tonight. I shouldn't get stressed out." He tugs at his pants, which are so low in the crotch he looks like he shit his pants. "You don't know what it's like to have all these people demanding things of you."

"I don't know?" She blinks at him and puts her hand on her hip. "Of course I know. But it's really important to them. They camped out waiting for you. Can't you at least look up?"

He rolls his eyes and looks up. Through the windows, I can see girls jumping up and down and screaming. Allegra gives him a kiss on the cheek.

"Quit it," he whispers. He tugs at his pants again. I remember reading about this rock star who actually lost his pants onstage because they were so loose.

"Don't be such a grump." Allegra tries to smile as they walk inside the airport. Fans scream.

Jonah puts on a big, fake grin. "I'm not being a grump. You're being annoying."

This conversation is painful. I'm just listening because I'm waiting for Jonah or someone to say the name of their hotel. I know his concert's at seven, and then, he'll go back to the hotel. I just need to sneak into his room before then and beg him to go with me.

Just.

Just need to sneak into a rock star's room.

Just need to get this jerkwad with pants down to his knees to do something out of the goodness of his heart.

They're in the airport now. Girls are thronging to meet Jonah. His bodyguards and the airport police are trying to hold them back. I wonder if they purchased tickets just to get through security, or if this many random fans are just wherever he is. Allegra is trying to interact with them, but most want nothing of her, only him. And he's ignoring them, talking to the balding guy, one hand firmly on his pants.

Please just say where you're staying before Drunk Mom comes back and I have to put away the mirror.

"Will the hotel be like this too, Harry? 'Cause I'm planning on breaking up with . . ." He nudges his head toward Allegra, who is hugging a little girl. ". . . so it would be nice to have some privacy in case she screams her head off."

The guy—Harry—shrugs. "I don't think there are any leaks, but these girls tend to find out."

"They'd better not," Jonah says. "Get extra security."

"I'll alert the Cornwallis."

Bingo. The Cornwallis is a fancy non-Disney hotel on Disney property.

"The Cornwallis?" Jonah shoves past the fans. "Nice British name. Will it be private?"

"We have a floor all to ourselves, you, Allegra, your staff."

What floor? What floor?

"What floor?" Jonah asks.

"The top floor," Harry says. "The floor below is a health club. People make all sorts of noise. She can scream as much as she likes."

"Good. I need to be rid of her. The stress is affecting my voice."

"Wouldn't want that," Harry says just as a fan breaks through and touches Jonah. His bodyguard pushes her away.

A few of the kids who didn't go to the lounge run past me. A blond boy is holding a handheld game, and a redhead tries to get it back. Just as they get to me, the redhead tackles the blond, barreling into my legs and almost knocking the mirror from my hands.

"Hey, watch it," I say.

"Sorry." The redhead stares at me. "Hey, how old are you?"

"Seventeen?" I say. "You?"

He ignores my question. "So you're, like . . . ?"

"A smaller-sized adult? Yes."

"Cool. I thought maybe you were from one of the other troops."

"How many troops are there?"

"Three, I think."

"Come on," the blond kid says.

"Okay." And they run off.

I notice a blue baseball cap lying under my feet. I pick it up and start to call after the redhead who lost it. But they're gone.

I have an idea.

It's one when the train pulls into the Orlando station ahead of schedule. Thirty little boys in thirty blue T-shirts and twenty-nine blue hats are herded as neatly as you'd expect out of the car. I follow them to their bus and put on the thirtieth hat. I make sure to move around, not stand by anyone in particular. I pull the hat low. I'm guessing no mom here knows all thirty kids.

"Hey, you!" One of the moms grabs my shoulder.

I freeze.

"Stay with the group." She pushes me forward into the line.

I follow the others onto the bus and sit in back. I keep my head down.

It's not a short ride, but I know if I make it, I'll be on Disney property. I can use their transportation to get to the Cornwallis.

Of course, getting to Jonah himself will be another story.

When we reach the All-Star Sports Resort, I find the red-haired kid and hand him his hat. "Hey, you dropped this."

Then, I run in the opposite direction.

7

An hour later, through a maze of transportation, I have gone from the All-Star to the Magic Kingdom, the Magic Kingdom to the Cornwallis Hotel's own shuttle. I let myself close my eyes on this one. I picture Celine, the way she looked that day we went to Target, smiling at me. I want her to smile again, even if it's not at me.

"That boy fell asleep," the kid next to me says.

"He must have had a fun day," his mother replies.

And it's not over. I open my eyes, and we're pulling into the Cornwallis Hotel. Parking attendants dressed like Cinderella's footmen, with powdered wigs and purple hats with giant plumes greet the shuttle. I step out, and they bow with a flourish.

I glance at my watch. Two-thirty.

So far this was easy, too easy.

I'm sure it will get harder.

I take the elevator to the twentieth floor. There's no lock, no restriction. But when I get off, a guy who looks like an extra on *Game of Thrones*—two feet taller than I am with a scar on his cheek that looks like it was made by a sword—comes at me.

"What are you doing here?" he growls.

"Just heading for my room. Twenty-fifteen." That's Harry's room. I heard them discussing it one of the ten times I checked the mirror while on the bus.

"Wrong!" the guy growls. "No one on this floor but Jonah Prince's people."

"I know. I'm with him. Harry, his manager's my dad." I start forward. One good thing about being my size. You can get away with stuff because you look nonthreatening.

"Hey, Otto," the guy holding me says. "You remember Harry having a kid who looks like this?"

He grabs my waistband and drags me over to another, even bigger guy. The disrespect is mind-boggling. He lifts me up. I almost have a clear shot at kicking the guy in the nose, but I'm thinking that might not be a wise choice. Instead, I yell, "Put me down!"

"Pretty sure I'd remember him," the bruiser says.

Of course, the bad thing about being my size is, I'm also very memorable. I had one shot to walk off the elevator, and I blew it.

The guy turns around and shoves me into the elevator. "Bye-bye, little guy."

Sighing, I press the button to go down to the eighteenth floor.

Time for another plan. Or a plan at all. Since I didn't know which hotel he'd be at, I hadn't been able to research the layout or anything. I'd thought maybe luck would be on my side. Like I could go up with a housekeeper. But even the minute I spent on Jonah's floor let me know there was no housekeeper there. They probably cleaned his floor first, so he could check in early.

The housekeeper on this floor is still working. A door stands open. I hear vacuuming. I wonder if I can talk her into sneaking me upstairs. Doubtful. I try the stairs, but the door to the twentieth floor is locked, so I come back down. The hallway is empty.

I pull out the mirror.

"Show me Jonah," I say.

The mirror does. He's in a fancy room, talking on his phone, alone.

"I'm seventeen, and I have a hundred million dollars. I don't need you telling me what to do." He holds the phone away from his ear to avoid what I'm sure are her shrieks. "Yes, I suppose I do want to break up. After tonight. Let's just get this tour over with. You're still coming to the concert, right? What? What?"

He paces back and forth, tugging at his pants even though no one's there to see him. "Is that a threat?" He nods. "All right, then. Call my mum. She's in New York, and she won't care, but go ahead and call her. Oh, stop crying. You know you never really liked me. It was all a publicity stunt. What?" Again, he pulls the phone away. "Just come to the concert tonight. We leave at six-thirty."

He hangs up. Then, he walks to the window and stares out, shaking his head. "Call a guy's mum, why don't you?" He must notice a crowd outside because he backs away and flops down onto the bed.

"Show me Allegra," I tell the mirror.

It does, switching to a similar-looking room. Allegra is collapsed on the bed, phone in hand, crying, saying, "He broke up with me. He's so out of control! He's not the guy I used to know. I had to stop him from giving these little girls the finger." She stops talking and sobs. "I know. You're right. Thanks."

She puts down the phone and sobs some more. I feel bad,

watching something so private. Still, I don't know what else to do. Also, I feel like I know this girl, having watched a gazillion hours of *What a Girl Needs* with Isabella.

"You're better off without him, sweetheart," I say aloud but, of course, she doesn't hear me. A minute later, she sits up and looks at the phone on her nightstand. She crawls across the bed and looks at it, reading the instructions, then picks it up and dials.

"Hey." She sniffles. "How do I get room service?"

A few seconds later, she says, "Hello, this is, um, Mrs. Kendall, room 2016. Can you send up, um, a bottle of wine . . . white wine . . . what *kind*? Um, I don't know. Whatever you recommend. Oh, and a hot fudge sundae."

This gives me an idea. I tell the mirror, "Show me the room service person she's talking to."

As the mirror melds into the person she's talking to, I start toward the elevator.

"Yes." It's a girl with dyed-black hair and a white apron over black shirt and pants. She rolls her eyes. "I understand it's an emergency. I'll send up the 2008 Didier Dagueneau Silex right away . . . and the sundae . . . my name. It's Kasey. With a K. Yes, I understand. It will be there in twenty minutes."

Twenty minutes. I have twenty minutes to work if I'm going to be part of Allegra's room service order.

"Isn't that a cliché," Kasey says when she gets off the phone. "Little teenybopper star wants to get drunk. And stupid room service is going to buy that it's her 'mother' calling."

The second the elevator hits the ground floor, I'm off and running toward the restaurant. I figure the kitchen's probably behind there. It's a dead time of day, after lunch, but way before dinner. When I stroll in, there's only one woman manning the maître d' station. "May I help you?"

"I'm looking for my sister. She works here. Kasey? The kitchen's through there?"

She nods and goes back to the game she was playing on her phone.

I keep my back against the wall as I enter the kitchen. The room has an island with high, stainless steel counters. I hide under one near a wheeled room service trolley that is already topped with a bottle of white wine. Kasey's standing by it. A tall red-haired girl is bringing over wineglasses. "How many?"

"Just one, I suppose." Kasey makes a tsk-ing sound with her tongue. "Poor little Allegra, drinking alone."

"And ice cream," says the second girl. "She got dumped for sure."

I peek over the counter. Kasey snaps a photo of the wine bottle. "Got dumped, and now, she'll get drunk." She takes a business card from her apron pocket. "This guy, he's a paparazzi . . . paparazzo . . . photographer; he told me to call with any tips. Said he'd make it worth my while. He'll love hearing about Allegra getting faced."

I feel a twinge for this girl I don't know. Well, like I said, Isabella loves her. I notice the trolley's about the width of the TV in my parents' bedroom, with a tablecloth over it. I could fit under it if I could get there. Then, if they pushed me up to Allegra's room, I'd at least be on Jonah's floor. Maybe they even have adjoining rooms. But right now, both girls are standing by the trolley. If only one would move.

"That's really mean," the tall one says. "Kick her when she's down."

"You have such a soft heart, Caitlin. How 'down' can she be, spoiled little starlet."

"My kid sister loves her. She'll be so disappointed. Why do they always turn out to be crazy, drunks, or sluts?"

Kasey shrugs. "Not my fault. Hey, make that sundae. Her majesty said she needed it quick."

Caitlin moves away. Kasey takes out her phone, starts to call someone. I make my move, sliding under the counter, which requires some knee bending, even for me. I get into the trolley, which requires more. It's tight. I'm short, but I have shoulders, and I'm not a contortionist who can dislocate them. At one point, the trolley starts to move. I hear the wineglass rattle against the cooler. Kasey doesn't notice. She's too busy talking.

". . . leaving in a couple hours. She should be stumbling drunk by then."

Finally, I stuff myself in, sitting on my feet, shoulders gathered around my ears. My left side aches bad, and I wonder if I dislocated my shoulder after all. In any case, I can't move except to give the tablecloth a tug. I hope Caitlin will hurry.

"There we go." I feel the thunk of a huge sundae above my head. "With extra whipped cream. I'm sort of excited to see her. Wonder if she'd let me take a picture."

"They'll kill you if you ask. Have some dignity."

Caitlin pushes the trolley. It barely budges. "Wow, I need to start working out." She gives it a big shove, and we're on our way.

She drives me through the kitchen, where Caitlin manages to ram into every possible counter, and into the dining room, which is carpeted, so the thing will barely roll with my weight on it. Each bump and thump makes my shoulder ache worse, and I grit my teeth to keep from crying out. Finally, finally, we hit a marble floor.

It's smooth skating for about twenty feet. Then, we reach the elevator, which is another death struggle as we get over the gap.

And off to the top floor. So I have a solid minute to sit and think about how much my shoulder hurts, how both feet are already asleep, how I'd love to clear my throat, scratch my head, burp, fart, or all four.

I try to remember that tomorrow, this will all be over. I'll have succeeded or failed, but hopefully succeeded.

And, if I succeed, Jonah will wake Celine. Jonah Prince is as close to a prince as we have, and she loves him.

So they can fall in love, and she can live happily ever after.

With that asshole.

I really need to scratch my nose. Why am I doing this again? Oh, yeah. Love. True love. Unselfish love.

And a fascinating topic for college essays about an obstacle I've overcome.

If I don't get arrested and can still apply to college.

Finally, finally, the elevator reaches the top floor.

I breathe out, though I have no idea why I'm relieved. It's not like I can get out and walk around now. Rather, I'm going to have to wait until Allegra passes out or leaves or, at least gets drunk enough not to notice a guy walking around her room. Depending on her drinking habits, that could take awhile.

I could come out of this experience a hunchback. Another good college essay topic.

I really want to crack my neck.

Caitlin wheels the trolley down the hall. I hear her explaining to the bodyguards who she is. They let her through. Finally, she knocks on the door.

"Room service!"

The door opens. "Thank God you're here." Allegra's voice.

Silence.

"Well, aren't you going to bring it in?" Allegra asks.

"Oh! Sorry." Caitlin pushes against the trolley. "I was just sort of . . ."

"Slow?" Allegra says.

"Awestruck. My little sister watches your show all the time. She won't believe I met you."

Allegra seems to gather herself. "I'm sorry. That's great! Can you bring the tray in now?"

"Oh!" Caitlin gives the trolley a shove, and I have to grip the bottom to keep from falling out. "Of course. I'm sorry."

"It's okay. Maybe set it by the bed."

By the bed. That's good because maybe I could sneak out and get under the bed.

In an hour or so.

Caitlin pushes the trolley across the marble floor for a long time, turning to get through a door or something. Finally, it crashes into the bed.

"Really, I'm sorry," Allegra says. "That's sweet that your little sister likes the show so much. Would you like a picture so she'll believe you met me?"

"Omigod! Omigod! Omigod! Really? That would be so awesome. I can get a selfie of us together. Thank you sooo much!"

"No problem." Allegra sounds happier. "It's great to meet a fan."

"You have so many fans," Caitlin gushes.

"Obviously not enough for Jonah," Allegra mutters.

"What?"

"Oh, nothing," Allegra says. "Do you have a phone with you? Okay."

I wish Caitlin would leave so there'd be one less person to notice if I tumble out of this thing. My legs ache, and so does my stomach. I had a burger on the train. Obviously, a mistake. What if I . . . experience gastric distress? Just thinking about it makes my stomach hurt worse. Actually, there's no part of my body that doesn't ache. My arms, shoulders, even my head are pulsing, pulsing, pulsing.

I think of Celine, comatose, feeling nothing. I have to hold it together.

Last night, I printed out some photos of Celine, the one I took at Target, one from the house, and one of her in the hospital. I did it since I wouldn't have my phone, so I could prove her existence to Jonah. They're still in my backpack, flattened against my back. I wish I could look at them, see her face. Maybe it would inspire me. I close my eyes and visualize her. I don't need the photo. Her blue eyes stare into my soul, and I see every detail, every eyelash, every freckle, every blush. Every time she smiled at me.

It works. I relax and can sit there on my sleeping foot while Caitlin snaps a dozen selfies and Allegra coos about Caitlin's sister, asking how old she is and if she wants an autographed eight by ten. It takes at least ten minutes before Caitlin says, "Omigod! Your ice cream's melting! I'm sooo sorry. Should I bring you a new one?"

"That's okay." Allegra's feeling better, it seems. "But I guess I should eat it now."

"Of course. Sorry. Thank you. I'll get going. You're the best!" She stumbles toward the door, and Allegra is left alone.

Almost alone.

I hear her taking the cover off her ice cream, then clinking the spoon. The trolley shakes as she digs into her sundae. Then, she bursts into tears.

"I hate you!" she screams. "I hate you, Jonah Prince! I hate you!"

With my unique view of the floor, I see her remove first one strappy sandal, then the other. I hear her hurl them against the wall.

I try not to move, to be very Zen-like, meditative, enlightened, planning my course of action. I'm in Allegra's room. After Allegra either leaves or passes out, I'll take out the mirror and contact Kendra. Hopefully, she'll have figured out the relation between Allegra's room and Jonah's. Hopefully. Hopefully, they're adjoining with a connecting door. If so, I can simply walk into Jonah's room and talk to him when he gets back.

And hopefully, he won't be a complete douche.

My neck hurts so much. So much. I try to adjust it.

And tumble to the floor.

For a second, time stops. I lie there, dazed, thinking—I don't know—thinking maybe if I don't move at all, Allegra won't notice a guy lying on her floor.

But no, I can see her eyes. She knows I'm here.

And she's winding up for a good scream.

"No, please!" I stumble to my feet. "Please don't be scared!"

It's hard to stand with both feet asleep, and for a second, I think I'll fall. Allegra gapes at me, mouth open but no words coming from it.

I say, "I am your *biggest* fan. I just had to see you in person. I'd never hurt you." I stare at her like I'm starstruck. "Wow, you're so beautiful!"

She really is. I see her decide not to scream. She closes her mouth, then opens it right back up again.

"You're . . . little."

You're . . . observant.

But I say, "Yeah."

"Sorry. My brother's about your size, my older brother. He's away at college."

Somewhere in the far recesses of my mind, I think I knew this, the way you just know things about famous people without actually knowing where you know it from. Probably Isabella. Kid is a storehouse of completely worthless information.

Or maybe not that worthless.

I say, "Do you miss him?"

And her face sort of breaks. She starts to cry, dark hair falling over her face. "I miss him so much. Caleb's his name. He goes to school in Louisiana, and he's always saying I should just . . . chuck this and come home. I miss him and my mom and dad. I miss everyone. I want to go home!"

On shaky legs, I approach her. What is it about me that makes women burst into tears in my presence? Still, better than screaming. Being from Miami, I'm a hugger. But that's out of the question. I keep my distance as much as possible, holding out my hand.

She reaches for it. "What's your name?"

"People call me Goose."

She shakes her hair away from her face. Her eyelashes are moist, with a bit of mascara under her eyes. "I'm Allegra. I guess you knew that. I'm so lonely I kept that room service girl here until my ice cream melted. I have no one to talk to, no one but Jonah, and he h-hates me."

"I'll talk to you." She still hasn't let go of my hand, so I squeeze hers. "Talking's my superpower."

She smiles. "My brother's like that too." Finally, she drops my hand. "You're positively not going to kill me, right?"

I shake my head. "If I was, wouldn't I have done it already?"

"I guess." She inhales a huge load of snot. "I could use a tissue."

I wonder if she usually has someone wipe her nose for her. "Let me get one. Which way's the bathroom?" Her room is huge, and it connects to another room, a living room, which is why it took Caitlin so long to push the trolley through. There's a balcony on one end of the room, but no connecting door. I glance into the living room. There's another balcony, an entry door, and yes, a closed door—maybe it connects to Jonah's room. I head into the bathroom and grab a wad of tissues. I hand them to Allegra. "Cry away, milady," I say in my Cockney accent. "Sorry, I was in the school play, *Oliver!*, and we talked like that."

Allegra sniffles into a second and third tissue. Her face is red and puffy. "I'd love to be in a school play. It sounds so . . . normal."

"Most people in my school play would love to be on a TV series."

"That's because they don't know what it's like to have your career be over at seventeen."

"You mean just because your show went off the air? You'll get another."

"No, I won't. People hate me." She picks up tissue number four.

"The girl who delivered your room service didn't hate you. She said she was a fan."

"No, she said her little sister's a fan. People watched my show when they were younger, but then they outgrew it, so they hate me. Do you know there are 'I hate Allegra Kendall' Facebooks, Twitters, Instagrams, and Tumblrs? One of the Twitters is called DieAllegraDie. People post about what a whore I am, or how I can't act. If I wear a bikini, someone takes a picture and says I'm a slut. If I wear a big sweatshirt, they say I'm getting fat. I optioned this book I liked, because I wanted to make it into a movie, and people said I was doing it because I had to pay to get roles. They hate that I date Jonah, so it should make them happy that he dumped me."

"He's kind of a jerk, isn't he?"

"Yes!" Her eyes widen, and she nods. "He's a total jerk. Cute only gets you so far. He's rude. He loogeyed on his fans once. More than once. But they love him and hate me. They're all just waiting for me to get drunk and do a sex tape. My agent thinks that wouldn't be a bad thing, prove I'm not a baby anymore."

I eye the bottle of wine which, I notice, is open but still full. "Is that what you think too?"

"Yes. I mean, no. I mean, I don't know why I ordered it. I guess because my boyfriend broke up with me, and you're supposed to get drunk. But I don't really like drinking. I like being in control of myself." She looks at me, like she wants my opinion.

"I think that's smart." This goes against my plan to wait until she passed out. But I guess that went out the window when she saw me anyway. Besides, I feel bad for her. I remember the room service girl, Kasey. If Allegra gets drunk to go out with Jonah, the paparazzi will take pictures and make her look bad. I can sneak into Jonah's room after Allegra leaves—if she trusts me.

And I'm trustworthy. I say, "If you get drunk and the press gets photos, won't it hurt your chances of getting into college?" She stares at me like I'm crazy. "Sorry. My mom's always worried about college."

She laughs. "Yeah, college. What a joke. I could never go to college." She takes the last tissue.

"Why not? Lots of kid stars go to college. Jodie Foster was a kid star, and she went to Yale. Natalie Portman went to Harvard. Emma Watson started at Brown, but she quit because she was working too much." More stuff I know without knowing *how* I know.

"High-class problems." She sniffles deeply.

"Let me get you more tissues." I go back to the bathroom and, this time, remove the whole Kleenex box from its holder and hand it to her.

"Thanks. You are so nice." She blows her nose. "I could never get into a college like that. I'm not smart enough." She starts picking up the pile of used tissues.

"I bet you are. Or just go to a normal college. Where's your brother go?"

"Loyola." She sighs and tries to stuff the tissues into her pocket. "Back home. God, I'd love to go to school with Caleb. I miss him so much."

"You should go. I bet you have a ton of money saved up. Then, if you still wanted to act, you could come back afterward, when you don't have to get drunk or pose nude to prove you're a grown-up."

"I would never pose nude," she says. "But you're right."

We talk like that for maybe an hour, maybe more. I tell her about the classes I take in school and how it's my ambition to play Boq in *Wicked* on Broadway. She tells me about her family, the TV show, and how everyone pushed her to date Jonah, to be part of Jollegra. But then, the teen girls hated her even more because she "took him" from them. "I really barely know him. We never once talked the way I'm talking to you right now. I have no friends. This is the longest conversation I've had in a year, and you're some guy who snuck into my hotel room."

I shrug. "Yeah, sorry about that."

"No, no. Don't be. I'm glad you did. You kept me from doing something really stupid." She glances at the clock. "Oh, gosh, I have to get out of here soon. Command performance with his highness. I bet I'm a mess."

"No, you're beautiful. Your eye shadow's just smeared. Here, let me help you."

I get the makeup I saw in the bathroom and help her clean up. Then, we tackle what to do with the wine, and with me. She's worried that, if someone knows about the wine, they'll think she drank it, and if they know she has a guy in her room, they'll say she's a slut. "I haven't done one slutty thing ever," she says. "They don't care."

"Don't worry about me. I'll sneak out after you leave."

"Are you sure?"

"I snuck in. And maybe you can give the wine to the maid, like a tip."

So we write a note to the maid and put it on the wine. Allegra takes a picture of the bottle with her phone, to prove it.

"Do you want a picture of us?" she asks me.

"Huh?" Then, I remember, I'm supposed to be her biggest fan. Also, if my parents don't murder me, I could show it to Isabella. "I forgot my phone. Can you take one with yours and send it to me?"

"Good idea. Then, I'd have your phone number, and you'd have mine. We could talk sometimes. You could tell me about high school." She crouches down beside me to snap the photo.

"And you could tell *me* about college, when you go back to Louisiana."

She squeezes my shoulder and takes another shot. "I think I might actually do that. I mean, yeah, the press will assume I'm pregnant, but I'll know the truth."

"So will I."

She looks at the photos. "It would be so cool to be friends with you."

"That's me, every girl's BFF."

And no one's true love.

She sends the photo to the number I give her. Just as she does, there's a knock on the door.

"That's Jonah. Gotta go." She looks at me. "Are you sure you're okay?"

I nod. "I'll think of a way out." I already have.

She leans and kisses me on the cheek. "You're an incredible person, Goose. You've really opened my eyes."

"I'm glad."

I hide behind the curtains as she opens the door. I hear Jonah's voice. "So, I suppose we're doing this," he says in his British accent.

"I suppose we are," Allegra says. "Look, I'm sorry about before."

"I don't want to get back together."

"No, neither do I." Her voice is calm, even happy. "I just want to get along and stop fighting and everything."

A pause. "Sounds good. Shall we?"

"We shall."

I hear the door close behind Allegra. I wait a minute, then two, before I move from my spot, in case anyone comes back. No one does, so I check out the living room.

The connecting door is locked from the other side. If Jonah's room is on either side of Allegra's, there's only one way to get to it.

Climb over the balcony.

Did I mention I'm afraid of heights?

After Allegra leaves, I contact Kendra through the mirror.

"You're still in Allegra's room?" She's wearing a black lace mantilla, but otherwise, she looks like Violet.

"Yeah, how did you know?"

"Hmm, magic. That's how I know you're in room 2016, and Jonah was next door in 2014, so you only have to get one room over."

"Yeah. Only." I look out the glass doors. It's so high, I can see Cinderella's castle in the Magic Kingdom. "And you still can't magically zap me there?"

"Still, no."

"Really? What's the good of having magic powers?"

Kendra grimaces. "I often wonder that myself."

I hang up or sign off or whatever you do when you talk to someone in a magic mirror. I ask the mirror to show me Jonah.

He's in a limo, sitting with Allegra, but pretty far apart. She's trying to talk to him. "I was thinking about going back to Louisiana."

He says, "That's nice." He smiles at his phone, takes a selfie, then stares at it. He picks his teeth with his pinky.

Terrific. They are well and truly broken up. That means when he meets Celine, if she does wake up, they can fall in love. He'll be available. And he's such a douche. I'm going through all this so a girl I like can ride into the sunset with a douche.

Maybe he won't like her.

Any guy with eyes would like her.

I visualize Celine's smile. Of course he'll like her.

I decide to wait in Allegra's room for a while. The concert's at seven, so Jonah won't be back until at least nine. Maybe if I climb over the balcony after dark, I won't be able to see the ground below.

I look in the mirror. "Show me Celine."

In the mirror, I see her, dark hair fanned out over the crisp, white pillow, her heart-shaped mouth curled into a tiny smile. Is she dreaming? Does she know I'm gone?

I remember what Violet said about letting her live forever, comatose. Would I rather not know if she could never love me than lose her?

No. I want her to be happy. She's been through so much, losing her mother, her dad. She deserves to be happy, even if it's not with me.

"I love you," I tell the mirror.

Celine doesn't respond. Of course, she couldn't hear me even if she was awake.

I stare at her another minute.

I decide to check out—just check out—the situation on the balcony. I pick up my backpack, open the sliding glass door, and head outside.

The balcony is a large one, spanning both the living and bedroom areas of Allegra's suite. At its front is a white aluminum railing. I don't know much about construction, but it seems pretty flimsy, with vertical rails about six inches apart and some ornamental scrollwork on top. I edge out, remembering the part in season one of *Game of Thrones* where Tyrion's imprisoned in the sky cells, these dungeons on the side of a sheer cliff with no wall on one side and an abrupt thousand-foot drop. At least I have a railing. At least I'll only fall into the pool area and have the remote possibility of just being a quadriplegic.

Except—oh, right—Tyrion was *fictional*.

Still, I have to look. I walk to the side of the balcony closest to Jonah's room. It's not a balcony that bumps out. I won't have to scale a wall. Allegra's balcony and Jonah's are only inches apart.

For an average-height guy, it would be a no-brainer, just lift himself over the railing (which reaches my chest but would reach someone else's hip at least), swing his leg over the other railing, and drop down.

Down.

I picture myself, swan-diving off the railing, splattering on the pavement.

Florida Man plummets from hotel balcony.

My parents will hear about it on the news.

My mother will know she was right.

And Celine will stay in a coma.

I look across again, aware of my breathing, which is crazy-hard, hard enough that it sounds like a car with a busted muffler, and my teeth feel like they're buzzing.

Okay, I need to go back inside, just for a while, a second. Slowly, carefully, like Tyrion in the sky cells, I edge toward the door.

Shit, there's someone in Allegra's room. The maid.

I rush to the corner of the balcony, sit down, and hide.

The good thing about being my size is it's easy to hide.

The bad thing is, I feel like I could fit through the railings.

I can't. They made it so kids can't fit through. Isabella couldn't. I'm bigger than a kid.

That doesn't change my racing thoughts and heart. If I could just be reasonable, I wouldn't have this fear. But that's not how it works.

I close my eyes and picture myself, over and over, splattering to the ground. Even the solid stucco wall behind me doesn't help.

I want my mother.

No. No. I don't. I'm here. I want to do this. Put on your big boy pants, Guzman. You can do this.

Once again, I take out the mirror.

"Show me Celine."

The mirror shows me her room again, her face. Kendra, disguised as Violet, sits in the visitor's chair while an elderly nurse checks Celine's chart. I watch until the nurse walks out.

Desperate *not* to look down, I ask the mirror to show me Stacey.

She's at home, in our kitchen. God, I wish I was in our kitchen. She's cleaning up dinner dishes. She hasn't noticed I'm gone yet. At least, she hasn't started worrying. I check my watch. Seven-thirty. Half an hour into the concert.

"Show me Jonah."

He's in his dressing room. I can hear the opening band in the background. He looks stoned, and he's meeting some fans who are posing for cell phone pictures.

"Show me Violet."

The mirror shows me the same elderly nurse who was in Celine's room.

"No, show me Violet."

Still, the nurse.

I get it. The nurse is Violet. But Violet promised to leave Celine alone.

Violet lied.

Of course Violet lied. Violet is at the hospital, disguised as a nurse. With access to drugs, access to needles.

And access to Celine.

I look at her name tag as she walks out. It says, *Lavinia Barnes, RN.*

"Show me Kendra."

"I still can't zap you into Jonah's room." Kendra still looks like Violet. This is really confusing.

"Listen! Violet's in the hospital." I tell her about Nurse Barnes, what I saw. "Please don't let her hurt Celine, and maybe . . ."

"What?"

"Maybe get my parents, my dad. See if there's something they can do to protect her."

Her face, Violet's beautiful, horrible face, shows confusion. "But if I go to your parents, I can't stay with Celine."

"I was thinking maybe you could use the phone."

She rolls her eyes. "Ohhh, the phone. Of course." She turns and looks at the old-fashioned beige phone on the bedside table. "How does it work?"

Geez. I walk her through it. Several times. Finally, she gets it. She says she'll call.

I've been trying not to look around too much, not to look *down.* Instead, I look out. It's after eight now. The sun is sinking into the orange pool of the sky. The mirror shows me Jonah, singing onstage. It's almost time.

I stare through the glass door. The maid is still in Allegra's room. She's drinking the wine Allegra left. What if she sees me? I walk to the edge of the balcony. Even though it's June and hot, I suddenly feel chilled to the bone. My legs, my arms, my hands are shaking, teeth chattering.

As I reach the very edge of the balcony, my hands shake harder. The mirror slips from my grip.

I hear it shatter to the ground, twenty floors below.

Shit.

Shit. Shit. Shit.

I dive to the floor in case someone below saw the mirror (how could they not?), guessed where it came from.

I look through the bars, down, twenty floors below. The ground swims up to my eyes, and I feel like a cartoon coyote.

On the floor as I am, I'm not worried about falling. That won't happen. I won't fall off the balcony. Even I know I can't fall from the floor.

I'm worried about the entire balcony falling, detaching from the building and crashing to the ground—but only after it hits every single balcony in between. How is it even attached to the building? Screws? Concrete? Who put it up there? Were they drunk? Disgruntled? Insane? I was able to push these thoughts from my head when I could look at the mirror or talk to Kendra. Now, with nothing to drown out the noise in my head, all I can think of is the screws that hold the railing up and when was the last time they were inspected?

Probably never.

I have no idea whether Celine is safe from Violet or when Jonah will be back. I know nothing.

The good news is, I hear nothing from below. Hopefully, they'll think some kid at the pool broke the mirror.

Because kids are always running around with antique sterling silver mirrors.

The bad news is, it's almost dark.

Or maybe that's the good news.

I reach for my backpack with a shaking hand. I fumble for the one distraction I have left. Celine's picture. I take it out and stare at it in the waning light.

The day it was taken was the first day I'd told myself, screw it, I'm never going to *not* love this girl, the day I knew it would never work with Willow or any other girl because I would never stop thinking about Celine.

She'd been so beautiful that day, in a sweater the color of iceberg lettuce that perfectly set off her pale skin and dark hair. They'd been practicing the scene before Oliver and Dodger meet, the scene where Oliver is bullied by Noah Claypool. This guy, Tedder Strasky, was playing Noah, which was perfect casting because Tedder's a serious bully, like the kind that puts guys' heads into toilets (not mine, but still . . .). Celine had been playing Oliver halfheartedly. Acting wasn't really her thing. But when Strasky said his line about Oliver's mother being "a real bad 'un," everything changed.

Oliver's supposed to attack Noah, and considering Strasky is about twice Celine's size it should have taken an impressive amount of stage combat to make it work. But as soon as Strasky said his line, Celine stood, launched herself at him, and practically pushed him off the stage. For a second, it was so real. I knew.

I knew, whatever happened, I wanted that girl on my side. She was a fighter.

Just like that day in biology class.

Now, she's in bed, maybe dying.

I know if our positions were reversed and it was Celine in a situation where she could save me, she would not be cowering on the floor. She would not be worrying about how the balcony was screwed in.

She'd be fighting her way into Jonah's room.

And that's what I'm going to do.

What I am doing.

I pull myself up on the railing. I feel it wobble a little, hear it creak. I drop back down.

No, it didn't wobble. It's solid.

I'm solid.

I take a deep breath. Okay, I take five. I'm doing this. I don't look down. I can barely see.

The distance between the two balconies is less than a foot. All I have to do is climb up on one, then down the other. All I have to do.

And if it falls off and crashes to the ground, I will just die. That's all.

I read a book once, about auditioning. It said that you could combat nerves by imagining the worst-case scenario. Like, you don't get the part, so you have no money so you starve and die. Death is the worst-case scenario. Some comfort.

But the worst-case scenario right now is that I *don't* do it and Celine stays in that cold, gray place for the next fifty years.

Worse than death.

Death, I'll risk.

I stuff the photo into my backpack, zip it, and throw it onto Jonah's balcony.

I take one last breath and hold it.

I pull myself up on the railing and over.

Maybe it's adrenaline rush that lets mothers lift cars off their infants. I pull up first one leg, then the other. I'm on top of the railing like I'm Spider-Man.

Okay, not exactly like Spider-Man, but pretty good. It holds. It's not crashing to the ground. But the whole thing is like slow motion, like I've been here for an hour, and just as my foot is searching for the other balcony, the sky lights up with an explosion of red and gold.

Fireworks. Disney fireworks, which means there are a lot of them. Fifteen minutes at least.

I freeze. The balcony, the building, the entire city is shaking with explosions, first from one side, then another.

Think of Celine. Be brave like Celine. For Celine.

My foot finds the other rail. I don't want to move. I want to stay, hug the railing forever.

No. I want to land on the other side, save Celine.

The fireworks explode like bombs bursting in air all around me. I wonder if this is how it feels to be in a war, like in the 1940s in London or Berlin.

The balcony's trembling, and I'm trembling with it. I picture Celine on the other side, arms outstretched, beckoning to me, telling me that loving her isn't a crazy idea.

My feet hit the ground.

I crumple to the floor.

"Hey, what are you doing here?"

11

Okay, so I know I'm small. And being small sort of skews your perspective. So, possibly, you might see someone who's just a little tall and think they look like Fezzik, the giant in *The Princess Bride*. Especially if you were already completely freaked out from hanging from a balcony two hundred feet up, during a fireworks display.

But really, I think this guy is literally eight feet tall.

And there are two of him.

Wait, the second guy is the one I talked to at the elevator, the one with the cut. He's only seven feet tall. My bad. And I get a good view of the cut on his face because the first guy is lifting me by the shirt collar. It's a festering, weirdly swollen, open wound.

"You really should get that looked at," I gasp as Fezzik strangles me with my own shirt because, even in stress situations, I can never just shut up. My mom says, no matter what happens, I always have my mouth to keep me company.

These guys aren't talking much, though, unless you count cursing. Fezzik carries me into the room and swings me like a pendulum against the wall, then drops me. He starts to pick me up again.

"Stop!" I yell, because that seems like a reasonable thing to say.

And, weirdly, they both do stop. They stop and stare at me like they think I'm going to say something brilliant. I try.

"I'm not here to hurt Jonah. I mean, how could I? Look at me." I stare at the guy with the cut. "Does that thing feel hot when you touch it?"

The guy holds his monster-hand up to his face. "Yeah, really hot. Is that bad?"

"I'm not sure." I'm glad no one's picking me up, and I'm trying to prolong that. As I said to Allegra, talking is my superpower, my only superpower. "It gets a little warm just because it's healing. But if it's really hot, it might be infected. I knew a guy with a wound like that, and he was seriously ill."

Actually, I don't "know a guy." It was a character from a movie. And he died. But I keep that information on a need-to-know basis. "Anyway, you should have it looked at."

The behemoth puts his hand to his face. "Thanks, man." He turns to his friend. "Otto, do you think it looks infected?"

Otto squints at it. "Could be. He's right. You should get it looked at." He turns back to me. "We need to get him out of here. He'll be back soon." He starts to pick me up again.

"Wait!" I scream. "Wait! Wait!"

He drops me again. Hard. My head is ringing. "What?"

"Please," I say, channeling Westley from the same movie. I'm on my knees, more because I'm already down there than because I'm begging. But partly because of begging. "I have to talk to Jonah. I came all the way from Miami and climbed over a balcony."

"What are you, in love with him? 'Cause he likes girls, lots of girls."

"I know. That's what I need to talk to him about, a girl. She's my friend. And she's dying."

"Haven't heard that one in a week." The scarred guy is still touching his cut.

"No, it's true. If you let me get my backpack, I could show you pictures of her. You could see." I wish I had the mirror. With that, I could prove lots of things, including the existence of magic. I could check on Celine too. I push aside my worries about Violet. Kendra's taking care of it.

But the mirror's gone. I have, as usual, nothing but my big mouth.

So I start talking, telling them the whole story, about how beautiful Celine is, and how nice, all the things that happened to her, her parents dying and everything. At some point, the scarred guy (whose name, I find out, is Sherman) does get my backpack. He takes out the photos and shows them to Otto. I've got one of Celine, lying still on the bed. When he gets to that one, I'm practically crying. And so are Otto and Sherman.

"So you see," I say, "it's really important that I find Jonah. Only he can help."

Otto looks at Sherman and shakes his head. "That little prick's never going to help. He'll probably fire us for letting him stay."

"Tell him it would look bad in the papers if Jonah's bodyguards beat up a shorter statured individual like myself." They look at me, confused. "A little person, a dwarf. If a big guy beats up someone smaller, that's . . . frowned upon." This has gotten me out of many a fight (when my mouth has gotten me into one), questioning the guy's manhood for hitting someone smaller.

"How would the press find out?" Otto asks.

"I'd tell them, of course. It would be right there on the cover of the *Enquirer*. I'm an actor. I love publicity. And then, it would be all your fault."

"He makes an interesting point," Sherman says.

"And, meanwhile," I say, "it would be really *good* publicity if he visited a sick girl in the hospital. And couldn't he use some of that after the thing with the bicycle last week? After his breakup with Allegra."

"He didn't break up with Allegra," Sherman says.

"Oh, I think you'll find he did. He was a total jerk and broke her heart. Even if my friend doesn't wake up, he could take pictures, prove Jonah visited. We could call *Extra*. It would be a lot better than another story about him getting drunk and doing something stupid."

"He's right," Sherman says. "We could ask Harry. That's his manager. And you seem like a really nice guy, um . . ."

"Goose," I say.

"Goose. We should try to help Goose, Otto."

But, just at that moment, the door opens. And Otto picks me up and drops me again.

12

You know in old cartoons, when someone gets beat up and they see stars going around their head? That's how it is. I literally see stars. Then, I realize it's the last of the Disney fireworks out the window. Still, my head really hurts.

Otto starts to pick me up again. Why did they turn on me?

"Man, stop!" I scream. "Dwarf tossing's been illegal in Florida since 1989!"

An aside: This is actually true. In 1989, the Florida legislature voted to ban the "bar sport" of throwing little people against mattresses. This may be one of the best and least-stupid laws Florida has ever passed. Makes me proud to be a Floridian. It's still legal other places. But there are actually people campaigning to bring it back, to "create jobs." If that's ever my job, just kill me.

Sherman's yelling at Otto to stop too. "Don't go crazy, man! Dude's tiny. God, this is gonna look really bad if the papers get wind of it."

And then, I understand.

When Otto picks me up the second time, he whispers, "When I drop you, stay down and act hurt."

"Shouldn't be hard." It comes out a grunt.

He drops me, and every bone in my body aches. But I get it now. It's a show for Jonah.

"I just wanted him to visit my sick friend!" I yell.

"What's going on?" A British accent. Jonah. Wearing purple diaper pants and a backward baseball cap. "You're beating up a . . . a midget in my room?"

"Actually," Sherman says, "that word is considered offensive. I believe the preferred term is 'little person.'"

"Right," I grunt.

"But you're beating one up. In my room. That's my point, really."

"Otto is," Sherman says. "I tried to stop him. I told him it would be absolutely horrific publicity if this guy went to the press."

Horrific?

"He snuck into your room," Otto says. "On the balcony."

"Ouch!" I yell, partly for show but partly because it really does hurt.

"Stop it," Jonah says.

The guys back off. Behind Jonah's back, Otto winks at me.

"Who are you, and why are you in my room?" Jonah demands.

"My name is Goose. Goose Guzman, and I want you to visit the most beautiful girl in the world in the hospital."

"Oh, brother." Jonah sighs.

I pick up Celine's picture, which has fallen on the floor. "That's her. She's in Miami. She's in a coma. And I think meeting you might be the only thing that will wake her up."

And then, I tell him everything else about Celine, how great she is. "I know you have a ton of fans, but this girl is special. And, what's more, she's an orphan."

"An orphan?" Jonah smirks. "Like Oliver Twist?"

"Exactly like Oliver Twist," I say, glomming on to the fact that he's British and has actually heard of Oliver Twist. "In fact, that's how we met, in a school play, *Oliver!* She sang, 'Where Is Love?' and that was how I knew."

"Knew?"

"What a great person she was. Like no one else. And you have the opportunity to help someone like that. And, frankly, it would help you too."

"What? How would it help me? Why do I need help?"

Is this guy for real? Does he have no idea that everyone thinks he's a complete turd?

"Well, after the pictures of you peeing on your neighbors' lawn last week and practically running over that kid in your Maserati, not to mention your big breakup with . . ." I stop, realizing I'm probably not supposed to know about the breakup. "Don't you think it would be nice to have some good publicity?"

"Now listen here," Jonah says. "It's not my fault the press follows me about and reports on my every move—normal teenage stuff like—"

"Like mooning a group of Catholic schoolchildren out the window of your limo?" I ask.

"Nuns are so funny!" He giggles. "They look like penguins!"

"Or when your monkey bit that waitress?"

"She shouldn't have tried to pet it."

"So you don't care that you're perceived as the biggest douche in the universe?"

"Girls don't think so." He glances in the mirror and adjusts his hat.

It's true. Celine liked him a lot. I always figured it was a blind spot on her part, that she somehow didn't see what he was like. It's like on *The Simpsons*, how Lisa reads *Non-Threatening Boys Magazine*, that girls like unattainable, girlish-looking boys because they're scared of real ones.

My head hurts. In fact, my whole body hurts. My brain hurts, and I just want a ride to the train station so I can go home—after calling my mom to assure her I'm fine and apologize.

"Fine," I say. "I'm sorry I thought you'd want to help this girl, who's a really big fan—and, incidentally, a really cool human being. My bad." I turn and start for the door.

"Actually, I think it's a fabulous idea."

Before me stands the biggest, blondest woman I've ever seen. She's wearing a pink suit and a matching hat with huge white roses all over.

I turn to stare. Jonah turns too. "Mum, what are you doing here?"

"Allegra phoned. I've come to check on the mess you've made of your life." She looks him up and down. "Pull up your trousers."

"Mess? I'm an international sensation." But he does pull up his pants, which fall back down as soon as he lets go.

"An international sensation with no soul." She grabs his baseball cap. "Take that off. It's disrespectful."

Jonah tugs at his pants and the cap at the same time. "Mum, what have I done?"

"You spit at that crowd of fans last week. You wore those horrible trousers to sing the national anthem at a ball game. The whole country saw your crack, the whole world, maybe." She gives them another tug.

"Mum, quit it."

"When you visited the Washington Monument, you said you

were sure Washington would have told a lie to get to one of your concerts." The roses on her hat tremble with each word.

"He might've."

"And you haven't been inside a church in a year. This is not how I raised you, Joshbekesha!"

"Josh—what?" I say.

"That's not my name!" Jonah snaps. "I'm having it legally changed when I'm eighteen."

"But you're seventeen now, and you do as I say. And I say you should do one nice thing for every ten rotten things you do."

Jonah nods. "Yes, Mum." He looks at me. "Perhaps I can help you out after all."

Jonah's Amazonian mother smiles at me. "Now, this looks like a nice boy who listens to his mum."

I feel my ears get hot, which literally has never happened. Between my olive complexion and my high threshold for embarrassment, I'm not a blusher. But I assume that's what's happening now. I say, "Usually, you're right. I am a great son with a great mum—uh, mom. But I'm afraid today has been an exception. If you'd let me use the phone, I could make it up to her, though."

Two hours later, I am—as hoped—on Jonah's private plane. We had to drive through what looked like a cornfield of teenage girls to get out of the hotel. I don't know how they knew he was leaving, or maybe they just live in the parking lot. I called my mother on Josh's mom's cell phone, and she only slightly freaked out. I guess she figured out where I was and was happy I wasn't dead or arrested.

"Can you check with Kendra?" I ask. I'm trying to figure out what to say not to get her more worried. But I'm worried, so it's hard. "Can you just . . . make sure Celine's okay?" I don't want to tell her about the evil nurse.

"Okay," Stacey says. "Just get home safe."

Jonah's sitting in the seat across from mine. He has on khaki pants and a blue button-down his mother brought him and sort of looks like a waiter at TGI Fridays. He's saying, "Yes, mum" a lot.

"Yes, Mum, I did notice how Goose called his mum so she wouldn't worry," he says.

"You're right, Mum. It probably wouldn't kill me to volunteer at a soup kitchen."

"Yes, I'll get a haircut. It would look nicer."

"Of course I'm not on drugs."

His speaking voice, like his music, is sort of . . . soothing. It's after 1:00 a.m., which means it's been almost a full day since I've slept. And, even then, I barely did because I was so worried about Celine.

I feel like closing my eyes.

Maybe I will.

Yes, maybe I will . . .

I will . . .

I feel a bump beneath me. I start awake. It takes me a moment to realize where I am. Across from me, someone is saying, "Of course, Mum. Of course I realize it should be about the music."

Jonah. Jonah's plane. I've actually succeeded. He's going to go to the hospital and kiss Celine.

Kiss Celine.

I push back all the feelings that causes. I can't think about how much it's going to suck to see him kiss her right now. Or ever. Celine is my friend, and I should want what's best for her. And if this . . .

"Really, Mum, how was I supposed to know I shouldn't text at a funeral?"

. . . if this idiot is what's best for her, then that's what I should want. At least he has a nice mom.

I look out the window. The night outside is black. At least, since it's 2:30 a.m., there shouldn't be too many girls waiting in the terminal.

Okay, I spoke too soon. As soon as we leave the secure area, there are *hundreds* of girls, crushing together, craning to see Jonah.

"Is that him?" one yells.

"Couldn't be, in that nerdy outfit."

"It's a disguise! It's a disguise!"

"Omigod! That's his mom!"

"I love his mum!"

"Who's the little guy?"

"Are you famous too?"

"Not yet," I can't resist telling them, "but I'm going to be."

Otto and Sherman and a bunch of other bodyguards I don't know fight against the surging mob. How did they even know he was going to be here? Don't they have mothers to tell them not to go to the airport at two in the morning?

Oh, yeah. They probably blew off their mothers like I did.

Finally, we make it to Jonah's limo, one of three limos that peel off in separate directions. Ours goes to the hospital.

When we get there, it's blissfully quiet. It never occurred to anyone that Jonah would go to a hospital instead of a club or a South Beach restaurant where you eat dinner in bed. We head for the entrance.

"Where's the photog?" Jonah's manager, Harry, is griping. "The photog was supposed to meet us outside. Damn, there's always paparazzi around when he's pissing on a monument, but never when he's doing something nice."

"Perhaps it's because he's so seldom doing anything nice," Jonah's mom says. "Go on, love."

"Maybe he could go up now and the photographer can come

when he gets there, when Celine wakes up."

Oh, please, let Celine wake up.

"I think we should wait for the photographer," Jonah says. "After all, it's the whole reason we're—" He's interrupted by the mother of all nudges from his mum. "I mean, of course I'd love to go up and meet the gi . . . young lady right now."

He looks to his mother for approval, and she pats his shoulder.

"Come on, then." I gesture for Jonah to follow me to the elevator. "It's probably better if it's just the two of us."

The elevator is one of those big ones that can accommodate a gurney. We stand far apart and don't talk. Jonah's probably tired from the tongue-lashing, and me, I don't have anything to say. I don't have anything to think. At least, nothing I *want* to think. If I was thinking—which I'm really trying not to do—I'd be thinking this is *it*. End of the line. If Jonah's kiss doesn't wake Celine up, maybe nothing will. Maybe Celine is really and truly gone forever.

The hospital is so silent, which is bad because it allows me to be alone with my thoughts but good because it's quick. Only one nurse gets on the elevator. She doesn't seem to notice Jonah, and she's going to the same floor we are, twelve.

I watch the numbers. I don't want to talk to Jonah. Celine thinks he's so profound, but really, he's an idiot. She'll be disappointed.

She'll be disappointed *if* she wakes up.

Five.

This has to work.

Six.

It will work.

Seven.

What if it doesn't?

Eight.

No point thinking about it.

Nine.

But what if it doesn't?

Ten.

Stop it. Stop it!

Eleven.

I'll know in five minutes. Two if we run. Almost there. At least the wondering will be over.

The elevator jolts to a stop.

"I'm afraid I can't let you boys off," the nurse says.

13

"What the—?" Jonah yells.

But I know. Of course it's Violet. She looks different than the nurse I saw before, but I know her by the expression on her face. And, um, the fact that she's not letting us move.

The first thought that flashes through my head is that I must be right about Jonah. I must be close. Violet hasn't bothered Celine until now. If she's suddenly trying to stop me, she must know that Jonah is the handsome prince who can wake Celine.

I lunge for the alarm button. It starts ringing. Jonah's screaming, "Help! Help! I'm being kidnapped! I'm a rock star!" But then, just as suddenly, my arm, my whole body freezes. Jonah's screams stop. I can see that he, too, is frozen, stone-like, like Medusa's victims. I can only move my eyes, and with them, I see Violet push the button for the roof.

"I'll drag you up and throw you off. Falling from a great height is your destiny, dwarf."

I feel the elevator start up again. I can't do anything about it.

And then, there's another person in the elevator. She looks like Violet. My eyes take in blazing red hair and high-heeled boots. "What are you doing here?" the nurse-Violet screams.

"Saving them!" the other Violet screams, so I know it's Kendra. "It's too late to save you. Violet, you disappoint me."

The elevator again jolts to a stop.

"Disappoint you? I always disappoint you," Nurse Violet mocks. "I disappoint everyone."

"That's not true. I thought you were the daughter I never had. It breaks my heart to have to stop you, to have to use tough love."

"Then don't!" Nurse Violet screams.

And suddenly, a ball of fire flies right at Kendra and me. I can move, and I duck to avoid it. Kendra somehow quashes the flame, but there is another, and another. Jonah is shrieking. The doors open, and Kendra screams at us to run, even as she uses a fireball of her own to hold Nurse Violet at bay.

"How?" I look out the door. The elevator is several feet above where it's supposed to be, hovering above the floor. The white linoleum floor looks slick and hard as ice.

"Just jump!" Kendra says.

And, amazingly, tugging Jonah behind me, I do.

I fall hard, but I don't die. Jonah lands neatly, and I yell, "Come on!" I don't look back. I hear the door close. I think, hope, we're on the right floor, Celine's floor. I check the numbers on the doors, 1201, 1202. Yes! We skid around a corner and almost hit an oncoming nurse.

"Slow down!" she yells.

At least it's not Violet. We slow. Jonah's been making frightened, incredulous sounds, combined with lots of cursing. Once we pass the nurse, he says, "What the hell was that?"

"A witch." I don't look at him. "I didn't tell you because you'd have thought I was lying. Or crazy. But now you know. A witch put a spell on Celine to make her go to sleep. I want you to kiss her, so you can wake her up." I keep walking fast, not looking at him. Eyes on the prize. Celine.

Presumably because of what he's seen, Jonah doesn't seem to think I'm crazy. "You think I can break the spell?"

"You're a handsome prince, aren't you? Or as close as we have." We reach a corner. I grab the wall to stop myself, then check around it.

"Oh, yeah." He's panting, but he grins. "Guess I am."

We round the corner at a fast walk, me working hard to keep up with Jonah's longer legs. I say, "So you'll do it?"

"Sure. Why not?"

Why not? Because you might be putting yourself in a witch's path. But I don't say it. Why would I? If he's too dumb to realize it, I'm not going to enlighten him. I just need him to wake Celine. He can leave right after. In fact, I'd prefer it.

We fast-walk around a last corner, then to Celine's door.

I open it.

She is so beautiful. It's been a day since I've seen her, and I am stunned by her like it's the first time. She lies there, so pale against the white sheets. Her black hair is fanned out behind her on the pillow, and her full, red lips are exactly the ones I've always wanted to kiss.

Please let this work. Please come back to me.

I jut my hand toward her, in case Jonah doesn't get *which* comatose girl exactly I meant. "That's her." It's hard to form words. "Celine." Something's wedged in my throat, making it hard to talk.

The idea that, if this doesn't work, maybe nothing will. She might never awaken, she might die, and with her, the possibility—however slight—that I keep with me every night as I drift off to sleep, the possibility that she could someday love me.

Of course, if it works, if Jonah's kiss wakes her, that possibility will be gone anyway. He doesn't know her, but once he sees how pretty and sweet and funny she is, he'll fall in love with her. Even a douche like him would know she's special. They'll walk off into the night together, like Andie and Blane, and I'll be left all alone—well, alone with a houseful of people, but without her. So, alone.

Still, I have to try it. I love her. She needs to be alive on this planet, even if it's not with me. That's what love is, after all, wanting the best for the other person, not yourself. I learned that the hard way.

Jonah looks at her, and smiles. "She's lovely." His admiration is genuine, of course. With his accent, it comes out all *loff-lee*, which is probably why girls think he's so hot. Maybe someday, I can move to another town where nobody knows me, pretend to be a Brit, and get all sorts of girls, short girls, tall girls, lots of girls. Just not Celine.

"She is," I say. "Loff-lee. She's nice too, and funny, and talented and . . . good with kids. She's like no one I ever met before, which is why I need you to help her."

"And you think my kissing her . . . ?"

"I hope so." *Do I hope so? I do.* "I can be straight with you now that you've seen the witches, seen what they can do. This is her only chance."

He shrugs. "Guess we can try." And then, without another word, he leans down toward her and . . .

I can't look. I turn away. This is what I wanted, dammit. This is what I wanted, the reason I traveled so far, lied to my parents, hid in the room service cart, and hung from a balcony. I want this. I just want her to wake up, no matter what.

The room is silent. God, are they still kissing, all this time? I want to look, but I don't want to see if she's, you know, enjoying it too much.

Finally, Jonah's voice says, "I don't think it worked, man."

My chest is a deflating balloon. My eyes ache like I just came out of salt water. I squeeze them together. I wanted it to work. I did. Now what?

I turn back, opening them. Jonah's staring down at Celine. "I was really hoping it would, and not just because I wanted the reputation of having my magic lips raise someone from the dead. I knew if you were willing to go to all that trouble for her, she must have been pretty special."

It's a really coherent thing for him to say. Still, the past tense about kills me. My eyes are damp, but I'm not going to wipe them, not in front of him. "She was. She is."

He tosses his hair a little girlishly. "So this spell, the spell the witch put on her, it said *I* had to kiss her?"

I shrug. "I don't know. In all the fairy tales, the girl gets awakened by a handsome prince. I was going with that idea."

He chuckles. "Perhaps not handsome or princely enough." He looks down, thinking. "My mum used to read me those storybooks. It was nice. I was a shit to my mum, wasn't I?"

"Yeah, sort of." I was a shit to mine too, and it didn't even help.

"You know," Jonah says, "most of my books talked about true love as well. Perhaps that's a factor. Perhaps that's what's missing, the love part. Beautiful as she is, I don't love her."

That must be it. Still, I say, "She loves you, though. She listens to all your songs, has posters of you all over the place, writes your initials on her notebook in pink highlighter . . ."

He throws back his head then and laughs. "But that describes half the teenaged girls in the world, these idiots who camp out in the airport. Do you think I can resuscitate all of them too?"

"They probably don't all need it." Celine's not an idiot, but he does have a point.

"Still, I think your definition of love may be a little thin."

"My definition of love isn't thin at all." I take Celine's hand and squeeze it in the silent room. It's so soft, and I remember teaching her to play the piano, one finger over the other. I love her fingers.

Jonah sees me and nods. "Surely there must be someone who actually loves her, who *knows* and loves her. She's quite pretty." He looks back at her, and now, I hate him looking at her, since it didn't work. He turns back toward me.

"She's very pretty," I say. "Nice too, and talented and fun. But she doesn't have a boyfriend, if that's what you mean." When you think about it, it's crazy that someone as cool as Celine doesn't have hundreds of guys in love with her. She once told me she didn't like guys who think they're hot. That describes most guys at our school.

Jonah tugs at his pants, then seems to realize they aren't falling down, since they're the geeky pants his mom got him. "Well, maybe not a boyfriend, but it strikes me that someone who went to all this trouble for her—I mean, someone who could have been arrested dozens of times. Someone who did get beaten up by my bodyguards—that, perhaps, that person may in fact be her true love."

Oh. Duh. He means me. Am I that easy to see through? Is he smarter than I thought? "Yeah, well, of course I love her. But that doesn't mean she loves me back. I mean, look at her, and then look at me."

"Of course," he says, and I sort of want to hit him for agreeing so quickly, but then, he says, "Ahem. I mean, of course, we don't know what she thinks, and she isn't awake to tell us. She could love you. You have rather a charming personality."

"Gee, thanks." This guy's getting less charming by the minute.

"But even assuming you're right, does it have to be mutual? If you are truly in love with her, might that not be enough love?"

"I don't know. I hadn't thought of that." I hadn't.

"Should you not, perhaps, try?"

I think about it. I've wanted to kiss her since forever, or at least a few months. But the thing that stopped me was her reaction, what she'd think of me. If I didn't kiss her, we could be friends. I could be with her all the time, like buddies, see her every day. But if I kissed her, it would get all awkward if she didn't love me back. I didn't want to upset things.

Now, she's in a coma. She wouldn't need to know I kissed her. In fact, I'll take it to the grave. Is that pervy? Maybe. Perhaps, as Jonah would say. But does that matter? The fact is, she holds my heart in her body, and if she doesn't awaken, I may die.

I nod. I step up to Celine. Her lips are so full in her heart-shaped face. I wish she'd open her eyes so I could see those too, so I don't feel like I'm taking advantage. But, of course, that defeats the purpose of kissing her. I touch a lock of the shiny, black hair on the white pillowcase. It feels soft like the satiny ribbons my mother uses on packages at Christmas or on my sister's hair. Celine used to do Isabella's hair in ribbons. I can hear her breathing, smell the sweetness of her breath. I imagine for a moment that she loves me. It's not so impossible, is it? I'm a great guy. I picture us sitting at the piano that one night, me playing "Clair de Lune," trying to impress her. She could have loved me then. I reach forward and adjust her face so it's leaning toward me. I feel like there's no air in the room.

It's not like I've never kissed a girl before. Just not this girl, the one that matters. And there's the part about her being asleep. I inhale through my nose. Then, my lips meet hers.

God.

I mean to give her a small kiss, a polite kiss, not be like one of those guys who waits until a girl passes out, then mauls her. I love this girl. I love this girl, but I don't want her like that, not by fraud. In my fantasies, she wants me too. And yet, when our lips meet, I feel a flash of something—call it electricity, call it magnetism, call it magic—binding us together, and I can't let go, I can't let go, and I'm kissing her like I've always imagined.

Finally, I back off. I more than back off. I pull my lips off her like a plunger getting yanked out of a toilet. I run behind Jonah, then out the door.

It didn't work. I knew it wouldn't. A regular guy like me couldn't possibly be the true love of the most beautiful girl in maybe the whole world. I'm not Blane. Heck, I'm not even Duckie. Still, I hoped it would work. I hoped it would because now, I'm out of ideas, and Celine's still in a coma and I am there with her. Maybe she'll die or just stay there, suspended, forever, and I will never have anyone to teach piano to or watch John Hughes movies with, no one to tell me I don't have to be funny for people to like me.

And, at that moment, with no one there to see except the nurses (who are probably used to it), I give way to the tears that had been threatening to seep out of my eyes for the past week. I bury my face in my hands and sob. *Celine.*

"You're here. You?"

What? A voice from inside the room. Not Jonah's voice. A girl's voice. Celine's voice! But how?

"I am here," Jonah's voice says back. "Was it . . . Celine?"

"Yes. I had a dream about you. You were in it. In my dream, you kissed me. I thought it was only a dream because it sounded so crazy. I mean, why would Jonah Prince be here with me? It's so incredible."

She's talking to Jonah. She's so happy to see him.

"Why indeed," he says. "A little friend of yours came to see me, to tell me about you."

No. No. Don't tell her I kissed her. It will ruin everything.

"A little . . . oh, you must mean—Goose! In my dream, you weren't the only one who kissed me. In my dream, Goose kissed me, and that's what woke me up."

What?

"Goose!" She's calling me. "Where is he?" Her voice holds a note of panic I can't help but imagine is from missing me. Could it be? I wipe away the embarrassing tears. My face hurts.

"Celine?" I step from behind the door frame before I have time to chicken out. "I'm . . . I'm here." Is she mad? Will she laugh at me?

She's half sitting up on the bed, leaning on her hands, her blue eyes wide open. When she sees me, her face breaks into this huge smile that wasn't there before, not even for meeting Jonah.

"Goose! You are here! You went away, and I missed you so much!" She adjusts herself on the bed, then reaches out her hand.

I run to take it. God. It's not like I haven't touched her hand before, but this is so . . . intentional. Almost like kissing her, but almost kind of better than kissing her because she knows I'm doing it. Is it possible? Could my kiss have awakened her?

"You . . . missed me?" I ask. "You knew I was gone?"

"Of course. Everyone thinks that people in comas don't hear anything, don't know anything. But we do hear or at least *I* did, and we have a lot of time to think, too, about . . . everything. I knew you were here all that time. And then, I knew you left. Why did you leave? I missed you, even when I was asleep."

She missed me. I get more daring. I squeeze her hand. I see the little burn scar I noticed that day. It's really her hand I'm holding. "I left to find Jonah, to get him to kiss you."

"Why did you want him to kiss me?" She squeezes back, only instead of just a little squeeze, she clings to my hand.

"Kendra said a handsome prince might break the spell. I thought . . . Jonah Prince. Prince. I thought he was your handsome prince, your true love."

She laughs, shaking her head. The light from overhead makes her hair sparkle like those black stones goth girls have in jewelry. "He's not my true love. I just like his music." She looks at Jonah. "No offense."

"None taken," he says. "You seem quite a pleasant girl, but I don't love you either."

"I do love your music," she says politely.

"But you woke up," I say. "How?" Because, even though the thought has been forming in my head, I want her to say it. After all, maybe it's just that I love her. That's what Jonah said. Maybe me loving her is enough.

"You silly goose! How could you have awakened me without knowing the answer?" I guess I'm still staring at her blankly because she says, "True love, right?"

"True love?" Obsidian. That's what those black stones are called. They're supposed to be magic. Her hair is like obsidian. "What? Who?"

She's still clutching my hand. With the other, I gesture to myself. "Me?"

"You." She loosens her grip. "I mean, if you feel the same way. Maybe you don't."

"If I feel . . . ?" And suddenly, my mouth is stretching so far, my face smiling so hard it hurts. "You mean you and me? You don't mean you love me as a friend, or . . . any of those other things girls say?"

She's just staring at me weird, and she says, "Nuh-uh. None of that. That first day at auditions, I was like, 'This guy is awesome.' You were so bold. And I agreed to be Oliver partly so I could know you better. And then, when I did, you were sweet and funny and smart. And brave. You protected me. You *saved* me, like a hero." It's like in my dreams, every dream I'd had. Her voice, saying she wants me, and it's finally dawning on me, what she's saying. "You're the one who woke me up after all."

"I did, but . . ." I step closer, wanting to take her in my arms now. "You really . . . ?"

"Perhaps I'll go get a nurse," Jonah says, "let her immortalize this moment on film to tweet to my fans and make my agent happy."

I guess he leaves. I'm not really paying attention.

"I read the poem," she says, "the one you wrote."

"You did? It's really . . . embarrassing." I'm still not completely wrapping my head around the idea that this is happening.

She shakes her head. "I loved it." Celine holds her other hand out, wiggling her fingers until I come closer. Then, she touches my face. Her hand is so soft. "It let me know you felt the same way I did. I hadn't admitted it to myself before then, even when Izzy flat out asked me."

"Really?" I wonder how long she felt this way, how long I was wondering when I didn't have to.

She nods. "God, you're so adorable."

"Really? Adorable? That's the adjective you're choosing? Like I'm a kid or a teddy bear?" But I'm thinking, *She thinks I'm adorable.*

"Oh, don't be stupid. People call big guys cute all the time. Adorable as in, I *adore* you. I adore you G . . . what's your first name? It's strange to love a guy called Goose. When I was sleeping, I tried to remember if I'd seen it in the program for *Oliver!*, but I couldn't envision it."

I laugh not because it's really funny but just because I'm happy. "Nope. It wasn't there. They listed me as Goose Guzman. That's what I told Connors to do." Now, I want to stop talking and kiss her again.

"But that's not what's on your birth certificate. At least, I hope it's not. I mean, when you graduate, your diploma won't say Goose Guzman, will it?"

I laugh again, all stupid-happy like our neighbor's shih tzu, who practically turns himself inside out from ecstasy when you pet him. "Nah. My father wanted me to have a big name since I was a little guy. His name's only one syllable, Jorge; two if you pronounce it the Spanish way, Hor-hey. They gave all of us big names, Antonio, Isabella, and me, Mauricio. It's a dumb name."

I'm talking too much. Less talking, more kissing.

She smiles. "Mauricio. I like it." She rolls closer to the edge of the bed. "Aren't you going to kiss me again, Mauricio?"

I do. I do, and the sparks and the magic and the fireworks are all there just like before.

Suddenly there are people in the room, and there's music, a guitar, and a voice, singing.

Sometimes when I see your face,
It takes me to a better place.
When I look into your eyes,
Walls fall down and curtains rise . . .

And I'm kissing Celine, holding, crushing her to me like I always wanted to and never dreamed possible. She loves me and I love her, and she's alive and safe, and we're together.

Finally, though, we break apart, and I say, "What is that music?"

"Oh, sorry." It's Jonah. "I was feeling a bit of the third wheel here, so I thought that, if this was a movie, there would be music. I do love a happy ending. Harry brought up the guitar, but perhaps it is a bit—"

"No." I grin. "There would be music."

"There definitely would be," Celine agrees.

The other people in the room are nurses, and then a doctor shows up too. And Kendra, who *looks* like Kendra and a little worse for wear too. I know I'll hear what happened later. They're all pretty shocked to see that Celine is, in fact, not dead, but I resist the urge to gloat. What are doctors supposed to know about magic spells? So we let them think they cured her. After some debate, they unhook Celine's feeding tube and everything, and after about six hours of tests and my dad (who filed an emergency petition to become her legal guardian, after Jonah and I explain about Violet attacking us in the elevator) filling out a ream of paperwork, and photographers taking tons of photos to prove Jonah was here, the hospital lets Celine go home. With us. With me.

"So what do you want to do when we get there?" I ask Celine on the way downstairs.

She squeezes my hand. "I was thinking we could make some smoothies and watch *Some Kind of Wonderful*."

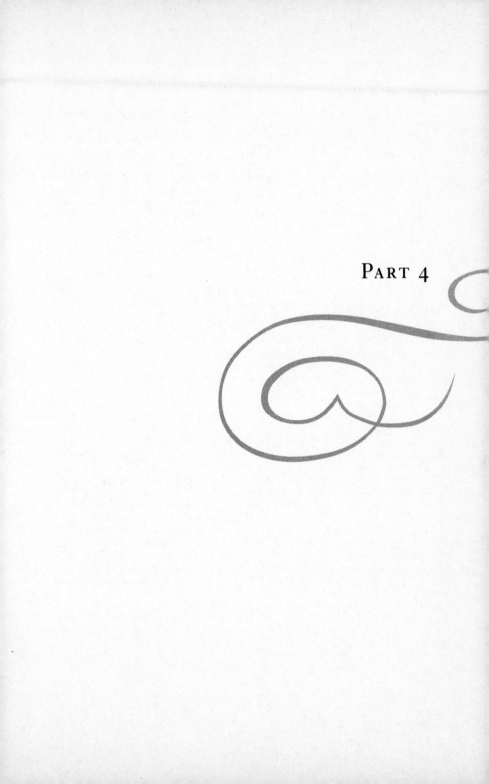

PART 4

1

Kendra

The elevator door slams shut behind them, and a ball of fire comes at me.

"Hey!" I yell. "If you don't stop, you're going to kill us both!"

"Does it really matter?" Violet asks.

"It does to me. I want to see how this turns out, whether he wakes her." For I have realized that Violet wouldn't be here if she didn't think Celine would wake. And I've realized something else. I've figured out who can wake her. It's not Jonah Prince.

I see Violet gearing up for another attack. Her magic is no greater than mine. It may be less. But she's more ruthless. She loves no one and has nothing to lose. I once felt that way, but now . . . well, I want to check on Celine. I can hold Violet at bay long enough for Goose and Jonah to reach her, I hope, but I can't stop Violet forever.

I've frozen the elevator on the fourteenth floor. Another explosion rocks it.

I dodge the fireball, putting it out with a neat blast of water.

"Play with fire," I say, "and we'll both get burned."

Violet smiles. "The difference between us is I don't care if I die. I don't care about anything."

"Then why hurt that sweet child?"

"Because that child is evil, the spawn of evil." She walks away as much as possible in an elevator. I know why she's doing it, to make me think she's pacing, make me let down my guard. But I never let down my guard with Violet. I did it early on, and I regret it.

"You think she's like her mother?" I say, eyes firmly on her.

"Her mother, or her father. Greg was no better. I see that now. He wanted Jennifer as a trophy, no more. That's why he preferred her even when we were both beautiful. She had more status."

"Maybe he loved Jennifer, and not you." I can't resist twisting the knife. What difference does it make? Being careful around Violet didn't help.

Violet ignores me. "He wanted her as a trophy. And then, when she was gone, he wanted me for the same reason. He never loved either of us, not really." She shakes her head sadly.

"Celine loved you," I say. "Before she knew you killed her mother, she loved you."

Violet looks over her shoulder at me, her face like a crumpled gardenia. "No one has ever loved me, not really."

"You know that isn't true." I walk over to her and lay a hand on her shoulder. "I have loved you like a daughter since the first day we met."

And, like a real daughter, she fights against me, pushing me away with hands suddenly burning hot. I cringe, and she says, "You don't love me."

"I do, though I did you a disservice, allowing you to change your-self so much."

I remember how she looked that first day, so small and pale, beaten down by those horrible boys. I'd had my own experiences with boys like that, and I'd have done *anything* to help her. I had done anything. I had given her my knowledge, my instruction, my magic, my heart. At what point did I give too much, do too much? And could I have stopped her if I'd tried?

"A disservice?" Violet murmurs, as if she hasn't quite heard. "I was miserable. You . . . tried to help me."

"But did I help you? Or did I make things worse?"

She shakes her head, still not looking at me. "I don't know."

A voice comes through the elevator's intercom. "Are you all right in there? We're sending help."

"It's fine." But, obviously, time is running out. I can't keep Violet in this elevator forever. She could leave if she chose. I only hope she'll stay. I must persuade her to make peace with Celine or, at least, leave her alone.

"Celine isn't who you think," I tell her.

"Of course not," Violet snaps. "I'm always wrong about every-thing."

"Maybe not everything, but this. You told Goose that Celine could never care about him. You were wrong about that too."

She shakes her head. "I wasn't. Little bitch would only want the captain of the football team. She'd never appreciate that kid, even after all he went through for her."

I pull a mirror from my voluminous skirt. Violet knows what it is because she has one just like it. I gave it to her so many years ago, and we have spoken through it almost every day. I say, "Show me Celine."

The scene in the mirror shifts to Celine's hospital room. Celine is awake, looking around the room. She says, "True love, right?" My heart feels tight in my chest. It worked!

Violet pushes the mirror back toward me. "That proves nothing. The pop star, he woke her up."

I angle the mirror toward her. Now, Celine is holding Goose's hand, gazing into his eyes.

"She loves him, always has. So you were wrong about that. What else were you wrong about, Violet?"

She stares at the mirror like someone in a fog. "I don't know." She takes it from me, gazing at the happy couple. "This is all I ever wanted. This. Love. But when Greg died, there was no chance left for me."

"No chance? You have every chance. You're immortal, magical. There is always another chance." It's a conversation we've had before, unsuccessfully. She doesn't seem to comprehend how long her life will be. I, with hundreds of years behind me, know that life stretches before her like a patchwork quilt with many experiences, some beautiful, some heartbreaking. "Go someplace where no one knows you, and start again."

"Someplace else." The mirror catches the ceiling lights. "Yes, someplace else. Will you take care of her then, of Celine?"

So you can always know where to find her? But I don't say it. She is staring so oddly that I wonder what she has in mind. "Of course Celine will be taken care of. But what about you, my darling?"

"Yes." Her voice is a shredded whisper. "What about me?"

And suddenly the elevator begins moving, down this time. It doesn't stop at twelve or anywhere but goes all the way to the bottom. When the door opens, Violet steps forward, then out. "Good-bye, Kendra. And thank you. I know what I have to do."

She presses the twelve button, gives a tiny wave of her fingers. They are, as usual, perfectly manicured. Everything about her is lovely, luminous. If you didn't know her, you'd think she was perfect.

She smiles as the door closes, and I know I will never see her again.

On the twelfth floor is celebration. Celine, Goose, Goose's father, Jonah, all celebrate Celine's revival. A photographer snaps pictures. It is hours before we leave, and when we do, I go in the car with Goose, Celine, and his father. Goose and Celine sit in the backseat, holding hands.

"I think you should stay with me," I tell Celine. "I can protect you in case . . ." I'm not actually sure Violet intends to do anything, but I realize I want Celine with me. "You don't need protection anymore, probably. But I'm alone and you're alone. It was meant to be." She can be my daughter, and I can do a better job this time.

"That might be good," Goose's father says. "If Goose and Celine are . . . together, it wouldn't be right for Celine to live with us." I see him raise his eyes in the rearview, but then he smiles.

"Hey," Goose says. "I thought you said you couldn't just zap people someplace. Looked like you kind of zapped into that elevator."

I shrug. "Every rule has an exception."

Celine says, "I'd like to live with you, Kendra. But you don't think Violet will try to harm me again?"

I start to say I don't know what Violet will do, but that I will try to protect her.

Then, something catches my eye.

Off in the distance, a plume of smoke, a brush fire maybe. But it's not in the right direction for a brush fire, not to the west. Rather, it's in the direction of—

I nudge Goose's father and point. "Drive that way."

"What? Why?"

But then, he too sees it, an orange blur, a flame, just for a second.

Celine, noticing, shrieks, "Oh, no! No! Do you think—?"

I shake my head. "I'm not sure."

We follow the smoke until we are on a familiar street, Violet's street. Celine's street. Celine's house.

The house is in flames.

I hear glass breaking, and a crow flies overhead.

2

Violet

Something is burning. It's my house. It's burning down. I myself struck the match, a wooden match from a restaurant matchbox, someplace Greg and I used to go. *Greg! Did you ever love me? Or was I just a poor substitute for someone else? Did you ever even love her?* A sob escapes my throat, or perhaps I'm choking. I am lying in the bed I used to share with my husband, waiting. If I rest my nose on his pillow, I can still smell him, barely. Except it's hard to breathe. I stare into the silver mirror in my lap, expecting to see the girl I was, the ugly girl. I'm still beautiful, but all I want is to die. What the dwarf said was right. Everyone hates me. It isn't my face, not anymore, but me. And yet, as the flames lap closer and closer to the bed, the mirror in one hand, my wedding photo of Greg and me in the other, I can't help but wonder if that could change. Maybe there is another way, another place. I could do as Kendra said, go somewhere else where

369

no one knows me, start over as many times as I need to. Change my appearance and fly like a crow to faraway places.

The room is hot. A window breaks, and I am sweating, blinking my eyes against the gray smoke. A mortal would have succumbed to it long ago, but I am no mortal and can only die from the pain of the flame. I dread it, coward that I am. I squint at the silver mirror. "Show me Celine," I tell it.

There she is, black hair and white skin, a beautiful girl, a girl who once loved me. A girl I loved. She's with the dwarf, sitting in a car holding his hand. Her eyes widen, and she leans to embrace him, gazing at him as if he is the most beautiful man she has ever seen. He turns and smiles, and suddenly, he is beautiful, dark brown eyes shining from a handsome face. I see his beauty as I wished others would see mine. I know I was wrong about Celine. I was wrong about so many things. Was I wrong about myself too? Can there be hope for me?

I feel a spark on my shoulder. The bedsheet has caught fire, and soon, I will be consumed by it. I am not tied to this bed, though. I can still flee. I make my decision. I take one final look at the photo, at Greg. Greg, who never loved me at all, not really. I feed it to the flames. I watch it burn.

There is nothing left of Greg but Celine. There is nothing at all left of Violet. Violet is dead. Quickly, I manufacture something, a dummy version of the girl I was, the ugly girl. I remember reading *The Picture of Dorian Gray*. In the end, when the beautiful main character died, he became the hideous old man in the picture. That was how they found him. They could only recognize him by the rings on his hand. That is how they will find me—or think they did—my charred remains lying on the bed. But I will be gone, far, far away from all of them.

Then, I make my escape, flying on jet-black wings out the window and away, into the warm summer night.

I will begin again . . . somewhere!

3

Celine

February, the next year

"You know we don't actually need to go shopping," Kendra says as
we pull into the Target parking lot where it all began. I'm driving the
red VW Bug Jorge helped me buy with money from the trust he set
up for me out of my father's estate. Goose taught me to drive because
Kendra definitely didn't know how. "That's one of the great things
about being a witch, no money needed."

"I know," I tell her. "But you know you like shopping. It gives
you ideas."

Boy, does it give Kendra ideas. Since I've started taking her on
weekly shopping trips, our entire house has gone from French provincial to Early College Dormitory with every kind of thing Target sells,
all in pastel polka dots. Kendra buys none of it. It all just appears.
"You know you love the dollar section."

"That's true. You think they have that mint foot rub?" She exits

371

the car, fluffing her purple tulle bustle. "Maybe I should get a job there."

Goose and I exchange a look. Kendra, work? Kendra, wear a uniform? Kendra, deal with the public?

"What?" She looks from one of us to the other. "It would be easy for me and give me something to do when you go away to college."

We start toward the shopping carts. There are tons of black birds, crows, or grackles on the lights overhead, and they're cawing and chirping so loud it makes my head hurt. I'm freaked out by birds, have been ever since we had to read "The Birds" in English class this fall. Goose loves that and loves to mess with me. "They're gathering, Celine," he says in a creepy voice. "They're making plans."

"Quit it!" I slap his shoulder. He recoils like I've hurt him, but I know he's messing with me. Still, I give his shoulder a pat.

Kendra has also been staring at the birds, but now, she says, "Come along, children." She grabs a cart and starts booking it to the entrance.

"Maybe you should take Kendra to some higher-end places," Goose says, yelling over the cawing. "Get ideas for a prom dress."

"Splendid idea," Kendra says, still walking extra fast.

I love Kendra, but since I've been living with her, she has this great idea I should dress like her. I'm more of a prep, but I'll occasionally let her design a dress for me. Just not for prom.

I try to change the subject. "Is that your way of inviting me to prom?" I ask Goose.

"I sort of thought it was a given we were going together, since I'm the love of your life."

"It is, and you are. But it's still nice to be asked." I was sort of expecting an elaborate "prom-posal" out of him. He's theatrical, after all. He's left roses in my locker twice, and once planned an elaborate scavenger hunt, involving teachers, students, even the football coach, all to give me my birthday present, a bracelet with charms representing both our families, and us. So I was expecting at least a song with the lyrics changed to include my name, sung at a pep rally. Which would be super-embarrassing, actually.

We've reached the entrance. I'm ready to go in, to get away from the birds. But Goose takes my hand and gets down on one knee. "Celine, my darling, will you accompany me to the prom?"

I laugh. "Of course I will." And part of me is thinking, *Get up*. But the other part of me knows he's perfect, that I need someone just like him, someone who doesn't mind being stared at, who helps me get out of myself. Who loves me for me. Finally. So I wiggle my fingers. "Now, kiss my hand."

He does. The birds are screeching, cawing. I tug at his hand to help him up. "Let's go in. The birds are freaking me out."

Just as I say that, one bird swoops down from the rest. It's a big one, and flying sideways, it looks like a black kite. It flaps its wings right in my face. I run behind Kendra and Goose, remembering my mother, her fear of animals. But the bird doesn't peck or attack me. Instead, it flutters down and rests on the shopping cart handle, right by Kendra's hand. It stands there, staring at me. I grab Goose's hand at the same time Kendra grabs my other one. So we form a weird human chain, me and the two people I love best. No one can hurt me, not with love and magic on my side.

The bird cocks its head to one side, watching us.

It blinks, then flies away.

I stand, holding Goose's and Kendra's hands, and watch it disappear into the sky.

4

Goose

And we live happily ever after.
    Really. That's all.
    The End